"They're out to get Mr. Edmund Trothe — *and anybody connected*."

Chief Superintendent Hockley of New Scotland Yard was warning Edmund Trothe of what he already knew — that two of his former friends in M.I.5 had penetrated his Anglo-Arabian oil empire.

The Pair, or the Dirty Double, as Trothe thought of them, had murdered some of his employees. They had turned his company into a domicile for spies. Except for his fiancee, Consuelo, (were they after her too?) there was no one he could trust.

And until it was too late, Edmund Trothe did not know how formidable his enemies were — and the enormity of their plans for him *and anybody connected!*

WHITE HORSE
TO
BANBURY CROSS

Richard Llewellyn

 PYRAMID BOOKS • NEW YORK

WHITE HORSE TO BANBURY CROSS

A PYRAMID BOOK

Published by arrangement with Doubleday & Company, Inc.

Pyramid edition published March 1973

ISBN 0-515-02963-7

Library of Congress Catalog Card Number: 70-78681

Printed in the United States of America

Pyramid Books are published by Pyramid Communications, Inc. Its
trademarks, consisting of the word "Pyramid" and the portrayal of
a pyramid, are registered in the United States Patent Office.

Pyramid Communications, Inc., 919 Third Avenue, New York,
New York 10022

CONDITIONS OF SALE

CHAPTER ONE

Big Ben struck eleven, and I watched a patrol of police cars back smartly into line, admiring expert wheelwork, but suddenly I couldn't see, couldn't hear, could only stand there, as our villagers say, mazed and a-wonder.

The seed of the idea must have sprouted in the humus of Consuelo's remark those weeks—or months?—before, when I'd been grumping through an early breakfast before flying to Teheran, and she'd said Joel Cawle was careless in hanging his pictures. I remember a momentary pause of surprise, because his father's collection had passed to him, and he always had a Picasso or a Nash or some other piece of nonsense in his office, possibly to annoy those of us who couldn't afford much more than something tastefully trite in the way of a travel poster or a simple, blockhead H.M. Stationery Office calendar.

"He wouldn't let them be *mis*-hung, surely?" I remembered saying. "He wasn't the sort I'd call unexacting?"

"Not mishung, but simply askew. I was only in that section a few days. I put them straight when I couldn't bear it any longer, and that girl of his—I can't remember her name—she was with the NATO team—wasn't she German or Austrian?—yelled the place down and I was transferred. I'm fairly sure it was for that. I've often wondered why."

"What sort of pictures?"

"Oh, nothing much. A Gauguin and a di Chirico, and I think a Miró, and a quite lovely Magritte. Every hair in place. Everywhere. And that collection of Japanese or Chinese black and white things he always had. He paid more for insurance than I earned. I didn't think it fair. I became a socialist on the spot. *Raus mit uns!*"

Also sprach Consuelo, before six o'clock in the morning, clear-skinned, shining as a seraph, though

5

why seraph and not angel I'm not sure except perhaps for her rather more than hint of lyric innocence. That, indeed, was hers, though how, conjoint with a wildly sensual passion was one of those minor, more delicate mysteries which helped to make her so gloriously, untiringly lovable.

I stood in the anteroom to Chief Superintendent Hockley's suite, looking out of the window into the inner quadrangle of New Scotland Yard. The idea hit me almost physically in the nape. I suppose there'd been some curious thinking among those who'd waited there before me, though I'd have posted a bet that none were more bizarre than mine at that moment. I saw nothing except a violent reddish-blue flash and heard a sound like a riptide electric drill.

It passed, and I was left with a clear answer to a problem that had puzzled the devil out of me for some time. I don't know if anybody's tried to explain the mechanics of proleptic thought—the extraordinary business of suddenly getting the answer to a question, and then having to go back and work out how it was got—and I wouldn't even try, but I hadn't a doubt I was right.

The door winged, Sergeant Evans held out a welcoming hand, and I walked in to meet the Chief Superintendent, looking, as ever, like a minor parish clerk, felt a dry grip, and sat in the green leather chair he nodded at.

"Mr. Trothe, I asked you to be good enough to come here, because I've had some nasty bits of news about the Lane-Cawle pair, and some of them concern you," he said, wasting no time, looking down at an open file. "We've had them pretty near the hook, but they just nose at it, and dive. Too smart. The years they spent at the game, can't be too surprised, can we? But there's no doubt they're out to get Mr. Edmund Trothe and anybody connected!"

I nodded. It was nothing new. Bernard Lane and Joel Cawle had been Military Intelligence colleagues of mine for many years until I'd left the Service. We'd worked fairly closely together at odd times, we'd been to the same school, knew more or less the same people, and I had every reason to believe I was the only one, outside their immediate families, able to identify them on the instant, in any circumstances, plastic surgery or not.

"You've had a couple of bomb attempts, a few snipings, a bit of messing about here and there, so I understand how you feel," he went on, looking down at the long page I couldn't see. "There's a lot here I can't show you. I'd like to. For your own sake. But you know the game, too, don't you? Can't be done!"

I lolled. It was a fairly comfortable chair. My ease and apparent lack of interest were not lost upon him. He stared at me over the half-moons. They were a policeman's eyes, black, bright, hard. I'd once been told he was known as a "real" terror, and I could quite see why.

"Don't look too flurried, Mr. Trothe?" he said, almost amused. "But I am. And I can tell you I don't get in a flurry too easy. That's why I asked you to come here!"

He turned a page.

"You're in twice-daily communication, by code, with twenty-seven radio stations, and you maintain a staff of eight operators on three eight-hour shifts," he went on, as if reading. "The operators are all pensioners, Armed Services or Post Office. This makes things worse. You *know* what they're doing. They don't. If they were arrested, they could go to prison, lose their pensions, homes, everything. Is that fair?"

"I'm operating under a blanket of licences of every kind. In this country, at any rate. What's your objection?"

He opened another file.

"I'm not going into it," he said, turning pages. "You're here to be warned, that's all. That's the top and bottom of it. I'm not asking why you're in contact with these countries. You could tell me it was part of your business. I couldn't argue. I know you're working in

7

most of the Arab States. That's all right. But I don't see why you're in touch with somebody on the Soviet-Turkish border. Or why you've got into the armaments business!"

That was a shock.

"I wasn't aware of it," I said, looking at a publicity still of a surprisingly pretty policewoman. "The Soviet-Turkish border, of course, *is* of value, because a pipeline will one day terminate at the port, there. But I'm really not in armaments of any kind. We've bought jet aircraft for fast freight, we've got eight small pipeline scouts, and about a couple of dozen automatic pistols and shotguns for our desert outposts. They're for wild animals, roamers, etcetera. Apart from that, nothing!"

"No contacts with the Israeli War Department?"

I laughed. It was rather a funny notion.

"Superintendent, you're the sort I'd like on my side in the event of—let's say—difficulties," I said, sitting forward, taking command. "Let me explain what's going on. We're an Arabian consortium with a small American banking interest. I control, because, in effect, it's entirely my Company. The Arabian shareholders vested all authority in me for the next ten years. We're constructing five pipelines to five different ports which we're building. For obvious reasons, we have no contact of any sort with Israel. If you follow me?"

He nodded, looking down at the page as if I were telling him very little, or not as much as he knew. I knew it, wondering how far to go and what *not* to say.

"You're not too friendly with Lord Blercgrove, I believe?" he said, reading.

"Not really, perhaps—"

"Head of your old Service? Seemed friendly enough last time I saw you together?"

"Shall we call it expediency? You were after our blood!"

"All right, let's look at something else," he said, still reading. "You buy explosives in large quantities, Poland, Czechoslovakia, Rumania, sources of supply, among others. What would you need rockets for?"

"Signal rockets? We use them as warnings, weather news, breakage, seepage, that sort of thing. They can be seen a fair distance, and the news passes on to base by the same means. Radio isn't always usable. It's often difficult to hear Morse, much less the voice!"

"These rockets are ten foot long?"

"Nothing like it!"

"It says here!"

"Have you checked the source? It *could* be the pair with their usual type of put-on, you know?"

"You don't use forty-foot boosters?"

I could only stare.

"What the devil for? A rocket, in my terms, is only a slightly larger version of schoolboy fireworks, bigger burst, longer duration, that's all. Look here, Superintendent, I don't want to waste your time or mine. Why don't you appoint a few senior officers, fly them out at my expense, and let them go where they please, talk to anyone they wish for as long as they think necessary. They won't be told what to do, or where to go, or tagged. On?"

He laughed, still reading.

"Arab countries aren't my business, Mr. Trothe. But it *is* my business when arms and munitions come into this country under the guise of ordinary commercial trade. I want to know what for, and where they go, and on what authority!"

I could feel patience, like thin gut, starting to unravel.

"I give you my word that nothing of the sort's happened, or ever will while I control. If you'll show me any evidence, I'll have Berry look into it. I think you know him well enough?"

He took his glasses off, rested his forehead on bony, square-tipped fingers with a long scar in ragged white gleam across the knuckles, and slowly turned a page.

"Glad you brought his name into it," he said. "He's one of my best friends. Joined the Force together. I recommended him for the job for a lot of reasons. But I don't want to see him busted and ruined for doing something he never ought to!"

9

I felt the string go.

"You're talking as though my Company were a criminal enterprise and most of us subject to arrest!" I said, not pleasantly. "Permit me to say that all you've told me is merest tissue. Berry's an extremely capable head of my Intelligence Section. Nothing he's done has been criminal. He'd be the last to obey any order he thought improper. He could never be got to do anything unlawful. You know it. Then why all this?"

"I'll accept that, Mr. Trothe. As I started by saying, you're here to be warned. Not accused. I hope that what I've said *has* warned you. You now know what's being said. What do you know about a certain woman, calls herself Lily Hong? Supposed to be Chinese. Got other names—"

"Don't I remember that name in the transcript of my son's deposition?"

"That's correct. She got him taking the stuff, first, and then supplied him with it to sell. One of Mr. Chamby's friends—"

"Hard to believe!"

"—and a partner of the pair. Very dangerous bit. Never since heard of her, or met her?"

"Never. I'd like to!"

"So would I. She'd do fifteen years. If she was lucky, and got a nice, softhearted judge. You know the Graf—or Baron—von Staengl, don't you?"

The change of pace almost unperched me.

"A brief acquaintanceship, that's all!"

He smiled over the half-moons.

"I'm not telling you anything, Mr. Trothe, but I want you to keep on remembering what you're here for!" he said, amiably enough. "Let's call them tips, shall we? I'm after Lane and Cawle, and every rat working with them. You're after them, too. You've said it before witnesses. You're reported saying you'll kill them. But I'm on the professional end. You're not. You can get into very serious trouble, and so can anybody knowingly or unknowingly working against the Law. That is, people employed by you. You know the extent of the

10

training the pair had. They were both bomb experts, for a start. You'll have to be even more careful. I'd think twice about driving alone. Or letting too many people know where you're going. Or making a habit of travelling to, let's say, Rome, on a certain day, at a certain time, a commericial flight, or taking the car ferry. They don't want long to catch on. They've got a big organization. And it works!"

He closed the file, tapped it with the half-moons.

"Worst case of its kind I ever had the bad luck to get into," he said. "I don't want to see you get hurt for the wrong reason. And you can!"

"I don't treat them lightly, rest assured. It's true about killing them. Not particularly because they're traitors. That's your business. They were responsible for the death of many friends of mine—"

"Your son-in-law, Mr. Obwepoway, or whatever he calls himself," he interrupted sharply. "Does he do any business with you?"

"So far as I know, not!" I said, with equal sharpness. "His affairs are entirely his own. Why?"

"He's invested a lot of money here, as perhaps you know."

"Has that anything to do with me?"

"Any idea of the trade he does in arms to Africa and the Middle East?"

"Again, what's that to do with me?"

"He never uses your planes or airfields?"

"Never. Take it from me. Never!"

"He's another one they're after. And your daughter, of course. Any idea where your son is?"

I had to think. I was being given "tips" and I should have felt grateful, but I wasn't. I was infuriated that some sort of gossip was being peddled as "intelligence" though I shouldn't have been. I'd served long enough to know how agents padded a report. Any bit of tattle was grist. But I knew that my black son-in-law was indeed a power in Africa, whether in banking, supply, arms, or the recruitment of mercenaries, though I had nothing to do with any of it.

11

Frederick, my son, was quite another matter. He'd been arrested on a drug charge, and I'd been grateful to the magistrates for putting him in keeping of the village doctor and permitting him to stay in house arrest under the supervision of our vicar. In almost twelve months he'd managed to free himself of the habit and, I thought a mighty effort, pass his Finals.

"You'll find him at St. Matthew's vicarage," I said, hoping I sounded more confident than I felt. "He's done very well—"

"He came off restriction a week ago. Officers of the Drug Squad report they've seen him a couple of times in the West End. Soho and Edgware Road, to be exact. Any idea what he's doing there?"

I shook my head.

"Can't do much about a lad that age," he said, and got up. "They'll do as they like. Too bad. I hope I'm not wrong, but I thought he was one of the few got over it. I'll answer the questions you're *not* asking, Mr. Trothe. We're keeping an eye on him because he might lead us to this Lily Hong. Or a go-between. Once we're that far, we'll be very near a lock-on to the pair. That'll be the day!"

"Frederick's a little piece of bait?"

"Call it that," he said, going to the door. "If I find out where he's staying, shall I let you know?"

"Most kind of you. Was *that* why you asked to see me?"

He pointed at the photograph of the policewoman.

"My daughter," he said. "My boy got killed in Aden. Nigh killed his mother, too. So I know what it is. If I can help, it'll be done. Take care of the family, and don't go out too much alone!"

The doors winged open, and Sergeant Evans came with me to the stairhead. I barely saw where I was going, but the scarlet phonebox appeared almost as a blessing. The village seemed to drift along the line with the houseman's voice, and I saw the polled oaks on the Common, and the holly hedge in the vicarage garden, and then I was talking the usual fluff about health and the weather.

"Where's Frederick?"

"Ahh—mm," the vicar paused. "Well, he went to London to see some friends. I spoke to him last night. He sounded perfectly well. Ahh. I don't *think* there's any danger, you know. He wanted a couple of shirts and things sent up by train, and said he'd be back on Saturday. I asked if he needed any money and he said no. Doesn't sound *too* frightening, does it? Doctor Norris agreed that he should go. Stretch the pinions a little. Got to face it some time, hasn't he?"

Indeed. That had to be.

But there were other things to worry about, not least Consuelo. Any thought of the pair's harming her brought on that cold, berserk feeling. I'm not sure why it is, exactly, but the mind seems to stop functioning, and squeezing a trigger becomes simple as that. Lane or Cawle in front of me, and I knew, beyond all appeal, I'd kill them with absolute pleasure, not particularly because they were traitors, but to remove any threat to her, first, and in doing that, avenging so many of my friends.

In that walk back to the office, I saw both, and so clearly, as they'd been those years before, and as I'd last seen them, Cawle as head of M.I. in Washington, Lane with the same job here. Thankfully enough, I'd left the Service, but they'd stayed on, so far as I was concerned, in the mire, the subnorm, subworld of espionage, though as agents, spies, however they were known, in my view, they packed with the rest of them, misbred dogs, and nothing more. Unfortunately, because of a wartime sense of duty, I'd become one of them. That was my regret. So many things I did, I hate, or let it be said, I despise beyond words.

I've been cause of many deaths, or plainer still, murders, that I'd never boast about, or try to remember.

They could all have lived, and so happily, as we all manage to live, without help of anyone like me and

13

my—at that time, painful—sense of duty. But what *is* duty?

In full possession of our senses, why do we accept an order to kill someone we didn't even know existed? How can we pretend to ignore that a woman sweated in pain to give them life?

I'm able to explain it up to a point, and then fall back on an excuse—duty—but I'm in front of my own judge and jury and it's not a comfortable spot. Because the question remains, what *is* duty? A compulsion to support the country? Very well. Now we can twitch into transports about patriotism and such, but it doesn't answer the question.

Especially in having to think of the Blur—as we called him—Lord Blercgrove—backed by the Lane-Cawle type, in absolute control of the Civil Service, exercising formidable pressure in the Cabinet, Privy Council, House of Lords and Commons, diplomacy almost direct, banking, commerce and all activity requiring an element of government support, virtually in charge of Armed Services, with far more than a finger in the Judiciary, the Church, and the political parties, and with complete supervision of Intelligence in all its branches.

This meant that his lordship was really—as Paul Chamby had once said—the Power behind power. Corridors of power is mere verbiage. Power's behind a desk in a suite of offices near Horse Guards, Whitehall. Very few of us in the Service ever went there, fewer still knew where it was. Unfortunately, not long before I'd crossed his lordship, and knowing how he worked, I was certain that his attempts to convince me of his solicitude for my welfare were poppycock. Bernard Lane and Joel Cawle had been favorite birds of his, perhaps because in his career he'd been Governor-General with the same feathers in his hat as their fathers. Therefore, the sons had to be encouraged, promoted, pushed on, regardless. That's what surprised most of us.

Anyone far less careful than the Blur must have taken notice of the reports which many of us got at first hand and passed to his desk. They could only point to

Lane and Cawle. In my case I had four, clear-cut, which I sent on. I never even got a line to say they'd been received.

It passed, as everything passes. That's the devil of life today. Everything passes. Everything's permissible. Even murder.

But any notion of Consuelo's being a target brought on that fit which took moments to control. Thinking of her got in the way. I was starved for the sound of her voice. I missed her, all of her, body, hands, mouth, the scent of her pelt, the long plaits, the luxury of kissing her, being kissed, caressed, caressing.

She'd flown to Jamaica a couple of days before to look after the estate of her mother's sister. I'd hated any idea of her going, but her mother wasn't well enough, and anyway, Consuelo's was the business head, and family is also a duty. Two ex-policemen had gone with her, but in view of the "warning" I felt there should be day and night guards, and notice sent to the Chief of Police in Kingston.

I couldn't go with her because I'd had to fly to Cairo that morning, and I'd got back the night before to find Hockley's message marked *URGENT* in red. Thinking back, I realized that everything he'd said had been a nudge where it wasn't an outright shove. If I read him correctly, I was being told to leave London, or at any rate, stay away from the office and the apartment, the usual restaurants, my club, and the other places we sometimes went to. It seemed absurd, but then, I knew the pairs' methods too well. I'd used them myself.

I began to realize that I'd become a creature of habit, and using the right type of tail, it wouldn't take the pair very long to compile a map of my daily round, pick time and place, and set up the knockout.

There was no question in my mind about where I should go.

I went to the Post Office in Pall Mall, and sent a telegram to Ulla Brandt Ben Ua, quite sure that if I used a little care in getting to that house on the beach between Derna and Tobruk, nobody on earth would find me, unless I wanted them to, and I could reach Consuelo by radio telephone at any time.

She was my single worry.

I dreaded to think of trying to live without her. If only for that, I was forced to accept Hockley's warning—"and anybody connected with you!"—at its full weight.

I put in a call to James Morris.

"Edmund! What a very great pleasure—"

"Would you care to see me for a moment?"

"Of course. Something on?"

"Our friends. An idea!"

"Tea's almost ready. Come along!"

CHAPTER TWO

"I can't see—except a little murkily—how it could have occurred to you, but I think it's brilliant!" James said, and put the cup down. "What d'you suppose made you think of it? What—ah—train of thought?"

"Perhaps what I was told at our smelterers. The people who make our tubing. They were taking photographs with this laser business, and I saw a couple of photographs of metal under stress. Well, they'd put a sort of glass screen in front which showed a graph. I suppose it reminded me of the type of thing I'd often seen on the walls of Cawle's office. Consuelo called them Japanese or Chinese—"

"They were neither!" James said. "We know exactly what they were. But a little too late, unfortunately. They're holograms. *Not* photographs in the usual sense, you see?"

"I fear I'm a little in the woods—"

"We're doing a lot of work with lasers. That's the basis of the hologram. It's not a new idea. It became a reality when we were able to use the laser light with it. The laser ray's coherent, that's to say, it doesn't wobble or pulse as the electric does. If we took a photograph of this room, for example, with an ordinary camera and film, we'd get a black, shadowy blob. Not enough light. But using the hologram process—*holo*-complete—and *gram*-message—we first of all know that any object emits light of some sort, and then we send in another light source to equal and strengthen it. Of course, if I go off into textbook guff we'll be here all night. Anyway, if you look at a film taken by this process in ordinary light, you'll be disappointed. But then, look at it by laser light, and it's quite another thing. You feel you could pick anything up, for a start, because it's three-dimensional. But even *more* than that, you can see *round* or *under* or *over* things, just by moving your head. Let me show you!"

He pressed a voice switch.

"Mildred, bring a couple of those holograms in file W E three-one-one here, will you? And get on to Mr. Foulds, and ask him to bring me the list of everything found in the offices of Messrs. Lane and Cawle, here and in Washington, and any photographs there may have been taken of any other office of theirs. Right?"

He pressed another button, and half the wall to my left slid away. There was some sort of glass screen shining, but I was a little too surprised to comment.

"Of course, both of them would have known quite a lot about it," he said, filling the teapot. "The process was being used in sonar and radar, and the space program, and heavens knows what, here and in the United States. All top secret, naturally. Every damn' detail passed across their desks. When I permit myself to think of what those two must have garnered and given away, I really despair. And their fathers were two of the best men I ever met. God, what a venal blight!"

"What I'll never understand is how they were allowed to get away," I said, and put my cup down for a refill. "And I can't think what's happened to the Blur. There were reports about them years ago. I worked with Lane just after the breakthrough in Egypt. I always thought it strange the Russians knew such a lot about what he'd done. Nothing about me, apparently. But we were both in the same field. He got a tray of decorations and one round his neck. I got a nice letter from an aunt of mine who'd seen my name in the papers. Chagrin I think's the word. Says it exactly. I didn't see him for years after that. I think I know why. I might have got his chitlings long ago. He knew it!"

James poured carefully, a steady deep gold stream which never showed a leaf. Evening light whitened his hair. The teapot's porcelain reflected in the luminous grey of his eyes, intent, glacial. I was remembering him with Mavis, that afternoon, long ago, in the garden of their house, pruning roses, joking, gentle, almost a yokel. But this was James Morris, whom we called the Banger, head of the Explosives Section of Military Intelligence, and I had time to wonder, again, at the expanse of the human personality. A rosarian at one end, an inveterate tea-drinker in the middle, and a disintegrator of people and all material things at the other, with I-wasn't-sure-what rounding it all out, and here he was, handing me my cup.

"Heard any more about that affair at Hauerfurth?" he asked casually, which I took as a wink to a blind horse. "We had a report, but extremely attenuated. I don't think we're as well served there as we ought to be. Nothing in the newspapers. How's Yorick? And the other chap?"

"Getting along, I believe. Bit of a wearisome job, though. You'd hardly believe it, but Yorick was running this bar in Fraglechshaben, and one night, he and the barman were simply whisked off. Next thing, his fiancée—d'you know Gillian Roule? Simon's daughter, of course—well, she told me he hadn't been on the air. Then a C.I.A. report put him in Hauerfurth Prison. That's when I came to you. We got him, and the son of a friend of mine out. But without your help, we couldn't have moved. They'd been injected for months with some sort of stuff that made them swell horrendously—"

"What was *that* for?"

"To make them talk. They couldn't have gone on much longer. Yorick, of course, had plenty to tell them. He didn't. What beats me is how the East Germans knew where he was, and how they got him over the border. They *must* have been told. One of us?"

"Wouldn't surprise me. We're still riddled. But I don't think there're any here, in this Section. They'd get short shrift, I can tell you!"

Since nobody on earth knew more about poisons, gases and explosives than he, I was prepared to believe it, and I knew at least two cases of untrustworthy staff dying, in what the Coroner later called Accidents of Unforseeable Origin, and others, where there'd been no inquests, because there were no bodies.

A short girl with bobbed hair floated on crepe soles

into the room, put three files on the desk, and mini-squeaked out. It struck me that I'd never seen a good-looking girl in that Section. Perhaps that was the idea. Faceless, formless, not easily recognized anywhere.

"There's your hologram!" he said, and gave me a slide, en route to the glass screen. "Put it in the projector in the ordinary way, switch on, and what do you see?"

The slide he'd given me was a greyish, cloudy affair. Holding it to the light, I saw nothing, a few specks, smoke. The slide on the screen was the same, but lit by the projector's light.

"Disappointing?" James said, almost jovially, but I knew him too well. "Obviously. But we're using house electricity, aren't we? Now let's put in the laser. *Abracadabra!*"

I almost fell off the chair.

Westminster Cathedral's interior is gloomy at most times, but here was a brilliant picture, three-dimensional, every detail in glitter, chalice, monstrance on the altar, vestments gleaming, banners in glory of martial color. But I really was almost stunned to find that in moving my head to the left, I could see most details of the banners *behind* the first, and *behind* the altar when I tiptoed, and *under* the choirstalls and pews when I bent down.

"That's one, and here's another," James said, putting in a slide of Portsmouth harbor at night, with every detail of the warships at anchor clear as in broad day, and again, the extraordinary experience of being able to see over, below, around and behind on what seemed nothing more than a flat plane.

"Now, how might this have been used by the pair?" James said, and switched off. "They had the equipment—it's not a great deal—and the knowledge, and if they needed them, they had the laboratory staff. Question is, why wasn't that work reported, and if it was, why didn't it give the game away?"

"Knowing the pair, I doubt that anything was reported unless they said so. Both could have inter-

20

changed this sort of slide-holograms-by diplomatic pouch. When was this system workable?"

"It was invented by Denis Gabor, an Anglo-Hungarian, here, in 1946, but he didn't have a laser. They had to wait till 1963. An American, Emmett Leith, first took it in, and then he and George Stroke at the University of Michigan brought the system to the point you've just seen. But Gabor's first efforts could certainly have holografed a micro-dot message. The result might have been rough, but perfectly legible. But if they *had* the micro-dot, and it worked, why change?"

"More to say? Drawings, despatches—"

"Ah, yes. Of course. No need for code, or anything else. And the advantage of this process is that it can be reduced to a pin's head, and then blown up, every detail as you saw it!"

"Special film, of course?" I asked, thinking of a break-in at my Rome office, and the police finding traces of film and flash bulbs, not on the market, that couldn't be traced to source. "Any sort of camera?"

"Doesn't need lenses, simply a pinhole. The film's not so difficult to get, at least it isn't now. But I must say, the laser job's not the handiest to cart about, though a couple of chaps'd find no difficulty. I think your idea's perfectly sound, but I can't quite see how it'd be of any real worth to the pair. Do you?"

"Could be pretty damning if photographs of any of our agents, with all that sort of detail, were passed to the other side. And the pair knew them all, of course. Ours, American, French, the lot. I always found it impossible to imagine how the other side could have picked up so many, hundreds, I suppose, on the same night, without a great deal more than oral or written description. By the way, could a hologram be sent by satellite?"

"No difficulty whatever!"

"Do we know when, at what time, Russian satellites approach Washington or London's receiving zone? Or one of ours?"

"Very soon find out. You mean they may have sent

21

this stuff by satellite? And received warning by the same means?"

"Everything—I mean, technically—was set for them, wasn't it?"

"Oh, yes. Had been for a few years. Come in!"

The tap at the door—a thump of knuckles—brought in a bustler of a fellow, a shock-head of grey curls, thick grey eyebrows, right slightly above left, a fine Grecian nose, and the deepest-set eyes I ever saw, in that light black, almost hidden by heavy eyelids, and a grin-that-wasn't, which I can only describe as malignant.

"Ah, George, you haven't met Mr. Trothe, have you?" James said, and took the set of files. "You made remarkably little of this, I must say!"

"Never very far from reach, that stuff, sir," Foulds said, in a thin, almost girlish voice, with an OxBridgian accent which I couldn't place, but the very pip of the pedant, widening the grin at me in acknowledgement. "I know Mr. Trothe by what I've read, and that's all. But it's surprised me that these relics haven't received the attention they merit. For example!"

He took a hologram slide from a short rack, and went to the projector. James held up a clip of pages.

"Everything found in their offices and apartments," he said. "Furniture, pictures, photographs, personal effects. They both, it seems, had to make a run for it. Very little time to burn anything, that's evident. Well, George?"

The light flashed the usual muddy swirl, and then the laser blazed, and a room glowed in extraordinary detail of red velvet curtains, a white bed, and the nude body of a girl, face horribly smashed far beyond recognition, blood, still wet, draining into the sheets, toes, fingernails painted bright coral, a pearl necklace, and what remained of the face in bloodied crests and troughs as though a bar had pounded inch by inch, methodically.

"Turn it off!" James shouted, and stood. "Great God, what *is* that?"

"A fitting souvenir, sir!" Foulds said. "There are four others. That's five obvious murders. But, you

22

know, what's so awfully strange is, they've never been mentioned in any report!"

"I find that hard to believe!" James said, and he looked as I felt. "Don't the Americans know about it?"

"I was sent over on the night they were to be arrested. I saw these, and knew them for what they were. They were probably taken for an amateur's errors, and put aside. By our people, of course. The Americans couldn't. Diplomatic immunity. But the Ambassador wisely allowed them an extremely thorough search after I'd been through. As you see from these photographs, Mr. Cawle left in a hurry!"

"I always thought Cawle was at the London end," I said, looking through photographs of rooms in disorder, drawers open, papers about the floor, though I didn't see a picture on any wall. "Curious he'd have pictures in his office, and none where he lived?"

"Lane and Cawle interchanged," Foulds said. "They could do more or less as they pleased. Cawle sent back the last of his oils about a month or so before. The entire collection was going to be shown for charity. But he *did* keep the black and whites. Here they are, and here's a photograph of each, singly. Nothing Chinese or Japanese about any of them, except the brushwork on the glass which framed them!"

I looked at all seven singles, and one of the group in their places on the wall. They made an attractive pattern, except that three—I remembered Consuelo! —were askew.

"Curious he'd appear to make a habit of letting pictures hang like that." I said. "It'd get on my nerves!"

"Until one realizes that *all* of them are holograms blown up to that size, and changed, sometimes, every day or two, and those tipped a little were portraits," Foulds said gently, in his ladylike way. "With this process, you see, it's possible to cover it with something opaque, like that glass, but put a laser through it, and there's the hologram!"

"But you need the laser and reflector to take the picture?" I said. "Where'd these pictures been taken?"

"Most of them in that office, others elsewhere,"

23

Foulds said, and switched on the projector. "Would you let me have the number of the photograph you're holding?"

"Seven!"

"The lucky one!" James murmured, and laser light blazed.

Projector light had shown a brushwork of bamboo shoots against the familiar smoky background. This was a startlingly clear layout of papers I felt I could have picked up and folded. I didn't know what they represented.

"That's a little job sneaked out of Cape Kennedy," Foulds said, and I gave him the rest of the photographs. "This one I took myself. That's Cawle's office. Just move your head a little to the right. What do you see?"

The photograph must have been taken from somewhere near the ceiling. The usual desk, chairs, armchairs, coffee tables, bookcases were all in place, but when I moved a little to the right, I saw, behind a draught-screen, a table affair of steel rods, legs clamped to the floor, something like an office tea-trolley.

"Notice the space, there?" Foulds said, and pointed. "That's where the laser rod had been. There's the high electrical input toggle. These three holograms are a series of portraits. Men and women. The murder shots I found at the apartment—"

"I'm not anxious to see any more," I said. "Except that the portraits may be of people I might know?"

None of them were. There must have been thirty, most, from the background, taken in that office.

"That's it!" James said, and switched on the room light. "Now, how d'you feel about your 'idea'?"

"Someone has to work on it. How did they get all this away? By satellite? Messenger? I can't think why it hasn't been thoroughly investigated!"

"Shared by some of us, Mr. Trothe!" Foulds said, at his most malignant. "It *was* reported, you may be sure. But I'm equally sure they're going to get themselves caught in doing something as clever as this. What defeats me is that neither of them could have feared detection. At least, for some time to come. They'd made no preparation. Why?"

"Somebody upstairs? Working with them?"

Foulds looked across at James, but he was busily assiduous in patting the photographs in order, and silence spoke, so far as I was concerned, eloquently.

"Do any of our American or French or other colleagues know anything about this?"

"There *have* been hints at a certain level," James said. "But no report, and hence, no reaction. No need to tell you what *I* think!"

"A most improving forty minutes," I said, and got into my overcoat. "And depressing. This is how they so easily could have informed on Yorick. I imagine he must have borrowed that identity—Primondi—from M.I. files. With a few pictures, it wouldn't take East German agents long to trace him. That is, given the word from our side. Explains many things, doesn't it?"

"I've heard the word 'traitor' quite a lot recently," James said, going to the door. "But I never fully understood its meaning as a taste in the mouth until these two brutes gave it a further dimension. I hope you're taking great care of yourself?"

"Indeed. In an hour I shall be leaving the country for at least three months. Mr. Foulds, thank you very much. James, God bless you, and unrhetorically, confound our enemies. We need help!"

"Amen!" James said, and I got the slight, double pressure, a warning to say no more. "I'd take the back way, if I were you. More cabs on the corner!"

CHAPTER THREE

I'm something of a hand at radio and electronics generally, and the set I'd built in the attic of the beach house was the most powerful I'd ever used. I could talk to all my offices in Europe and Arabia, and on a small screen I could see who I was talking to. They didn't know that.

As virtual owner and sole director of a £100,000,000 oil-gas complex, I had double responsibility. I had to give half of the shares back in ten years' time to the sons of the four Princes who'd entrusted it to me. I intended to see that trust was earned, and that the capital value increased at least ten times. We were pumping mineral gas across the desert to small ports being built on the Mediterranean and on the Arabian gulf, because later, I intended to pipe into Pakistan and India, and ship to South America. Meantime, the main complex at Beyfoum had another four months to go before we could start operations, though by then we'd have all lines linked.

We'd be in business.

I'd promised everybody the party of a lifetime on the night Prince Abdullah pulled the switch, because Consuelo and I were to be married that night, and apparently the entire princely family was turning the Middle East on its ear to make the nuptials an event in space. That was no exaggeration. They had a rocket on order which was to be shot up when we came out of the church—built for the occasion—which would carry our names round the earth, visible everywhere it overflew, until it burned out. I wasn't sure how long that was going to be, but I was quite certain everybody on earth would be thoroughly sick of us by the time it did. Could that—it suddenly recurred—be the rocket that Hockley had spoken about? I had to tell him.

I switched on, and went to London, Paris, Geneva,

Zurich, Rome, Athens, saw the same managers, got the same report. I went over to Ryad, our head office in Saudi Arabia, and then to the basecamps, outposts and store dumps, and down to the ports. All went well, all in good heart. It was fine exercise for my languages. I had my mind set on an international business, with every country being served by its own nationals. I never saw any sense in aliens occupying top jobs. By all means serve time abroad, but when the job's been learned, take charge.

It also applied to the women. I had a problem with the children. We needed medical centers and schools, and that meant physicians and teachers, surgeons and dentists, masters of trades and tools. It wasn't easy to find them, and neither was it simple to site the schools. The majority of my men were Arab laborers. The job was the best they'd ever had, and for the most money. Their rations and quarters were something new.

"Air-conditioning?" Logan, my Chief Superintendent whispered, almost in a spin. "*Air*-conditioning? What, for Arabs? They'll think you're sun-tapped!"

But they didn't. Coming out of that oven—and truly the desert *was* an oven—into a cold shower and a cool bunkhouse was an experience I shan't forget, and the expressions of disbelief, changing to blank enjoyment on the workmens' faces more than paid for the installation. Even when I explained how it worked, they still didn't believe it. I wish I could have got inside their minds to find out how they thought. But their children were far brighter. Unfortunately, their families suddenly appeared wherever Daddy was working, and made do with whatever there was. Those women were extraordinary—by our standards—and without seeming to make much of an effort, they kept families of children comparatively clean and well-fed, and built shelters overnight out of five-gallon cans and moth-eaten skins, until the camps began to look like pioneer towns. That, of course, was what they were.

That in mind, I'd brought in a young architect, Denis Lincoln, to look at all the sites and give me an idea of

27

what we might do in constructing a skeleton township that could grow. Water had to be brought in by truck, but we were hoping to tap a well, or pipe in when the main construction job was done. I'd seen the first roughs, and a model was being made. I'd had triple-roofed huts of sheet concrete put up, with chairs and desks made in our own shops. Getting teachers was the problem. No money was enough to attract them. I can't say I blamed them. A basecamp in the desert is the most forsaken place on earth. There can be little social life. Half a dozen surveyors and engineers made a large gathering, and the majority were married, wanting nothing after work except a drink, a bath, a meal, and bed. There were the nurses, but they made twice-weekly visits for an hour or so, and flew the worst cases back with them.

Not much of a life for a girl, or anybody else.

But I wanted those schools filled immediately. I intended to ask one of the Princes about it next time we met. I hadn't seen any of them for more than three months. They didn't give a damn about the business. I knew that two of them were in South America looking at racehorses, two were in London for the Season, and the Prince Abdullah was at his palace in El Bidh, getting over an operation Popular education, beyond instruction in the Koran, wasn't their idea. But I'd had to warn them that control of an industry could only be held by schooled men, technical ability, years of study. Shareholding and finance was quite another matter.

I hadn't convinced them.

I got a yellow flash from Geneva I'd been expecting, and pressed the button.

Ex-Chief Inspector Mohr of the Swiss Federal Police came in focus on the screen.

"Good morning, sir," he said, in his very good English. "At the Central Bank, a woman fainted yesterday, and other women and the bank staff assisted her. She was there for about forty minutes. It was a very good faint!"

"She was old, and everybody was very sorry?"

28

"I regret, sir. She was young, good-looking, well-dressed. She went back to the Carlton. In three taxis, two trams, one omnibus. From the bank to the hotel is, at most, seven minutes even on a crutch!"

"Passport?"

"British, sir. In the name of Renée Saddler. It is being checked. She flew to Hamburg on the late flight last night. She stayed at the Adlon. She flew this morning to London. She is at 243, Revers Road, Kensington. Mr. Berry has been informed!"

"You did very well. Where did she faint?"

"Near the last desk, close to the gate of the strong room, sir. It is why I report!"

"What could she see?"

"The desk turns left there, sir. Nobody saw when she fainted. She could have been lying on the floor at three-fifteen when the director and the staff open the strong room gates. I have tried. Every operation can be seen and photographed from there. It is the only place!"

"You've re-doubled your guards?"

"I have taken measures, sir. They can always get in. But they don't come out. Except to a police truck!"

"Thank you, Inspector. That's our Achilles heel. I'm sure they're going to try. Keep me informed, please!"

I got on to Berry in London. As I'd thought, he was out, and his ex-policewoman sergeant secretary, Miss Hammond, a dark girl with glasses, severe until she smiled, told me he was at the address in Kensington.

"Any signs?"

"Not a word, sir. Nobody answers the door. Mr. Berry doesn't like it at all!"

At nine o'clock, I began to call the outposts I'd established, from London, to the little town on the frontier between the Soviet Union and Iran, where I'd been enormously lucky in finding a woman I'd known for years before. All of them had one of my "clix," an extremely small radio, that couldn't be located by any direction-finding equipment, that even X-rays wouldn't find if it hadn't been in use immediately—at most a few minutes—before. They were all excellent people, all of them had an account to settle with the pair, and they were all part of a milieu where, at some time or other, both would appear.

I knew more or less where to look, and it hadn't taken long to find the people I wanted, and put them to work. I knew that sometime or other, in some guise or other, the pair must appear somewhere. It wasn't my intention to kill them one by one. To kill one would be to warn t'other. I knew they both had people working for them in the United States, Great Britain and Europe generally, in Government and Industry, in the Civil Services, in the Arts, and in private life. I hadn't an inkling how it had been done. Those people had to be paid. I knew what it cost me, and I'd only just started.

The pair of them were wealthy men, and they'd both married wealthy women. Their banks had made an exhaustive check, but nothing in their accounts suggested they'd ever made a single ex-parte payment anywhere.

Obviously.

I understood that very well. They were working with other funds.

Whose?

That was the prettiest question of all. That was the answer I most wanted to find.

Who'd spent millions over past years so that those two—and the people working with them—could do what they'd done? The record, now that we knew it, was crystal clear. Hundreds of people had died because of the information the pair had passed to "other" sources. We weren't even sure of "those" sources, or "that" source. On the evidence, I couldn't make up my mind, and in any case, I didn't want to think about it.

My sole desire was to kill the pair of them.

That done, I could think of other things. But it hadn't for a moment left my mind that in this time, both of them were working with many another to put *me* away. That was only because I knew too much. It sounded a little pretentious, but it happened to be the fact. I'd been the only one in the Service who'd worked with both, and over many years.

Apart from that, I'd been at school with them, I knew the people they knew, I had rather more than an easy acquaintance with most of their colleagues, some were close friends, and more importantly, I knew how they went about their business. With me out of the way, they could move freely anywhere. Both were masters of make-up. Perhaps I was the only being on earth able to spot them in any form, at least, now that I was alert. They'd both, on occasion, and more than once, taken me in. Lane had pulled my leg, but I'd been singularly offguard. He could never do it again, and he was far too sharp to try. Joel Cawle had done a lot more than pull my leg. I'd sat beside his desk in Beirut not long before, talking to him as an area supervisor in my own organization, without for a moment recognizing him. That, indeed, had been a rough surprise. There had also been others, and I'd swallowed them. Each time the net closed a little. The more the repertoire was exhausted, the shorter the road in front.

I was convinced they'd go for our strong room at the Central Bank in Geneva.

We had the treaties, and all the diplomatic correspondence about the project held there, and since many of the countries were members of various Pacts and Organizations, whose other members, for the most part, had not been informed, the material was highly explosive. Any publicity could easily put us out of business. I didn't like to think of having to negotiate those treaties again, especially with the successors of ministers who might have been shot or imprisoned. Nothing, of course, had been done without money. Once the facts were known, detail must follow, heads would fall.

The pair knew it.

I was sure that Geneva was their target number two.

I was number one.

I never lost sight of it.

Ouran Khadesh slapped down the path in front of the butler carrying my breakfast tray. The "butler" was his eldest son, Arefa, being trained to serve Ulla when

Ouran led his camels and flocks back to his own oasis in retirement. That was a few years yet, and I was grateful. I'd come to rely on him. He knew the desert, dune and track, and all its people by name, and nothing moved anywhere without his knowing. He was a true Bedouin, a strict Mohammedan, and there aren't many better men. His son took after him, a good lad, slight but wiry, fine features, fluent English learned from Ulla, but he'd broken his right leg bird's nesting and had to wear an iron, which stopped any idea of becoming a dragoman after his father. I asked Ouran if the lad couldn't do something better than butling, and offered to find him a job.

"He was born here," he said. "He knows the house and the work. He loves the Madame. Why does he need more than he has? How many have as much? What is his use outside? He is a nesting bird. Besides, when I leave, I know everything is with one of my name. God is good!"

He waited for Arefa to set the table, turned a cup to the correct angle, whispered a scold, and when the boy jingled away, looked at me. He wasn't happy.

"Two men and two women in a car were in El Garh yesterday," he said, with a forefinger in the side of his beard. "One of the men asked if you were known, and where you were. They offered money!"

I went on eating an Arab skilly of fresh baked wheat, curds, honey and small sweet currants, a delectable mix. Ouran didn't expect me to say anything, and I didn't. But it was a shock. Nobody, not even my office, knew where I was. Khefi, of course, knew. But as Commissioner of Police, he wasn't likely to tell anyone.

"A message is up and down." he said. "When they are seen, I shall be told. Their car will stop. If you please, we go and see them?"

"Not before ten o'clock," I said. "After, yes. How d'you know they'll wait?"

"If the car stops, it will stop till we get there," he said. "If you find the people dangerous, *they* will stop there. For a long time!"

32

He touched heart, mouth and forehead and slippered away, leaving me with the ends of a puzzle. How could anyone know where I was? My air tickets were in another name. I'd flown from Athens, and I was certain I hadn't been followed there from London. I'd landed in Cairo, and after Customs dealt with my baggage, I'd gone in Khefi's car to Eilat airfield and his own plane.

I was hanged if I knew what to think. I couldn't imagine Consuelo's saying anything. The office didn't require to know. I was in touch by the attic radio day and night.

I had another cup of coffee, picked up the towels and went down on the beach, to the steps cut in the rock of the long, grey headland, choosing my place in the sun from a dozen, all cemented smoothly in different tints of pink, lilac, blue and amber. I put the towels down and lay flat, aware that the sun was hot, and life was good.

It could have been a lot better with Consuelo.

And if I'd known who those four people were, or what they wanted with me, or how they knew I was anywhere near North Africa, I'd have lost that small worry, which seemed to be hanging straggles of windblown tape in my stomach.

I knew exactly who, and what, I was up against.

CHAPTER FOUR

My morning cable from Consuelo came in via Khefi's office and put me in a far better humor. Following hers came the morning report from Gregson, her senior bodyguard, all well, tickets booked for the 17th, time of arrival at Cairo to be sent next day. I made up my mind to meet her, take her to dinner at Frascati's, stay at our office and fly back by the dawn plane.

It was then about ten to ten. I went over the five bands of my clix again, but nothing flashed. I set the switch to the call position—so that I could hear it anywhere in the house—and went out, gratefully as ever, into that wonderful pre-noon sun, only then noticing how cold it had been in the attic.

A couple of hundred yards out, a small fishing boat sailed in for about the middle of our beach, with an Arab astern, holding sail lines and the tiller. I counted heads and made seven, but they were all whites, and at least three were girls, judging by the length of hair. I was wrong. When the boat slid up the beach, there were five girls, and two men, both bearded. The sailor wore Arab trousers and a wrap of cloth about his head. The girls were loosely tied in what the French call a *sex câche,* and a bra that did little more than hold. The two lads sported thready shorts.

I heard Arefa jingle near me, and his face mooned in a shrub, though I don't know how he got there. He rolled his eyes toward the group, and lifted his eyebrows, asking me if I wanted to talk to them. I shook my head, and lay back on the towel. But I was startled, looking up at the sky, to hear at least a couple of Cockney girls' voices, then Ouran's gutturals, and the sailor's reply becoming an argument, and a guitar, strummed quite well, and a girl singing some sort of shanty.

I raised my head again.

The group stood on the beach, and the singing girl

dabbled her feet from the gunwale, still strumming, while the others pointed fingers, used their hands, and the sailor called Ouran a miser for not wanting to buy the net of fish. Another girl was in the garden, calmly picking flowers.

I felt it time to intervene. I got my shorts on, and a shirt, found my sandals, and stood. Ouran saw me, and came in a spread-toe shuffle. The group didn't move. The girl went on picking flowers. That annoyed me. They were abundant, but I think it proper to ask.

"They want to exchange fish for bread and flour, and cigarets," he called. "I told them we've got plenty of fish, and no stores to spare. We don't want them here every hour of the day. They've got a camp up there. About a hundred of them. They're a pestilence!"

"Send Arefa to the house for a carton of cigarets," I said. "Give them a couple of loaves and a bag of flour. I'll deal with them!"

"Who's the spokesman here?" I called, going toward the group. "Don't you ask permission before you enter private property and pick flowers? Which of you is British?"

"None of us *are* anything," the taller, fair man said, in a North Country accent, Huddersfield, perhaps. "We all *speak* English, if that's what you mean. She can only pick so many, can't she? Leaves you enough, doesn't it?"

"Don't bear 'scussion," the dark man interrupted. "Flowers don't 'belong' to nobody. Everybody's enjoyment, they are. Tell us we can't look at scenery next!"

"Those are the last flowers you pick, and this is the last time you come here," I said. "You're not welcome, is that understood?"

"When a few more like us get the word, we'll have a colony here," the fair man said. "Run things ourselves!"

"Flowers, me arse!" the dark man said. "Common property!"

They were all a wonderful color from the sun, all bright with health, and I couldn't see a sign of vice or

35

anything else I might have expected in that sort of an enclave. They didn't look seraglio-wan. The girls were beautiful, particularly the flower-picker, coming toward us with an armful that hadn't made the smallest difference to the garden. Her eyes were a pale grey that shone white light, strange, and rather a pleasant surprise. The girl behind me on the gunwale began an Afro-American threnody I didn't know, and they all hummed with her.

I thought of Frederick, my son, and Patricia, my daughter, both in this age group, and wondered what I'd have said to some self-righteous old curmudgeon who'd reprimand her for picking flowers, merely because nobody's being there, she couldn't ask formal permission. It seemed childish, and worse, mean. But, the curmudgeon nagged, the land had to be bought, gardeners had to be paid, seeds and roots had to be sent for, fertilized. Everything cost sweat and money, and some idiot can do as she pleases?

They weren't taking any notice of me. They didn't stand as though they'd ever worn shoes or clothes. They were graceful with youth. But none of them had ever had a lesson in comportment, of that I was certain. They couldn't walk, and I'd heard them speak.

I wondered how Consuelo would have looked in their company. She *could* walk. And flaunt, without appearing to. But she was so far apart from all of them. I realized, when I saw the dark girl's healed pinkish corns, that I was being the primordial snob, a plain and unvarnished specimen of all I'd thought I detested in certain of my countrymen.

I felt curiously alone, alien, separated.

They had nothing to say to me. Apart from a feeling of shame that I could think about them in such a stupid manner, and a desire to do something for them to mitigate it, I hadn't a word to say to them. I couldn't think of anything.

We were all in our place. They in theirs, I in mine, put there, not so much by any social order, but by a school which had taught me to think, speak and act in certain ways unknown to them. We were of the same nation, but of a different caste. Caste was still alive everywhere, as an old friend of mine, Samdhas Gupta, had once said. It was, he said, a matter of the soul. The rude, the vulgar are also born among the *aristo*. Birth doesn't bequeath caste. I still don't know if I agree with him.

"You see?" the fair man said, suddenly, pointing up at the rise behind the house. "That's plain as y'd ever want, isn't it? There's the beach like it was about four thousand years ago. Before the seas went down. I bet y'll find seashells up there!"

"That's correct," I said. "If you'd like to go up there, you'll find all you want!"

"Certainly would," he said calmly, in a side stare. "Just like to show these unbelievers one small item of evidence. Trouble is, they don't read, and they won't use their eyes. It's only since they've been here they've learnt anything. Make a start?"

"Left hand path, right at the statue, straight on through the date palms!"

The flower-picker ran in front of me and I saw that the *câche* was only for social reasons. Most of the day they must have been in the nude from dawn on. No pale patches. For a moment I seemed to catch a side glance from Consuelo. She liked the nude, but not in public.

The group stood, back to me, up on the brow of the rise, against a blue sky. Except for the legs and shoulders of the men, they all looked the same because of the length of hair.

Curious, but until then I'd had nothing but contempt for long-haired males, a carry over, certainly, from the post-Oscar Wilde trial period, when longhairs came to be regarded as not quite the thing, apt to carry an orchid, and quote Sappho with a lisp.

But no man was ever more male than my Grandfather, and he wore his hair to his collar, and swathed his head in a silk bandana when he washed it. My father was only a little more conservative, and I, at school, never had a chance. We were at the barber's

37

every ten days, until I never thought twice about a hair cut. Hair had to be so long, fairly short back and sides, and no nonsense. Anything else was freakish. That's what we'd been taught.

To find myself sympathizing with those young men up there was something distinctly new. Why shouldn't they grow long hair if that's what they wanted? They'd lose it soon enough. Gather ye rosebuds, and bald pates. I was amazed to find a sneaking thought tiptoeing round the corners of my mind, regretting I'd never had as much freedom when I was their age. I wondered if I'd have had the initiative to come out to North Africa to set up a colony with a lot of quite lovely girls? The idea was certainly attractive.

These youngsters, I realized, suddenly, and on a blue morning, were teaching me something I wasn't quite certain I wanted to learn, and wasn't at all sure what it was, exactly, and to be truthful, felt rather nervous about. Once the thought passed, I wondered *what* there was to be "nervous" about, couldn't answer, and cursed the sudden broil in a mind that supposed itself to be fairly stable.

I walked toward the group. They'd gathered a mound of seashells of all sorts and sizes, some of them gigantic.

"Ah," the fairhaired man said, seeing me. "I suppose you won't mind if we take these along? Informative and utilitarian. Make lovely plates and salad bowls!"

"Take all you wish," I said largely. "Did you have any breakfast?"

"If you say *café*, I faint!" the flower-picker said, faintish. "And toast!"

"Ooooh!" the darkhaired girl groaned, and fell against the guitarist. " 'at dough stuff vey fwy down there. *Eee-urgh!*"

"Coffee, toast, eggs, bacon, porridge, if you like," I said, always the practician. "Downstairs on the outer patio in fifteen minutes. Bathroom's along here, left. You'll see a silver chamberpot with a rosebush growing out of it. That's the girls'. On the other side, there's a large burial urn with a cactus this high. Don't touch it. It's poisonous. Towels, everything, inside!"

The fairhaired man looked at me without a smile, and in a sudden clumsy move, offered his hand.

"Thanks," he said, still no smile. "We thought you were one of the rest. That's why we're here. Get out 'their' way!"

" 'n vat's *dead* vight, vat is!" Kix, the darker Cockney girl said, having some rather attractive trouble with her r's and w's, "Ve lost all ve uvver fuss. Names, addvesses, families, birf sustificates. Don't have none. Dumped!"

"Burned the lot, with the collars 'n ties, and all that crock!" the dark man said, for him, affably. "We've found all we want, and we're sticking with it, I'll tell you!"

"Haven't you anything more than what you're wearing?" I asked, "Isn't it rather cold, sometimes?"

"Some of us weave," the guitarist, an American, said. "We've got prettier things than you could ever buy. Tight for coin, that's all. Have to pay for wool, and stuff!"

"Revisionist," the dark man said. "Have us all in boiled pudd'n' cloths next. Never satisfied. Remnants of burjwah imperalism!"

"Comin' from a dirty fascist beast, that's ve'y good," the darker Cockney girl said. "You're a half-hard Cohn-Bendit. Only you don't know it, do you, Nub?"

He shook his head at me, and turned his back on them going away, arms about each other, laughing, a delightful line of almost-nude, deep-gold naiads.

"No hopes for any of *them!*" he said. "They've lost it. Soft life's muddied their brains!"

"If you haven't any names, why do they call you 'Nub'?" I asked.

He laughed about three teeth up at the sun.

"Nub'dy loves me!" he said, and walked toward the cactus.

Ouran Kadesh, a ghost under flowering shrubs,

39

raised a finger, sign that it was time for me to start work again. I went to my room, put on flannels and a heavy shirt, and hurried out.

The bath house pulsed with a song sung in parts by the girls against the shower's whisper, and rhythm rap-a-boom-tapped on the benches and partitions, adding a brighter note to the house, and memory.

But I wished Consuelo were there, wished the solo voice were hers, wished she was in front of me going into the shower, wiggling marvellous hips to drop the bikini. She taught me the meaning of wiggle.

Wished.

She'd taught me the meaning of that too. I'd never known or realized it had a muscular meaning. I'd always thought wishing was mental.

It's not.

CHAPTER FIVE

Arefa met me with the morning coffee, the mail, and the papers, and I sat in the shade to enjoy the news.

The first letter, from Berry, was a jolt.

Lane had been reported at Plummy's Club in London.

Meryl Armitage, the manageress there, couldn't have been mistaken. She'd known all of us for thirty years or more. But how could Lane be so stupid as to ask if she'd seen me? And what were our people in the Service doing? He could be picked up anywhere on sight. He knew how search parties worked, once the word was out. How he got in the country I didn't bother to ask myself. He and Cawle must have had enough false paper for a regiment. But to walk barefaced into Plummy's was a suicidal thing to so. Unless, of course, he had a working agreement with someone near the top. I couldn't imagine it. But facts told their own story.

The news that the Russians had gone into Czechoslovakia gave me a certain melancholy pleasure. I felt sorry beyond words for the Czechoslovaks, but I was sure the Communists and their congeries would regret the error for the rest of their history. By that ineluctable act of barbarism, they'd shortened it.

However, I had two very good men, and an excellent woman there. I had to get them out. They were merely keeping open an office for import & export which didn't do much business, but it paid for itself, ready against a time when the Company would need it.

I got Ouran to send a man in the jeep with a couple of cables, one asking Miss Pearlman to meet me in Rome, and the other to Athens, asking them to instruct Gleitz and Kober to report to that office soonest. That, I thought, would bring all three out of trouble.

I'd begun to tell by Arefa's jingle what sort of message he was bringing. This was full speed ahead.

The car with the four people, sir!" he called. "It's at Hamoun. My father has the car ready!"

I ran back to my room, got into a pair of Arab drawers, knee-length shirt, rawhide slippers, and a blue and white burnous, slipped on a pair of sunglasses, and even Consuelo wouldn't have known me.

Ouran waited in the front of the car, with Ahmed and Halif in the back. I got in front as a good servingman should, and we started off.

"Maurice send the message, sir," Ouran said. "They in the soukh buying carpets. They still asking always for you. The car was hired in Derna. They gave a name, British passport. The name is too difficult to hear, even for Maurice!"

It occurred to me they'd narrowed the circle of enquiry, because El Garh was a little more than thirty miles to the east. Hamoun was twelve miles or less west. In between there must have been at least ten villages. They were covering quite a lot of ground. My little friend and talisman sat in its shoulder holster, ready. It was a comforting thought. If those people were anything to do with Lane and Cawle I intended to kill the lot, and I had the men with me to find a place in the desert where they'd be picked clean overnight.

Hamoun was a ball of dust, a lot of little tents on the outskirts, a few mud huts nearer the oasis, one ragged soukh of stalls, a couple of two-storey houses with walled gardens, a clump of palms all round the pools, camels and families in the shadow, and a petrol pump outside the cafe-cum-rest-house.

Maurice, a veteran of LeClerc's Army, had lost a leg at El Khebir and married the Arab girl who'd found him after the battle and nursed him into sanity. He lived in one of the two-storey houses, her mother in the other. He owned most of the action round about and financed the rest, and she and her mother could buy him outright and not—as he said—know which pocket they put a hand in. They lived modestly as the Bedouin do, but because of a yearly visit to Paris, the house inside was surprisingly luxurious—surprisingly, that is, by comparison with the camels, mud, dogs,

42

puddles and dust outside—and they'd often been over for coffee after dinner as they did when Ulla was at home. Ben Ua bought the land for the house through them, and I was hoping to buy a place a few miles farther up. Maurice was doing the talking, and since he'd contracted to build, I left everything to him.

I didn't want to show my face for the moment, because if things had to be done, I preferred to do them quietly, with a minimum of witnesses.

We stopped outside the oasis, where the houses hid our dust and the car wouldn't be seen, and walked through the tented area, among dozens of children and dogs, and got on the wide track up to the water. Oasis is a pretty word, but that brack could only attract thirsty camels. It was little more than thin mud at that time of year, though Maurice's filtering system gave their house and Ulla's something of a purity and taste really out of the ordinary.

We got into the tented shadows of the soukh, and eased with the strollers. There might have been a thousand people altogether, marriage parties, buyers from the interior, families with children, laughing, haggling, squatting for coffee, up to the petrol pump, and crowding the cafe tables. I could see Maurice, hands in pockets, shirt open, cigaret dangling from the corner of his mouth, listening to somebody, and shrugging, hobbling, up-down, up-down, into the garage. We turned the other way, and Ouran found Sergeant Mahmed in a space between the tinsmith and leather buyer. He said our party was in the carpet tent a few yards down on the right. Their car was stalled in the garage. Maurice had "attended" to it.

I went first, a slow pace behind a noisy collection of brats, all yelling to be fed, and it didn't matter that the father shouted it wasn't time. They screamed back, pointing to their mouths and rubbing their stomachs, and the mother howled with them, and an older woman came in with a time-stopping screech now and again. But then the father caught my eye and winked, and I saw it was a family joke.

They'd given me the opportunity of stopping at the

carpet-seller's tent opening while the crowd passed. In that shadow I was only another Arab.

I let Ouran go in, and went behind. At the back of the third tent, one leading into another, the carpet seller had a pile beside him, and one stretched the width of his arms. He was making a price, and somebody was translating into English.

No doubt about that voice and accent.

I went behind the carpet seller, took the carpet out of his hands, and Ouran pulled him gently to the side.

"Now, listen!" I said, imitating the voice. "A prize hunk of Kairouan, and you don't want to fork out a couple of measly quid for it? What do I have to do? Tie it round y' bloody necks?"

Errol, still too fat, laughed open-mouthed, silently, on a pile of carpets. Gillian shrieked and threw herself at me. Angela Masters, even more beautiful than I remembered, stood with Paul. Hands in jacket pockets, he just looked at me in the old way, blank.

"Knew we'd find you in some dunnigan like this," he said tiredly. "Any chance of a gulp of something iced, like a case of beer? If you haven't got a few stowed somewhere, I don't know *you!*"

"Don't talk about beer!" Gillian said, hanging on me. "Let me just look at him, and adore!"

"Mind the latter part," Errol said. "We're getting married, remember?"

"Why the get-up?" Paul asked.

"Cooler," I said. "Suits are no good in the desert. Didn't you know?"

My Xth sense, the one that warns, burned somewhere in the middle of my head. It's been too great a friend to disregard. Something was wrong with Paul. He was half-shaven. There was still dried soap in his nostrils. His eyes were not those of the Paul Chamby I'd known. The Little Cham, as we called him, I'd thought of as my best friend. We'd worked together for years, in the Service and out, and he'd preceded me as Director-General of my Company—he'd invited me to join him—until he went into a nursing home for a drug-addiction cure. I wasn't sure if he was "cured" or not, but he certainly didn't look it.

Errol was still pastyish, jowly, weak in a languid don't-bother-me-manner, quite unlike himself. He walked on with Paul and Angela, and Ouran told them about the soukh. Gillian strolled with me.

"I've *got* to talk to you alone!" she said, looking in front, and without moving her mouth. "Make some excuse, will you?"

Paul turned at that moment, and left the three to wait for us. In the sun, I was a little appalled at his appearance, and the hint of a crafty smile in his eyes. But craftiness wasn't in his nature. Something was wrong. He'd obviously left the nursing home too soon.

"What're you two muttering about?" he called, in a jokingly hapless way that set my teeth on edge. "Think I'm a write-off, do you? *I'll* show you!"

"Don't doubt it," I said, and turned into the garage. "This is where I keep the beer. Stand to!"

CHAPTER SIX

By the time I'd introduced Maurice and Haza, his wife, cold beer had been served in the garden, and we all went out there, a long, wide, high-walled joy, flowers and rose bushes at this end, fruit, vines, and vegetables at the other. Haza took the girls to see the twins in the flax tent under the trees, and Maurice stumped inside to find something to go with the beer.

I wanted to get away without inviting them to the house, or saying anything about it. There was a curious silence between Errol and Paul. Neither looked at the other. Both had been ill—still were not well—and I'd have thought that would have brought them closer.

"No use asking how you two are," I said, as a gambit. "But what brought you here?"

"Why are *you* here?" Paul said, looking down the garden. "What's wrong with the job?"

"Nothing's wrong. I'm studying sand-shift, that's all!"

"Why not study it in our own desert?" he asked. "Plenty of sand there, Christ knows!"

"It may have escaped your attention, but the French have also studied sand. And the Eygptians. I'm simply consulting, let's say, other knowledge. We don't know it all, you know!"

"Don't get shirty," he said. "Asking's no crime, is it?"

"You may like to know what we're fiddling about here for," Errol said quickly, in almost his old way. "Gillian met Angela last week and thought she wasn't looking at all well. Her father was flying to Algiers—it's his aircraft—and she invited Angela to come along. Thought she'd make a goodish chaperone. Paul thought it a fair idea, and we made the party. Since then, we've been to Tunis and a couple of other places. We sent the plane back from Tripoli, and came on by hired cars. Wonderful country. And this sun, of course, makes one distinctly chary of the embalmer, don't you agree?"

"You've been near enough to know," I said. "Everything going well?"

"I've heard all this," Paul said rudely. "I'll look at the grapes!"

He walked away with his glass. Errol turned his head to watch him.

"He's becoming, or else he always was, an absolute lout!" he said, almost to himself. "Answering your question, I'm distinctly better, thank you. Huge appetite, which Gillian controls, shots every day, but not by any means back to form, as you see!"

"I never thought you'd look as well as this," I said. "I often feel guilty, thinking of the others."

"Don't, Edmund. They're better off dead. If they're not, then mercifully, they can't be far off!"

"How do you think they got you?" I asked, taking the bottle over. "It's puzzled me. You were supposed to be an Algerian of Italian descent. All papers in order?"

"Georges Pontvianne got them for me," Errol said, through a sip. "I sweated through the detail for months. I couldn't tell myself apart from Ugo toward the end. It really seemed I'd been born in a bar. We made a lot of money, too!"

"What happened to the man with you? Could he have been the tattler?"

"Best chap in the world," he said gently. "I had the necessary enquiries made, of course. He 'disappeared' on the night I did. A policeman found the bar open, pail still there—we'd been swilling down—cash register untouched. Not a sign of anything. Ugo Primondi and Carl Rosberg *kaput*. But we *did* find that on the same night, an unidentified man was taken to the mortuary. He'd been crushed by a truck. The tattoo marks on the arms were the same as Carl's. I mourn him!"

"Von Staengl, in the West German Embassy, seemed to know where you were," I said. "Could he have had something to do with it? He was extremely disinclined to talk!"

47

"I'm really not sure," Errol said, lying back in the long chair. "The only reason I'm here's the prison doctor. Very good man. He saved me in the early days. The governor used to have me down for question-and-answer sessions. No possible doubt he'd been given the tip. He used something new in gadgetry. New to me, anyway. Felt like a bucket of scalding water. No joke. The doctor told him point-blank, either I could take the daily shots, or else *he'd* have to stop the sessions. One more, he said, and the patient will die. I would have done, too. I could feel it!"

"Before they get here," I said, with an eye on the tent, and pouring more beer. "How do *you* think they got on to you?"

"Don't know. Nobody knew anything about it. The Blur may have had a small idea. I told him what I was going to do, but I didn't say where, or how. Many ways he *might* have got some information. But not from me. At least, I have the satisfaction of knowing I did a great deal more than I'd thought. The poison was slower than I'd been told. It took three, sometimes four days. No pain, no trace. Very good stuff. Never a breath of suspicion. My great advantage was that the club was upstairs. They held three of their 'parties' while I was there. I don't know who they were for. I simply picked out the chaps they *sieg-heiled,* first, and then any chance member who looked like a stormtrooper. Nobody died actually on the premises. I was glad of that. Enquiries, autopsies, whatnot. But whatever's said, Edmund, the Nazi party's back. I can't see what's to be done. I've talked too much. Or it's the beer. Do please forgive me!"

He lay back, eyes closed, seeming to sleep.

I felt a tremendous pity. Remembering other days, Errol, in that state, was indeed pitiable.

I understood Gillian's look, that menace of "empty" eyes looking directly up at me. Hell certainly hath few furies to touch a woman whose love's been cruelly tortured. I was certain she was waiting for a move from me. I had every intention of employing her. She was, in cold fact, a gift of God. She had a first-class brain, she

48

knew the Service high and low, had the necessary social position whether as daughter of Simon Roule, of Roule Brothers, the bankers, or as the future Lady Imbritt. Apart from that, she'd been friendly with both the Lane and Cawle families, naturally, since they moved in that circle, she'd been to school with Lane's daughter Alethea, and joined the Service at about the same time. I had to find out where Alethea was. I'd forgotten about her. Could she have been her daddy's Little Bird? Or the Blur's?

The girls and Paul came out of the tent, and along the path between rumples of scarlet, yellow, pink, white roses. Wistaria ran mauve along the shadowed wall. Maurice stumped his broompole leg out of the house with a girl bringing a platter of small chicken pies in a flakey crust I'd had before.

"Try these," I said, to Errol. "They're delicious!"

"Diet," he said, nodding at Gillian. "There's the gorgon!"

"Nothing till midday," she said, and took a pie. "But that doesn't mean me!"

"*Hola,* what shame!" Maurice groaned and bit out a half. "How you can treat him like this? So nice girl!"

"He's used to it," Gillian munched, and patted his knee. "I went without for days at a time when I first got to the clinic. To keep him company. Then Doctor Lev made me sit in front of him and eat the most colossal meals. I was dying of starvation. Just because he's a fatty and mustn't eat!"

Paul looked at his watch as if he meant us all to see it.

"Time we got along!" he said, nodding at Angela. "I want to look through that rug market in Alexandria. Just make it if we start now. Come on!"

That was my opportunity.

"You mean you were going away today without seeing me?" I said. "All this way for nothing? How did you know I was here?"

A curious silence began. I could hear Maurice chewing. The children in the tent were laughing.

"Well, we went to your son-in-law's agency in

Algiers," Paul said, almost as if he'd been waiting for someone else to speak. "He wasn't there. He was down the Gold Coast, somewhere. With Patti. We wanted to see how she was. His manager said he'd telex London when I asked if you'd been there. Well, they didn't know in London, but they said a cheque of yours had passed through recently with a Tobruk cancellation. So we were coming down this way, anyway, and we thought we'd stop off. That's all!"

Nobody looked at anybody, and nobody said anything.

It was a curious moment.

I knew my Xth sense had been correct. No cheque of mine had ever passed through Tobruk.

"How did *you* find *us?*" Angela asked, speaking for the first time.

"Camel telegraph," I said. "Useful. That cheque *was* a giveaway, wasn't it?"

"You picked the closest-mouthed neighborhood *I've* ever hit against," Paul said. "Even a bribe won't do it!"

"I'm a long way out," I said, and stared blank at Maurice's entirely French look of disbelief. "May I offer you lunch? It's only a couple of hours!"

Maurice's delicate fingers took another pie almost as a penitence. I could have laughed, but didn't.

"Alexandria's a bit far for that," Paul said. "We're shipping out of Dar-es-Salaam next Monday. I'm taking Angela to Australia!"

"We're flying to Khartoum tomorrow," Gillian said. "I've got a cousin there I haven't seen for ages. And lots of sun for Errol. Second half starts next month. Doctor Lev won't let us call it a treatment. Errol's not ill. The difference between now and when I first saw him's simply confounding!"

"I'm not quite so handsome," Errol said, getting up. "Hostesses used to fight each other to carry me up the stairs to the aircraft. Really was worth living. Distinctly palatable, some of them. *And* matey!"

"*Not* when I'm about," Gillian said. "A lecher *redivivus!*"

"Suppose we cut the fancy talk and make a start?" Paul said, suddenly and shockingly. "Alexandria's a good way. Come on!"

"We shall stay in Tobruk, or wherever we please," Gillian said edgily, in open warning. "You do as you wish. Edmund, d'you think you could get us a car?"

"Maurice has one ready, I'm sure," I said, and he nodded. "I could reserve rooms at the hotel for you—"

"Come on, Angela!" Paul said, peremptorily. "This lot's over!"

He went out, through the garage. Angela looked at me in a way I could only think of as infantile appeal, didn't look at Errol or Gillian, and walked as if she might fall at any moment.

"My God!" she barely whispered. "I'm tired of this!"

Maurice took my nod, and stumped after them.

Errol and Gillian looked at each other almost happily.

"Can't *believe* it!" Gillian whispered. "They've gone!"

"We've got to get Angela away," Errol fretted. "The snake-and-rabbit act's gone far enough. I don't know what he's doing to her or to himself. I don't know how she puts up with it!"

"Darling, supposing you go and see them off?" Gillian said, curling up her knees, comfortably. "I've been snappy. I couldn't wish them a fondish. Utterly false. Angela's welcome as the flowers, she knows that. Tell her to leave the brute and come with us!"

Errol nodded and went out, head down, splay-foot, ponderous. Gillian looked at him, and up to me.

"Far better than he was!" she said, and drew a breath. "I had the impression Paul was deliberately trying to make him worse, d'you know? If you hadn't come along today, I was going to put my foot down. No more of it. I found we could fly to Cairo from Tobruk. But that's not what I wanted to say. I think Paul's back on drugs again, and I also believe we're been followed everywhere!"

"Why?"

She gave me full benefit of that menacingly "empty" look. I'd always thought she had black eyes. They were lovely blue, at the moment frozen. I'd once considered her plain. She wasn't. She had every right to be called quite lovely, deep blond hair in a bun, petite, beautiful legs, and above all, extremely feminine, in these days most uncommon.

"We haven't much time," she said, looking toward the door. "Errol has to be taken care of. That's why we're going to Khartoum. We'd be well-warned of strangers. Europeans can't move an eyelash here, unless it's known in the right place. My cousin's got that in hand. There's no time to tell you the details, but there were two attempts on Errol, one on me, and another on Angela. Errol was shot at in the grounds of Mellonhamp, and two nights later dynamite or something went off when his car passed. Somebody almost ran Angela down when she was riding last week. She had a very good mount and she took a hedge. But it was a deliberate attempt. My car blew up in the garage. I'd phoned down to have it ready, and the poor garage man was dreadfully injured. So my father said, that's quite enough. Out of the country, and give the Police a chance to link up. That's why we're here. But Paul wasn't asked, and that story about your cheque didn't come from your son-in-law's agency!"

"Oh? Where *did* it come from?"

"Errol saw the manager, himself. They knew nothing about a cheque of yours, and they'd never heard of Paul!"

"Apart from that, there was never any cheque!" I said. "I encouraged him to see how far he'd go. He's ill. That's clear. Do you want to work with me?"

She sat up, clasped her hands, smiled happily.

"More than anything!" she whispered with a side glance at the garage door. "Tell me what I'm to do!"

"Put out all lines for Lane and Cawle," I said, and instantly her smile went. "They're at the root of this. Not, perhaps, in person. These recent attempts look like second-string stuff. When those two start business they won't make *any* mistakes, you know that. I want to know who warned them in Washington. How the warning was given. I'd like to know where Alethea Cawle is, and what she's been doing. I want to find out who told the East Germans where Errol was, and how they got him over the frontier. Who told them that Ugo Primondi was the Lord Imbritt? Was it either of the Washington pair? Who told *them*? Chiefly, I'd like to find those two snakes and put a boot on them!"

She stood, suddenly. Her teeth held her upper lip for a moment, making her look distinctly feral.

"I'd pay for their graves myself," she said. "But only after Errol's gone back to the clinic. Before that, I can only write or cable. You can always get me care of Daddy. What about Paul?"

"He'll have a tail he won't lose from the moment he reaches Cairo. Angela'll go with you, if you want her?"

"Oh, but of course, poor girl!"

"Then she'll be on the same flight. Log your expenses in the usual way. I'll open an account for you in Zurich. Anything else?"

Maurice came to the door, held both jambs, and looked extremely French, one eyebrow up, one well-down, cigaret in half a leer.

"The other car has gone, and the lady's gentleman is waiting," he said, and flicked ash off the cigaret without taking it out of his mouth. "He is a little impatient!"

"Every right to be, poor lamb!" Gillian said, and turned. "I heard from Consuelo. Apparently she's an heiress. I know Banbury Cross. It's a lovely house and beach. Is she quite safe?"

"She has two bodyguards!"

"Do with two more. Jamaica's a quiet place!"

"Glad to be sustained in self-argument. She'll have them there tomorrow morning!"

"Love to know why we're singled out for attention," she said, on the way to the garage. "Are they going to make things uncomfortable for everybody they knew?"

"I believe they'll try to put away anyone who knew them rather well. It's a matter of identification. With a few people out of the way, the authorities haven't much more than a dossier and perhaps a few ancient photographs. They could both operate pretty well as they pleased, and even if they were picked up, it wouldn't be easy to nail them as themselves. How was Paul let out of the nursing home?"

"Refused to stay there, and made a bolt for it," Gillian said. "We didn't know that, or he wouldn't *be* with us. Daddy told me when I called him the night before last. Oh, Edmund, I'd never have believed it. I *know* him. I've worked for him. Absolutely the very finest type. But now? He gets drunk, he fights, he's horribly rude. And he's dirty!"

"He's not himself," I said, with a very heavy heart, because I knew what I'd have to do. "Keep the best of him in your mind, and forget the rest!"

"That's an order!" she said, and tiptoed to kiss my chin. "Can't tell you how really happy I am. Errol's comatose. Just as well. These roads roll that poor tum about and make him groan. *And* curse. I never heard anything so funny!"

Errol seemed to have gone to sleep in the back of the car. Gillian got in with him, set his head more comfortably, leaned to shake hands with Haza and Maurice, and in a perfect Arab *ulula* and clapping of hands, the car went out to sunny dust.

Maurice, cigaret a-dangle, squinted at me through the smoke.

"You live a couple of hours from here?" he asked, mildly. "I say nothing, eh?"

"I didn't want them there, and I don't want anyone to know where I am," I said. "I hope that's clear?"

"Clear," he said, nodding. "This first man, he want to know how to reach where you camp if they turn back from Tobruk. I say, go through here, right to Derna. Then you ask the gendarme, and they take!"

"Well done. What made you think of that?"

"If he is your friend, why he don't ask to you? If he is not you' friend, he will come through here, certainly. And I will tell to you, and in Derna, make a special arrangement, no?"

"Yes," I said. "Thank you, Maurice, I believe somebody *will* come through here. And quite soon!"

He opened his hands, and shrugged.

"I am ready," he said, and nodded at Haza, coming through the crowd with a parcel. "More chicken pie, and a special kous-kous. I don't tell you what. You eat!"

"What did you think of that man?" I asked, getting in the car. "Leave any impression?"

"What I think?" he said, and turned down his mouth. "I think he has a *cafard*. I know it. A sickness of the mind. It is not well, you know? He is not strong!"

But strength of mind, of spirit or anything else were qualities I'd always believed Paul possessed. Besides being the sharpest brain, the coldest thinker, and I suppose the best all-round man I ever met. I held my present position because of him. I wasn't forgetting it for a moment. I intended to find out what was wrong with him, first, and then with Angela. She was no ordinary girl. She was going to be his wife.

Her tears, that were quite foreign to her character, had a great deal to tell me.

I rankled and rambled round it all the way to the house, and ran, because the call hummed everywhere. I got up to the attic, and sat down, switching on, running up the band, and suddenly flashed a "blue."

It came from a prism I used as a warning instead of a bell or buzzer. It had never come on before. I hadn't expected it to. My known callers were tuned exactly on.

But it hadn't come on in the right place.

I sat there, in that blue light, knowing that somebody, somewhere, was "on" to me.

Deliberately.

The cold I felt was not of the room.

CHAPTER SEVEN

I went downstairs and got the transistor set I used for news.

I knew I was wasting time, but I swept the bands, trying to find a local whoop, though obviously whoever-it-was had a locator of considerable power and he'd managed to get one pointer on me. When he got the second on, I'd be pinpointed. I had to pin him, first.

I got on to Khefi in Cairo, but he was out.

The blue still came on, went off, sometimes bright, then dull, back again to bright blue. Whoever it was knew his business. He wouldn't hear anything when I was working except the scrambler "rip" whether of speech or cipher. He wouldn't need anything else.

What then?

We were fairly lonely. Ouran, Arefa, a few gardeners and watermen and myself, were the only males for miles. I saw I had to recruit a company of light sleepers and very little conscience.

I called Ouran.

"I want you to recruit riflemen of your own choice," I told him. "They'll be hidden day and night in all-round defence of the house. When I leave, twenty will stay on for three months. After that, ten, at all times. I want everyone to know this house is a fortress. Station half-a-dozen or so pairs of ears in El Garh, and another half-dozen—I leave it to you—in Hamoun, that is, in addition. Put whatever men you please on the high ground between us and the road. Get a full report every morning and night about traffic from Tobruk or Derna. Private cars and trucks should have a special check. Or people renting cars, or using private planes. Put the word out to the seamen. There'll be a reward for all information. As soon as you please!"

He touched heart, mouth and forehead, and slippered off.

I went up to my stores, and found a couple of locators I'd intended for another job. They were the latest, put together by artificers in my own workshop, small, powerful, accurate. I wired one of them, and switched on.

The blues were intermittent, dull. He seemed to be sweeping, trying to find me. My locator needle circled, dipped, and went back to normal. My friend had switched off.

I left the locator on, and took the other with me, changed into shorts, and went down to the boathouse. Getting the boat into the water was a matter of pressing two buttons, one to open the door, the other to send her down the slipway. She was the prettiest cutter I ever saw, designed for rough or smooth, with a Rolls-Royce engine, built for Ulla Brandt Ben Ua's husband, and since modernized. She handled like a bicycle and made no nonsense of twenty knots in a sea about as lively as a glass of water. I went due north for fifteen minutes, and turned due west for twenty, which I thought would give me enough of an angle to hairline him.

The water was choppier and the wind had freshened, but it was still pleasant in the sun. I went aft, letting her roll, and switched on the locator.

The needle dipped, trembled, steadied, and *stuck!*

I almost yelled.

But the fact was sobering. He wasn't far off, and he had two sets each a few miles apart. This wasn't a Service or a Post Office job. They work on another principle. All he had to do was get a needle on my signal with each set, and where they crossed, I had to be. All he need do, then, was look at a map, use a compass, and follow his nose.

I didn't like it a bit. What really annoyed me was that I'd never even considered the possibility. I left the locator on, so that the needle would still—even if he switched off—point to him, and turned for home.

First, I decided that Consuelo couldn't come back.

57

She'd have to stay in Jamaica, or go to New York, and wait there until I had things settled. Secondly, I had to find both stations and destroy them, together with anyone I found at either place. Thirdly, I had to move.

I'd made quite a good plan, but obviously it had gone awry. How? Who knew? Who could have talked? Not Khefi. Of that, I was eternally sure. Or somebody in Tobruk? Maurice?

It's curious how the mind works—or almost panics—at such a time. Every ridiculous suggestion comes up for assessment. The obvious is nearly always forgotten.

How had Paul known where to look for me?

The business of the cheque had been a flat lie. Paul had never been a liar. It wasn't in him. I hadn't until then realized the full implication of his manner and appearance and the way he spoke. He wasn't just ill. He was a changed personality.

He was not the Paul Chamby I'd worked with.

It took a little time to sink in. It wasn't the most agreeable idea. How it could have happened was somebody else's business, but I knew that my first thought had been correct. He'd have to be put away for his own good.

I got back to our beach, and Arefa waited to send the boat up the slipway. I hurried up to the attic, taking a heavy towel from a maid as I went. I needed it. The attic was really cold.

The locator needle pointed where it had, and the secondary crossed it on site. I switched off and on again. Both needles dipped to the same position. I went to the wall map and took the protractor, tracing a line from my position, and another from the boat's.

The site was on high ground this side of Derna. I tried to recall that tract of country. There were houses round about, but few. I didn't know the area well enough.

I took a smaller map out of the desk and went downstairs to find Ouran. The maid told me he was up at the gate, talking to some men, and I sent her to get him.

The Tobruk operator outdid himself in putting me on to Khefi.

"Ah, but Edmund!" the familiar voice grated. "I have been trying to find you, my friend!"

"Now that you have, what?"

"Our friend, Mr. Paul Chamby has been here—!"

"When?"

"*A*-bout fifteen minutes *a*-go!"

"Impossible, Khefi. He left me at Hamoun by car something over three hours ago, if that. There's no flight from Tobruk till five. He was going by car to Alexandria—"

"But I know Mr. Paul Chamby!"

"Khefi, you're mistaken. I'll fly to Cairo now, and you can put us together!"

"Well, Edmund, this is a very interesting surprise, I shall say? I had no doubt of him—"

"I'm going into Tobruk. I'm asking Chaddid at our office to get me on the London flight tonight. I'll be with you at about eight?"

"I hope to have *a* Mr. Paul Chamby waiting for you!"

Arefa had brought in the locator from the boat. The needle had returned to normal, but the secondary needle still marked the other station's position. I compared it with the attic's and found them true, on site.

I ringed the area map, put a cross exactly on the spot, and dressed, waiting for Ouran. When he stood, a shadow in the brilliant doorway, sunlight tipping silver in his right eye, it took me all my time not to laugh outright. No cat ever lapped fatter chops after a maul of canary.

"Sir," he began, palm to me, fingers spread out. "I have the Sheikh of 'moun al Amoun in our pay, with all his people. The older women and younger children will stay in El Garh, Hamoun and the other oases, to listen, and report. With them will be boys to ride with the messages. The rifles, about eighty, are round us. You will never see them!"

"How do I know they're there if I don't see them?"

"I know they are there!"

59

"Good enough. Now, look at this map. What's at this cross?"

He took the map into the light, squinting the sun-furrows, and looked up as if he heard the answer.

"It is an estate of one I have never seen," he said, and put that forefinger into the side of his beard. "He comes once a season. There are five servants, two European, one Somali, one Algerian, one Bedouin. I have seen them in the soukh at Derna. There are eight women. Most are young, two from Sfax, mix-European Arab, two from Ghardames, Touareg, sold in the market, three Ouled, also sold, and one Somali. She is the cook. A good woman. I spoke to her. She wanted to come here, but the Madame permits only Bedouin!"

I saw light.

"Now, Ouran," I said briskly. "There's a very good idea. See if you can talk to her. Find out who's there, names, everything. Take a few of the Sheikh's men with you. They won't be seen, of course. I'll be one of them!"

He seemed to grow inside the burnous, and blood shone in his eyes with the smile. We'd been on a few outings before.

"God is good!" he said, and touched heart, mouth and forehead. "I call Maurice for cars? Or by horse?"

"By water truck," I said. "We shall be workmen going home. Twenty of us should be enough. All arms hidden. The rest remain here!"

I got on to Chaddid in the Cairo office, and gave him a list of things to do, and then I called Van der Luyn in the control tower at Tobruk.

"Anything ready for Cairo?" I asked him. "In a couple of hours?"

"I've got a Dart," he said. "Just came in—"

"I also want an extra passage on the five o'clock. Miss Angela Masters—"

"Already been asked for. From the hotel. I've had several enquiries for you in the past few days!"

"Take any names?"

60

"She didn't ask. They came here two or three days ago. Yesterday a man asked for you. I wasn't here. He, and a woman. I told the girl. Say nothing!"

"Who were they?"

"The woman was tall and fair. Very fair. Platinum, I think it's called. I didn't hear them speak. The girl called me too late. They said they were friends of yours, and they wanted to speak to you urgently. The girl told them to go to the Consul. I called him. They didn't go there!"

"Next time, make a fuss of them. Try to find out anything you can. Any idea where they went?"

"They took a car. I could find out?"

"See what you can do. And never mind who it is, you haven't seen me for six months!"

I was beginning to be distinctly worried. I'd thought I had North Africa to myself. Something, somewhere, had gone wrong.

I couldn't think how.

The water truck wasn't a comfortable ride. About twenty of the most unappetising ruffians I ever saw hung on to the clamps, or sat astride the tank, or stood on the chassis, holding on to the rail. I crowded in front with the driver, the Sheikh himself, a fat fellow indeed, swaddled in a magnificent deep-red burnous, and Ouran. With the exception of the Sheikh, we each had about a corner of one cheek on the seat. For the rest, we bumped and balanced. The windscreen was too greasy to see through. Our wiper didn't work, but anyway, I knew the road fairly well, sandbanks, potholes, dunes, and farther over, scrub, dwarf olives. I shut my eyes, trying to make up my mind where to begin, but the driver turned off the asphalt before we got to Hamoun, and took a track I didn't know. We were going the right way, and Ouran didn't say anything. He'd covered his mouth to keep out the dust. I thought that a sound idea. In the heat and petrol smell I dozed and swayed. We stopped bouncing, and floated again on asphalt, hummed, whined, turned, jolted over rough patches, tipped wheels on rocks, came out on the road again, sang a song of sandy tires spraying crystals, turned lurchingly uphill to the left, and stopped.

Ouran reached over to open the door. We were in an olive grove about thirty yards from the road down below. I got out and stretched. All the men had gone. I couldn't hear a sound. Ouran pointed up, and I followed. I heard a curious thump-dot, thump-dot behind me, which I thought familiar.

I wasn't wrong.

Maurice grinned in a particularly "French" way—nobody else can—shrugged inside the burnous, and jerked a thumb forward.

Ouran was at a door in a high, embrasured mud wall. He brought down the palm of his hand in a sign to halt, pointing into the ground, pushed open the door and went in. The door creaked shut. Maurice pointed to the top of the wall, and made a back underneath an embrasure. I kneeled on him, stood, gripped the top and pulled my eyes just over the edge.

The arched terrace of a long white house faced the sea. A garden gone to weeds stretched about fifty yards between me and the earthenware-tiled surround of a pool. A car roof shone just beyond the pomegranates. In a red-and-black striped awning, at the near end, a girl in a white suit talked to a man over a tray of drinks.

No mistaking that silvery plait.

I'd met her months before, in Capri, under curious circumstances.

No mistaking the man.

Joh Pensen, a pianist of the jazz variety. I'd seen him not long before in a place and at a time which stuck in my mind like a fistful of thistles. I lowered my head, knelt, and slid off Maurice's back. He put his good foot in my linked hands, and I lifted him for the few moments before he signed he'd seen enough.

His eyebrows were up, his eyes smiled surprise, but I went on, down the path, in sand that covered noise. Under the olives, I stopped.

"There was a car over there," I said. "They're

dressed ready to go. Know anybody at Derna airstrip, and the harbour?"

"Both," he said, and put a cigaret in the corner of his mouth without lighting it. "I call them, I want to know where these two go. It is strange, no? Four people the same, here—but here!—in one day? They are like *le cafard*, and that tall girl, this morning. But they are not. What do they pretend?"

"In what way?"

"The tall one this morning, she has a beautiful legs. This one is too thin. The hair of this one is too long down the back. *Le cafard* is tired, a little stupid. This one is not. But for somebody, they look the same, no?"

Ouran came down the path. From nowhere that I saw, all his ruffians began to close in.

"Four people have been at the house," he whispered. "Three men, one woman. Two men by boat. The man and woman by air. Two men have a room upstairs, always locked. There are sounds like many bees, and also in the night. The man is not the owner of the house. He has two planes, one small. It is in the garden. The other at the airfield near, on the coast. Also a boat. He goes today with the woman. There are two telephones. Many calls!"

My mind steadied. I seemed to see everything in ice.

In looks and dress this man, Pensen, and the girl, could easily be taken for Paul and Angela. Could that mean there might be danger of a "substitution" somewhere between here and Cairo? But then, who could have been the "Paul" Khefi had spoken to? Why should somebody be impersonating Paul?

It occurred, of course, that one was providing an alibi for the other. Why? Could one of the false "Pauls" be one of the pair I was after? I suddenly went hot to think I might have my hands on one or both.

"Get down to Derna," I told Maurice. "See that the aircraft is put under seal, and get the boat taken care of. Find out who this man's supposed to be and who the woman is. Send a good car back here for me. I shan't see you for a few days—"

63

I heard the splutter over distance. Under the trees, and with the wall between us, we couldn't see the helicopter take off, but it was rising away from us.

"Come on, Ouran!" I said. "Send your men in there. Maurice, take that car in the garden. I'll go back by truck with the men. Go!"

We ran up the path, through the side door, and along the grass borders to the terrace. In the dining room, beyond the long salon, two men were eating a meal. I went in, touching heart, mouth and forehead. The younger stood up, chewing, a little surprised, the other, inclined to be annoyed, went on heaping rice on his knife. There wasn't time for them to talk. The doors slammed open, and a dozen of Ouran's finest leapt at them. They hadn't an earthly. They were mummified in table linen, and flung in a corner.

I followed on behind the horde. Four rooms upstairs had been occupied. There was bath powder and an empty perfume bottle in one. I could almost *see* Consuelo! On the third floor two maids cowered in a corner. Ouran sent them downstairs with a tap on the rump, and I went into a fair-sized room with enough radio equipment for a couple of big ships, all in first-class order. The first thing I saw was the locator.

The needle pointed at Ulla's house. It shouldn't have been a shock, but it was. It had no secondary needle. I wondered if the other set had been in the helicopter. It would explain the blue prism's bright-and-dull off and on. Everything was bolted to the tables, but it didn't take long to chop legs off and carry the lot down to the tank truck and rope it on. I didn't leave a tack behind, and I went all over the house to see if I'd missed anything. It looked the usual sort of place for a summer hideaway, nothing expensive, just enough furniture for comfort. I couldn't find a single piece of paper, or curiously, a book, and there was no piano, or sheet music. I didn't talk to the servants. I left that to Ouran. I went in to question the two I'd left trussed in a corner of the dining room, but Ouran, outside, on the pool's surround, saw me, and waved a forefinger.

"Gone!" he called, and waved a hand beyond the walls. "They won't be found!"

"Back on the truck everybody," I said. "Were the servants happy with their money? You told them what to do?"

"I have three men here," he said, smiling. "Everybody is paid well. Nothing will happen unless I know. Nothing comes, nothing goes!"

We all went down to the truck. The driver had wiped off the windscreen, and the cabin stank of petrol, but at least we could see where we were going. We'd come more or less uphill all the way, feeling the rise, and the pull of the engine. Now we had the benefit of descent, through olive groves, pomegranates and vines, then the dunes, when we turned off to bypass Hamoun.

I was in the middle of a fine daydream about the Pauls, the one I knew, and Khefi's, deciding that the Paul I'd talked to that morning *was* Paul Chamby, and trying to imagine what sort of game the other might be playing, and Ouran straightened, stared, and turned to me.

I saw the smoke furl grey against blue sky just over the sand ridge in front. We went further down, and then had to climb, but at the top there was a still higher ridge. The driver did his best. We fairly rocked to the top, and Ouran threw up his hands.

Down on the beach, little figures were running through heavy smoke. The house was hidden by trees. Flame burst red over the tips.

CHAPTER EIGHT

My suite, the servants quarters at the other end of the house, and the gardener's store, water tanks and generator sheds in between were burning in a curious wispy sort of way. The house escaped because the pool was full, Ulla had a new type of extinguisher all round the place, and we'd got back just in time. With the main building safe, we went at the rest. Surprisingly, although it had looked as if we might lose everything, we got off very lightly.

A chemical must have been used. That was obvious from the smoke and flame marks. When everything was beaten out, and not so much as a breath rising anywhere, I pointed them out to Ouran.

"Now you have to find out who came here," I told him. "Someone got in and set many eggs. Ask the women!"

When he came back to tell me that nobody had been there, and the first anyone knew was smoke coming through the kitchen window, we seemed to get the idea at the same time.

"The little one!" he shouted, pointing up. "Arefa told me he saw it. It was out. Over the sea!"

But that was all the boy could tell us. If the helicopter had come over the house or anywhere near, everybody would have seen it, all would certainly have heard it. Ouran's face seemed to have creased another twenty years in wrinkles.

"Take the jeep back to Hamoun," I told him. "Tell Madame Maurice I want the workmen out here immediately. I want all this repaired and repainted. From now, I want a twenty-four-hour guard. You see what happens?"

He shook fists in fury of silent rage, tremblingly touched heart, mouth and forehead, and went off behind the black ruin of my suite. I heard him scream for the jeep boy, and went in, walking over pools of drying chemical. There had clearly been an explosion in the bedroom. Had I been lying down, as I usually did at that time, I'd have been nicely put away.

There was little doubt in my mind, then, that the pair had indeed got on to me. I had even less doubt that the fire was started by one of James Morris's "stickers," and the explosion had been caused by one of his discs. James had to be warned about it soonest. The pair had enjoyed unlimited choice of anything in that arsenal over the years. They must have had quite a variety of goodies saved up.

As, indeed, I had.

But somebody hadn't quite enough time to place the charges correctly. The disc explosive should have been stuck against the outer wall, behind the head of the bed. It would have wrecked the entire building. As it was, it must have been stuck to the outside bathroom wall. Inside, a fall of water came down like a smooth curtain over the entire area. The water had cushioned the effect, but the wall was blown out.

Somebody seemed to have been in a hurry. More, whoever-it-was didn't know the place very well.

I called Arefa.

"How many people have been here today, apart from those brought by your father?" I asked him.

"Nobody, sir," he said, still red-eyed from smoke, with a singed shirt, and violet anti-burn jelly on hands and forearms. "Only those men and women, those without clothes. I told them you had gone, and they went away!"

"Those who had breakfast here?"

"Like them, but not the same," he said. "A girl asked to pick flowers, and I took her to the lower garden. A basket, no more. They didn't ask for coffee or cigarets. She filled the basket and they went out. Did I do wrong, sir?"

"How long ago was this?"

"One hour after you went. They were at sea when I came from the kitchen. You would like lunch, sir?"

I looked at those little, doggish eyes, innocent as the sand he limped on, and nodded.

"Whatever there is. On the patio."

I went through the house, surprised at what little damage had been done. Maids were scouring floors, wiping furniture, brushing smoke-webs out of corners, still weeping, looking at me with the eyes of does, dark, tragic, as if they were to blame.

It was time to consider whether to go to Cairo, see Khefi, and clean up there, or to stay, and get the flower-children, or hippies, or hopsters, or whatever they were, lined up, and put in place. Among such a collection, there was ample room and plenty of cover for odd types ready to do quite another sort of job.

But how could anybody have been "planted" there to work on me? There hadn't been time. I'd decided to take the house without telling anyone except Ulla, in a cable to her place near Oman, and then in terms we both understood, though I doubt that anyone else would. Her house was called, in Arabic, Nest in a Sheltering Branch, and I'd cabled "Homing Branch, Iliad."

Nobody, except Ulla, could possibly make head or tail of that, I was sure. Not many knew we'd been in a Nazi prison for three days, at any moment expecting to be taken out and shot, and while we were in that cell, with God knows how many others—it was dark—I told her the story of the Iliad, in the words I remembered, if only to cut us both off from the disgust of that present time and to take our minds from the stench of our living selves. Ulla, a great girl, clean as the South of the World, a New Zealander, one-time schoolteacher, widow of an Arab oilman, grieving for him down to the day, had always told me to take the house when I wanted it. She went there only in those so few days after the spring rains, when the desert suddenly smiles color in miles of wildflowers to the horizon.

Those were the days she loved.

So did I.

I wanted to take Consuelo—without telling her—at the end of winter, in blackish skies, and mists cold as the skirts of Astarte, and let her wake up in a tent one morning in the first yellow springtime sun, to see the

68

desert open in a mat of leaf that tomorrow would bud, and then the flowers, everywhere.

Arefa set down the silver tray, and took off the cover of a couple of dishes.

"How did you see this one, this blossom picker, without your father's permission or mine?" I asked him.

"She came with the others in a boat, sir!"

"Which was she?"

"A dark one," he said. "The hair is fair. But when she walked, I saw she was dark!"

Those eyes were not quite so innocent as I'd thought. But in his ironed and starched white shirt-cum-kaftan he appeared the very hoop-la of boyish guilelessness, especially with the steel and leather straps of the boot curling away from the buckles.

"Anyone else?"

"Three, sir. The man, a dark one, was rude. He pulled off my headband, and when I stopped him, he kicked!"

The garden tremored in shades of pink. I dislike bullies.

"You told your father?"

"Not yet, sir."

"Tell him. The men of 'al Amoun will be here at ail times. They will guard the beach, as well. Nobody will come here. For any reason. This order I give you in the name of Madame. Also, the dark one will pay for the kick. This is my word!"

He touched heart, mouth and forehead, and jingled off.

In the silence of the garden, the distant sough of the sea, and the patient whisper of scouring brooms, I settled to make another plan, with little to go on, except that I'd thought the first would keep me hidden for at least three months, and it hadn't. I had to take a great deal more trouble, making sure, first, that Consuelo was safe.

The hipster lot, for the moment, could wait.

CHAPTER NINE

My Dart made smooth work of the flight from Tobruk to Cairo, and I climbed the new stairway up to Khefi's bffice with a mind that seemed sore with thinking. What I really wanted to do was put my head in Consuelo's arms and cleave—what a lovely word!—to those hardish breasts and the nipples, that in closed eyes, and under a touching tongue-tip felt a yard of Paradise long.

Khefi had a secretary—for the first time since I'd known him, a smart policewoman—but she knew my name, and showed me in without pause.

Khefi wore a gray suit. That was strange. He lolled in a new black leather chair. He didn't smile, get up, or offer his hand. Not a bit like himself. The matchbox still swung between the finger and thumb of the left hand, but the perenially unlit cigaret didn't point to the right of the bridge of his nose as it always had. It pointed at me, and the nail of the third finger plucked at his bottom teeth.

I was a little puzzled.

"I have questions to ask," he said, in his official voice, possibly the most intimidating I ever heard, mixing, as it were, Arabic gutturals with the interrogative impersonality of the torture chamber. "First, have you representatives in Israel? Second, do you employ Israelis? Third, does your business take you into Israel? I ask a fourth question. Have you been faithful to our friendship? Do you use my name to take advantage?"

I was more annoyed than surprised. I thought I'd better answer in the same tone, in my own way.

"I have no representatives in Israel!" I said, loudly, so that the policemen I could see through the half-open door in the next room might hear. "I employ Hebrews, yes. Three have American passports, two have French passports, and four others, British, one Tunisian, two

Czechoslovak, one Polish, one South African. None of them is Israeli. My business has nothing to do with Israel. The pipeline under construction doesn't pass within a hundred miles of the Israeli frontier. Finally, so far as I know, I have never taken advantage of our friendship. What leads you to believe I have?"

He seemed to understand that I meant what I said. The cigaret turned once again to the right, and he smiled, in the eyes at least, and sat up.

"Mr. Chamby told me a long story," he said, in a more humorful tone. "He is sure he was taken off the directors—what is it?—he lose the position because you are his enemy. You are of the C.I.A. and so are most of your regional supervisors. You are working only for the Jews, financially, and when you are ready, you will ruin our brothers!"

I heard him out, but only just.

"Look here, Khefi," I said, I hoped reasonably. "Let's consider this. You know the circumstances? D'you really think I'd give away an absolute empire for any reason? What good would it do me to work for Israel? They haven't got enough of anything to buy a fraction of what I hold. D'you think I'd sell my name? D'you think I'd risk earning the contempt of the Princes? Being able to look a man in the eye is worth more than money. Do you believe I'd *be* here—knowing you—if I'd been a traitor? I can look *you* in the eye, and ask you to bring in Mr. Chamby!"

He stared down at the pad, eyebrows up, nodding.

"You don't share our desire to see Israel destroyed?" he said, not looking at me. "You don't hope for our victory?"

"I'm on shaky ground, Khefi. I don't want to see either of you 'win.' It's going to be a pyrrhic victory, at best. You'll damn' nearly destroy each other. And the whole world's going to be the poorer. What I'd like to see is a little commonsense discussion between both of you. That's so easy to say, isn't it? But you're both 'soukh' bargainers. You don't need any help. You're peoples of the same stock, same root. Islam and

71

Hebraism are both matters of faith, thoughts, theories. Allah and Yaweh are one and the same. Why don't you get together, and stop bothering the rest of us?"

He put his head back, and laughed fine teeth at the ceiling, ya-ha-haaa!

"When you say it, it's so, as you say, easy!" he said, and looked at the secretary holding the door open. "Bring in, please, Mr. Chamby!"

"You've got him?" I said, surprised.

He nodded, straightfaced.

"I am no longer of the Police," he said. "I am in the Special Branch. With other duties. To preserve the country against enemies. We have many. But the worst enemy is the friend who isn't with us!"

"Meaning me?"

He nodded.

"I expect much more from you. After so many years and secrets, I am entitled to expect it. At this moment, you require a favor. Why should I listen?"

"Which favor do I require?"

"The release of Lord Imbritt and the two women with him!"

I had to swallow what felt like a flight of tin locusts.

"For what reason would you arrest them?"

"He is a Jew. The one woman is a daughter of Simon Roule. He is known to be an important factor in Israeli finance in London. Lord Imbritt is a partner in that company. The other woman, Masters, is known to be an agent of your M.I. Her father was advisor to Chaim Weizmann and Ben Gurion in the creation of Israel as a State. She worked in Tel-Aviv two years ago in the potash development. Do you deny it?"

"All of it," I said, knowing I was up against a wall of prejudice, and almost seeing the snake-fangs of the informant. "First of all, the Lord Imbritt is not a Hebrew. His mother is. He was brought up as I was. Secondly, Gillian Roule, one of the women, who's going to marry him, is certainly daughter of Simon Roule. But I know, as a fact, and you must accept this, that any dealing he may have with Israeli finance is part of the day's

72

business. Just as your own banks deal, day to day. They can't help it. A bank, after all, is simply a clearing house for commerce. As for Angela Masters, you may take it from me that she's employed by my Company as a principal secretary. She has about as much to do with Israel as I have. And that's not a hell of a lot!"

He was looking at me, smiling in a resigned sort of way.

"Let us talk to Mr. Chamby," he said, and reached to press the button.

I was in a far from happy state of mind.

To lose Khefi as a friend was catastrophe, replete. That Errol, Gillian, and Angela were under arrest was black news, indeed. Beyond calling the Ambassador, I didn't see what I could do. And I doubted that he could do much. Extraordinary, the effect of a few years. We weren't the Power we'd been.

The door opened quietly.

Two policemen came in with a sergeant behind, and he stepped aside for Paul Chamby.

He looked at me, and creased his face. It wasn't a smile.

" 'lo, Edmund!" he said, and laughed, eyes shut, shaking into himself, as if he wanted to settle into a smaller mould. "Got you where you can't snake out, eh?"

I could only look at him. He seemed drunk.

"Very well," Khefi said loudly. "Mr. Chamby, sit down!"

The secretary came in with a file, put it on the desk, and went out.

"Mr. Trothe," Khefi said, in the old way, as friends. "I am not going to interrogate you on this statement of Mr. Chamby's. You are free to leave!"

I got up. I didn't quite know what was on.

"Thank you, Commissioner," I said. "I'm perfectly willing to answer any questions you wish to ask, and provide proof—"

"Wharrya mean, proof?" Paul shouted. "Biggest liar ever was. Known for it. Couldn't see the truth stuck on

73

a plate. You don't believe him, Khef', for Christ's sake?"

"You may go, Mr. Trothe," Khefi said, nodding to the sergeant to open the door. "You are at liberty to leave the country as you wish. See me at any time. Thank you for your visit. Good night!"

It was blank dismissal. I didn't argue. I didn't look at Paul. I wanted to. I wished I could have found out where he was staying, or if I could help him. He seemed at the end of his tether.

But the very air was against me. Khefi's attitude warned. I hadn't any notion what was behind it. I wanted to ask about Errol, Gillian and Angela, but it wasn't the time. I simply walked out, bowed, in passing, to the secretary, and went steadily down five flights of stairs between lizard-green walls, and out, into warm night air, and the peaked face of Chaddid, supervisor of the Cairo office.

"Your air tickets, sir," he said, almost in a quaver, giving me an envelope. "The car will take you to the airport. You have just time. The bag is here. I am so relieved to see you!"

"Glad to be here," I said. "I'll call you from Rome tomorrow!"

I got in the Cadillac with a feeling of having slipped the leash, and away we went. I quite expected to be stopped and taken in arrest at any moment. I don't know why. I wasn't even thinking what I was doing. I just wanted to get airborne. I've never been in such a state. Perhaps Paul's appearance had something to do with it.

There was no longer any doubt in my mind.

He was insane, and I was sure that Khefi knew it.

We went into the airport and I had to scramble to get the flight. Fortunately, the chauffeur was known to the porters. My bag went up at the double, my ticket was scribbled on—I've never understood why airclerks have to do such a damned lot of scribbling and wasting time—and I was at a trot down the ramp, up the steps, and the steward shut the door.

A hostess took my hat and coat, and I sat down, buckled the seat belt, and heard somebody say "Well!"

I looked round, to my right.

Errol and Gillian sat in the two seats over the aisle, and behind, Angela smiled at me.

"Compliments of Khefi!" Errol bent across to say, in a tiny whisper over the rising whine of jets. "I don't know *what* we owe him. Settle accounts one of these days, what?"

CHAPTER TEN

Angela came over, slid across my knees, buckled herself in, sitting back, eyes closed, legs stretched, a tired girl.

I went through the entire business, detail by detail, from the morning on. I couldn't put it together. Paul could only have got to Cairo before me by flying. But why had he lied to Khefi? What earthly good did he expect to get out of it?

He could, of course—if Khefi hadn't been a strong friend—have ruined me. I'm not sure how I could have defended myself against a charge of being an Israeli supporter. In that office, with an unfriendly Khefi behind that desk, realizing the power he held, I wouldn't have stood a chance. He didn't need a warrant to arrest. There was no such thing.

"Do you wish to hear *anything* I have to say, Mr. Trothe?" Angela asked, sitting up. "I don't intend to tell tales or anything of the sort. But there *are* two or three things you ought to know!"

"I'd be glad to hear them," I said, a little surprised. "I shall rely, as ever, on your discretion!"

She laughed for the first time since I'd seen her, but so painfully, I was hurt for her.

"Well, you know that Paul and I were going to be married. That's off, unfortunately. It began by being a—wonderful—well, sort of adventure. At least, it was for me. We went everywhere. Arabia, Afghanistan, Uzbekhistan—"

"I didn't know that? In Soviet territory?"

"Oh, yes. We went all through the Caspian oilfields. Up to the Russian nuclear testing grounds. We saw a rocket take-off—"

"You were allowed there?"

"There didn't seem to be much trouble about it. Of course, we weren't very near. But we were treated very well. We came back through Moscow, Warsaw and Berlin. That was just before the Beyfoum project began. We went down there to see the ground broken. That's more or less where it began, I'm beginning to think!"

"What?"

"The drug horror. We were in that new hotel. The suite on top that belongs to the Company. We gave a party up there for about fifty people, engineers, architects, all our top people. When the rest'd gone—it was quite early but everybody had to be up at the creak—we were about a dozen or so. Paul, the man in Beirut—Finlayson—and Mr. Logan, from Ryad. And do you remember Dorothea Ferris, Mr. Lane's onetime secretary? Very clever girl—"

"Indeed! What was she doing there?"

"She was with Mr. Finlayson. Which rather surprised me. She's by way of being the austere type. He's distinctly not!"

"You met Joel Cawle, didn't you?"

"I worked in his section for a few weeks, years ago. I only saw him a few times. Not the sort I'm fondest of!"

"You never saw any likeness between Finlayson and Cawle? Physical, mental?"

She touched the tip of her nose with a forefinger, thumb under chin, staring up at the blanket rack, and shook her head.

"I wasn't near either of them long enough to notice," she said. "And neither of them were the type I'd willingly inspect. Of course, I think Daddy was so right when he said that Cawle got where he did by being an albino rat. Colorless, with hardly any except a rattish, behind-the-wall personality, nothing but a current opinion, and *the* most *wicked* backbiter. He was always that!"

"And this party? By the way, are any of these people, except Mr. Logan, still with the Company?"

"I'm really not sure. Mr. Logan didn't get on very well with anybody. He's very much North-o'-the-Border. He had a couple of hearty scotches and lost his temper with Paul over the sort of women coming in—"

"Which women?"

"We'd entertained a dancing troupe somewhere or other, I think it must have been in Iran—one of those nights-out in a small town—and they were touring. Nothing vulgar about them. They weren't the usual. About ten of them. They danced marvellously. They came to our table and had a drink, and Paul said if ever they got as far as Beirut or Damascus, or anywhere we had an office, to get in touch and he'd put on a performance for the staff. Well, they'd been flown in from Basra. Of course, when they came to the party they were all in make-up, and Mr. Logan said his piece—he's Calvinist, and practices—and off he went. Well, the drinks went round, and the dances went on, and quite soon, so far as I was concerned, everything went round. I remember being a little surprised to see Dorothea Ferris whip all her clothes off, and dance. I'd never have suspected anything quite so uninhibited. But one really can't tell about those *secretive* types. Well, when I woke up, it was morning. I was in my room, and I didn't ask how I'd got there. Well, you know, I don't think I ever met anyone who could hold a lot of drinks and still be absolute master of himself to compare with Paul. But that day he failed. He didn't get up. When he did, I had to call the doctor. He said it was an overdose of sleeping pills. Paul got so angry when I mentioned it. He'd never talk about it. I'm sure Finlayson and that little half-Chinese thing were at the back of it!"

I said nothing because I didn't want Angela to know more than she did. I was waiting for something else.

"Did you ever see him with the little Chinese piece after that?"

"Once in Rome, once in Beirut, and about half a dozen times in London. She seemed to be with Finlayson. I didn't take much notice. At that time."

"Did you ever go to Stockholm?"

"To see Professor Tamm at the University? Yes. Once. Never again, though. The same dancers were there. They did a tour of Europe. Paul was getting worse. Unconscious for two days and more. I tried to ignore it, but it's not easy, and he was always so utterly repentant. Abject. Then he went in the nursing home, and I thought everything would get so much better. When he suddenly appeared in Leicester—when was it?—five, six days ago, he said he was cured, and he wanted to take me to Australia and get married en route. Well, he was so much his old self, I couldn't resist. I'd met Gillian in the meanwhile, and she'd mentioned the air trip, and Paul said 'Great!'—you know how he is?—and off we went. One thing seems burned in my mind. I was riding on the morning before we left, and somebody tried to run me down in a car. I caught a glimpse of his face, just before I went off the road for the hedge. It's a horrifying thought, but I can't escape it. I'm surer still, now. It was Paul!"

That was what I'd been waiting for, though I wasn't prepared for it.

"Sure it wasn't someone who looked like him?" I said, matter-of-factish. "I know at least one case of Paul's being impersonated. Fairly easy to do. Early morning light, closed car?"

Tears were rolling from the corners of her eyes. The poor girl wasn't far from a breakdown.

"I'd like to think so," she said, steady. "But the past few days have been awful, and the scene in Tobruk I'll never forget. He went absolutely berserk when I said I wouldn't go with him. The Inspector of Gendarmes and some of his men had to hold him off!"

"How did he get to Cairo before you?"

"He was put on the Ilyushin. It was waiting there. I believe for some Russian engineers. Anyway, I never want to see him again. Oh, yes. The thing I almost forgot. In London, the night before we left, we went into Plummy's Club, among other places. I'm sure he met Bernard Lane there. I'm certain it was he. I couldn't follow them to the members' lounge to make sure, of course. But what ties it up is that Paul wouldn't let me go to the Grosvenor Street flat. When I called the maid, she said a man was staying there, a friend of Paul's, and

79

she wanted to give notice. She didn't like the people he brought there. He'd been there three days. He'd arrived with a note from Paul. I talked to Paul about it, and he flew into a rage, and told me to mind my own bloody business. I'll give large odds it was Bernard Lane!"

That, too, was what I'd been waiting for—I suppose—though without in the least expecting it. Plummy's was very much a private club. Some of us had got together to open a place for late nights, when we couldn't get a drink elsewhere, didn't feel like going to a night club, or our own clubs, or home, where we could take friends, or a girl, and have a meal at any hour, in pleasant company of those who didn't gossip. It was a perfect place for Lane, Cawle and coterie. The flat in Grosvenor Street was in Angela's name. The free use of both, and at night, gave a perfect combination of silence and privacy. And obvious compliance on the part of M.I. It must have been known.

"Any idea why Errol and Gillian are going to Rome instead of Khartoum?" I asked, as if what she'd said was of no importance. "I thought they had a month's stay there?"

"They're going to meet his mother in Venice. There was a cable waiting for them. She doesn't like flying by herself. Neither do I. I *hate* flying!"

I pretended to sleep, and did. I find flight a calmant of sorts. That background drone creates a noble music all its own. I woke up when people started bustling about. I've noticed that some passengers are always off the aircraft first, through Passports and Customs while I'm still looking for my hat. I don't know what they do with their saved-up moments, but they're generally in line for a cab behind me, so I take my time.

Errol and Gillian waited outside on the concourse.

"I'm glad you had a talk to Angela," he said. "There's nothing useful I can add, except that we're not going to Khartoum. We've left a little paper-chase, though. We're going through to Andorra. See if we can't disappear in the Basque country. Where shall we find you? If necessary?"

"Cable me at Beyfoum, and come and stay with me

whenever you please. You heard about Plummy's and so forth?"

He nodded, looking away. Gillian stared up at me with that "empty" look.

"Don't like it," he said, and held her shoulder. "I'm not in condition to challenge. For the moment. Not up to it. But there's a deal on—there must be, or they couldn't parade all over London—and something's got to be wrong up top. That's why we left, primarily!"

"The Blur, d'you think?"

Again, he didn't look at me, though Gillian hadn't taken her eyes off.

"Don't know, Edmund," he said shortly, tiredly. "I'm as much at sea as you are. He was a close friend of my father's and I have every reason to believe, of mine as well. One doesn't like to imagine things!"

"Daddy's dining with the Prime Minister on Friday," Gillian said, in a small, murderous voice. "He's going to have what he called a 'quiet word,' and Daddy's 'quiet' word's never less than nuclear. If we run up against the slightest trouble, Edmund, I shall cable you!"

Angela joined us after a Customs argument about the carpets she was sending on to Leicester. She was red with temper and quite beautiful.

"*Bloody* people, those Customs!" she fanfared. "Same everywhere, that type of bastard!"

"But, *Miss* Masters!" Errol said airily. "I must say your sojourn *chez* Chamby greatly improved the dialect."

"It's neither sojourn, nor dialect!" Angela said. "It's outraged human nature. I don't like the foreign claws in my bags!"

"Scratch, what?" Errol said. "Are we all ready?"

I waved them off in a private-hire car for the Rome Terminus, and went to the Western Union Counter. I'd had an idea.

CHIEF SUPERINTENDENT HOCKLEY NEW SCOTLAND YARD LONDON, I wrote. LANE SEEN PLUMMY'S CLUB AND AT CHAMBY'S

GROSVENOR STREET FLAT. MUST BE AN AGREEMENT AT TOP LEVEL THEREFORE SUGGEST CAUTION. REGARDS. ANON

WASHINGTON D. C. UNITED STATES OF
The second I sent to MRS CRIGHTON BARRETT STRETTON JR 1700 WASHINGTON AVENUE AMERICA. LANE SEEN PLUMMY'S, SUPPOSEDLY USING CHAMBY'S HIDE GROSVENOR STREET. PROBABLY A DEAL UP TOP ADVISE CAUTION. PPX

Mrs. Crighton Barrett Stretton, Jr., alias Druxi, probably, together with Indira Gandhi, Lisa Meitner and a few others, among the most remarkable women of her time, was queenpin of the C.I.A. unknown, unsung, unmedalled. She'd done perhaps more for her Country—and the rest of us—than many a Fleet, Army or Air Force Command. That's no exaggeration. I know, because I'd been part of what went on. I hadn't the slightest doubt, if Hockley didn't get there first, she'd show him. She was that type, which is, of course, why all of us who'd worked with her, loved her.

CHAPTER ELEVEN

The plate-glass walls and marble-floored lobby of my Rome office held a feeling of sanctuary. I tasted it, while Busso came behind me with a pile of correspondence. I liked my office in the East Room better than any other, whether for width, height, parquet or furnishing. The only drawback was a lack of radio facilities. I hadn't had the time to instal what I wanted.

I put in a call to Consuelo, and began opening letters. There were the usual field reports, auditors' certificates, office expenses and tradesmens' receipts. A little pencilling made it an average good week. But a note in handwriting on the Tou'm El Mis' basecamp report caught my eye on a flip-through. I always looked for the handwritten remark. This was from Heumann, a Swiss engineer, first-class at his job, in charge of the advanced pipeline camp about three hundred miles northwest of Beyfoum.

"It is the second time I have a visit from Chinese or Turkestani engineers. We are not on a road or track. We find a way by compass. Therefore, they also come by compass. They are in Chinese and also Russian trucks. I ask myself how they find me. They always go back by the way they came. Perhaps on a back-bearing? I think we need a small airplane to make flights every day, to find where these people come from and where they go. Only one in each party spoke English, not well, and the rest look at what we do. They are all courteous. They all smile. Worst of all they drink my coffee and brandy and I have none left."

I went upstairs to the common-or-garden radio I'd installed to talk to my head offices. I knew I'd find an operator on duty at Ryad, and I got him immediately. I told Logan to send the Avro up there on round-the-clock duty, pick up and track all visitors, follow them back to base, render a full report, and send up a double issue of coffee and brandy, with my compliments.

I didn't like the sound of it. So far as I was concerned, any Russian or Chinese visitor was unwelcome. But there was nothing to stop a party from visiting. All they'd see were men at work, and a pipeline stretching back to Beyfoum, whatever good that might do them, beyond a little chat, and a coffee and brandy in an air-conditioned hut.

I wrote to Heumann, thanked him for a useful report, and to keep on foot-noting down to the most trivial detail. Trivia can often be important straws.

Busso tapped, and came in with the night tray.

"Sir, Miss Pearlman is at the hotel, and she calls every hour," he said. "If you would like to see her? It is, she says, important!"

I hadn't forgotten Miss Pearlman from Prague, but I'd thought it a little late.

"I'd like to see her now," I said. "Send a car for her. Have one ready for me."

I called Arturo, a cafe owner, an ex-agent who'd been keeping an eye on the office, what went in and out. His wife, one of our girls in the old days, now sentinel of the cash register, answered. She, sensible girl, kept her voice down, asked me how I was and when I was coming to see my godchild, all in Italian, and then Arthur spoke, but only two words, Veni, Vedi, which meant he wanted to see me urgently.

"At the usual place in one hour from now," I said. "I have somebody to see, first."

I'd barely put the phone down, and Busso tapped to announce Miss Pearlman. I'd forgotten she was in the hotel only a moment away down the hill.

I shall never forget the pathos of that face. Her eyes were grey, enormous, shadowed. She hadn't a touch of paint. She wore black.

"Mr. Trothe, I can never repay you," she said, when I put her in a chair. "On your cable, I was given a permit to take out my father and mother, they live outside Prague, and my brother and his wife. It was the first day of the crime. We could take nothing with us, but at least we have our minds and our lives. We are free. We

84

may think as we wish. We say as we want. It sounds strange to you?"

I shook my head. I couldn't have done anything else. Reading about it, or listening to a radio, is one matter. Looking at a girl in her late twenties, talking about being able to think and say as she wished, as if it were a privilege, was quite another. She knew the verities.

"What's going to happen?" I asked her.

She shrugged, pressed her lips together.

"Spirit and flesh does nothing against steel," she said. "We are rebellious inside ourselves. We show it in the face. But we do as we are told. Of course. We must live. Imagine a boy throwing a stone against a tank? What is one to say? How is one to feel? It is an incident. How many were squashed bloody in the streets? Who cares? But who forgets? Ah, sir, *who* forgets!"

"Indeed," I said, keeping a placid tone. "Have you anything about the office to tell me?"

She looked at me with that degree of sorrow approaching contempt I've often seen in others who've been through the firepit, and believe themselves deserving—on that account—of vastly more considerate if not more respectful treatment than the norm.

"I have already heard from Gleitz and Kober," she said slowly, in her careful but excellent English. "They are in Athens with their families. They too, are more than grateful, Mr. Trothe. At these times, we Jews have so few friends!"

I cleared my throat. I wasn't to be drawn into that type of discussion.

"How did you leave the office?" I asked.

She pulled her shoulders in, and looked at the ceiling.

"Everything was in order, sir. Mr. Kober left the staff—there were eight typists, five bill clerks, one messenger, one porter, one cleaner, one woman who made lunch for us—two years' wages at the Bank. They crushed their hands to see us go!"

"Rental?"

"It had already been paid for three years, sir. You said we would need larger offices at that time. Mr.

Gleitz also went to the Cathedral of Saint Wenceslaw to ask for one years' Masses, as you instructed, but the priest would not accept money. They will be said until the land is clean. Sir, you have a powerful Faith. I wish all were as strong!"

"Religion is a personal matter," I said. "I intend that Kober shall go to Istanbul. He speaks Turkish, French, English and Russian. Gleitz will take charge of engineering supplies for Europe in the Paris office. He has many friends at the Elysée and among the Press. You will be in charge of the office here, for the time being. Unfortunately, I can't send any of you to the places where you'd be most useful. That's in any of the Arab countries. I'd like you in Beyfoum, to take charge of schools for the Company's children. There are more than a thousand of them. But not at this time unfortunately. Life wouldn't be comfortable for a Hebress!"

She was staring down at her hands.

"You know, sir, I hold a Czechoslovak passport," she said. "There's no need for religion to appear. I am ready to go to Beyfoum!"

"You have the necessary qualifications," I said, trying to hide what I felt, and exultation was not too strong a word. "I shall approach the authorities for sanction. Are you prepared to do your best, not for yourself, or any belief, but for my Company? The children are my sole interest!"

Those big, shadowed eyes looked at me—I could have kissed her feet—and she sat back and laughed like a happy girl.

"Ah, sir!" she said. "This is such a different world. I would love to teach again. Commerce, I don't like. Nations, I don't like. People, I like. Children, I love. I would love to teach what I know and *feel!*"

"That's all I want," I said. "Take charge here for a few days, and wait for a call!"

I got up to take her downstairs, but in a sudden move she knelt and held my hand to her cheek. I didn't quite know what to do.

86

"I thank you for the children!" she whispered. "You will never regret!"

She was up, and at the door, and down to the Otis, that golden birdcage. Busso had been waiting to shut the grille, and tug the rope, and we dropped down a floor to the lobby.

"Busso," I said, "Miss Pearlman is in charge of this office from tomorrow morning. Warn the night staff. The order will appear in the bulletin tomorrow!"

He bowed, and hurried to open the main door. The car waited.

"But, sir, I can walk!" she said.

"But, madam, you cannot," I said. "This is Company property, and that's the Company's car, and you are the Company's representative in Rome. Permit me!"

I put her in the back seat, and wrapped the blanket. She looked very small. Black clothes joined the car's black leather. Her face seemed to float in night. Suddenly I saw her and her sisters frightened in Prague.

I was almost ashamed of being human. We'd done nothing for them. Except beat our breasts and sick-up the usual, arid nonsense. *Fainéant*.

"Sleep well," I said. "It'll all come right. Nine o'clock tomorrow morning!"

Busso shut the door, the car went away, and the one for me came behind.

"The Grand Hotel," I told the driver, and got in.

CHAPTER TWELVE

The main buffet at the Rome Terminus must be one of the world's busiest. Generally I saw Arturo outside, and he'd amble in a few minutes later, after watching for anyone who might have been following me.

But I didn't see him until I'd been at the counter for an appreciable time—I'd read a couple of pages of *La Stampa*—and he slid into the space beside me, not the Arturo I was waiting for, but a workman in paint-splash overalls and a ragged felt hat.

"The McGowan murder's still giving them trouble," he said, pulling a salami rind from his mouth. "They had another case the same in Milan a couple of weeks ago. The forensic surgeon here was sent up there. Friend of mine. They could never find out what sort of weapon was used. He was all cuts. Very deep, like razor cuts, but no razor could have cut like that. The edge cuts fine, and it's a bit of time till the blood comes. But the back of a razor's thick. If it goes in too far, it makes the wound gape. Blood goes easier. McGowan was cut to bits. All fine wounds, but deep, except in a few places, and they were all long, S-shaped. Then this girl got cut up the same way in Milan. Funny thing is, they both had their faces flattened. He told me. She was beaten flat. Couldn't see who it was. Turns out this girl was working in your office here, up to a few months ago. Name's Teresa Gigetto. Worked as a secretary in the Economic Department. She left—I remember her—and it seems she went to Milan to live with somebody, name's Giorgio Finotto. They're looking for him. They haven't got an idea where he is, or what he does for a living!"

My memory's computer clicked overtime. McGowan had been working for me when he was murdered. I was fairly sure that the pair had realized he was dangerously near putting a rope round them, and got rid of him. I remembered the girl, small, quite beautiful, with a degree from Rome University. She'd been working in the department Thanatos-Finlayson and-how-many-other-aliases had been part of, and obviously knew too much. Mr. Finotto, I had no doubt, was Thanatos-Finlayson et al, either Joel Cawle or Bernard Lane, I wasn't certain which.

I had to think a little more, put two and two in order. "Anything else?"

Arturo tore off a small crust, threw it in his mouth, drank some chianti, smacked in fine Roman style, and nodded to the barman.

"There's a woman from Czechoslovakia been calling you every hour since yesterday. She's—"

"That's Miss Pearlman. She's in charge of the office from tomorrow. Take care of her!"

"One more little matter which you will enjoy, I believe, sir? You forgive me? A male clerk, in the Air-Despatch Department, Basilio Civetti, a modest man, very timid, has a lodging on the other side of the river at the address I have written on the border of page nine of this paper. After seven o'clock he leaves the house by the back way, and takes a bus to the Barbieri. He walks up the hill to the bar on the right hand side. He has a coffee or beer, and goes to the mens' room. He walks through the passage, and generally takes a taxi to Parioli. He has a room in a house which lodges single men. It has a side entrance. He changes clothes, and leaves at about nine o'clock. He walks to the Borghese. The addresses are written on the border of page ten. The third is a large apartment. He has a key to the garden door. There is no porter on that side. The rental is three times what he earns, without the other two. With you, sir, I leave this little domestic mystery. I have nothing to do!"

"Why?"

He wiped his mouth, took the cash register tab the barman held out, chose a toothpick, stuck it between his front teeth, pushed the paint-splotched felt a little farther back, and belched, apparently a well-satisfied client.

"I am happily married," he said, making fine choice of words, and time. "I am a father. Of two wonderful children. I have a flourishing business—in which you, sir, own a sixty per cent interest—and I have no intention of depriving my wife of my company, or of allowing a complete stranger to inherit her and the best cafe in Europe. It's not so big as La Coupole, but it will be. That man is dangerous. That was why I wished to speak to you urgently. Good night, sir!"

He finished the chianti and left. Nobody would have known we'd been talking. I had my elbow on the paper. Somebody else came beside me. I picked up my tab and put the paper under arm, left a tip, and shuffled through the crowd to the cashier, paid and walked out to that enormous foyer, strolling down to the arrivals board. A look at the names of stations brought that deep feeling of nostalgia. Reggio Calabria, Cantanzaro, Brindisi, Florence, Assisi, Capua, Verona, Parma, Gobbio. I saw villages on mountainsides I'd slept in as a god, tasted again those meals I could never forget, picked grapes by the wrist-bending bunch, felt fishing lines tighten round my hands, saw the small Etruscan bronzes dug from hidden tombs.

But all the time I had Mr. Somebody, of three addresses, well in mind.

I had no doubt whatever that he was one of the pair.

I went to the public telephone and called Colonel Perrine at the Carabinieri Headquarters. He wasn't in his office, but they put me through to his home. The man servant said he was dining, and I gave him the pass word *Redentor*.

"Perrine!"

"Edmund Trothe. I want at least twenty of your tallest and most bad-tempered lads. I believe I have one of the kites. Where shall we meet?"

"On the corner of Piazza Venezia, left, as you look at the monument. What's the address of the kite's shitheap?"

90

"The Geronimo Edifice. Via Gloria, number 315, apartment H, near the gardens!"

"Fifteen minutes!"

I took a cab outside the station and got to the Piazza in a little under nine minutes. Three minutes by my watch later, four cars stopped just in front of me. Less then two minutes passed, and Colonel Perrine, in plain clothes, got out of his staff car, and saluted.

He didn't ask me how I'd got my information, and if he had, I wouldn't have told him, and in fact, we didn't say much till we got to the apartment building. I found the entire area staked by the Celeri—Roman brethren of the Flying Squad—which I didn't think a good idea at all. Their jeeps were on every corner. One look out of any window, and warning was plain.

"I suppose they sounded their sirens coming into position?" I said.

"Ah, no!" he said, shocked. "They know much better!"

"I was sure of that. I've counted eight jeeps. They muffled their engines, possibly? On a quiet night like this, they wouldn't be heard, of course?"

He looked back to answer, thought better, and led the way into the lobby. A porter read a paper behind a table. He looked at us over his spectacles, and a sergeant waved him down. About a dozen of us got into the lift, and up we went to floor H.

One of them rang the bell, another tried a bunch of keys, and turned one. The rooms were well-furnished, no pictures, no photographs, a table laid for three with three soup plates, spoons in them, soup fairly hot to the touch, dinner of mutton chops on a silver platter in the kitchen, parsley garnish, ready to be served, the back door open, and nobody in the place.

I stood there and whistled under my breath. The rest did whatever Colonel Perrine told them, but it was all deadend.

I wondered how it had been done, who'd warned Basilio Civetti, and that, at the last moment. Had it been the jeeps in fine array? Or had it been a tip?

91

I knew I was short an air-despatch clerk, and that the other two addresses would yield nothing. Air despatch, of course, was about the best intelligence post of the lot. I saw how I'd been spotted from London to Athens to Cairo—cancelled tickets went back to that office—and all he need do was alert somebody at the other end.

From apparently nowhere, an idea sparked.

I left them at it, got back in the lift, went out to the street and called a passing taxi. I didn't know the address but I knew where to go, and told the cabman, round here, round there, and here we are.

Mama Guillermina's house was a *pensione* for single girls, where Miss Greig, a secretary of mine, now in London, had stayed, and I knew at least one other was still there. I'd seen the address on her pay check.

Mama was still up, and came to the door, a mass of rustling white. God only knows what she had on, but her skirts touched both walls of the passage. She rustled in embracing me, and I heard the strength of that peasant contralto vibrate through the layers of starched linen—or whatever it was—smelled the ironing, the fragrance in hair and body of a healthy, well-bathed woman, and ah! that pang in thinking of Consuelo!

"Come in, come in, come in!" she bellowed, and shoved me almost, in front of her. "How many times we have spoken of you, sir. A glass of wine? Don't say no, eh? It is from my brother's vineyard, and it's half mine, and if you say no, I am insulted, he is insulted, and he is a terrible man. He's *this* size!"

She held a hand a little lower than her hip, staring those big black eyes. I nodded, naturally, and she opened the glassfront case, and took out two beautiful Murano goblets.

"I want you to call Miss Zanetti," I said, to stop the flow, "I have a matter to discuss. You will please remain here while we talk. I want you as a witness!"

She didn't hesitate. The flask, a straw-covered balloon holding about five gallons, was left on the table, and up she went. I heard her tread the stair, and her voice reverberated. A door opened, and Miss Zanetti tippi-tapped downstairs, overlaid by the weight of Mama's tread.

Miss Zanetti was in rollers—I don't know how women manage to sleep in that self-infliction—it's-even horrible to look at—and a flowered wrap. She was in her beauty grease, which didn't help, but she was intelligent, and smiled, as if to say All Right, You've caught Me, So Go to Hell!—which I respected because I'd have thought exactly the same—and Mama came in behind. She sat between us, and poured the wine, broke the long loaf, cut the cheese, as a matter of course.

"Miss Zanetti, you knew Giorgio Finotto?" I began, through a crackle of crust. "He was a friend of Miss Gigetto's?"

She nodded, looked at the wine, not at me. I knew there was something there.

"Then you know Mr. Civetti?"

"To work with," she said, still looking at the wine.

"Were Mr. Finotto and Mr. Civetti friends?"

She frowned, looking at me.

"Perhaps they were, sir. Mr. Finotto often lent Mr. Civetti his car. I know, because I went out with him!"

"Neither of them ever came in this house!" Mama said, lifting a forefinger.

"With Mr. Civetti?" I said, over the rumble.

"Twice, sir. Never with Mr. Finotto. He didn't work at the Company. He used to meet Teresa—Miss Gigetto—outside. I was horrified at the murder. I haven't been out since!"

"True!" Mama tromboned, in upward scale.

"Was the murder the reason for not going out again with Mr. Civetti? Or was that before the murder?"

Again Miss Zanetti looked at the wine she hadn't touched.

"It was before," she said, quietly, and turned to look at me, direct. "Sir, why do you wish to know?"

"Mr. Civetti will not be working with us any longer. I'd like your opinion. What sort of man was he?"

Suddenly, startling in that quiet room, she made a clawing grab at Mama's hand.

"He kept a cat in a glass tank!" she said in eyeshut horror. "I only saw it once. That night. It was black. Perhaps the glass made it seem bigger. But he put in a cat he'd taken from the street. I tried to stop him. I screamed—I fainted—I came out—I was bleeding—he hit me. He was watching the tank. The big cat was eating the little one. Blood on the glass. I ran. Ran!"

Mamma wrapped the big arms about her.

"Finish!" she whispered. "You've told that story often enough!"

"Where was this," I asked.

"In the house at Villa Setta, sir. I don't remember the number. I can't think of anything to do with it!"

"How could you work with him after such an experience?" I asked more or less conversationally. "You saw him every day?"

"He worked upstairs. I've never been in the canteen since. He's called here. He tried to talk to me in the office. I got Mr. Bresson to tell him to go away. He was beating my desk so hard, he almost broke it. He had that ebony ruler. You should see what he did. If Mr. Bresson hadn't been there, I don't know *what* might have happened!"

"When was this?"

"Last Tuesday, sir!"

"She was home here two days," Mama said, proprietorially. "Wish I'd been there. I'd break the stool off him!"

I stood up. I'd heard enough.

"I'll look at that desk," I said. "I'm very grateful to both of you for your patience and hospitality. Please forgive me for disturbing you. Mama, that wine is excellent. I'm coming again for dinner!"

She held out those enormous arms.

"A favor to me!" she sang, in basso. "The five best plates in Rome. A spaghetti with shellfish. A dish of

94

veal cut in whispers with green grapes and white wine. A suckling roasted in apple juice. A cream of fresh beans, new potatoes and the first carrots. And my own whip of eggs, oranges, brandy and curacão. You enter your size, you go out mine. I have thread for the buttons. *Eat!*"

CHAPTER THIRTEEN

My first job was to find out how Mr. Civetti had ferreted through our Intelligence Service. A couple of moments thought convinced me he'd have no trouble. Forged references would be child's play. No amount of enquiry would do the slightest good. But I had to see how he'd managed to break through the net, if only to patch against another try.

I had to pay considerable attention to the underlying reason. There had to be solid ground for either of the pair to take the inordinate risk of entering my organization, knowing that the commercial record they presented, and all phases of private life would come under scrutiny. Why would they do it? What, for example, would an air despatch clerk learn that could be of any use to the Secret Service—ridiculous title!—of another country, or, perhaps of some other commercial interest? In a word, plenty, whether it concerned personnel in transit, or the type of engineering supplies passing from source to base, name and address of manufacturer, supplies agent, and banker. But why? The answer was obvious. My organization was first of its kind, and a competitor would have a rough time in trying to follow, whether in building, or entering any market. I had treaties with all the countries whose territory I was passing through and supplying with mineral gas. That was a firm foundation. I had too much of a head start to be stopped. But if I could be displaced, or replaced—either by death, or economic disaster—then another organization might take over the Company's assets by outright purchase, or try to make a new start from a different base. But that was no simple task.

Treaties were not to be signed overnight. It had taken our legal department all its sealing wax, and the Princes' friendship with the men involved, more than four years, in virgin ground to get the paperwork done. The financial basis had to be ample, and without preponderant Arabian capital, the Euro-American banking consortium, with a less than twenty per cent holding, might have thought twice. With everything in our favor, it had still been a difficult job. For somebody else, even if they had the capital, starting from scratch would mean years of treaty work, together with an enormous forward outlay in machinery and stores, again not to be got overnight, which in the event of failure in negotiation could become of little more value than scrap. There was every reason for getting rid of me, first, and then a Prince or two, bringing work to a halt, and going in with an offer.

Our strength was in the amount of work already done, the daily advance of the pipe-line, the rising construction of the Beyfoum complex, and in our capital, which cost us nothing, but which, on short term loans across the world, yielded generous interest.

Our great weakness, and it often worried me, was that we had no government behind us except the Arab States, and we were passing through countries that were not always friendly. But in the event of real trouble, we had nobody to turn to. We were simply another private company, and we could be gobbled without recourse, except for a little polite chatter in the United Nations.

I had some notion of what to expect, there.

I knew I had to send a first-class Intelligence team from place to place, sorting all junior employees' records, and then instal a central office to investigate all applicants anywhere. I hated to do it. I detest any thought of poking about in peoples' private lives. But it had to be done and when I got back, I put through a call to Berry in London.

Consuelo had been through twice. I got that call replaced, and I put in another for Khefi, and as an afterthought, for Kober in Athens. Busso brought in a sandwich tray—which I needed—and while I was in the middle of a most enjoyable chopped egg and water-cress slice, Khefi came through.

He had a diplomatic line, of course. I'd forgotten that.

"Edmund, I am so glad you called to me. I have another favor to ask!"

"Anything you please!"

"Where can I find Mrs. Ulla Brandt Ben Ua? I have tried everywhere. She is not there!"

"Khefi, if you were not in your office, and somebody asked me, as a great favor, where they could find you, what would you expect me to say?"

"Edmund, I appreciate very much. But where shall I find Mrs. Ulla Brandt Ben Ua?"

"Are we scrambled?"

"No!"

"Have you got a copy of the old Police Code? Five-letter groups?"

"Certainly!"

"You'll have a cable in the next couple of hours. Now I require a favor. Reciprocal!"

"Anything!"

"I want Paul Chamby put in the best nursing home there is, and given the best possible treatment until he's certified well and in his right mind. Could you do that for me? I am responsible for all expenses!"

"But, Edmund—"

"He's suffering from an after-effect of a recent illness. I want him taken good care of. I was going to call Boussaf at the Pharmacy. He'd know—"

"Well. We had a most pathetic—ah—time with him, you know? There was nothing to do. He is committed to the Military Hospital for the moment—"

"Khefi, if you're any friend of mine, get him out immediately. Doesn't matter what the cost. I'm sure Boussaf can help!"

"I call him, I shall see everything is normalized. I like to make my friends happy. Edmund, I hope I shall have a friend like you, you know?"

"In turn, I'll rely upon you!"

I went to the safe, and took out the bound dogears of twenty or more years back. The little code book had been handled so often that it barely held together. I

98

wrote the message, flashed for Busso, and went back to the sandwich tray.

Blues shone for an outside call.

"Through to Jamaica, sir" Marcanti on the switchboard, said. "Person to person, your return call to Banbury Cross, sir!"

"Where?"

"Banbury Cross. Private number, sir!"

I heard Consuelo, faintly faint, a wraith caught in a bubble of glass, and I shouted.

"Darling!" she murmured, almost in my ear. "Your telephone manner's quite deplorable. You *bawl!*"

"If you were anywhere near, I'd make *you* bawl!"

"Well, I'm not, so you can't. But I *wish* you could. I'm sick of being single. It's rather unhealthy. In a way. My sweet, how are you? That tired note in your voice. I don't like it!"

"I'm not a bit tired, except of being so far away from you. Thank God, aunts don't die every damn' day of the week!"

"Ah, poor aunt May! I only saw her a few times. When I was at school. She always brought me enormous hampers from Fortnum's. We were all ill for days. Now she's left me this most lovely place. It's all mine. I signed the papers today. I can't believe it. The beach—are you listening—?"

"—with three ears. The beach?"

"It's almost the length of Park Lane, and *private!*"

"Ploo-oot!"

"Plut' or not, I'm enjoying it in most plutocratic style. I have eighteen servants. They've been here since they were born. They're really the happiest people I've ever known. And wonderful to me. By the way, Gregson tells me two more bodyguards arrive tomorrow. But what for? I've got a private army. Nobody could get in, much less move about. There's a high wall, and a night guard. The local police are something really special. I think you're being overcautious and hopelessly extravagant!"

"Can you feed them, and put them up without any great trouble?"

"Oh, but of course!"

"Then let me be best judge, will you? You can't come back here—"

"*Can't?*"

"That's right. The dirty double's playing a game. You might go to New York, and I'll meet you there. Or if you can manage to stay where you are for the next four or five days, I'll fly there—"

"Oh, darling, I do wish you would. It'd be simply *heaven*ly. Our bedroom looks across a glorious garden to the beach, and the sea. You never saw such a color!"

"Yes, I did. When you look at me—"

"Mm. I get out of bed in the morning, and go out of a dark room on to that terrace, and fling off everything—"

"What're you sleeping in? Court gown and Inverness? What happened to the deerstalker?"

"Only my maidenly armor, darling. I find it *most* uncomfortable. I can walk about naked, in the *sun*. For the first time in my life. There's nothing else to compare with it. I believe, you know, I'm rather more than a hint of savage. I wouldn't give this up for anything in the world. When you're here, I think I'll simply lay me down, and *expire*. From sheer joy!"

"You can count on the laying down part, anyway—"

"Is that awfully good grammar, or syntax, or—"

"Everything else'll be very good, and you can call in experts—"

"As if I would. Did you ever meet a Mr. Maylor while you were serving in Lagos?"

"Maylor? No!"

"He called me yesterday. He's rather down on his luck, and he'd like to sell me some old silver. My aunt had a wonderful collection. You'll see it. You don't think I should?"

"Don't allow him in the grounds. Ask the Police to look into it. I never met any Maylor, or heard of one in Lagos. Or anywhere else. I'm very glad you've got four hefty lads somewhere near you!"

100

"I'd have thought you'd have been rather worried. The two already here are extremely handsome. Big mustaches, brawny—"

"Is Leverson still Chief of Police, there, d'you know?"

"He was here today, with the Justice."

"Would you please ask him to call me and reverse charges? As soon as possible?"

"Is *he* going to take care of me? He seemed perfectly willing!"

Yellows were flashing.

"Between hairy guardsmen and lascivious coppers, I think it's time I got over there. I flew from Cairo with a team of mannikins, those creamy Arab *bints*—"

"*When* did you say you were arriving?"

The yellows were longer. That meant a caller, in person.

"I'll be in London tomorrow for about two days, I think. I'll try to fly on the second night. Take great care of yourself. Never go anywhere alone, except to bed. And don't do *any*thing!"

"As if—"

"As if, naturally. Darling mine, I have to go. There's someone waiting. I'll be on again this evening—"

"Is that 'someone' one of those creamy jobs?"

"Wouldn't surprise me. About five thousand peach-packed kisses, and keep yourself warm. For me!"

I put the receiver down at about the same time Busso took his thumb off the button and the yellows stopped.

I touched the release, and the door slid.

Ulla Brandt Ben Ua opened her arms.

I could barely get out of the chair from absolute surprise. But I made up for it in a headlong rush, and wrapped her. She was then somewhere in her sixties, but she didn't look forty, fairly tall, slim, lightly sunned, henna-red hair, hennaed fingertips—and I suspected, toes as well—an air of being completely apart from everyone and everything, and, as usual, soigné. I love the sort of woman who comes off an aircraft after a flight of hours and looks as though she'd just left her boudoir.

"I've barely put down the phone from speaking to Khefi. He wanted your address—"

She pulled back in alarm.

"Don't give it to him, Edmund, for God's sake! *Yet!*"

"I gave him the Muscat palace, of course. Why? Something wrong?"

She put bag and gloves on the desk, slipped out of her coat, and sat, picking up a sandwich.

"I'm famished," she said, in a bite. "I can't eat on a plane. I've just come from Damascus. Look, Edmund. There's a new move on, somewhere. You know Garagesh, don't you? D'you get along?"

"Very well. Out for the odd penny, but you can trust him. Don't you find that?"

"He was an assistant of Ben's. Been wonderful to me in many ways. I trust him completely. Well, he wrote to me, it's a funny sort of letter, and we had a plane going up to Damascus, so I took the ride. We met for lunch, but I didn't eat much. There's something happening in the Army and Air Force, and in the Universities. It goes right through, and it's strong. There's going to be a *putsch,* not just in one country, but the lot. The little sheikdoms and sultantates'll go first. They're easiest. Then the bigger countries, one by one, or all on the same day. The only thing that stops it now, is politics, a bit, and religion. More than a bit. But the youngsters aren't like the older lot. They can get together and agree to disagree. After all, the plums are black and shiny and they're dripping syrup. Hanging there for the eating. We're dealing with ambitious youngsters, Edmund. All captains and lieutenants on down. They're the ones that fight the battles. The older lads lie back. Well, this time *they're* going to do the commanding, and they'll shoot everybody in their way. I'm told I'm among the number ones on the list, because my little place—which isn't so little—yields more barrels than all of the other little places put together. I'm told we're all due to go at about the same time. Well, my dear, I have no intention of letting it happen. That's why I'm here!"

"Tell me what you want me to do!"

She opened the handbag and took out a package folded in three.

"You remember Colonel Hamid? My administrator?"

"Very well!"

"He drew up this plan for all-round defence. If they attack by air—there's always a possibility—there's not much we can do except get in the shelters. They're being built. But if they come by land or sea, we should be able to kill most of them, and by that, warn the rest. I want twenty armored cars, twenty propelled guns—it's all down here—with recoil-less rifles and a lot of other gear. I don't know what it's all about, but I *want* it. I also want—at the earliest possible moment—three hundred white mercenaries for day and night duty. I'll take them on for a period of two years. There's a lot of other detail. It's all here. Can you help me, Edmund? Or d'you know the man I ought to see?"

"Leave it with me. What did Hamid advise?"

"He said any arms agent would do. I have an address in Paris. It's here—"

"Could Colonel Hamid meet me in Paris tomorrow?"

"I'll see he does!"

"My office, any time after ten. That is, in the morning. I'm glad you intend to fight it out!"

She got up to put her coat on.

"Ben's buried there," she said, while I helped her. "I intend to be. He'd have fought. God, would he? I'm just doing what he'd want. Catch him crawling out!"

"One small item," I said, on the way to the door. "You have some idea of what this could cost, I suppose?"

"You'll find a cheque attached to those papers," she said, careless as air. "If you need any more, let me know, won't you? I'll be at the Plaza, New York, for the next three weeks. I'm flying now to get m' flying all done. Couldn't be tireder than I am!"

"And Khefi? He's a good friend, you know?"

103

"Sure! But I know the Egyptians'd just love to station their own troops in there and other places. When'd I get them out? I'd rather do it my way till I'm proved wrong. If you follow me?"

"Wise girl. Have a good trip. Don't be surprised to see me in a few days. I'll have the news you want!"

Busso floated the Otis up, and she turned to kiss me, a hummer, on the cheek.

"Oh, Edmund!" she whispered. "You're so much like Ben sometimes. No, just leave me here. Bye!"

I nodded the Otis down, waved to a bent head, and went back to open the package.

The draft was for five million sterling, made out to me.

I had to look twice.

The paper wad, clipped, and badly typed, was signed by Hamid, an appreciation of the enemy's strength and possible lines of attack, and a detailed account of what defensive measures might be taken, with a list of armament and munitions required. It was a thorough, soldierly essay, with all the marks of the Staff College and his years with the French Colonial Army.

But he hadn't mentioned what to do about possible traitors inside the country.

There was always a lot of movement in that little port, and a great deal to and from the hills. He seemed to have no intention of defending the town itself, but only the palace and gardens. In that case, armoured cars and the rest was nonsense.

I had a series of what Consuelo calls my "nasty" ideas. I don't like "nasty" ideas, but I'm given to them, simply because experience has taught me that all isn't always as it might appear.

On reading through again, paragraph by paper clip, I had a distinct feeling that Colonel Hamid was playing another game. Certainly not Ulla's. I'd met him a couple of times, a French-trained Arab, of good family, always courteous, never hail-fellow, little to say. That, in itself, had given him the reputation of being rock-solid. He'd been in charge of the Police in a couple of Trucial

States, and went to Ulla's little territory south of Muscat just before I'd joined the Company.

Ben Ua wasn't so little. But it *was* wealthy.

I cabled my son-in-law OBWEPOWAY, LONDON. NEED TO SEE YOU URGENTEST LONDON TOMORROW OFFICE 2100 HOURS BRING PATTI AND MY BEAUTIFUL GRANDDAUGHTER IF POSSIBLE. IF NOT YOURSELF WITHOUT FAIL. LARGE CONTRACT SPOT. EDMUND.

I decided, then, despite Ulla to call Khefi. He'd know as much about Hamid as anybody. I put the call through, and blues flashed for another incoming call on the International line.

"Berry here, sir? Can you hear me?"

"Perfectly!"

"Been a strange go, here sir. That woman at Revers Road? I tried to get in all day. She got there in the morning. Nobody'd answer the front door. So I got one of my lads to go up and smash the glass in the back door. Make it look like a break-in. We called a constable off the beat, and he went up and found her. Been dead about six-eight hours, the surgeon said. So she must have been murdered about the time I got there this morning. Nothing in her clothes or handbag. Fingers and palms burnt over the gas stove. No finger or palm prints. That means she's probably got a police record somewhere, or Interpol knows her. Face smashed in. Death by fracture of the skull, that's how it looks. Any further orders, sir?"

"Did you see the body? How was the face smashed?"

"I saw what was there, sir. Smashed it was. Flat. Must have taken a bit of trouble about it. Couldn't see anything!"

I saw that hologram in James's office, again. I heard Arturo's voice, speaking of Mac, and the girl in Milan.

"I hope to be in London tomorrow night. I'll stay till the day after. See what you can manage to gather in the way of detail, and we'll meet. Thank you, Berry!"

I sat back to stare at acanthus entwined on the ceiling.

It looked as though one of the pair had been busy again.

Could he also have been Mr. Cat-in-a-Tank Finotto? Why would he take a fancy to Miss Zanetti? I'd thought her nice enough in her way. What would be her attraction for him? Except the usual? I had no doubt whatever that Mr. Finotto and Mr. Civetti were one and the same Joel Cawle. Or was it Bernard Lane? But why would he be such a fool? I saw I had to have a closer look at the sort of work the girls were dealing with in the office. I hadn't asked. That had been a careless oversight.

Blues flashed.

"Athens, sir. Mr. Kober!"

"Please!"

"Sir, Mr. Trothe? My English is too poor to tell you how I am grateful—"

"Mr. Kober, I want you to go to Istanbul, and take charge of the office there. I shall send Mr. Argyopoulos instructions to issue your tickets and cash vouchers. You will fly via Rome tomorrow, and we shall meet here before I fly to Paris. Is that clear?"

"It is perfectly clear to me, sir!"

"Have you anything further to report?"

"Sir, I shall say everything tomorrow, if you please?"

"Anything you feel I ought to know now?"

"Sir, it is too many people here. I speak tomorrow!"

"Why are so many people there at this time of night? Who are the people? Is Argyopoulos there?"

"No, sir. It is the Police, here. I am free. I can go. The Captain gives me a pass. I can meet you in Rome. Tomorrow, sir? The tickets?"

"Go to the airport, now. Wait there until notice of your flight arrives. At Rome, there will be further instructions. Be calm, do as I say!"

"I thank you many times, sir. I have a great debt!"

I put through a call to Teddy Taphamides, at the Greek Foreign Office, and went back to my chair. What the devil were troops—I knew perfectly well they weren't Police—that was Kober's quick grasp—doing in our office? It was fairly large, in a new building we owned, and Argyopoulos was a first-class man. He knew I didn't allow politics of any kind in the Company's business. He, and all my managers, had strict instructions about it, and he wasn't the sort to ask for trouble.

I telephoned the airport and spoke to the airline supervisor, gave her instructions, and asked her to call me at any hour when Kober's tickets were delivered in Athens.

Blues flashed.

"Cairo, sir," Marcanti hollowed, as from a pit. "Four-oh-four B!"

"Khefi!"

"Edmund? I'm glad. What is the matter?"

"Disregard the telegram you're going to get. You'll find our friend at the Plaza Hotel, New York, from tomorrow morning. Do you know Colonel Hamid, her administrator?"

"Of course! We were cadets. He was a fine man. I regret!"

"*Was?* What d'you mean?"

"I have a report, he died five weeks ago in Ain Harah. Near Bône. For this, I will speak to New York. You understand?"

"I'm supposed to be meeting him tomorrow. We shall be discussing the defence of Ben Ua!"

"You will be planning the capitulation!"

"Oh? Who *is* he?"

"A friend of Chamby!"

"How d'you know?"

"Chamby was flying to Basra en route to Dar-es-Salaam. He had the tickets, and the Ben Ua address. So I enquire from my friends in Alger. Hamid died in the hospital at Bône. Of a peritonitis. Caused by a bullet!"

"Who killed him?"

"The present Colonel Hamid. The police traced from the statement before death. He was there to buy arms. From a man called Merzel—"

"Merzel? I know him!"

107

"Aha! I like to get that pretty dog here only five minutes!"

"I can imagine, let's say, three of them. But if he *does* meet me in Paris, what's the form?"

"I remember the expression. It is very nice. Very well, the form. Make an excuse, fly with him here. I give such a welcome!"

"I don't think he'd bite, Khefi. But if he leaves Ben Ua, can't you do something?"

"I shall see. He would probably fly to Karachi tonight, and take the Paris plane. It doesn't touch Cairo. In that case, I can do nothing. But I do not think he will go to Paris. He is too careful, huh?"

"I'll let you know, anyway. The address I've given you is safe enough isn't it?"

"Good night, Edmund. If you insult, I finish to speak!"

"Merzel" had been one of the first aliases of either Lane, or Cawle, and I had yet to find out which. Both had worked together closely over the years, and obviously they'd rung the changes to confuse any investigation, first, and then to provide an alibi, one for another. In their official jobs they had more or less unlimited choice of movement, and when airlines permit luncheon in Cairo and dinner in London, or breakfast in London and tea in New York, time's not very important, but geography can make a cast-iron alibi.

They were a cunning pair.

I wondered why they'd exhume the "Merzel" identity. I didn't doubt they'd have excellent reason. My son-in-law had met "Merzel," had done quite a lot of business with him until he was warned by the Algerian counterespionage Service that the munitions "Merzel" had ordered weren't going to Arab insurgents, and for that reason, had to stop.

There was never a moment's suspicion of dishonesty. That was enormously in the pairs' favor. They always paid cash, cheques were met, and their system of banking must have been the work of a committee of sorcerers. Despite every kind of enquiry, bank to bank,

108

world-wide, we could never find out where the cash originated. We still hoped. A small error would give the game away. It had yet to be made, and I certainly would not have bet a farthing it would turn up.

Blues brought my call to the Greek Foreign Office, but my friend wasn't there, and I spoke to a secretary, who might have been English, and asked if she knew of any trouble at our place. She told me to hold on. I simply sat there. That's an advantage of my Vox system. Press a button, and listen, or talk. There's nothing to pick up or put down.

"Mr. Trothe, I've got quite a full report from the Special Service," the quiet voice said, almost a shout in the room's silence. "I don't think you'd like it at length over the telephone. You have a Miss Renée Saddler on your staff. She was thought to be coming here from Prague, via London, under another name, Genia Pearlman. But she didn't arrive. Two other men did. Cuziel Gleitz, and Tamuz Kober. One of them had copies of your Prague paylists. The name Saddler was not there, and they swore that nobody of that name had ever been employed in Prague!"

"They were correct. Further, please make a note that I have no woman employee of that name anywhere in my Company. Miss Pearlman is here, in Rome. This woman Saddler. Is anything known of her?"

"We know she has worked as an agent for East Germany. Perhaps for Russia. She had an English father. Polish mother. She married a man called Pensen. A concert pianist. They divorced six years ago in London. Recently she had a beauty salon in London, and in Paris. She was put under surveillance in Paris because of a letter in the Poste Restante. We were informed. I have other details, but I am sorry, this is a long document!"

"Please accept my thanks. Would you be kind enough to inform Mr. Taphamides that Renée Saddler was found in London this morning. She'd been murdered. Scotland Yard will supply the details, I'm sure. Good night!"

That would teach Teddy that we had a fairly sharp 'I'

system of our own. But I saw I had to stop off in Paris and try to see Georges Pontvianne of the French Service. Why hadn't he got in touch with me? That was an extremely worrying thought. Georges, I'd imagined, was a close friend.

Something was happening in and around my Company which I knew nothing at all about, and those who did seemed disinclined to tell me. It appeared that Madame Saddler had done all she was instructed to do in Geneva, and was promptly put out of commission. But I wondered why, in such a manner. There were other, quieter ways.

Except, of course, that had she not been "tailed" by my own people, her identity might have remained her murderer's secret for a considerable time. She might never have been traced. There was, indeed, method in lunacy.

CHAPTER FOURTEEN

I used Prince Azil's apartment in Paris, easily the most luxurious, without being in the least decadent, I've ever seen. It was, as he once told me, his treasure house of the items he'd bought because he liked them, and not because agents thought he should. There was a Roman room to match the glory at Herculaneum, a Greek room better than anything in Athens, an Egyptian room that might have been stolen from the museum in Cairo, and the other rooms made a superb gallery, though it took time to realise that da Vinci nudged Braque without collision.

My own favorite smiled in a niche outside the library, a palely golden Ceres—I suppose—nobody knew, and he'd had most of the knowalls there to look at her—brought up by his own pearl divers from a bay near his house at Oman. He had, he'd told me, more than ten years diving booty there, whether Greek or not he didn't know, but I'd promised myself a visit one fine day. At the back of my mind, I thought it might be *the* place for a honeymoon, away from everything, well-guarded, quiet. Ulla's house had been my first choice, but not as things were. I didn't feel like going back, though I knew I must, and I had no further intention of taking Consuelo there for any reason.

A stack of letters lay neatly smeared on a salver. One from Consuelo I put in my pocket, one from Denis Lincoln had the pleasure to inform that the model and working drawings were ready and available at my earliest convenience. I scribbled "London, tomorrow, noon, office. Call cons: company. Have senior engrs there."

Three begging letters from old hands, humbugs, two from "disease" societies, worse, one, handwritten, heavily sealed, by messenger, from my old friend, Sir

Chapman Ryder, of the Canal Banking Syndicate, made me sit down.

"I'm not exactly certain of my facts for the moment but I have good reason to believe that something in the nature of ten millions sterling, or more, in bullion on the unofficial market is being transferred from Paris to Geneva in the near future, apparently in the name of one of your Company's subsidiaries, Marine and Offshore Holdings Ltd. Since we have had the pleasure of acting for you in other matters, and because this information comes to me in a most unusual way, I wondered whether it mightn't be advisable to acquaint you of, let us call it, a rumor, and to ask if we might conveniently quash it, as it were, stillborn. In this, I ask you to believe, we have your best interests at heart, because the bullion, it is being said, is to be used as a first payment on fighter aircraft which you are buying for a country on the other side of the Suez, which, of course, happens to be our home ground, and where, as you know, we are extremely well-informed. Please be kind enough to telephone me as soon as you may. I shan't enlarge on the effect elsewhere of this rumor. But it ought instantly to be denied in the proper quarter. I have no need to tell you that if the movement of bullion is verified, and the rumor is in any part confirmed as fact, it can only mean your absolute overnight ruin. I send this by hand from London, since I am informed that you will be in Paris this morning. Yours ever."

It was like being punched in the face. I lunged for the Out dial, got his office, and I was put through to his house at Sittingbourne.

"Ryder? Your letter. There is strictly, I assure you, not one iota of truth in any of it, whether it touches bullion—I haven't ordered any since the last consignment through your office—or aircraft of any kind except five light scouts for our own desert survey, and as you must know, for obvious reasons. I've never even written a postcard to Israel, much as I might like to. Does that satisfy you?"

112

"Perfectly. And I must tell you how delighted I am to be able to deny it!"

"Any idea where it began?"

"I fear I'm going to hurt you, Edmund, but this is not the time for the pretty touch. It came from your son-in-law's office in Algiers, and the manager there got it from no less an authority than the Lord Imbritt!"

"Absolute nonsense!"

"It seems to have been partially confirmed by the visit of two of your American directors here, and in Paris—"

"I have no American directors. There are representatives of the four contributing Banks on the twice-yearly Finance Committee, but that's all!"

"On your letterhead, in front of me, they are Robert Ingleby, U.S.A., and John Alvin, U.S.A.—"

"On my—on *our* letterhead? The Company's? Impossible!"

"It's in front of me, Edmund. It asks me, in your absence, to smooth any difficulties they might have in meeting the directors of Rand Bullion, with a view to transfer of certain purchases, between London, Paris and Geneva!"

"Signed by?"

"It looks like Bertil. Jules Bertil?"

"I don't employ anyone of that name, and the Paris office hasn't been working officially for a considerable time!"

"Oh!"

"If the two are in London at the moment, would you please call Chief Superintendant Hockley, at Scotland Yard, and give him the facts, and ask him to move? Those men are imposters, and the letterhead is a forgery, and there *is* no Bertil. This one's for the Fraud Squad. Did they take any money off you?"

"They cashed a check for eighteen thousand dollars which was met while they were in this office. On the Chemical Bank of New York—"

"You might get in touch, and ask whose account—"

"That's been done. The account was left with a credit of twenty two dollars odd. No details are known of the client, beyond a business address in Washington, a silk buyer, apparently, and a home office in Manila!"

"I doubt he's still in London. Ingleby or Alvin?"

"Alvin. Both of them quite presentable. Seemed to know what they were talking about. Nothing but praise for you!"

"I'd give them praise. Might we have breakfast in the morning?"

"Eight o'clock here?"

The famous pair were at work. They'd given substance to a carefully planted rumor by enquiring about a transfer of bullion in my Company's name, and they'd "proved" themselves to be acting for me by use of the letterhead and—I'd have bet—other devices, and I quite understood how Khefi, among others, might have felt when the rumor blasted, as it must, almost at the moment it was broached. I felt even more grateful to Khefi because he'd taken my word. That sort of implicit faith is rare indeed. It was the only bright spot in the entirely maddening business.

I had to tread very carefully.

I saw then that I'd been more than fortunate in having to leave North Africa. A few more days in my hideaway, and God knows what damage might have been done, and that, with little more than forgeries and whispers. Any smallest hint that I was helping Israel would have been enough.

There was no time for the breakfast I'd promised myself, with the early Georgian silver, the view from the terrace and all the newspapers. The car got me round to the office through the rain, and as I expected, Madame Berthe was there, a big busty woman, extremely efficient, and pleasantly surprised to see me, though without any fuss.

The main office was dark, typewriters were covered on desks glistening in shadow. Madame Berthe used a small comfortably "modern" room on the ground floor, translated and filed reports, and kept lists of personnel and goods passing through France to or from the main base at Ryad.

Without saying anything to her, I went through the in and out air travel lists, saw nothing out of the ordinary.

"Any visitors lately?" I asked.

She looked at me a second longer than necessary, almost a challenge of black eyes, and opened the desk drawer to take out an envelope, unfold a couple of sheets. One was a scrawled-on printer's specimen, and the other held a couple of lines of type.

"The representative of this company called here yesterday," she said, in her brisk way, seeming to be talking out of the side of her mouth. "He gave me these two sheets and this envelope, and asked me to sign for an order of five thousand top pages, and two thousand continuation, and three thousand envelopes, ordered from London by Miss Furnival. I said absolutely not, until I had authority from London. He said he'd been given the order, personally, by the Prince Azil!"

I looked at the sheets. The paper was an excellent quality, the type in embossed Roman, just what I'd want, but the two American "directors" were very much there, with two more, Albert Boyne Rogg and Colman Marcus. I mind-filed the names, ready for any future clash, and handed the sheets back.

"You might write a letter to all tradesmen dealing with us, and say that because of an attempt at fraud, the greatest care should be taken to ensure that your signature is on any request for samples, and that without your signature, no order is valid. In this case, ask them to erase the names I've crossed off, and let the order stand. But be severe!"

I saw by her attitude that she meant to be, and the flush that bloomed and went. In that sentence I'd made her our representative in France, instead of a glorified caretaker.

"Your salary will go up commensurately," I said. "I take it you wish to work for me?"

She clasped her hands and really, truly blushed.

"Ah, sir!" she whispered, "with all my heart. If I have doubt, I shall communicate to London. I believe two of these men came here last week. The office-cleaner was here, it was early, and I had not yet arrived. They wanted to enter, but she is a good woman and she kept the steel gates closed, as I told her. They said they were directors, and wanted to use the telephone, and write letters. She said I would call them when I came in, but they were not at the Georges Cinque a few minutes after nine, and their names were not known. I thought it curious?"

"Pay the Inspector and the policemen on this beat to take a special interest. Debit petty cash. I shall be in London tomorrow, and New York on the day after, at the Plaza Hotel. That is confidential. Any really serious matter, cable me direct. Use, of course, the Company Code—"

I had an interview with Georges Pontvianne, of the French Service, in twelve minutes, at his little office not far from L'Etoille. It was over a perfumery on one side—"it is more agreeable if one works on dirty things in a sweet smell, no?"—and a tailor's on the other—the backa-chacka-bocka-chicka of the sewing machines came through the wall, if the lettering on the window made it clear that all work was by hand—then a cafe, where we'd done most of our talking over really good coffee and croissants, and sometimes a *fin*. I had a feeling that the entire block was owned and staffed by the Government.

Nobody except an extra-light ghost could climb that rickety warp without being heard up at the Opera. Georges came out of his office to meet me, as usual in shirt sleeves, pen behind his ear—I never saw anyone look more like an overfed delivery boy in a run-down village grocery—all part of the job, of course, and a simply lovely—but a glorious—the more one looked, or goggled, the more exquisitely beautiful, a she, an apparition, came out behind him. In blue. I almost saw the bones of her hips. With a white collar and cuffs. About a mile high. In that shadow, sunshine at night.

Georges looked at me, around at her, and back to me. Georges, let there be no mistake, was a *fatt!*—with two t's—man.

"Mm-hm" he grunted, a master of tonal accusation. "Oh-ha? Nu-hf? Same effect. Collapse. Complete. We take a coffee?"

He reached inside the doorway, took a jacket off the hook, speared the pen toward the desk, and came down. In that space he couldn't get the jacket on, his bulk hid the goddess, and I had to turn and go down in front of him. I helped him on with the jacket outside, and we went into the cafe, noses in air, both knowing the piece we were acting. We'd played it since we'd first met, those years ago, when he'd taken a girl away from me—I'd meant him to, and she'd done a splendid job which he'd found out about later—and I'd taken two off him, one he'd meant me to, and one he hadn't, and we both pretended we'd forgiven but not forgotten.

"No flowers, no chocolate, no telephone, no little visiting cards, nh?" he said, legging out a chair. "She is sacrosanct. She will marry a Lieutenant Colonel of the Republican Guard, I hope. Her father is a Cabinet Minister, her mother a Duchess, and her seven brothers all champions of back-street karaté, and known murderers. It would provide a defence. None of these things, unfortunately. She is American, single, she doesn't like to marry, she is a psychologist, mathematician, she has degrees from Massachusetts and the Sorbonne, twenty-three, an assassin. Not a man survives. She is with me, thank God, for only six months for training. After that, I make a suicide with pleasure!"

"She's the daughter of someone we know?"

"How do you guess?"

"How? She's exactly like her mother!"

"We don't mention a name, eh?"

"I'm glad she's with you. Risky on our side?"

"Regretfully. For the moment!"

117

"With all that out of the way, what about a woman called Renée Saddler, and why wasn't I told?"

He switched those fat man's pale-blue eyes at me. He wasn't playing.

"You were told, at the moment I knew," he said, in his official voice, that cut like a grass blade, finely. "If you haven't the good manners to answer, I cannot be responsible!"

"Where was I told?" I asked, easily.

"At your London office, the address you gave me!"

"I make no excuses. I've been out of the country for a little time. If anything was sent to London, it should have been forwarded instantly. It wasn't. I shall be there at about four o'clock. I shall find out why, and I'll let you know. Satisfy you?"

He shook his head, but the coffee came, and I sat back to think. I'd been in touch with London twice every day, and any letter or message or piece of paper that came to the office addressed to me or to the secretariat was relayed. There'd never been a word about Paris.

"How was the message sent?" I asked, when the waiter had gone. "I'm alarmed, I must tell you!"

The whiz and clack of the fan overhead covered our voices.

"I was sure there was something not in order," he said, helping me to sugar. "To put all our eggs in their proper boxes, your lines are tapped, you have microphones in your office, and at least one of your operators works for someone else. Possibly M.I.?"

"How does all this become known to you?" I asked trying to lard my French with some of the aroma of Paris streets. "You have a system of magic?"

"It does more than enough. My men went one better than your own system you told me about, one day, here, at this table. You remember, bluebells, and buttercups? Blue for international, yellow for local? My assistant, Mylés, the black one? From Dahomey? He took his case to your office. He sold the notebooks with plastic pages, a marvellous product, which, of course, only we make. He was very well treated. He was not called a black bastard or a dirty nigger, which—uh—I must aver with regret, after such a magnificent period of civilization, when we have saluted Kings, Queens, Presidents, and Popes with Christian prayer and fine words, yes, poor Mylés, it often happens. But not in *your* office. He was given a cup of tea, and a sandwich he swears on his knees was the best he ever passed between his teeth, and he sat, he actually sat, with your porters, and smoked afterwards. The poor man came back to me in a swoon. He also brought the case the books are displayed in, all in sets of colors, very well done, and I shall say it, attractive. But in the lid is the, what you call, business, nh? The system of bluebells and buttercups also now has the Recamier rose, and the springtime mignonette. Where wires are tapped, your bluebell shines. Where microphones record, your buttercup glows. Where outgoing messages are not on your usual wavelength, the rose blushes. Where incoming stuff isn't received on your own set, the mignonette writes green. Here is a copy of the graph. Frame it, and I will write with love from Georges, and his devoted staff!"

I almost lapsed into straight Left Bank. I'd been outflanked, mired, and blissfully stuffed. By people I'd thought were amateurs.

"I express incontinent admiration," I said.

"An English expression," he murmured, a deliberate and premeditated insult in thyroid glaze at the ceiling. "We don't know it here. You do odd things to the language!"

"I'll level with you before very long, butternut. One question. Why do you think they're after me?"

He shook his head.

"You give yourself airs," he said, in Churchillian tones and Harrovian English, always a graceful combination in a French mouth. "They are also after me. My wife and two children are not at home in our

119

seasonal house at Saint-Malo for that reason. They can not enjoy the beach. You think I am pleased? I do not enlarge. *But I pay attention!"*

The sudden lapse into the language of his fathers held all the shock he'd meant.

"I'll give the question another twist. Why d'you think they're after *us?"*

"Us? And a few more? It is in the nature of what we do. Or what we have been doing, nh? Their attention seems to be on the Arab countries. We don't know why. For you, I think you have the desert. In the desert is oil. You are a prince. You command a principality. Of a kind. Oil confers power. That is, let's say, for the moment. Without you, what? Who knows what to expect? From which side? Who will control in your place?"

"You speak as if it were fact!"

"Except for your 'absence'—however regrettable, and one or two more—it is!"

"Any idea what this woman Saddler was doing?"

"She had close links with Western Germany. For the moment I don't know why. She owned completely a good business as a beauty-specialist. Just near here, in the Rue Colomby. Above, she had her apartment. Of a magnificence, I must say. Whoreshop Victorian. Nothing spared. Even the feelings. Our first report came from Poste Restante. She was receiving mail from many countries, most of it commercial, in her own line. Advertisements for cosmetics, and that sort. Innocent, nothing. But I have smart girls. They asked our agents in those countries, an idle enquiry, you understand, for particulars of products. They were sent. They didn't, in many cases, exactly correspond with the advertisement. It caused no surprise. The advertisements were looked at again, and as you have no doubt guessed, they were in part a code. It took my team many hours to break, and so we knew we were confronting something important. The place was supervised from the moment. It, I mean, the business and upstairs, was a resort of Lesbians, in these days unsurprising. My agents professed a horror, as all virtuous hebes should, but to arrive at their target, they had to become targets themselves, and perhaps unnaturally, they acquired a taste. And they blame me? But, as I told them, my business is the report you place on my desk. Your miseries are your own. What is it?"

A man had come in quietly behind my chair. He gave an envelope to Georges, a thumb went under the unstuck flap, a folded note came out, and Georges flipped the envelope back.

"Economize," he said, in dismissal, looked at the note, and reached across to stand it, like a tent, in front of me. "Read it later. Very well. These advertstisements came from all over the world. But from Vienna, Warsaw and Budapest, they were partly in code. The instructions are always to travel somewhere, to London, to Bonn, to Brussels, every detail carefully timed, who she will meet, where, when. Everything exact. Except that we picked up the mail, before she saw it, copied it, and had an agent with her wherever she went on her last two little trips. Before Geneva, she went to Rome, and met there Mr. Paul Chamby, gave him a package for which he paid three thousand pounds in notes, and returned to Paris. I thought it might be drugs, possibly, and she was a go-between. Mr. Chamby returned to London that afternoon, and next day flew to Algiers. She came back to Paris by train, stopped at Villefranche, met Mr. John Alvin, an American who is not, or he uses a British passport, false we discover, of course to our shame, occupied the same room that night. We assume he slept fully clothed on the divan, or she did, today's customs being what they are, and my agent was left to ruminate all night, poor boy, on the *mores* of his time. Two days later, La Saddler went first to Neussen, a new industrial town in West Germany, and attended a concert given by Joh Pensen, a pianist, who takes a Bechstein with him, very popular everywhere, and he autographed her program. She went that night to Bonn, and flew next morning to Geneva. She took a room under her own name, and went to another hotel and gave the name of Mauer. Here she

121

was met by a man we don't know. She was given some-thing we don't know. She went to the Central Bank to cash a cheque for two thousand francs on the account of Mr. Colman Marcus, also an American, apparently, and poor woman, she was taken with a faint. I have made up my mind always to employ women agents in future, that is, when we have a woman in view. She can enter places sacred to women, you see. A man, you will not be sur-prised to hear, cannot. Therefore he lost her. She had gone back to the hotel where she had given the name Mauer, and met someone, a man, also staying there, named Woitin. He left and so did she, for the hotel where she'd given the name Saddler. Then she went to London, and you know the rest!"

"Alvin and Colman are most probably the two we're after," I said. "I'd never heard of Saddler before. I haven't heard the name Woitin, either. Pensen may be working with the C.I.A., but I'm not sure. Is it your idea that Saddler was working with the drug ring?"

He shook his head, shut his eyes.

"Bigger than that. No drugs passed at the salon here, or in London. Straight business, both. The Lesbian ca-chet was repeated in London. It confines the clientele. An intelligent fence, you agree? She was there generally two days a week. But it was too short a period to com-pile a substantial report. I think she worked for M.I. But through the Indian—I mean the Hindu or Pakistani or Arabian woman in your office—that is to say, on this last two of her little trips!"

I stared.

"There isn't one!" I said, blank.

His smile reminded me of a deflated camembert.

"Your problem!" he murmured. "I'm not responsi-ble. Mylés from Dahomey assured me she runs the translating department, from what he saw. Also, she seemed to be the link between La Saddler and her employers. She attended the salon twice and sometimes three times a week to have the long hair washed, hn? She always took an envelope for her combings—not to be mixed with others—religion, they are strict. In that envelope was sometimes a small Japanese package, the kind with the garden, you know, you put in a glass of water, it grows flowers, colors, very pretty. Ah, but beautiful!"

"Georges, get a move on!"

"But of course. The pattern told her which advertisement here, in Paris, she must look for. Of the many dozens she was sent, how would she know? She would waste a great deal of time. So? We didn't have time to find out who was behind the Hindu. La Saddler did her part, and sent her report from here in the diplomatic pouch of a certain country, I prefer not to say which. Why surprise? Where you have Lesbians and 'pouffiasse,' you have always the means. In London, it was picked up from that Embassy and taken to the office, you know, near the Embankment. Isn't it M.I.?"

His innocence was misplaced. He knew exactly what he was saying. He also knew that his warning was well-taken.

"This opens several possibilities," I said, talking out of one side of my mouth. "All interesting, none for comfort. There's a link between the Saddler woman and M.I. If Joh Pensen's C.I.A., link there, too. But I doubt anything's known officially either in C.I.A. or M.I. about it. Pensen's probably doubling, and so's somebody in M.I. What's puzzling me is why my organization's being honored in this singular way!"

Georges raised his hands, let them fall, palms open, staring at the roof. He looked like something in mosaic at Ravenna.

"You have radio and international telephone lines and telex, no?" he said. "They are in use twenty-four hours? But then, they can't be used by others for other purposes? It isn't singular. It is extremely sensible. No trace!"

"You haven't got any of those advertisements, or a Japanese packet I could see?"

"I can show you photographs of the advertisements, and of the water glass with the pattern. They will be in the case you may wish to take to London. But I must warn you. Your visit could be your last, you see? I believe there are one or two people waiting for you. My friendly advice? Go in as somebody else. You will learn more. And live!"

"Thank you, Georges. Anyone waiting for me'll have to be patient. What idea have you formed about this?"

He sat forward, as near the edge of the table as bulk would permit, and laid clasped hands flat behind the coffee tray. He was sharp as anyone I'd ever met, he'd spent years in the business, and I valued his opinion because, in his position, he knew so much more.

"Edmund, I wish I could tell you that I had formed anything so constructive as a working hypothesis," he almost whispered, staring at a boss on the pot-handle. "I think your organization is being used in many ways, in the correspondence, air, and sea mails, and in radio and line. You reach across Europe to the Middle East, certainly. But the same means could go far beyond. It is not only the Arab versus the Israeli, in that area. There is also a potential enemy of all of us further off. I don't name any country. I say, and I permit no contradiction, that a great deal of money is being spent to foster certain ideas that many of us would reject, because we were educated in another way. Others' wills and brains are not yet formed. They can be influenced. I believe your organization is being used for that purpose!"

"Any reason for thinking so?"

"I shall give you radio reports my monitors took from your station in London. I shall give the telex messages, and some telephone calls, let me say, of a length. These, I suppose, could only be for publication. Or broadcast?"

"All of them, allow me to guess, with a distinct flavor of Mao's hand-picked, hundred-flower-petal tea?"

He laughed shut-eyed, silently.

"We share the same thought," he said. "What led you to it?"

"The stuff. We can only thank our stars its badly translated. But when they get a few good pens at it, I'm

124

a little worried about what the effect's going to be. Communism's played out. That red guard nonsense can have a distinct pull!"

"I looked on the idiots once as puppy comedians," Georges said, pushing back his chair, fingers clawed on the table, ready to leave, mouth a small o, one eye shut, looking at the note still tented in front of me. "He—and naturally, she—both deserved, I thought, a certain affectionate indulgence. They were the youth of our time. Give them a chance, hn? He, with his poetic hair —after all, youngsters can't afford these seigneurial prices for a haircut—and whiskers—he must show bristles to prove virility—cowboy trousers naturally—he is prisoner of his concept of liberty—and she, more appealing with a small skirt show the legs, cheese in the mousetrap, no? Then the drugs, the marijuana, the heroin, *merde,* you call it? The lisergic acid, the horse. And the freedom of sex. Very well. Then the Sorbonne riots. We wake up so suddenly. Now, it's no longer puppies, eh? Puppies don't burn cars, peoples' property. We deal with what? The educated? They will occupy our positions in ten-twenty years? Hm? What type of life do these devoted students offer for my old age? I speak always of myself, you notice? Can the hundred-flower-petal tea provide an answer, I wonder? Edmund, I believe we have two problems. The indolence of ourselves, and then the Other-Thought, which touches the imagination of those who don't like discipline. And we don't want to fight them, because they are young, hn? We are stupid, my friend!"

He pushed the chair back, and eased his waistband.

"Read your note, and come upstairs for the case. I want you to believe me, you see? It should provide an amusing entracte!"

"Whoa! What's this Hindu woman's name?"

"The Christian name, I don't know. The surname, Bavayani."

"I'll have a look at the lady," I said, and picked up the note.

CABLE ADDRESSED INTERMOIL LONDON
RELAYED OFFSHORE PARIS, KINDLY FIND
TIME TO FLY HERE AND SEE ME. ABDULLAH.

Several thoughts found a way out of the welter.

It hadn't taken long for the rumor to reach El Bidh.
The French Service had a tap into our office lines, or
into the lines of somebody doing the tapping. I thought
that more likely. So might M.I., and who else? However
carefully we'd toothcombed, somebody had managed to
infest the London office. Working for the pair, or M.I.?
Or both? Did Renée Saddler work for M.I.? Was all
Company radio transmission monitored by M.I.? By
whose order? My signal from Ulla's house could have
been located from London. A ship of our Mediterranean fleet could have made a certain fix on my position.
The Blur had probably known where I was from the
start. Had the pair known? Had one of them told Paul?

I felt I'd been batting a fool's bladder.

In that little white-tiled cafe, with the whiz and clack
of the fan overhead, I decided I had to cancel what I'd
planned and begin again at cold prime. I'd been
fondling a couple of unmuzzled dog foxes, always a
dangerous thing to do. I'd hoped I was setting the scene
for a double kill. Instead they'd yapped laughing rings
round the hunt.

I had to warn Consuelo. I had to do a number of
things.

But I intended to take that case to London, first, with
the buttercup, the bluebell, he rose, and the mignonette.

I wanted to get into the building as a complete
stranger—I believed Georges when he said I could be
put away—to find out if any extra-official radio
transmission went on, and where. It was a development
I hadn't expected, at any rate, in my own office. That
inspection couldn't be done as any ordinary person,
certainly not as myself, a princeling-o'-sorts.

But it was certainly possible as my favorite fellah-of-
all-sorts, Bul-Bul, the Zoroastrian, to whom the past
and the future were one, and the present a merest

unkempt harry through purgatory, with the lily-gardens of Nirvana not far on, and manna to eat—"can't you *smell* the honeyed bake of the crust hot from the sun? But you are not i*mag*ining, sir. You are re*mem*bering, you see, from your other life, certainly. It is a vindication of my teaching"—a crystal drip of moonflowers to assuage, and the thirty-nine Dianic kisses, a restless and wondrous provender for livelong, spaceless time.

That was my boy.

Bul-Bul, Zoroastrian, the Invocator.

CHAPTER FIFTEEN

I thought about him on the flight to London, trying to "get" that accent again, remembering the hours we'd sat up on the night of a market day in a Central Province's village, while he told me another Thousand and One Nights. I'd had to put him in chokey for his own safety. Hindu rustics are perhaps the greediest humans on earth, and he'd been selling them sticks of "solid" gold—"from the golden branches of the sacred tree of Krishna, at the very umbilicus of the Ganges, our most holy river!"—until somebody broke one, found the lead, and a mob chased him. I wish I'd had his hands, that palmed five red billiard balls a yard away from me, opened both hands to show them empty, rubbed them together and gave me five red, and a blue I hadn't expected.

I never saw how it was done.

I'd copied his manner, his patter, accent and appearance many times in later years, each time, I suppose, getting further from the original, but I retained the bun of hair, the tortoiseshell comb, the black pillbox cap, and the ruby in the nose. It seemed to fascinate. I was often asked if it was real.

I telephoned Mimi Prôche from Heathrow and told her to get Bul-Bul ready. I'd been waiting for her little yelp of delight.

She was a curious bird, I suppose in the early seventies, a lovely fluff of white hair, perky as a bantam hen at whatever hour. She might have been Roumanian, I don't know. I'd found her leaning against a lampost in Marjoram Street one rainy night, and took her along to St. George's Hospital. They'd diagnosed malnutrition, in her case a euphemism for starvation. I found she'd been a dresser for Pavlova, among others, knew the history of costume, in textiles, leather, metal and jewels from the earliest ages, and her work with the makeup-box was a constant marvel. Unfortunately, she had bouts of heavy drinking. She'd go for months without, and then be off for ten days or more, and come back with that heavy reddish face, tousled dun hair, lidded eyes, shaking hands, and a smell of sour vats she wouldn't lose for a long time. She never apologized or said she was sorry, or any of that nonsense. It was a plain case of take it or leave it, and I preferred to keep it. I knew I'd never find anyone else to touch her.

I'd inherited a couple of houses off Sloane Square and in one I let her have the small terrace flat at the top. The rest of the house was let to Denis Lincoln, my architect, and since he and his staff were generally out by seven-thirty, she always had a full measure of the silence she prized.

The other house was let on three floors to an electrical appliance designer. Each house had a car-dive at the side, and each garage led to the other through a long cellar running under the back gardens, part of it walled, where I had my own radio workshop, with a lift to my apartment built in two floors over the roofed-in space of the garages.

I'd had a large wardrobe there for many years, and the make-up room was probably the world's best. Even my family had never known about it, Consuelo didn't, and I was sure it was one place the pair would never find. I always took great care about going in, and leaving. I went in one car-dive and left by the other in the street behind, though never in the same car.

It hadn't taken Mimi long to get back into her old position as mistress of the wardrobe. She'd overhauled every stitch at the start, and from that time, the place was always ready to give me any change I wanted. She'd never asked a question. I'd never said a word. I'd had her checked by M.I. Her record showed her as dresser and wigmaker, unreliable because of alcohol. It didn't worry me. Her life was her own.

I went direct to the sauna and stayed there, broiling, till Mimi tapped on the door. I came out feeling pounds lighter. My face was thinner. I took the requisite pills, drank a cup of honeyed tea, and went in to dress.

Bul-Bul's clothes were on the rack, ready. I got into

the ankle-tight white linen jodhpur, the long, tucked and embroidered shirt, bound a raw-silk neckcloth, slipped into worn patent leather shoes made a shade too big to ease off my heels, and sat to let her clip beard and mustache. She tinted the ends a grey-blond, touched eyebrows and lashes, set the wig, a masterpiece, with a bun at the back held by a fine tortoiseshell comb, and pinned on the little black obloid cap. That wig could be tugged at, but it wouldn't come off.

My idea was simple. If Georges had an agent in my office, I wasn't going to make him a gift of a report that I'd appeared there with the famous case. That, at the moment, was downstairs in the workshop, being transferred to a Bul-Bul affair of papier-mâché.

Apart from that, to appear at the office as myself, besides presenting a target for whoever might be waiting, would give all the warning necessary to get rid of any electronic gear which oughtn't to be there. The pair didn't make that sort of plan without careful thought for emergency. I had to take the case into the main office, verify, where possible, that other circuits or microphones were at work, leave everything as I found it with no hint of suspicion, and then, with a team of Berry's men, go in, make the arrests, and call the police.

Any other way was simply providing an outlet.

When Mimi stood away, I dialled Berry.

"Can you get a dozen men and keep them at your office till I call?"

"Certainly, sir. Armed?"

"Might be better!"

While Mimi helped me on with the frock-coat, I looked in the pierglass, front, and back, and profile, adopted the hump, shrank the shoulders, bent the knees, clipped in the extra teeth, and smiled.

Behind, Mimi clapped her hands palm to palm, fingers away. Nothing so delighted her as any odd appearance she'd had a hand in creating.

"All right, Mimi," I said. "You will begin to think of Evariste Fromentin Bézé, ex-officer of parachutists in the Algerian campaign, now in business selling domestic furniture, apartment in the Boulevard Zulier, seaside cottage near Nice, children at school, Peugeot car for him, Lancia for his wife, financially sound, against socialism, hating Communists, *vive la France*, sings the 'Marseillaise' on all occasions fervently, but, of course, bestially out of tune!"

"As if it mattered!" she said, in a large wave. "I see him perfectly. Always a tweed suit of impossible cut, brilliant linen, a perfectionist wife, a fine fork for the same reason, a small *pôt*. Not yet embonpoint, but wait a little, eh?"

"Have him ready for me. I'm glad you mentioned the *pôt*. He's had a car for years. Obviously, he doesn't walk any more. When he does, it's on the inside of the heel. His hat?"

"Probably the wide-brimmed Borsalino he bought in Milan last year? Italian ties, narrow, with a small pattern. French socks with a clock. Colored border on the handkerchief. Cufflinks of Algerian coins he acquired in the campaign. A pipe and pouch, a metal cleaner on the key chain. A gold wristwatch telling the time everywhere he hasn't been, and also under water, but he can't swim. I think fattish lobes to the ears, teeth not very good, a short-clip mustache, a triangle under the heavy underlip. *Voilà!*"

I put my hands together in the Hindu salute, got in the cage, went down to the car-dive. I practiced the walk out of the other back door, holding the umbrella by the bulge, handle at cheek level, case jogging at my side.

I'd made a few alterations in its contents. I had no peddlar's licence, but I had a passport. I didn't want to be caught with a lot of stuff. London policemen can be inquisitive, and I had no wish to spend a night in custody. In the false lid, my men had brought Georges' detector down to half its size, and about a finger width high. It was covered by a letter pad and envelopes, pen and pencil in loops, cheque book, passport, letters, all in a fine state of wear, and the case was filled with a cardigan, a pack of nut paste sandwiches, an apple, the usual small brass wash pot, a glass with one of the most chapfallen toothbrushes I ever saw, one large and one small tissue-wrapped package, and a worn-to-tatters pack of Tarot cards. I didn't think a policeman would have much to say about any of it, but I wasn't in a position to take chances.

I got a cab to Pall Mall, and slip-slopped into the marble, steel and plate glass lobby of my London office, almost ready to dance with joy. Instead I fixed Regimental Sergeant Major Kerrigan, Irish Guards —his name, rank and regiment were on the desk tab—with Bul-Bul's benign eye, held the umbrella as a Bishop might his crook, and bowed in a slant of the head.

"Sir, I am coming from Rome, and I am being asked to deliver forthwith and immediately to Miss Toverell for the purpose of relieving myself of all responsibility to this office," I began, in one breath. "In fact, I am being late by virtue of a slight misapprehension with the omnibus which required to be paid in coin of the Realm, which I am not having, only lire, by dint of a peregrination to Italy, and hence my unfortunately tardy appearance here at the request of Miss Consuelo Furnival, I hope we are agreeing, a lady of incalculable estimation and pulchritude. I am hoping to find complete accordance if not substantial affinity!"

Kerrigan's grey eyes looked through me. Without hurry, he took a slip out of the box and put it in front of me, with a pen.

"Be kind 'nough t'put y'name 'n address down there, y'business, and anybody y'wish to see," he said, in the same tone. "Be takin' a seat in th' waiting room, if y'please!"

I wrote Bul-Bul on the same line, and Invocator in the Business, and in quilly flourish along the top, "Miss Toverell, with sublime and complimentary regards and elevated tokens of respect, B-B."

I went into the waiting room, put the umbrella on a chair, and my case across my knees. I snapped both locks, and touched the button to open the lid a fraction.

132

All four prisms were alight. A fifth, which we'd added, opaque white, showed the locator needle pointing diagonally left, and steady I judged the stranger to be along the corridor to the main office, and left, somewhere in the three suites in a row down to the back wall, Planning, Survey, and Market Control. The heads of those sections, all first-class men, Ockleby, Anderson and Howell, had been cleared months before and had never left London. But among those departments were perhaps thirty men and fifty or more women, most of them copyists in Planning, and the majority hadn't been looked at.

I had to be careful what I did because the electric eye watched me unseen, but timing the light and dark phase of the blue prism, I saw that a three-second signal was being sent at twenty-second intervals, possibly to "place" us. The yellow and red light were on. Radio messages in and out were being monitored by a set in the building. Green showed a message being unofficially transmitted.

Under everybody's nose, how was it done?

The radio room was two floors above, as I sat there, behind my back. The four operators were ex-servicemen, specially picked. I saw I'd have to put a locator and a warning system in there, and work out a plan with Berry, so that a signal would automatically lock all doors, and a search party led by an operator with the locator would then uncover the cuckoo.

The electric-eye glass doors opened in a *whump!* that startled me for a moment. Miss Burrows, Consuelo's secretary, smiled at me. I was glad to see that callers were kept downstairs. But it was my business to get into the main office and find where that extra equipment was, and then call Berry. It wouldn't take him two minutes to get there.

"Mr. Bul-Bul?" she greeted, gently. "I'm sorry Miss Toverell's not in. May I help you?"

I had to cut the original idea altogether.

"I am being asked to deliver two small packets to Miss Toverell, to be given to Miss Furnival on arrival,

133

and to take a receipt, and to hand over a pack of cards for Mr. Edmund Trothe because they have great value," I said. "There is no expense, and I am glad to have the opportunity to be a useful friend, free and gratis, no obligation, if you please!"

"Thank you," Miss Burrows said, in her pretty way. "If you'll follow me, I'll take charge of them and make out the receipt. Please?"

I went behind her, up the short stair, along the corridor and into the main office. There were fifteen girls and five men at their desks. Some of them looked at me with the Londoner's blank—nothing surprises them —and went back to what they were doing. I followed Miss Burrows through the glass partition to her office next door to Miss Toverell's, then a waiting room, Consuelo's office, and my suite.

Miss Burrows touched a chair for me, and went to the typewriter. Somebody moved outside. I heard the whisper in carpeting.

I put the case on the desk, opened it, took out the two packages and the cards, and deliberately let the apple drop on the floor and roll out to the corridor.

"Please, please, no matter!" I said, and she sat down again. "Kindly be so good to open the paper to ascertain the cards are seventy-eight in number. I am disappointed not to have the autograph of Miss Consuelo Furnival. An imperially sovereign type of graciousness, no doubt?"

Miss Burrows took both packets—one held a microphone, the other a volume control—and as I'd hoped, put them in the one drawer of her desk with a lock.

A heel tapped off the runner in the corridor, and then a move, more pressure of footsteps in carpet.

"Please to pardon me," I said loudly. "I must pick up my apple!"

I was at the door with the last word, and turning right, bending to reach, I caught the flash of a woman in black, pale stockings, thin legs, fair hair.

I'd seen her with Joh Pensen a couple or so days before outside Derna. A glimpse, but that was enough.

I picked up the apple, and looked at it. My mind sang like a buzzsaw. For that moment I was slightly tipped. Georges had known what he was talking about. If this one had found a way in, then others even more dangerous might have followed.

She'd turned into the main office. I had no excuse for going up there. I didn't want to alarm anyone, and I *did* want to preserve the get-up. Bul-Bul had been useful, and might be again.

Miss Burrows had almost finished typing the receipt when I went in, rapped out a final line, flipped out the sheet and signed.

"There!" she said, all smiles. "I think you were most kind. You're not going back to Rome?"

"I am flying to Bombay," I said. "Mr. Trothe was speaking of a translator. I have humble accomplishments in many languages—"

"Simply write for an appointment" she said, and gave me the envelope. "And thank you *very* much!"

"You haven't got the Miss Bavayani here?"

"Miss Bavayani's away. I'm sorry. This way please!"

I couldn't ask to use the telephone, because all calls were tabulated in the switchboard room, and Berry's number was one of our own. It hadn't occurred to me before, but an operator might well be working for the pair. Yet the locator had pointed to the other side of the office, away from the radio room and the switchboard.

The fair girl's being there really did worry me. She wasn't in the main office when we passed through, the corridor was empty, and so was the lobby.

"Thank you, Mr. Bul-Bul," Miss Burrows said, at the top of the stairs. "I shall look forward to seeing you. Mr. Kerrigan, pass, please. Good afternoon!"

Kerrigan pressed the foot-switch, the lobby doors opened, and I was out in the warmer air. The doors *clicked!* behind me, and I had fifty yards to go to the nearest call box.

I slip-slopped across, dialled Berry, and—suddenly—froze.

I'd made two fatal mistakes.

135

If somebody was inquisitive about calls in and out of Berry's office, the tabulator would tell them. All they'd have to do was pick up the inter-line receiver.

At that moment I didn't feel I was worth the trouble of kicking. I was sure, then, that the first call to Berry had been picked up.

I dialled, and Berry answered.

"Immediately!" I said, and cracked the receiver down.

I held up the umbrella for the taxi going by, and told him to go to Sloane Square. The cab braked on the corner to let a car pass, and I looked up at our side entrance, a green door let into a recess in the heavy stones of the ground floor. A man came out with a carton on his shoulder, and crossed the road. ACEY-DEUCE CLEANERS in red tape crawled over the back of his overalls. I watched him mount a tricycle on the other side, and caught a movement at the door.

Three men came out, two putting on their overcoats, and a woman in a fur coat and cap, greyish stockings, black shoes, nearly as tall as the men.

I heard myself groan.

The cab started. I tapped the glass, held out half-a-crown, opening the door as he pulled in. I sprinted for the corner, using will power to keep those shoes on, but the four must have gone into the Square. I went up that rise in fair time, but among the few walking behind parked cars I couldn't see three men together, or anyone in a fur cap. I doubled down the pavement next the garden. Further up, a gunmetal sports car turned out and went away. Even in a cab I couldn't have caught it, and by the time I'd squeezed between a couple of cars, the number plates were too far off to see. I trotted up to the corner, and found the parking attendant squatting on the stone surround.

"There was a gunmetal car here—perhaps a Jaguar—belonging to a friend of mine," I said, in a rush. "He's just gone. Do you happen to know if he comes every day?"

"Jag?" he said, raising his eyes. "Just gone? He's been coming the past week, yes."

136

"Don't happen to know his name, do you?"

"Not my business!"

"Do you remember the number of the car?"

Neuter pupils darkened, became sly.

"If I did, you wouldn't get it," he said. "You shove off, 'fore I call a copper. Then he might find out what sort of 'friend' *you* was. Twig? Bloody wog!"

I seemed to be doing everything wrong. I should have slipped him a couple of notes, and then asked. I turned my back and walked away. Sweat soaked my shirt. I could only thank my stars once again that I'd got back in time. I was fairly certain I'd been spotted at Ulla's house and the information had been passed on. Who'd done the spotting, and who'd passed the word to whom? In that little time, those four, perhaps more, had managed to join the Company, and while I admired that sort of initiative, I intended to find out how they'd been able to dodge "I," and if any others had been taken on elsewhere.

One matter stuck out, stark.

Except perhaps for Consuelo, I couldn't trust anyone, however faithful. Excluding Berry, nobody knew what was going on, or what we were up against, and for many good reasons I couldn't say a word.

I was at the top, in sole charge, alone.

It wasn't a healthy position. However confident I might be, I saw that I had to find partners, and so divest myself of the responsibility of leaving—in the event of my death—a healthy Company on the rocks. I knew it wouldn't take long for the Princes to find someone else, but I felt fairly sure he'd be a marked man from the moment he sat at the desk.

In all of it, shadily in rear of my mind, I had yet to explain to myself exactly why I thought the pair were interested in the Company. The financial advantage was obvious, though where, except in the Soviet Union and its satellite countries, would they be able to enjoy it? Everybody in their own world was looking for them.

help, there comes a moment when the very soul seems Yet, I knew from experience that while disguise may to rebel against the will, and one *has* to become one's

137

own self, if only for a few days. Consulting memory and feeling, I knew—or I thought I did—why Bernard Lane had gone into Plummy's as himself. In all probability, that was the reason.

He was revelling in the self he was lonely for, and reckless of what came next. In that mood, killing is the same as eating or drinking, and perhaps as enjoyable.

But I was sure I had to see the Blur.

I had to ask him point-blank if he had any idea why the pair were after me and my Company. I could give a few reasons, good enough in their way, but they left too many questions unanswered. That I was possibly the one man in the world able to identify either of them on the instant was, I thought, stretching it. That they were anxious to do something, and I was in their way, seemed more reasonable. The two together made a fair basis. But they were taking a great deal of risk and spending a lot of money for what return? I went round and round but I couldn't find an answer that satisfied me.

I lit a most un-Bul-Bul cigaret, and sat back, trying to imagine where the pair might have a crack next. They had almost half the world to choose from.

It was being forced on me that I hadn't the first notion where to look for either of them.

It was hard to get used to.

CHAPTER SIXTEEN

I paid off, scuffed along to the car-dive, through the passage, to the lift, up to my own place.

"Come on, Mimi! Quick clip, my own clothes!"

She snipped the tinted ends off beard and moustache, levelled the "cut"—an expert job—and I flew for my room. It had taken exactly twelve minutes from taxi to my own car, and I got back to St. James's Square in just under twenty-five.

Berry waited in the lobby.

"They're all a bit snitchy about having to stay in, sir!" he said. "Can't see anything going on. Nobody here shouldn't be!"

"Ask the cashier to let me have the names of people taken on in the past two weeks, and where they work!"

He looked up at me, over the spectacles.

"The only ones are the people you sent here, and the translator Miss Furnival sent," he said, scratching his temple. "We only had the letters of introduction to go on. Anything wrong, sir?"

"I wrote no letters. I'm sure Miss Furnival didn't. Why were they allowed to begin work without investigation?"

Berry folded his arms, shaking his head.

"Couldn't argue with your signature," he said. "There's a man, Gouldsden, in Buying Control. There's another, Spiers, in Accounts, and the other's in Machine Tools Dispatch. The woman's in Translation. From what Miss Burrows says, not too bright. There's another, Connors, hasn't been here long enough!"

"We'll go to Buying, first. Ask the others to go to my office waiting room."

I was sure we were wasting time. The pair's emergency drill was too good.

We were at the barrier. The staff sat at their desks.

"Sorry to have kept you!" I called. "Shan't be a moment. I have a small announcement to make!"

I went on a tour of inspection. Heads of departments stood and smiled as if they'd rather not, and I got down to Buying Control, a smaller suite of offices, between Planning and Survey.

Ockleby got up. I gave him no chance for small talk.

"What sort of a man's Gouldsden?" I asked him, quietly.

He stared at me for a moment. I saw previous thoughts being put aside, and new light faltering between Berry and myself.

"Not the sort of man I'd have chosen, sir!" he said, slowly. "Too much of the old school tie, too much running in and out next door. Too many larks with the girls!"

"Fair enough," I said. "Let me see his desk, will you?"

He led into the next office of three secretaries, to the larger room at the back. Gouldsden's desk was tidily stacked with the green, pink, blue and yellow copies of orders, his trays were empty, pencils and pens were in the rack, and the blotting pad was a new sheet of white.

The drawers were locked.

"He's got the keys to it, sir," Ockleby said. "He's only gone down to Cline's. They're experimenting with a new sort of coupling. A light alloy, cheaper by about forty per cent. Heat makes no difference—"

"I've got a key, if that's what you want," Berry said, and took a bunch from his pocket that looked like a balled-up spiky steel centipede. "Want me to try, sir?"

It took two or three turns and the master drawer slid open. He pulled them all out, and stood looking down at the bottom right-hand.

"Hullo?" he said, "What we got here?"

I leaned across the desk. I knew what to expect. The drawer held a small trans-receiver, as good as anything I could have produced for its size. The wire to the mains was coiled on top. I went round, saw where the controls pointed, switched to zero, plugged in, and turned on the speaker.

It was a powerful set.

I went up the band carefully, and got the tail end of a

signal. Just a touch further could have blown our ears off. I began to write a six-letter group message, got it all down, and waited. Air was live. O-T-U was sent three times. A smaller signal came in faint, and I turned up volume. A message began, and while I wrote I wished—how I wished—I'd had a locator there.

But Hanley, poor scut, the office page, suddenly came bustling in with one of the girls, and a tray of tea. It hadn't occurred to me to tell anyone to keep quiet. Berry, of course, was watching me.

"Care for a cup of t—!" Hanley trolled, and in a blast of rage, I bunched a fist at him, and Berry grabbed him by the lapel.

No use.

It was a very good two-way job. Anything going or coming was heard at either end without switching on or off.

Air was dead.

Hanley took his glasses off, poor fellow, pale with shock. The girl stood there with the tray.

I switched off.

"Might as well have a cup," I said. "Where does Gouldsden live? As if we'd ever catch up with him!"

I gave Berry what I'd written.

"See what the cipher team can do with that," I said, and took a cup of tea, helped myself to sugar. "You'll have to disregard 'notes' from me in future. Obviously you don't know my fist from a bull's foot!"

"I took Miss Furnival's word for it, sir. She sent it to me!"

"Miss Furnival's had nothing to do with anything for almost the past month!"

"Well, sir," Berry said, without feeling, "If I'm not told where anybody is, how do I go on?"

I took the radio out of the drawer with help of a steel rule, and Berry's right hand.

"Get that taken to pieces, and see if you can find out where the parts came from. We've got to sit down for an hour or so, evidently. What was Gouldsden's address?"

"I've sent a squad round to Cline's, and his house, to

wait for him. If they get him, they'll call. Same for the others!"

The girl took the cups, clattered them on the tray, and left.

"If I could say a word, sir," Ockleby said, over the bridge of his nose, "The address my secretary heard given for Gouldsden isn't the one she had for him!"

He gave Berry a red-print *DON'T FORGET* office note.

Berry looked at it, and dropped his hands.

"243, Revers Road?" he said, and looked round at me. "Kensington?"

"Thank you, Ockleby," I said. "Get a replacement for Gouldsden. Berry be good enough to bring everything to my office. Pity you can't bring Gouldsden and company!"

CHAPTER SEVENTEEN

We had a couple of hard hours making a reference guide for employment of staff. All seniors would start on a one-month training program with pay. During that period "I" would have a chance of looking into their records. No junior staff were to be engaged unless they were recommended by the technological school or secretarial college which had trained them.

"That's a makeshift, but it's better than what we've had," Berry said. "That Gouldsden, he's a fly boy!"

"Did you get a good look at him? Would you know him again?"

Berry looked very much like a policeman.

"I don't know about 'know' him," he said. "I got a complete set of his prints, though. That's much more useful!"

"Unless he was wearing plastic tips. They're made, y'know? Might look into that!"

He sat back, taking off his spectacles, rubbing his eyes with a thumb and forefinger.

"Funniest job I ever ran into, sir!" he said, looking from here to there. "I don't think I'm *such* a fool at this game. I didn't ought to be. What's really worrying me is this. D'you mind me saying this, sir?"

My turn to sit back.

"Please do. We probably agree!"

"Y'see, sir, after you've had a few years on the Force, you find out the innocent ones are the liars, and the ones you'd lay odds was liars are innocent. It takes a bit of getting used to. Then you start having a sort of 'feeling'. I don't know what it is. But you don't have to be told. I knew Gouldsden was a bad 'un. Very nice man, very well educated. Dirty fingernails. Thumbs bit down to the quick? Something wrong. I put a man on him, minute he left the office. He lost him. He kept on losing him. I put another man on. Gouldsden come up

143

to him in a coffee house in Piccadilly and wanted to buy him a cup. That's the sort he is. Clever. My man never said a word. He come back to me. Done the job in. Gouldsden had this address in Cromwell Road. I had two men outside, one in, a waiter. He never went there 'cept twice. He had this Jaguar. Couldn't catch it. You see, sir, we can't order barriers up the road. We have to take what we get. We go too far, we get into trouble. See that, sir, don't you? No excuses, just facts. Now then, all that of one side. What's worrying me, like just now, here, this afternoon, he goes out, the excuse is, he's seeing Cline's. Look, sir, he won't come back. Where *do* they get the 'off'? I've been to the phone operator. Gouldsden never had a call this afternoon. The wireless set? Was that it? All right, whoever it is the other end, where do *they* get it to pass it on? That Hindu woman, or whatever she was, went off yesterday. Who told *her*?"

We looked at each other.

I sympathized, because I'd been trying to find an answer.

Not a soul knew I was coming back to London, and certainly, not a soul could know I was after Gouldsden. Had he finished the job he'd given himself? What job was it? He couldn't do much damage in the Buying Department.

But his office was between Planning, and Survey.

Ockleby had said he'd done too much running in and out. Old school tie. Larking with the girls.

"Let's have a look at Planning," I said.

We went downstairs. The main office hummed in the cleaners' floor machines, and a wastepaper wagon was being pushed by someone we couldn't see. A pair of arms came up, emptied a basket, and sank. A door shut.

Survey was a long room with half-a-dozen planning tables, green Plastex, being washed. All original work was locked in the safe. Along the corridor, cleaners washed down in the Blueprints section, wheeling the boards out to suction the lather.

Copyists never knew what they were doing. They simply drew on a transparency.

But I saw what a stupid mistake had been made. All original drawings in Survey went into the safe at night, but here, because it was only the copyists at work, unfinished tracings were left on the boards.

But the boards, at that stage, held the series diagrams of the cooling and anti-fire systems at Beyfoum. There was no lettering, nothing to show what those curious designs meant. But any engineer would read them off the top of his head.

Just a little "larking" with the girls every day would bring rich reward. A wristwatch or finger-ring camera would never be seen or heard. But anything on a board would be on a negative. A few sets of microfilm photographs blown up, day after day, as work progressed, would give a competitor all he need know.

The Beyfoum project was first of its kind. There were installations there I wasn't anxious to advertise. I was paying heavy patent royalties, a good investment so long as the Company held control. It looked as if a few of them might have left home.

Again, I was forced to wonder who the "competition" might be, or who the pair could be working for. It had never been established. At first, naturally, it had been thought they were Russian agents. They'd got away to Moscow, or paragraphs in a few newspapers had reported they'd held a press reception there. The reports seemed to have come off the news agency wires, and yet, the few hardheads I'd talked to on the accredited correspondents' staff in Moscow hadn't seen the pair, hadn't been to any reception, knew nothing about them.

But working newsmen of that rank in the profession are seldom blarneyed. The three I'd talked to had made enquiries among their colleagues. Nobody, at any time, had seen the pair. The agencies appeared to have taken their stories from Tass, the official Soviet newswire. But I had all the cuttings, in all languages, and I'd found that Tass appeared to have picked up the report from somewhere else, because its only paragraph was timed twenty minutes after one from Teheran. But when I enquired there, I was told they knew nothing about it. The top man was a friend of mine. There was no need for him to lie. I didn't think he had. A news agency feeds, and is fed on. The rest gets lost in the tape basket.

That was how any investigation of the pair began, and ended, in a puff, a damaging whiff.

They'd done a very good job for many years between them, and they must have had some competent people working for them. And money.

The money began to occupy my mind.

Where was it coming from, and how?

It isn't simple to pay people large sums in any currency and keep it hidden. The money has to come from somewhere. If it comes from a bank, it can be traced, all the way back, anywhere on earth, while paper exists.

We'd never been able to get a whisper, world wide. Their cheques and drafts were always met on time, and the original funds were invariably paid in banknotes, sterling, dollars, francs, or gold. They had the advantage, there, of being able to work where we were blind. It wasn't until a cheque appeared that we could start an enquiry. By that time, scent was cold.

Who were they working for?

Russia? China? Neil Collinson, new vice-chief of M.I. 6., had wondered about an American or European combine—several were enormously powerful—wanting to enter various markets, upset political regimes, put in their own people, that sort of thing. I'd heard it all before. I'd seen it done, at times, but I couldn't believe, in view of their past, and from what I knew of them, that those two deadly traitors had the smallest hand in anything so healthy as normal commerce, or for that matter, with the C.I.A. or any other European agency, working for the West.

What was left?

Nothing much except me, sitting in an empty office,

with the cleaners, a group of green-clad and turbanned female gnomes, glowering at me, waiting to finish, and Berry under a light in the corridor, leaning against the wall, hands in pockets, looking down at the toes of his boots.

CHAPTER EIGHTEEN

Madame Berthe telephoned from Paris to relay a cable, sent from Abadan, that Colonel Hamid was unavoidably detained, but would be honored to receive me at Ben Ua, with deep expressions of regret and compliments.

I looked at Ob, my son-in-law, across the table, stretched in an armchair. He seemed even bulkier and blacker than I remembered. He had a curious habit, when thinking, of staring those enormous eyes at one place on the ceiling with rarely a blink, putting the left thumb under the left hand side of the jaw, and stroking the jaw and down the neck with all the other fingers, slowly, rhythmically, curling them away into a half-fist, and starting again. I wondered where, against which leaf-thatched wall, and when, that mannerism had begun. He was first generation of his kind. I wondered about the second. My granddaughter, among them.

"Very well," he said, still looking up. "I see no complications. I shan't need all that money. There's a lot of very good stuff ready. I can ship it in the next week. The recruiting, I'll begin tomorrow. I have a retired General of the United States Army, and one of the old German Army, not a Nazi, and I'll send them there, with their wives, as tourists. They won't arrive at the same time, of course. Within ten days, we should have a report on the possibilities of the defence of Ben Ua from two points of view. They've never yet been wrong!"

"How about this fellow Merzel?"

He shrugged.

"I don't believe that Merzel, or whatever he wants to call himself, or anyone else can do as he pleases in Algeria today," he said. "If it's the Merzel I know, he's

148

marked. That's all. You don't fool with Boumedienne. I'm thinking of this young officers' plot, the students and the rest. That's far more worrying. They know they have the power and the numbers. A little more from somewhere, that's all they need. Their only enemies are the older men in politics. Get rid of them, they have a direct approach to the people. Then a general revolution leading to war is very easy. All they want is the *JEHAD*. Make a holy war, strike hard from every side, a Soviet navy along the seaboard, and the sack of Jerusalem could be repeated—when was the last? —Hadrian? That seems to be the idea. Then the young men take over the Governments, and spend the money. Paris is still with us. Girls are still girls. We speak of *our* time!"

"Not very hopeful?"

"There's too little power in command. Nothing to respect. Nothing holding at the top. A few men, armaments, any little lieutenant or major can take over. All they have to do is murder. Or imprison. In the past month I've been from country to country. People are trying to do business. But there's nothing to protect them. Nothing under their feet. Look at Biafra. Hopeless. Mali. Gabon. Impossible. We live in an unpublicized disaster!"

"What about trade?"

He moved only his eyes to look at me.

"Half of five years ago," he said, sharply, "It should be fifty times more. Who's allowed to trade? Some of the 'boys' in power? There aren't the conditions. For the moment, foreign loans are keeping things going. But this bankers' business, of one Government lending another funds is absurd. We all know it. It rarely does what it should. Only the private businessman creates a country's trade. Naturally. But where have we a chance? If you took my company out of the half a dozen countries I've just been to, what would happen? No business. Why do you think I have bodyguards with me? Many would like me out. Then it follows a collapse here, another there. Then a take-over by the worst elements. And what? An empty shell, where another fish can make a home!"

I'd never heard him talk like that before. I thought I'd push my luck just a little.

"Any idea what type of fish is likeliest to move in?" I asked—as it were—offhandedly. "I'm fairly sure we're beginning to feel a touch of it!"

He got up and buttoned his jacket, in my experience, an unconscious form of self-protection.

"My own agents are busy in the matter at the moment," he said, looking away. "It doesn't do to talk too much. I know there is Chinese capital. I've used it. There are nationalist and tribal elements among us, very active, and Red Chinese financial interests behind each. We've already found in many cases the same banks and agencies are behind both sides. But those interests aren't really financial. They use money to create unrest. Paying for sabotage, mercenaries, gun-running. Strikes. Fires. Everything. Economies in Africa are delicate. We are loose. We have only desires. It's not enough. We are amorphous. No schools. Few educated. One who reads English or French is immediately a power. But what do they read? And who supplies the worst inflammatory stuff? It will surprise you, I think? Your own company here!"

I couldn't do much more than stare.

"Come along, now, Ob, m'lad!" I said. "All very well, talking anti-us. Let's have a fact or two!"

He pointed to the neat packet he'd put on my desk.

"When you have the time, please look at those," he said, and laughed. "Patti told me you couldn't be surprised. I have a pleasant shock for her!"

"Distributed in all these countries, or just one?" I asked, ripping the paper off. "I'll put a man on this, first thing!"

"They've gone to many countries, and there's no imprimatur, no author. I know it comes from here because a British plane brought it from Gatwick. It was taken

150

there by the Riteair delivery people, another small surprise, perhaps, from this address!"

His face was a block of guileless ebony, not so much black as a darkly vital blue. I was just beginning to know him.

I had no need to look at the address he gave me. The type of print and paper, the makeup generally, was that of our own printer, Stanshead, one of the oldtime craftsmen.

I dialled him at home.

"Oh, yes, Mr. Trothe!" he said, as if he'd been eating. "I'm very glad to hear from you. I asked your secretary to let me know—"

"Who gave you this booklet job? This 'Britain, the faithless,' and the other rubbish?"

"It came from your office in the usual way, sir. My head proofreader called my attention to it. Most offensive stuff I ever had in the place. If it hadn't been one of your jobs, sir, I'd have refused it. But I thought you might have something in mind, I mean, like the other jobs, so I got on to y—"

"What other jobs?"

"Well, sir. There've been several. Two in French, two in Arabic, one in Spanish, one in Portuguese—"

"I know nothing about any of them!"

"Oh? Well. Serious as that? Thought there was something very wrong. Never get hold of you. Always got put on to someone always said I had to write for the letter to be forwarded, meantime exceptionally 'portant job an' underlying reasons. That kind of pile-up!"

"When you called here, did you ask for me?"

"You or Miss Furnival, sir. The operator—it wasn't Hines, sir—I know his voice, and he knows me—"

"What time did you call?"

"Generally about when I came on. About nine, or a little after."

"One of the Mayfair numbers?"

"No, sir. Your old number—"

"Thank you, Mr. Stanshead. I'll get back to you!"

I switched off with a feeling that I had more than one snake in my hammock. The slightly open bottom drawer of my desk showed the thinnest crack of white light, which meant that my little "box" was killing a family of planted microphones. The set in the drinks sideboard was recording all radio signals in and out, and the "clix"—my own make—recorded all the telephone calls being tapped, including the one I'd just made. Half a dozen of my own technicians from Sloane Square were all over the building with Berry's men, and I expected to have the information I required before I took the Company's jet to Abadan.

Ob had pulled aside the blind to look out at our fair view of London. Lamplight greened the trees over in the park, reddened the brick of St. James's Palace, touched a sentry's scarlet tunic, silvered the bearskin cap, glinted off the roofs of cars, pooled amber daubs in asphalt sheened as satin.

"I'm sorry you must lose all this, one day!" he said, quietly, nodding outside, "I feel it should be preserved. But there's no hope, is there? I feel sorry for all Europeans. In Africa, we know we must have at least another five hundred years of tooth and claw. We must kill to survive. You also know that. Better than anybody. But you don't like to say so. It's not Christian. But you *aren't* Christian. Or, not as I was taught in *my* school. Everybody talks. Speeches. Everybody a plan. So wise. Based on the latest economics. But behind all of you, we see a rocket. On television, you are so kind, you show it to us. It will burn the world. Instead of a savage like me, with a big spear, going out to kill other men, you have a man with a button, sitting comfortably in a clean bathroom. He will burn the world. This, here, and everywhere else. And so we should believe you? Why?"

"It's out of *my* hands I'm afraid. I don't think I feel any better about it than you do. But there isn't much to be done, is there?"

"In these democracies? Where the people have the power? Where you believe you have an answer for everything? Because you all have a vote? And you always tell us what we should do? So, so kind. But, Edmund, I'm sick of this humbug, really. Why do you make such a prepotent god of the vote? Who votes? Who uses the power? We think you're all stupid!"

"Very easy to say," I began, hopefully, looking at the clock. "We can all preach. It's an accusation, of course. But I have to leave in fifteen minutes—"

"As I have told Patti!" he said, picking up hat and coat. "You are all cut from the same piece. I see a pattern. I had an interview with a Minister this afternoon. The moment we began to speak of an issue not on the agend—the agenda!—what is a *real* talk for?—something relevant to me and many of my people—he had an appointment. You wonder why you lost an Empire? My dear sir, you all had an appointment!"

"I have a few things to do, and then I'm going to Heathrow. Are you coming with me, or do you intend to stand there blathering?"

He tipped sideways, a rag doll tugged on a string.

In darkness I felt the heat and flung up my hands. I floated. Air burned my nose. I fell on my shoulder and upper arm. My knee hit me in the jaw. I thought I'd landed beside the bookcase. I lay there. Without a breath. I could smell heavy dust. Lights were out. My ears stung and pained. The floor shook and part of the masonry collapsed. A cut lip was salty. I heard a rumble of settling stone, small shouts, glass in long shatter.

The floor tipped down toward the window, trembled, steadied. Dust was too thick to see anything. All I could smell was powder, acrid, in the head, beyond the ears. I crawled face down toward where I thought the door had been. I couldn't feel where Ob had fallen. There was no staircase. Far down, I heard a hammer smashing at metal. Perhaps the lift doors.

I put my head on my forearms, smothered mouth and nose.

It was no consolation to know that the pair had scored.

But there *was,* though, a certain purely childish satisfaction.

They hadn't killed me. I felt like sticking my thumbs in my temples, wagging my fingers, poking my tongue out.

Ridiculous. But I remembered a tongue-out photograph of Albert Einstein. In extremes of anger, in resentment, we revert to the primally untinged feelings of childhood.

It's healthy.

CHAPTER NINETEEN

I took White Horse Five, the Company's new jet, and got to Abadan in excellent time. The sleep did me a lot of good. A stiff scotch and soda and three stitches had put Ob on his feet, and I didn't need the stitches.

I let the staff deal with Customs, and while I soaked in three-minute hot, three-minute cold plunges, I went over what I'd discussed with Chief Superintendent Hockley. He was putting a man in the Planning Office, one in Survey, and two women in Pay and Accounts.

"Nobody'll be able to work for a couple of weeks till they've got it all back to normal, anyway," he said. "That gives us time to have a thorough look at everybody. I'm surprised that's never been done. I mean, knowing what *you* do!"

"I didn't like sacking people just becaue they'd been taken on in Chamby's time. Most of them have been checked, except the minor clerical staff."

"That's more than seventy people, though. In London, alone? Eh? Bomb planted inside the building. Switchboards tapped, microphones, odd wireless sets? I mean, there's nothing missing except a loose robot or so. Still, can't say it's out of the ordinary. Day before yesterday I was in Court to see a staff-sergeant out the Royal Air Force sentenced to twenty years hard. Traitor. R.A.F., mark you. And we know there's more. By the way. That Revers Road case. Very strange. The dentist reconstructed the jaw of that poor girl, there. Her name's not Saddler. It was Dorothea Maxwell Ferrers. Knew her, didn't you?"

I'd known both her mother and father. I felt the most utter misery for them. I couldn't feel much for her. Pity is far more self-sympathy for having to feel anything.

"Very well, indeed. She was assistant to Joel Cawle for some time. And to Bernard Lane before that. The pair we're after. First-class girl. Excellent family."

"They can be just as rotten as the rest. I saw Mr. Collinson. You know him, of course? She left the Service some time ago. Opened a beauty place here and Paris. Doing great. I don't know why they don't stick to honest business. What is it, among these people? A disease?"

"She was a girl of strong character. She might have told them she wasn't interested in further business?"

"Knew too much for their book, most likely. They're a right couple of hounds, y'know?"

"I always think of them as a pair of mangy foxes!"

"Not too far wrong. I'll lay you a small bet if you like? Just on what I know. One of 'em's going to stop the other!"

"Who's your choice?"

"Lane!"

"No bet. It would never be Cawle. He's afraid to be on his own. He relies on Lane. Works through him. But don't underrate him on that account. He can give Lane pointers in quite a number of things. Ever met the public school weasel?"

"Thought they was foxes!"

"As a pair, yes. Alone, Cawle's a weasel. Always was. It's his nature. But he didn't kill Dorothea Ferrers!"

"Oh? Who did, then?"

"I'll give you a hundred to one. Lane!"

He held out his hand.

"You know them better than I do," he said, as if it didn't matter. "But those odds. I'll take you. And I'll be glad to lose that quid. Almost honest. Only if I've got him nice and comfy inside, though!"

I'd forgotten how hot the Arabian sun could be. The first fierce blast hit me in leaving the bath house with those warning stabs of prickly heat, and I turned thankfully into the cool airport coffee shop. The Prince's Rolls-Royce hadn't arrived. I had some very good coffee and hot biscuits with the aircrew, saw that their quarters were comfortable, and the manager came to say that His Highness' car waited for me.

156

The khaki-colored juggernaut seemed to ogle me most unfavorably with its headlamps. The aide shut the door, got in beside the pennant-holder, and we turned out in the dust.

It was still fairly early. Camel caravans lolloped toward knots of palms, laying up for the day's heat. A few cars and a couple of watertrucks passed us, but nothing seemed to be going to El Bidh. We turned on to the narrow tarmac leading up to he palace. Sometimes, at first, a couple of hundred feet down, I saw the waves break slow, creamy lace on red rocks, but for the rest of the way we had a sheer cliff on both sides, and with the headlights on, it might have been night. I knew that sentries up above watched us every foot. If the aide hadn't waved the blue pennant under checkpoints from his window in front, we wouldn't have got very far. I'd been there twice before, but I never lost the feeling we might at any time, somewhere in those miles, be crushed under tons of rock.

We came out above the artificial park the Princes' grandfather had planted at the beginning of the century. It was still an agreeable surprise in sudden flush of whitest sunlight to see the palace's arches, and gold cupolas and the stalk-slender minaret on the further hill. The garden glowed, green everywhere, red peaks all round, and the road's white hairpin turned among a glory of blossom, rose gardens in stone walks, beds of gentian, masses of marguerites, magenta pinks, water-lilies in the ponds, while lilac, scarlet asters, to the tunnel in the main wall, a solid yellowy-red mass of gilly flowers, and the car hoists up to the ground floor.

I hadn't seen a soul, so far, but when the doors opened on the top level, an aide in a white uniform and gold aiguillettes tapped his spurs together, and in a courteous gesture led the way to the waiting room.

The air was pleasant with a familiarly faint musk-cinnamon-clove and Egyptian tobacco aroma. The waiting room could have made a comfortable mausoleum, walled and floored in white marble with a gold mosaic dome, teak and red-leather chairs, a small fountain in the middle filled with plants, and a large, gold-framed colored photograph of the Princes' grandfather looking as if he'd caught someone peeping at the conjugal register. It was said he'd had more than three hundred wives. Those eyes seemed to follow me. Perhaps vindictively.

A servant in black and gold livery brought a coffee tray. Halfway through the sherbert I awoke with a jolt, realising I'd been rather more than a little torpid. I hadn't been met by Hassan Farad, the Prince's secretary.

Mark of acute disfavor.

That rumor, of bullion for Israeli fighters, it seemed, had been taken seriously.

I crossed my knees, closed my eyes—I knew I was being watched from behind the lattices—and marshalled my facts. I had most of the paper with me, and I'd done a couple of hours' work aboard the aircraft, so that with Khefi's questions to guide me I felt reasonably confident, that is, except in the case of the hard-line Arab. In my experience he's exactly the same as the hard-line Hebrew.

They don't think as Europeans, haven't that mentality, feeling, or outlook. Where they believe themselves cheated, no apology will suffice. Revenge is all, and method won't matter. In that, both are helped by their history. The solitude of the desert, the long pace of the camel, the stench of ghettos, the atavistic rejection of defeat or insult, and grimed-in-the-soul spiritual travail over generations, seem to have become integers in national character, whether of individuals or as peoples.

Time is theirs' or their sons', and Allah-Yahweh is good, and they can wait and suffer, but a Day must come.

The aide tapped those spurs behind me and inclined his head. I picked up the briefcase and followed him down the red runner of a long corridor, into a rotunda of five other corridors, went down the northeastern, with small doors on both sides under arabesques, which I thought were offices from typewritertap, and he knuckled a gold bell twice at a massive iron double-grille.

The outer leaf opened, and the inner. A white-bearded guard in scarlet, scimitar drawn, bowed, stood aside, and we went in.

Prince Abdullah sat in a gold throne at the end of a red baize table, with about sixty people on each side, so far as I could judge, and one with his back to me. Nobody wore European dress. But instead of their usual robes, they all wore the desert brown or white. It didn't augur well.

I walked up the right hand side, looking at Prince Abdullah all the way, trying hard to appear airily affable, fearing, however, that my expression came out as little less than covertly inane.

Hassan Farad slightly disarranged his cheeks in a grimace which deceived nobody, and half-bowed to the chair a yard away from Prince Abdullah's throne, and the saluki, a handsome blondish fellow wearing a diamond collar about four inches wide. I sat, and crossed my knees. I hadn't been greeted. The dog sniffed my shoe, seemed to find things rather too aseptic, and lay down in a sighing moan, resting his jaw on a forepaw. I sympathized.

The room was quiet except for the breath of air-conditioners. Everybody sat still. Only a blink here and there told they weren't all wax. I didn't know any of those I could see. Protocol forbade my speaking before the Prince. I didn't move. I had plenty of time.

"Well, Mr. Trothe, it is my duty to welcome you!" he said, in English, and half-turned his head toward me. "You arrive in time to attend a meeting of my family and the retainers loyal to me. I do not wish you to speak for the moment. I want a reply to these questions. First, has our Company transported war *matériel* to Israel? Has our Company ordered war *matériel* for Israel? Has our Company used its funds to order, or finance, or in any way to assist Israel or any sub-agency? Has our Company an office in Israel? Is any

159

Jew in charge of any of our departments? Does the Company employ Jews? Does the Company help the funds of the new Nazi party in Germany? Have we an office there? Is there an office in East Germany? Have we recently transported war *matériel* from either of those countries to Israel? Do we maintain aircraft flying between East Germany and Poland, to Tel Aviv? Finally, for what reason was a warhead, and by a warhead, I mean an explosive charge which is part of a rocket, flown from West Germany to Bell's Fosse in England, where the Company's aircraft are now kept? These are all matters of some importance to us. I am patient for your reply!"

I was willing to hope my face was blank as my mind.

It took me a little time to stop the kaleidoscope. The Israeli questions could be denied, out of hand, and on evidence of Company accounts. The employment of Hebrews could be defended. But the East German and Poland business, the ordering or purchase or financing of war *matériel*, the warhead flown to Bell's Fosse, our new airfield, was something very different. I had to think fast. Clearly he'd got his information from a hard source. Arabian Embassies, and their businessmen are no less clever than others, and neither are their Intelligence services less keen.

Something, somewhere had leaked.

The pair had been busy.

"Your Highness," I began, in drillhall style, so that my voice would carry to the end of the room. "Your questions about Israel are answered in a general and emphatic *no!*"

I waited for the echoes to fade.

"I have asked the Company's accountants to forward a copy of the balance sheet as at midnight last night," I went on, sensing relief in the air, seeing many hands go to the cigaret boxes. "As you know, they keep close watch on all disbursements of any nature. Nothing can be spent, not one postage stamp bought without their knowledge. The purchase of bullion, for example, would be queried in the normal course, and verified by

160

my signature and the chief accountant's, and would appear in the book entries of that day. That's where rumor collides with fact!"

Prince Abdullah looked down the table, nodding to the older men.

"Then, I am to understand there has been *no* dealing with Israel, or *any* sub-agency, or *any* work of *any* sort done by the Company?" he said, markedly less frigid, but still distant. "I am very glad to hear this. The employment of Jews?"

"There are eight Hebrews employed in senior posts," I said, knowing I was dancing on a pathway of eggs. "Two are chemists, among the most distinguished in their field. Both are American. Three are British, one is a chemist, the other a surveyor, and the third is a translator. One is Tunisian, a Hydrographer. One is Czech. The other is French, a computer specialist. So far as I know, none of them is linked in any way to Israel. They hold their country's passports. They are among the best employees we have. They've worked hard, and if Beyfoum is the success we hope for, we shall owe it to at least four of them. They were given three-year contracts in Mr. Chamby's time, and I'd be against terminating them for any reason!"

Prince Abdullah put his forearms on the table, and looked sideways at me.

"Nobody to take their places?" he asked, faintly surprised.

"With that degree of efficiency, no." I said jussively. "The men who'll one day take their places are still at their universitites. They're all Arabs, and when they graduate they'll all be under them for training. Men of that distinction don't grow on trees!"

Prince Abdullh opened his hands in a wave of dismissal.

"You know best!" he said, and—so far as I was concerned—let in a ray of hope that almost lit the place. "Now, this matter of war *matériel* being flown from West and East Germany and Poland. I want you to read this file. Not now. Then this, of a warhead flown to Bell's Fosse. I thought it was a private airfield? How was this done?"

"I know nothing about it," I said, loud as ever. "I wish you'd told me at the moment you knew. It's a very serious matter, and the Police should have been informed!"

"Here's the file," he said, and passed it across. "How is it that people seem able to speak so badly about the Company? How is our name used in so many items which are not true? What excuse is there?"

I had to choose my words.

"Your highness, I could leave this room, and whenever I wanted—let's say, in Paris, where you have many friends—I could make anonymous telephone calls. I could say or write anything. Most wouldn't be believed. But gossip makes rumors. That's the only excuse I can offer. But I shall sift all these matters. I'll cable when I have the answers!"

He half-turned the throne toward me, and the two guards helped it round until we were face to face.

"You will read those files, first, and let me know what you think," he said, almost his normal self, but still aware that many ears listened. "I am very concerned about that warhead!"

"I share your concern!" I said, and stood. "I leave my files with you. Kindly give particular attention to number three!"

He pulled Hassan Farad by the robe, whispered in his ear, and nodded smilingly at me.

I wasn't comforted in the least.

I could be kept there without an earthly chance of getting out. Paul Chamby, at a time when I wasn't in the Company, had been held there for almost a month, only because he'd agreed with Azil against Abdullah. He wasn't ill-treated. He'd been honored as one of themselves, and even had his own harem. But he swore he'd never go back there for any reason.

"A luxurious dungeon, Edmund!" I heard him saying, again. "By Christ, they'll never get me back there's

162

long's they've got a hole in their loose ends. That bloody garden. The *miles* I traipsed!"

I was thinking of him while I followed Hassan Farad down the wide corridor toward the Prince's suite of offices. Every five paces on both sides, a guard stood to attention and moved the scimitar across his chest. Those blades were like razors. We stopped at another grille, and Hassan rapped the bell with a knuckle. The soft chime brought a squeak of iron hinges and the grille swung out.

Not ten paces away, an escort of guards from outside the palace, in brown burnous, taller men, darker, more dangerous-looking, marched toward us. The guard at the gate halted them with a sign, and bowed us on.

I don't know what I was thinking about, but I was behind Hassan, following him down the corridor into the lift up to the offices, and I heard my name called loudly in a voice I knew but for that moment couldn't place.

I turned, trying to see round the guard behind me.

In shadow, as the grille closed, somebody in silhouette stood out of line, grey flannel suit, red carnation, waving, trying to stop the guard from closing the grille.

"But, Edmund!" he almost shouted. "I thought you'd be simply enchanted to see me again!"

I tried to go back, but the guard stood in my way and others came off the wall.

"Who is that?" I shouted, while the grille closed.

"One good guess!" he half-laughed, walking away, waving.

I knew the walk in a flash of light as he passed the window, almost afraid to believe my eyes.

Bernard Lane.

CHAPTER TWENTY

Hassan saw me to the smaller office—with four guards!—told me to order what I pleased, and went. I sat down, trying not to think of what might be going on downstairs. Here was about the most excellent site that could be imagined for the death and burial of Edmund Onslow Perceval Trothe. I'd never be heard of again. Nobody would know anything about me. There'd never be a whisper anywhere.

It would be highly proper, then, for Bernard Lane to take the Chair, same contract, same terms, with, presumably Joel Cawle as his second man.

If, of course, that was the idea.

I put it all out of my mind, and opened the first file, a series of reports dating from twelve days before, of the rumored purchase of aircraft for Israel, the companies, agents, type of craft and armament, supply of air-to-air missiles, with a number of names I didn't know. But I wrote them in my notebook.

The second file was a hair-raiser.

Bell's Fosse was on land of mine and a neighbour's, near my house. We'd put down a runway and two hangars without disturbing, to any large extent, the tilth, and the two cottages we'd moved had been rebuilt and modernized on the other side of the copse, and everybody was happy. The hangars housed the jets recently bought, and the turbo-transports making the biweekly flights with stores, a Customs warehouse, a control tower, a radio station that reached all our bases, aircraft in flight and ships at sea, a kitchen and dining room and a bunkhouse for the aircrews.

The West German reports cited cargo manifests, times of departure to Bell's Fosse and the names of the aircrews. The warhead was described in detail. It was sent from Barnbruche. I'd never heard of it. The crates were not deposited in the Customs warehouse, but carried to a bay in a hangar and left on a trolley for the morning flight.

The entire file was a clever forgery, with one exception.

The crews' names were correct.

Reading carefully, I was encouraged to find there was nothing to prove that any warhead had been flown in a Company aircraft. The warhead folio was separate. The cargo manifests gave the number of crates, index and catalog codes, but the warhead, live ammunition, arms, were not listed.

English is a curious language. A lot may be suggested. But fact imposes the duty of choosing a requisite sequence of words to state a meaning.

It wasn't there. I took heart.

The third file showed a series of payments to the Nazi Party made through our West German office—we didn't have one—and the *matériel* which had passed to East Germany via Czechoslovakia, on our aircraft, routed through our East German office—we'd never had one—and East German and Polish war *matériel* flown in our aircraft to various bases in Israel via airstrips in Beirut and Damascus.

I had to sit back.

Everything looked solid enough. Copies of manifests, order forms from manufacturers, Xerox replicas of receipts, cheques, cash payments. I had at least a month's work in checking. But before I did anything, I saw I'd have to take full page advertisements in the newspapers of West Germany, Holland, Belgium, and France, to begin with, warning of fraud being practised in the Company's name, and legal action to follow.

Reading on, there was a long report from the agent in charge of Arab munitions supplies, Waddid Garagesh, brother of the man I knew. He'd got on to the Barnbruche warhead story through his transport manager in Neussen. The name of that town, Neussen, brought a reminder of the Saddler-cum-Ferrers trip to see Joh Pensen, the pianist. Things appeared to be fitting together, though I wasn't quite sure how.

Waddid mentioned the order for the rocket to be used at the wedding—I assumed, our wedding—and detailed how it was to be flown in sections to Beyfoum, and enquiring about landing facilities for jets. Then he went on to report the flight, that afternoon, of certain *matériel* via the Company's transport, a VCIIO, to Bell's Fosse, and asked if the rocket sections could be routed that way instead of through Czechoslovakia and East Germany to save time and expense, and more importantly, why the bulk of all minor items couldn't be flown by the same route.

It was a fair question.

All incoming freight, generally from the United States, for pipeline construction, and not destined for the United Kingdom, went into Customs Bond, and stayed there under guard until released to be flown out. Because it was marked elsewhere and sealed, it wasn't liable to examination except in special circumstances. I could see that incoming freight, at two o'clock in the morning, going out at three, would stand every chance of being off-loaded, on-loaded in the waiting aircraft, and out, before anyone could look at anything.

It was a clever dodge.

It might work a few times before the Customs' officer hooked on. When he did, the Company would be in serious trouble, and I stood every chance of appearing in Court charged with everything from smuggling to a breach of security, to say nothing of crimes citing paragraphs A to Z of the Defence of the Realm Act, or whatever had taken its place.

I saw a legal scrimmage of historical extent behind each page.

I also saw the masks of two leering foxes.

One of them was downstairs.

I wondered what the other was doing, where.

I looked up, at filigrees of colored tiles threading here and there across the ceiling, no less complicated than the patterns in my mind. I gave up any idea of planning. I could only take all precaution everywhere,

166

wait for the first move from the other side, and try to counter.

An amazing flash of light seemed to illuminate all I'd been thinking.

Was that how Errol had been taken across the border into East Germany and Hauerfurth Prison? On a Company aircraft? Had Paul Chamby been privy?

Neussen was only about forty miles from Fraglechshaben. Supposing—just supposing, and I didn't want to—that the details were known, down to the letter code of the aircraft. How could I defend myself? Or the Company?

The pair, of course, would let it be known.

I had to see the Blur without delay.

I had to get out of El Bidh.

But I had four guards, locked grilles, many other guards, twenty miles of chasm, and forty minutes on the flat between me and flight to anywhere.

I looked at my watch. I was four minutes away from "clix" time. I knew that the eyes behind the lattices round the room were never off me. I had to be careful. Fortunately, "clix" was part of my wristwatch, and I had only to hold the left wrist with the right hand and the Morse signal movements were covered.

I wrote down all the names I could find in the files, and I was making a note of the manifest which had taken the last lot of crates to Bell's Fosse, and I caught an entry I'd missed in Pilot's instructions. It was a carbon copy, the fourth, on pale blue flimsy, and the writing was faint but "Para: Kretzgros" was plain enough, and some figures I took to be a map-grid fix. Parachutes aboard our aircraft were someimes used to dump cargo on landing strips socked in by bad weather, though that was only over desert base-camps, not in Europe. I'd never seen an instruction to a captain to make a parachute drop. That was his business to decide.

What had been dropped by parachute? I'd never heard of Kretzgros. It sounded German. I looked round

167

the room for an atlas. The walls were solid escarpments of books, but all Arabic. There wasn't an encyclopedia. I'd have showered gold on a Britannia salesman if he'd come in then.

A command outside, the guards stamped their feet apart in salute, the door swung, and Prince Abdullah came in with Hassan Farad behind, and the dog. He came to me in a hairflop gallop, jowls framed in a dazzle of diamonds. Even his spittle gave off sparks. He pushed his nose in my hand, stood on hinds, and I got up, pulling out the length of an ear, scratching behind the delicate edge of the skull.

"I have decided that you leave, Edmund!" Prince Abdullah said, looking at the dog. "You have much to do. Of value to us all. I see nothing further to discuss. For the moment!"

"Couldn't I have a word with your other 'guest'?" I asked, forcefully, with a weight of distaste. "I have good reason to believe he's responsible for most of this!"

I pointed to the files.

Prince Abdullah looked at Hassan Farad. From a mutual attitude, I was sure they agreed.

"Unfortunately, he is, let us say, the agent of a power friendly to us at the moment," the Prince said, scratching the dog's head. "I don't want any incidents here. But I'm curious to know how two such excellent Englishmen appear on opposite sides!"

I heard Hockley's voice—"What is it with these people? A disease?"—and perhaps for the first time wondered myself. Why should Lane and Cawle, thinking of them as schoolfellows, same background, English, of excellent family, choose to help an enemy, or at any rate betray their own country? What reason could they possibly give? Not in extenuation, but simply *a* reason, to account for conduct, over years, inimical to the interests of a Nation which had trusted them so far as promotion to high office. Politics? Knowing the pair, I could hardly believe it. The Prince had just said that Lane was agent for a "friendly"

168

power. But to the Arabs. Not to us. But why? They were both well-off, on money earned in Great Britain, they'd both married wealth and their fathers had been officers of State, with many another in their wives' and their own families for generations.

"I don't know how to answer you," I said abruptly, though I didn't mean to be. "Probably it's a case of the small boy punching his father. Being rude to his mother. Permissively. Then they grow up, still punching authority, still being rude. That's all. But I wish you'd give me five minues with him? Alone, of course!"

He shook his head, smiling, looking at the dog leaning against me for more earscratch.

"As I told you, I don't want incidents at El Bidh," he said, snapping finger and thumb at the dog. "I would like you to investigate this matter of the warhead. The papers are not clear. Where did this thing go? To Israel? For their engineers to copy? I want to know. I rely upon you to tell us!"

"But, sir, that could lead to an embarrassing situation" I said casually. "I'd have to send someone into Israel, or go myself. Couldn't be done. I'd be accused of fraternization, perhaps? It's idle for me to say there's as much truth in this as the story of a bullion purchase to pay for Israeli aircraft. I can only tell you it's a farrago, very well put together, but it hasn't quite gone according to plan. But why *should* you take my word, rather than the creature's downstairs?"

He put his hands behind, and looked across at the long shelf of gold-framed photographs of Ataturk, Ibn Saud, some I didn't know, his father, a couple of uncles, three brothers, Allenby, Glubb, Montgomery, Russell, Hoover, Roosevelt, and Paul Chamby, younger, perhaps during the time he'd been counsellor in Palestine.

"I have just had a bad operation," he said. "Ten years ago, I wouldn't have lived. The things which interested me before don't interest me now. I have a distaste for the sophism of this time. I don't trust what we pretend we are. I have no faith in the Western way

169

of thinking or doing. For me, not any longer. I rest on instinct. Especially the instinct of the animal. It is pure. He cannot hide what he feels. He is not civilized. This dog, Grock. With you, he is a friend. He went for the throat of the other!"

He shrugged, held out his hand.

"I must go back to the conference, Edmund. Hassan will see you to the car. Let me know what you find. Remember, always I am your friend. Until you are shown to be my enemy!"

"One question," I said. "Ulla Brandt Ben Ua. The defence of her property. Do you trust Colonel Hamid?"

"Ah, but Hamid is dead!" he almost whispered, craning his neck. "I preside now over a conference which has to do with this matter. We shall not permit Ben Ua to be taken. I know you are helping. It made a difference in your reception today. It was not cordial? It could have been less!"

"Who is the Colonel Hamid in Ben Ua at the moment?" I persisted. "Madame is a friend of many years. I want to know she's protected!"

"In this, we all are one, Edmund!" he said, sombre, decisive. "If Ben Ua falls, it's the end of all of us. We don't intend it. This Colonel Hamid, you must not worry. I am in constant touch with your friend, the Commissioner, Mahmoud Nas'r El Khef'. If that one, Hamid, leaves Ben Ua, I have the men ready to present him in Cairo!"

"I devoutly hope you succeed," I said. "But who *is* this Colonel Hamid?"

The Prince pointed behind.

"The friend of this one," he whispered, with a grin that held a knife. "Now we find out what he brings to offer us. I keep him here as a guest until I am satisfied. What I find out, I tell you. But, I assure you, we have an enormous conspiracy under our feet. You have your work. I have mine. Go, Edmund!"

I picked up the files, bowed, and followed Hassan, almost ready to sing from sheer relief. I hadn't attempted to carry the talk any further. Prince Abdullah was a man of moods, and he was very much a master in his own demesne.

All I wanted was to reach that airport, sit my thankful self in any aircraft, and get the hell out.

I had an idea about that paradrop.

Hassan touched heart, mouth and forehead, shook hands, and the aide closed the car door. We went down, and turned out in white sunlight, whispered through ramps of flowers, turned left, and I thought I saw where Lane had got his scarlet carnation.

It was no use complaining, or slopping tears in spilt milk, but that was my one real regret. Azil should have been presiding at that conference. He'd have let me have a few minutes with Mr. bloody Lane. One of us would have earned that carnation.

In sudden spate, for no reason, I was clawed, clutched, seized and immersed in a yearn for Consuelo, the sweet of her silk, her lips, her hands, her tenderness, her voice, herself, the glory of her orgasm.

Her.

If the Prince Abdullah was master in his own little piece of the Earth, then so was I in mine, and I thought I'd earned a day or two with love. It's Earth's rarest essence, I was in need, and all I had to do, since I was a lucky one, was say the word. I put aside any rot about responsibility or what I should or should not be doing, and managed to contain myself as far as the airport, that wonderful place, met Captain Bulkeley, and said it.

"Jamaica!"

CHAPTER TWENTY-ONE

I'd sent the usual nightly cable to Consuelo but I didn't tell her to expect me, and so I wasn't met at the airport. It was just as well. The sun wasn't up, nothing was open, and I had to wait for a cab.

The end of the night lazed in a cooling breeze, starlit, warm, with a smell of spice I couldn't name—perhaps a vanilla, or nutmeg?—light, faint, and a silence that seemed to whisper the furious life of a myriad insects without any sound I could hear.

We went through quiet streets, lamplight in trees and gardens, whitening walls and houses, and I felt I was back in the seventeenth century, seeing only the eyes of a line of Negro women with huge bundles on their heads, and a man, barefoot, in white trousers and shirt, wide-brimmed strawhat crushed under a crate almost as big as himself.

The cabman seemed to know where he was going, but I was lost in a maze of narrow lanes. We appeared to be bumping west, from a glimpse at my compass, over to the other side of the island, and I wasn't wrong. At about first light, a wonderful bluish-pink, I saw the sea, mauve, not far off, over surf, and we stopped at the gates and lights of Banbury Cross, in iron-work scrolls, and the electric torches of four khaki-uniformed guards.

I handed out a card, one of them trotted off to telephone, and I sat back, more than happy to see the place well taken care of, with a swinging lantern down the road showing boundary guards marching back. The man at the telephone chirruped, pointed through, and the gates opened. We went in to a gravel driveway reddening in morning sun, round and round, a surprisingly long way, through a wonderful garden, that suddenly opened on one of the finest lawns I ever saw, and the house, of two storeys, porch of tall columns below, double windows shuttered upstairs, red-tiled roof, long chimneys of curlicue brick.

Banbury Cross.

Exactly the sort of place I'd expect to find her ladyship in. And she owned it.

A footman in starched whites slipped down the steps to open the car door.

"I'd like you to call Miss Furnival's maid," I said, getting out. "My name's Trothe. There are four guards here—"

"One here, sir!" Briggs called, coming down. " 'Morning, sir. Nice to see you again!"

"Glad to see you're taking care of things," I said, looking at the .45 in the belt holster. "I don't want to disturb Miss Furnival!"

"Just follow me, sir!"

We went in to a wide lobby, to the right hand side of a double stairway, up to the corridor running the length of the house. Amber lights made a glow on polished mahogany panelling, copper panniers, silver.

Briggs stopped at a door, tapped twice, waited, tapped again. A bolt slid back, another, and a key gritted teeth.

A solid thickness of timber opened on a chain.

"All right, Big Mary!" Briggs whispered. "It's Mr. Trothe!"

I suppose Mary was the thinnest woman I ever saw. Barefoot she stood taller than me, at least half as wide, with enormous black eyes, a thin nose, narrow lips, black hair in smooth fall below her waist, not pretty, or even handsome, but beauty was inside her, and she beamed honesty. I took to her at that first smile.

"Been 'spectin' you, s'!" she whispered. "Leddy Conswell-oh, she don't talk nothing else. Her room, first right, s'. Your room, first lef'. Master room, leddy d'house room. Bathroom, dress'room, off. You like tea, coff', s'?"

"Tea, strong, and a large cup, please," I said. "For two!"

She shook laughter without a sound, and led through the foyer to a door on the left, opened it.

173

"I bring d'tea, s', I ring d'bell," she said, closing the door. "I leave 'm here, or come in?"

"Come in, why not? What do you expect to see?"

Her head went into her shoulders, and I caught a flash of teeth, squeezed eyes, a breathy heh-hee! and the door shut.

I was in a room that really was seventeenth century, with pirate chests in brass-studded leather, bed and chair carved magnificently out of an almost-milkwhite driftwood, two walls floor to ceiling of battleships in oils, and two walls hung with models of sailing ships in glass cases, all labelled, each a gem of its type. I knew I'd have to invite Sir Chapman Ryder. This collection beat his. The floor gleamed in wax about the colour of pale honey, and the roofing must have come from the stateroom of a clipper, heavy beams, with the brass ports hanging open along the surround. On the top of a perfect example of a skipper's desk, three daguerreotypes of Captains in Royal Navy dress uniform, one with a cocked hat, looked at me from copper frames. If I needed any reminder, I was made aware what sort of man commanded battle-sail in that day.

Brutes.

Heroes, by accident of victory.

In essence, brutes, because they had to be.

I took up the three of them, and opened the top drawer, put them in, among leather-bound books, possibly ship's logs, which I intended to look at later.

For the moment, I was using, as it were, the front of my mind. The rest, as far back as I could feel, was in a millrace with one thought cut solid.

Consuelo.

In bed.

Next door.

I went in the bathroom and turned on the hot shower, went into the ice cold, had a shave, slapped on the Knize, put on pajamas and a gown, and about the time I thought I couldn't stand it any longer, there was a knock at the door.

Mary's smile, of eyes and white teeth, hovered

174

behind a tea trolley, dipped in a curtsey. The room was dark. Shutters were still closed.

"Thank you!" I whispered. "Don't let me hear a murmur that size out of anybody before I ring the bell!"

"Yes, s'," she said innocently. "You don't want no bands, no singing?"

"No nothing!"

"That's right s'. That' what I said. He don't want nothin', I says, down there. An' 'at's *good,* I '*greel!*"

"You married, Mary?" I asked.

"No, sir, not yet," she said, going to the door, half-turning. "I di'n' find him. Else he di'n' fin' me. When he do, well, sir, this whole isl' goin' t'be in a rumble a couple o' days, take money. I jus' get the toast plate 'n kettle, s'!"

I went to the right-hand door.

I was looking at a piece of timber at least three hundred years old, polished by many a serving hand—what had all of them been thinking while the shine came up?—and what had been in the mind of the doubtless many, years before, like me, pausing perhaps, thinking of someone on the other side, hesitant to waken her, almost ready to go back till she woke, one memory stupidly persistent—"I don't care *what* time it is. I'm *wid*dershins, I'm *rav*enous!"—and almost tipsy with psalms and poetry I hadn't got a word for, rigid, pulsing, nothing in mind except that first, glorious influx, a conscious dream after, and her breath, her whispers, her hair, her silken pelt, her strength, for wonder and comfort.

I opened the door. It didn't make a sound. I shook hands with the carpenter. The room was faintly shadowed. Shutters were closed but the windows were wide. Voile curtains puffed a small voluptuous morning dance. The bed gleamed with a headboard of cherubim, a baldachino with white pom-poms, a dressing table between the windows in glitter of glass, a pair of slippers, one this way, one that, beside the bed—I could have eaten them—and a mound in bed.

Two mounds.

Two heads, one fair, long, a plait with a bow.
One black.

I was frozen in thought of bodyguards—"handsome!"—and policemen, days left alone—"the beach is a mile long!"—and the nearest mound turned, shook aside the plait, murmured something.

"Consuelo!" I barely whispered, though it must have sounded like a foghorn. "Darling? It's me!"

My voice bounced off the headboard. I don't think I ever heard anything so fatuous.

She straightened, opened her eyes, saw me, gulped a huge breath, and flung off the clothes.

"Darling mine!" she sleepily screamed in half a voice. "You're here!"

That dark head hadn't moved, and her arms were round me, and I squeezed hard, but she sensed.

It didn't take her long to wake up.

"Who's that?" I said, and nodded at the poll.

She looked up at me, halfway round, and knelt.

"Darling, you'll have to forgive me!" she whispered. "I asked him to—to—well, not *sleep* with me, exactly, but just, you know, keep me company. Oh, Edmund, he's so gentle, so—so—considerate—"

She leaned away to tug back the sheets, pulled, and threw up an extraordinary shape that seemed to bounce in darkness.

"It's Eddie!" she whispered, through the tiny rattle of the trolley next door. "The doggie you bought me in Paris. My stand-in love. Darling. *Don't* tell me you want *tea!*"

CHAPTER TWENTY-TWO

When I woke, the place beside me was cool.

I sat up. The shutters were still closed.

I knew I'd slept a fair time. I felt rested, but thick, and it wasn't far to the shower. There's nothing like coming awake in a sparkle of water. My toilet case was laid out, so that I knew Consuelo had been busy. I had a really clean shave for the first time in months. The beard had been useful, but I'd got tired of scraping round the edges. There's nothing like a clean face. But when I washed the soap off, I found I was burned blackish across the nose and forehead, and pale as a worm down below. I knew how to cure that. A bath of strong tea and lemon juice now and again in hot sun does wonders.

I found shorts and jersey, and opened a window into what felt like a blast of molten gold, full in my face, sunshine whiter than the African sun I'd got used to, and, I could feel, less hard on the skin.

The sea stretched a pale blue dream with streaks of electric green in front and as far as I could see on either side. About 500 yards off, to the right, a white boathouse and yachting slip ran out, with three or four large craft tied up. White sand showed over the edge of the terrace, running the length of that side of the house, banked both sides with flowering plants I didn't know. Further up, to the left, a loveseat swung under a blue and white awning. A coffee tray glinted half in, half out of shadow. A hand came out to take the coffeepot, a beautiful hand, slim, Consuelo's. The little-finger ring I'd given her made fierce dazzle in light, and went, in shadow.

For those seconds in time, which seemed aeons in my life, I knew we must marry, and soon, even that day.

The business of living with, or making love to, whatever terms are used—and I detest the Anglo-Saxon shorter word—is all very well, but it doesn't bring much except nervous release and certain marvels of the senses. There's always a nag that debts aren't being paid. It's a selfish mess. Nothing's steady, sane, in order. One's merely run-o'-the-mill with any other brute and some drab. Responsibilities none, social conscience none, sense of honor, none. But civilization isn't built or held together by that sort of dishwash, and I determined, decided—I don't think any word could describe my feeling, then—to marry, put things right socially, give Consuelo the peace of soul she was entitled to, and at the same time, smooth a few of the larger crinkles out of my doubtless tender conscience.

I felt I was thinking in an old-fashioned, thoroughly bombazine manner, remembering the boys and girls on the beach somewhere near Derna. No question of marriage there. All very well, I suppose, and I might have enjoyed being with them. For a time.

But, the little voice said, a living world isn't built or maintained on that sort of withdrawal to please the wilful self. Only a healthy economy founded on the hard work of millions can tolerate the few in idleness. But at the same time, if it tolerates the bone-idle among the rich, why not among the poor? And how about forced unemployment among the masses? And if they, of their own free will, wanted to withdraw, what harm did it do? Tramps and hermits always had. The world's Unemployed had, without wanting to. Perhaps the hopsters were simply tramps and hermits of the new age, or another sort of Unemployed living off dreams instead of the Dole. Or the monks and nuns of an era without religion—as we'd once known it—except, of course, they didn't run hospitals and schools, or for that matter, teach or console anyone except themselves, or in general do anything except exactly what they wanted to do.

But that's all any of us were doing, and some of us got paid for it.

I sensed an element of confusion somewhere. I hadn't the patience to analyze.

"There's a way out of this tangle if I can find it!" I said, aloud, and heard the *"Oh!"* "I never saw a more restfully lovely place, or a bluer sea, or imagined anyone as beautiful as you, and oughtn't we to take every advantage and get married? Now? Whenever you please?"

"Well, what a sell!" she complained, tranquilly, in shadow. "I expected to be asked. Not challenged. Not even a handkerchief to kneel on. No stammer. No passionate declaration. Just the same old 'how about it'? What do you expect me to say? Come *here!*"

She wore a red and orange flowered bikini, and a blue voile pull-on reaching to her waist, a garland of white blossom in her hair, and her office spectacles on the end of her nose, which she knew made her eyes seem twice as big, and even bluer, because I'd once told her so. They added a lustre, perhaps, of wisdom or sapiency, whatever it was, which I found inexpressibly kissable, and didn't waste any time.

But I had to be careful of the coffee table, and was.

"You must be starving!" she said. "Was I right about this house?"

"Never imagine anything like it. What's the taste of bacon and eggs, here? Any different?"

"That, or lunch in twenty minutes? This coffee's cold. Let me get you some. Read this for a moment!"

The blue notepaper I'd once seen in my office in the old days.

Gillian's.

I didn't take much notice of the first four pages, except that a skim down the middle gave the Basques top marks for hospitality, food, kindness, music, hours looking at clouds lying in pasture among shepherds piping to sheep, and Errol getting thinner, stronger every day.

I sat up for the footnote.

"Please tell Edmund that A.C. is working at Corledge Trans Inc. in the satellite TV and Radio department. That's all I've got, so far. I'll be back next week. More, then."

Corledge Trans, I knew, was a powerful communications company recently formed by a merger of several others. What was Alethea Cawle doing there? Unless she'd had to leave the Service? I couldn't for the life of me see them keeping her on, though it seemed hideously unfair to sack a daughter because her father was a traitor. I itched to get at a telephone. I wanted Berry to find out what she was doing, and how she got the job.

I hadn't seen demarara sugar in crystals for years, but the bowl Consuelo brought with the coffee took me back to Onslow Common and old Freeman's grocer's shop on the corner, savory in smells of tea in open chests, and varieties of sugar in sacks along the counter, smoked bacon, haddock, kippers, a plethora of all the goodness in the world, and I could still smell it.

That was the best cup of coffee I'd had for years, and only because of the sugar. It gives another richer taste.

"I didn't want to inter*rupt* you," she said, with her dying-duck expression, staring almost cross-eyed, head bent, hands loose in lap, a Botticelli virago, and dangerous. "Something about getting married?"

"That was this morning," I said. "You know me. I change with the sun!"

"I see," she whispered. "Scarlet letter stuff. I take it you're abandoning me? In the gutter?"

"Right kind of gutter to get abandoned in," I said, looking round. "Not an ice-floe anywhere. Which reminds me. How about some ice in a bucket, and a bottle, and I'll make a real carmens' pull-up champagne cocktail?"

"Right behind you. Sort of imperative detail I *never* forget. And it's *Krug!*"

Two footmen were bringing a table, an ice bucket with a magnum, napkins, glasses in a bowl of chipped ice.

"We're drinking to our joining in matrimony, which I've fixed for tomorrow at an hour to be decided by the Reverend Brother Teague, of the Franciscan Order," she whispered. "Think you can twist me round your little finger? You can try. I'm a nice size for my age. This is Perkins and that's Dollison. Perkins is silver pantryman. Dollison makes the best punch in the Caribbean. He's the head cellarman. Is the champagne fit to drink?"

"Let her sweat 'nother ten minutes, she' going to be right!" Dollison said, twiddling the bottle. "I had her in the ice house, 'long with the others. We di'n' know's you get' married, leddy Con-*swell*'? Big Mary's act like she the whole show, *and* the' bells. But there's us, too. We all like to 'sist!"

"You get the chapel ready for tomorrow, and let's see," she said. "Call Brother Teague, will you, please? I *must* talk to him!"

They seemed to share constant laughter, padding in step, giants, even taller, broader than Ob, slightly paler.

I looked at her.

"What are you wearing for the ceremony?" I asked her, on my knee. "Something local? No use grumbling if I don't match the social scene. My morning coat's in London. Best I've got's barathea. Lightish. A little demode?"

"This time tomorrow we'll be sweeping confetti under the bridal litter," she said. "There's ample time to call London, and have all you want on the next plane. Dimwit, or tightfist?"

"Little of both. Get on the blower. I want to speak to Berry, first!"

"I'll get him. In the silver parlor. Down that stair. Give me an extra*ord*inary kiss. I'd love to feel just once like a blushing bride. But I don't think I've got much of a blush left!"

We kissed in the gentlest way. I knew I'd been right. Bodies are all very well, but the mind *will* keep on thinking, reminding. I could almost feel Society—the part we belonged to, at least—breathing down our necks.

She, I saw when she walked away, *could* wear a bikini. I thought of the naiads near Derna. No comparison, snobbery or not. Schooling, grooming, social

181

drill, the more genial disciplines, nothing took their place. All the naturalistic, grow-as-you-please nonsense was exactly that, and coldly proven by results. Inferiority, superiority, as complexes, were never plainer than when the schooled and un-schooled met. The difference glared, even in memory.

All that, at any rate, from my own, I suppose, restricted point of view.

The naiads were beautiful as they were, no question.

But what, in ten, twenty years' time?

Gather ye.

I went down the stair and took a header into a blue pool that froze so much, I could barely swim the length. I came out wider awake than I've been for the past ten years, perhaps, and splashed under the fresh-water shower, got a towel and found my way back to the room.

I was in trousers and shirt when I was called downstairs.

Consuelo gave me the receiver and a kiss, and left.

"Your call to London, sir? You're through!"

"Mr. Trothe? Berry!"

We got a lot of buzzes, hoots and assorted grunks for a moment or two, and I realized he was putting in the scrambler.

"Right, sir? Lot been going on, here. Five people didn't turn up for work, Gouldsden, Blois, Palmer, Hoyt, and that Miss Connors, in despatch. There's another one, Miss Bavayani, in the translating office. They've cleared out. I had the explosives lads here. They don't know at the moment what caused it. Construction's going on. I had all the drawings and the stuff you pointed out, it's gone to the bank. There's a sealed packet from Mr. Obij-Obji—anyway, I'm sending it on with the portmanteau. Then there's another packet from Marie-France Belac, from Paris, secretariat of H.H. Prince Azil, and I'm sending on the findings in that Saddler-Ferrers case. That manageress of Plummy's Club, Mrs. Meryl Armitage, she's not daft. She knew they were looking for Lane, but as she says, y' never know who's who these days, so she didn't tell anybody, but she got the waiter to put cloths on all the stuff him and his friends—there were three of them, one woman—they used at the bar and the table, and she saved them. I've got four nigh perfect sets of prints. They're being checked now. Round at the Grosvenor Street flat, somebody got there before me, and who-ever-it-was done a clean job. I talked to the part-time waiter. He's from the pub round the corner. He's clear. He just helped with the drinks. The barman was Chinese, he said, and there were half a dozen or more others among the guests. Two women. I looked for prints but everything was neutral. Traces of powder. Either Lane or Cawle, or somebody else must have been busy. It looked as if whoever was staying there got out quick. The maid went in the following morning, and he was gone. Left everything except his clothes. She cleaned up as usual, couple of hours work, and when she went in the *next* morning, everything he'd left behind was gone, as well as his laundry. Who could that have been?"

I was glad Druxi's lads hadn't been idle. I wondered if they'd managed to bag anybody. One of those Chinese might give us a useful lead.

"Well, now, look here, Berry. Get on to Corledge Trans Incorporated. I believe their head office is in Queen Victoria Street. Make a file in detail of Alethea A-l-e-t-h-e-a Cawle. See what she's doing, who introduced her and when she started there. Quietly. I don't want anyone to have an inkling, d'you see?"

"Corledge Trans? Like picking daisies, that is, sir. My old colleague at the Yard, he's there as security officer. I can just walk in!"

"Don't lose any time. Try to get on to me tonight, will you?"

"Certainly, sir. And there's a messenger-delivery letter marked urgent, just in. It's OHMS and signed by a Mr. James Morris. Be sent on, sir!"

The letter from James could have been his analysis of the explosion, which I didn't think would help much. I was a little worried that I couldn't get on the air to my stations. I had to have a set installed in the house, because obviously we were going to spend a lot of time there. It was no punishment.

The ground floor was one large room after another, windows to the sea in front, to the garden behind, with the vestibule and staircase making a half moon wall in the middle room, covered with a magnificent collection of old prints of the Caribbean. The south wall, floor to vaulted ceiling in original flower paintings by Fantin-Latour, faced another, solid with fishes of the Isles, and between the windows, a really lovely Burne-Jones of a nude, lightly wrapped—possibly in her own breath —which the brass legend gave as "Evadne, At Dawn."

The model, Consuelo's aunt Evadne May, must have been for that day, at any rate, quite a girl. Posing in the nude wasn't done. Her beautiful body was about on par with Consuelo's, except that she had a little more under the apron—"That's through eating those enormous breakfasts and umpteen course lunches. They thought it did them *good!*"—and her hair was a shade paler, a little longer, but so far as I could see, not so thick.

A lot of people pretend to despise Burne-Jones, though I don't know why. He could certainly paint a woman, in glory absolute, and that's no small accomplishment, and if for some a photograph does the job just as well, it doesn't, for many of us carry the fragrance of those hours while the canvas filled, the charm of unheard talk, the possible caress, and too, the delicacy of thought inherent in graceful lines, lovely colour, and the wonder of the working hand.

CHAPTER TWENTY THREE

I finished a list of radio parts on cable blanks for Perkins to hand in at the Post Office en route to the market. Consuelo gave him her shopping list, and arms about each other's waists, we strolled.

The garden was a joy.

It had been destroyed by a tornado a couple of years before, but it didn't show a sign of anything except care. There were six gardeners, all trained from boyhood by Aunt May, and she'd been a blue-ribbon collector at the world's flower shows for most of her life. I never saw anything like the mass of color, though most of the flowers were coming into bud, and the rose garden was still green, an expanse of bricked walks, sunk in a surround of rock plants and climbers about twelve feet high, for color and profuse growth in a class of their own.

"I often feel I'm dreaming!" Consuelo said suddenly, while we walked through the greenhouse, racked in sprouting plants. "Sometimes I can't believe I'm awake!"

"Why?"

"It's all mine—ah—ours!"

"Comforting, anyway. When you need money—"

"I'll show you the bank statements. Uncle Joshua died about twelve years ago. Extraordinary man. He came from Nova Scotia. Aunt May was staying in New York. He met her at some friend's there, and they were married two days after. He was never the social sort. They lived here, and travelled everywhere in his cargo ships. She sold the company for an enormous sum, and simply retired, that's all. People thought she was a miser, but she wasn't. I've just found out what she sent Mummy year after year. It's the only reason we could keep that place of ours after Daddy died. And that I went to school as I did. I have a lot to thank her for. Including all this!"

"Why did she leave it to you?"

"I think it's because I wrote to her every single week. They're all upstairs. In bindings, if you please? And that's where she sat every afternoon. Her favorite place. Isn't it lovely?"

Between the two greenhouses, a glassed-in birdcage affair had been built as a winter-garden, filled with the rarer plants, fountain in the middle keeping the air cool, a wide, flat, balustrade all round with huge balls of wool in baskets, magazines and reviews, and an enormous wicker armchair, circular back and awning top, piled with cushions.

"I can almost see her there!" Consuelo whispered. "I've been writing to you from that chair. That's where I'll study. I think I'd be foolish to waste all that time and not take the finals, don't you?"

"I hope you've made up your mind you're not going back to London?" I said, to the water. "It's not necessary!"

"Perhaps it's wiser for the moment. There's still a great deal to be done here. I don't like the way the servants live. Doesn't agree with the time. Aunt May kept them in the old style. They didn't bother her. She was generous enough. But I'm going to rebuild their houses, bathrooms, gas, electric light, and then see about a better school. I'll take the examination next year. Then I'll come back to the Company. What did you decide about the schools?"

"Genia Pearlman from Prague's starting the basecamp school at Beyfoum. She needs help to find teachers. Any advice?"

"I'll write to my old headmistress. Where are you going to stay? Any hotels there?"

"Problem one!"

She put her arms round my neck and sat on my knee, and I had time to think. It was a very small waist. There was a lot in my lap. Warm. I breathed her in.

"Don't you think I ought to come back with you and have a look at the place?" she said. "Just to get an idea?

186

Letters don't tell much, do they? A few days, a lot of notes, and I'll know what I'm doing!"

"Right. But I insist on staying here at least till the end of the week. Or are you throwing me out?"

She squeezed.

"Now that I've almost got a ring on this finger, you'd have to crawl through it. But there's one thing. I shall have to stay somewhere else tonight. I've got to sleep in a maiden's room, and enter the gates in the morning, carried in the old sedan. The servants insist. Big Mary—you met her—she's the sort of chief witch— says it's always been the custom of the house. Can't break it. The jinns'd be after us!"

"After dinner tonight, you go to your maiden's room, and I'm going to the hotel. That's the best thing. I'll get here about half-past ten in the morning, and that's that. Which reminds me. How far's the church?"

"I don't want you to see it till tomorrow. You've noticed there's nobody about the place? They've all gone dancing off there, cleaning, polishing, oiling the woodwork, heaven knows what. They all want a hand in it. Hadn't been touched for yers. The gardeners are going to put on a show all their own. They asked me as a special favor to let them have their own way, so I said yes, I'm not allowed there. I'm not even allowed in the kitchen, if you please? The cook's getting extra help for the wedding breakfast. Insists it's all got to be done here. I'm told the cake's taller than Big Mary!"

"Since this morning?"

She looked up at the sun, white in the glass roof.

"Well, I'm the 'leddy' here, and I told them to get un-braked. They didn't need much urging. They *love* weddings!"

"How many are you expecting?"

"Everybody on the island's welcome. Things won't stop till the last crumb's gone, and the last barrel's empty. I rather *like* that sort of do, don't you?"

"Indeed!"

A footman tapped the door and pointed to the telephone.

"Yes, Dilyard?"

187

"Super'ten' Lev'son like to talk, leddy Con-*swell!*"

Consuelo reached.

"Mr. Leverson? Yes. Oh, yes. The notice'll be in tomorrow's paper. Wasn't time for today. There hasn't been time to send invitations. I only knew myself this morning!"

She laughed, tweaking my ear. She knew what it did to me. But I had a fair revenge. Bikini and shirt aren't much protection on a lap.

"I'll be most happy to see you, and the mayor, and council, and anybody who's kind enough to come here," she said, pretending a frown, keeping her voice level. "Yes, the silver *will* be out. Well, all the rooms have to be prepared tonight. I think that's most kind of you. It might be safer. So *many* policemen? You know best, of course. Thank you very much. I shall expect you and Mrs. Leverson. Goodbye?"

She put the receiver down, and the battle might have started then and there—the chair was wonderfully spacious—but somebody else tapped, and a voice muttered among the leaves.

"What?"

"Lunch's ready, leddy Con-*swell* 'n cook tell it's go' spoil'!" she said, louder, in a pad of bare feet, and a closing door.

I must say, though, I was hungry.

"Have to be careful what we do, and where!" Consuelo said. "Bad example. Perhaps it's what they need. Let's come in one afternoon, and *really* scatter cushions!"

She went up to put a dress on, and I got into trousers. I don't know why it feels "wrong" to lunch indoors in shorts, but that's the way I've been taught, or as others less charitable might say, brainwashed. Whether or not, I feel better in trousers. We lunched in the breakfast room because everywhere else was being decorated.

It was a delightful place, panelled in a deep red, polished wood I hadn't seen before, that must have come from a captain's cabin. His lamps, taper-holders and condiment set were on the top tier of the lazy susan table. The second, below, with the dishes of food, rotated so that each could serve himself, and the third was the table proper. We had a soup of oysters cooked with lobster meat, new potatoes the size of a thumbnail in mint, and steamed lettuce hearts. I managed one pancake with a date and ginger stuffing, and I was ready to lie down.

"Bed!" Consuelo said, and pointed upstairs. "I've got a lot to do. I'll bring tea in when I'm sure you're awake. Just bomble about a bit to let me know!"

It was the sort of sleep I went into, and came out of, as if it might have been a most satisfying bath. I was in the shower when the telephone rang, and I was in more than half a mind to ignore it. There's nothing more tiresome than having to wrap a towel, and dab through a room, dripping puddles, to pick up a receiver.

"Trothe!"

"Berry here, sir, at Corledge Trans. There's no trace of the name we spoke about. I've been right through the personnel files with the head. Nothing of that name, or anything like it. Could you give a description?"

"I'm afraid not. It's many years since I saw her. She'd be about twenty-three or four. Fair to brunette, I suppose. I believe she got her degree at St. Margaret's. She was at the London School of Economics and did very well. Can't be many girls with that sort of record!"

"If her file was cooked, we won't find St. Margaret's or anything else, there. They'd keep that quiet. Another thing struck both of us just about the same minute. If she was in the satellite communications department, I mean, there's about six hundred employed on one thing and another, all in sections with their own jobs, and some of them monitor the stuff going over the Atlantic. They're always improving, y'see, sir? Well, supposing she heard that call this morning? Or somebody told her?"

"I suppose your friend's alive to all this?"

"Oh, yes! In his job, he's the first to want to know who's pushing the boat out!"

"Why not consult your friends of the Oxfordshire

189

Constabulary? They might have a way in to somebody at the University. The young lady has at least a record there. They might be able to pick out a few incidents, you never know. *Could* lead to the new identity. If there *is* one!"

I hadn't any reason to suppose that Gillian might have been misinformed. Her news always came from the top. That Miss Cawle didn't appear on the books was what I'd expected, and pointed to another rat, weasel or vixen. Then again, ashamed of her father's conduct and all the publicity, she might have changed her name for a new start. At her age, and entering a career, the name was a burden, and if she were an honest girl, I felt for her. That is, if. But if she was of the same clip as her foxy sire, I intended to treat her in the same way. However, if Gillian knew, then someone else must—possibly M.I.—and I didn't give her much rope. M.I. waited just long enough for the evidence.

But I thought of the Blur, and wondered.

CHAPTER TWENTY-FOUR

I woke up that morning and felt the world was mine on a cushion of pink roses. I looked at my watch, and waited for the minute hand to touch seven o'clock, and on the point, as I'd known, Groves tapped on the door and brought in the tea. I like punctual people. He'd arrived on the Company's jet late the night before, and we'd met him, got the baggage past Customs, and then I'd taken Consuelo to Mrs. Brophy's house, where they'd decorated her "maiden" room in white, with a huge pink satin bow on one side of the bed, pale-blue on t'other. Maiden's choice.

"I should have brought snow-specs!" Consuelo whispered, when we said goodnight. "But it's nice to have a *feeling* of innocence, isn't it? Reassuring. I suppose you're going to a night club?"

"Naturally. I'm going to drink all the champagne I can see, and I'm going home with the front row. I'll learn 'em what a bachelor night is!"

"If I so much as see you with another woman, d'you know what's going to happen?" she said, eyes so close to mine, I was cross-eyed. "I won't bother about hairy bodyguards, 'n odds. I'll set Big Mary on you. She's the most quietly terrifying character I ever met. She's—I don't know the terms—don't want to—it's something like mameloi. A kind of priestess, I suppose. It's a sort of religious practice. Brother Teague was most reserved about it. Anyway, she told me you were in great danger, and I was involved. Second-sight? Prophecy? Don't know. But I'm a little worried, because Mrs. Brophy, here, swears by her. You've got to be careful, and I'm going to be careful *for* you. You're *not* going to a night club, are you?"

"Fine way to frighten me off!"

"Give me a virginal kiss. Not too much. Just take the bloom off, and *run!*"

191

Groves brought in the clothing while I read the local paper, listened to WOR and WNEW, New York, got on to Paris, found a station in Germany, and on the hour, listened to the BBC from London, switched to Armed Forces Radio, and again I was surprised at the vast coverage of the American stations, and the parochial skimp of ours.

"You'd think the news cost them part of their pay," I said. "Indolent lot!"

" 's right, sir!" Groves said, grey hair plastered, butterfly collar, black cravat, white pique jacket, black trousers, shoes glistening. "I don't listen to 'em no more. Football, yes, boxing sometimes. But the news and the other stuff, it's that dry, the missus said y'might just as well listen to the weather. We look at the tele, most often. We like the old films. The big ones. Takes y'right back, don't it, sir? Remember 'em when we was courting!"

My morning coat was on its own hanger. I was glad it was more or less new. I wore it when the Princes attended Company meetings. They always came in morning dress, because, as Azil said, they liked it, and of course, I had to. And I liked it. But I was happy I'd given away the other I'd worn to marry Melt those years ago. It had been a hard decision. So many memories making a Pandora's box out of a shape in cloth, some braid, buttons. Now, it drooped on the shoulders of old Stevenson, head sidesman at St. Matthew's, and his smile when I gave it to him was worth those hurting moments. Go back almost twenty-five years and two children, and *some* memories sting.

I had a light conversation with Consuelo—there must have been a dozen people yelling their heads off in her room—and she couldn't hear a word I said, so the soulful rubbish I tried to say, and which I thought fitting for the morning didn't penetrate, and I got off lightly with the start of a sore throat, which was just as well.

Superintendent Leverson came up in dress whites to salute the groom, and we had a glass of champagne and a little nostalgic chatter about the Sudan, Kenya and Zanzibar where he'd served his young years, and so had I. We had plenty to talk about, but no real time, and we agreed to make a night of it, later.

"Look here!" he said, with one of those "curious" glances I shall always remember. "You're not in any sort of trouble, are you?"

"Trouble?" I said, warned by the complete change of tone. "So far as I know, no. Why?"

"Just wanted to know, that's all. Everybody's away with the Prime Minister. There's a conference on. The Chief Justice's in charge. There were three men on this plane—they said it was R.A.F.—this morning from London. They asked for him, and a car from the Justice Department met them. My man seemed to think your name was mentioned!"

I tried not to let him see it, but instantly I froze.

Months before, when the pair had still been active as heads of M.I. in London and Washington, they'd almost managed to put me away—I still thought, with the connivance of the Blur—by inviting me to fly to Trinidad for a few days' rest while a particularly nasty business blew over. It was one of the few places where I could be extradited without fuss, taken back to London, and put inside without a soul the wiser. It hadn't happened because Errol Hinter had put on a show at the airport, and I'd got away, so far as I was concerned, lifelong in his debt.

Those times had changed. The pair were uncovered and on the run, and I, thank God, was no longer part of H.M. Civil Service. But I was still H.M.'s loyal subject, technically, and I could certainly be arrested by warrant of extradition on the terrain of a Commonwealth partner. We're still fairly medieval, and Habeas Corpus doesn't reach very far.

I'd never even thought of it.

He'd put his glass down, looking at me, a policeman's look, officially direct, blank.

"If that sort of nonsense is tried, what's the best defence?" I asked. "Who's the best lawyer?"

"You *are* worried?" he asked, picking up his cap. "If they've got the sort of documents I think they've got, a lined-up team of lawyers won't help you. You'd better cable London. Get a few to meet you!"

"I'm going to proceed with the morning's business, and if anyone tries to prevent me, there'll be trouble, I promise you!"

"Look, Mr. Trothe. If they've got a warrant, there's nothing anybody can do. You'll go inside!"

"If they've got a warrant, it's certainly not for me!"

"Your name was mentioned!"

"Can't you call whoever-it-is and find out?"

"I'm not supposed to know anything about it. What I'll do is go down there, and see what's happening. And try to call you. Or get somebody else to. But don't try to leave the hotel!"

"Is that what you came to tell me?"

He nodded.

"There are two men downstairs. I shall know why later. Take a friend's tip. Stay here!"

He went, and I poured a little champagne, and sat down to think.

Of my own free will. I'd walked into it.

Captain Bulkeley and his crew were at the airport with White Horse Two, a Company jet. If I knew anything about the process of arrest, an embargo had been placed on craft and crew. I picked up the telephone to call the airport, but the operator said all lines were busy.

"Could you get me London?"

"There's a three hour delay, sir. Shall I call you?"

"Thank you, but it'll be too late!"

I'd heard those words before, so far as I'm concerned, some of the most benighting in the language.

Two avenues blocked. I went to the window. I was on the second floor. An awning was open above the window below which could make a fair breakfall if I tried a jump. But a policeman looked up at me from the main door of the hotel to the left, and another saw me down on the right. I didn't catch a signal, but they

194

began walking toward each other, and I put my head in.

Even if I jumped for it, there could be a fight in the garden, and that, of course, would make a local charge, apart from there being no guarantee I'd find a car to take me to Banbury Cross, or perhaps anywhere else except the island prison.

It was getting late. I bathed and shaved, and got into my finery, feeling that I knew how condemned prisoners looked at things, easing into new duds on the last morning. I tied the grey cravat with the flourish my grandfather had taught me, stuck the folds with his pearl pin, buttoned on the dress slip which holds the cravat in place and gives that note of white between it and the waistcoat, and got into the morning coat, shot the cuffs, adjusted the handkerchief, and went over to the mirror to have a look at myself.

I hadn't gained any weight, and I might have lost some, though I don't suppose I'll ever touch minimum for my height. Sun the day before had reddened the bronze a little, and a couple of dabbings of strong tea and lemon juice had restored the color to cheeks and chin. Hair seemed to have stayed dark on top, white over the ears, and there wasn't much wrong with the teeth.

I felt distinctly marriageable, and I suppose there's nothing more exhilarating, though it might have had a little to do with the champagne.

A moment's thought convinced me it didn't.

But I had to get to Banbury Cross in twenty minutes, or suffer the displeasure of the leddy Con-*swell*. No sooner thought than acted on, and I picked up her present, made sure I had the ring, and in the same moment wondered if she'd chosen a Best Man. I hadn't thought of it, and didn't bother.

I opened the door and walked down to the stairway head. Nobody waited. The lift came up, and I pressed the button for the lobby.

Except for the receptionist, there wasn't a soul.

The hall porter saw me through the glass doors and took his cap off, waving a pair of gloves. A black

195

Cadillac nosed, and the chauffeur got out to open the door.

I looked left and right.

Nobody, not even a gardener. Grass was brilliantly green, gravel seemed to shine red, and spray drifted prisms from a fountain.

The car turned out, along the drive, into the main road, and found the narrower streets. We got held up twice for traffic, the first, a horse and cart, and the other a cyclist, and on we went, to broader roads, of fine houses and gardens, shops, and out again to narrow lanes.

I'm not sure what I was thinking during that time—I was very much the crow's nest lookout on an old caravelle, eyes always on course, ready to yell "Land-ho!"—and I was brought to my senses by the quiet gong of a police car.

I looked back.

Blue light flashing, three uniformed men in front, three or four in plainclothes behind, the big car was gaining. The blue light went out, a red of extraordinary clarity came on, and the gong struck, only a few times, softly, a gentlest warning to pull in.

My chauffeur reached back, without taking his eyes off the road, opened the glass divide, put his foot down, and we leapt. I saw the needle go over the 100.

"P'sess y'soul, sir!" he said, smilingly quiet. "They ain't jus' got to *catch* me. They got to *see* me. 'n they ain' goin' see *noth*in'. We *gone!*"

He was right. He was perhaps the greatest "rough" driver I'd ever known. One hand on the wheel, one flat on the car top, he turned corners of almost ninety degrees on the brake, blinded through dust—which couldn't have helped the lads behind—came out on a wider road, screamed along asphalt, turned off—looking back, I couldn't see the police car in the entire stretch—went slower along a narrow lane, turned off to bump over dried ruts in one narrower, took a corner to the right, and stopped, a few feet from a line of women in dresses neck to ankle of a shouting whiteness in that sun, which made their faces blacker, and their smiles so much bigger, teeth more refulgent.

Getting out of the car, I saw the white-kerchieved butterfly-knotted heads stretching all the way down, hundreds, solid, silent, no move.

A smaller, older woman, in front, came toward me, holding out a white waterlily in both hands.

"We come to take you to Ba'b'ry Cross," she said, and stared behind me at the sound of the police car gong coming nearer. "Nobody do nothin'. We all peaceful. Goin' raise d' palmleaves, sing hymns all the way, get d'leddy Con-*swell*' ma'd, make two one, give a heart each, take a life each, make happy. No wrong in *'at!*"

Loud voices echoed behind me. All the women were still. I never heard a more "dangerous" silence.

"All right, out' the way" a man shouted. "You, fancy Dan, there. Come on!"

I saw the idea. It was perfectly good. Rather than arrest in the hotel, with promise of trouble, noise, publicity they didn't want, they'd given me a chance to get out in the countryside. Whatever kind of fight I put up, seven of them were pretty sure of rolling me up, bundling me in the car, and quietly putting me aboard any London-bound aircraft.

"Your name Trothe?" the tallest of the plain-clothesmen called. "Edmun' Trothe?"

"That's my name!" I said, loud in the quiet. "What do you want with me?"

"Got a warrant here," he said, bringing a long blue paper out of a breast pocket. "Under the 'ficial Secrets Act—"

But no officer of the C.I.D. would dare make an arrest in such a manner.

"Let me see who you are!" I interrupted. "This sounds like a practical joke—"

"You'll find out how 'practical' it is!" he said, and called over his shoulder. "All right, close in!"

A drum ruffled behind the first few ranks of women, stopped, ruffled again, tapped once, and stopped.

Three uniformed men and three in plainclothes came toward me, splitting three and three to come in from either side. The man with the warrant stood off.

The drum ruffled, a louder beat, went on ruffling, and a bass drum began a double thump. All the women I could see had closed their eyes. They all held fronds of palm, and they swayed, slightly, one foot to the other, in time to the bass drum.

I'd buttoned my coat, ready for it, and the six had stopped about two yards away, left and right, spreading a little, and the man with the warrant flicked his right hand.

The six came in as one.

The air suddenly filled with drumcrash and the women raised the fronds in rustling whisper running past me. I was held back by the smaller, brushed by flying white skirts, appalled by the drawnout shriek from open mouths, seeing only glimpses between white heads of black fists raised and fronds clashing down.

I didn't try to go back. The smaller woman held my arm, threw the waterlily up while the crowd still ran past, and the drops of water sprinkled us both.

" 's a *sign,* 's a *sign!* " she shrilled. "We get the bless'n'. We don' *need* no more'n the bless'n. Them boys, they go back fishfood. They' *pulp!* "

"What about the Police at the house?"

"Doin' what they paid for. Guard'n stuff, mind'n nobody get runned over, keep ever'thing quiet for the ma'ge party. Just like it ought to be, way we want it. No strangers comin' in here, make trouble. Big Mary don't let 'em. Two brothers, both 'the *Po*-lice. She d'plain boss, 'n nobody say *noth'n!* "

"What's going to happen to these men?"

"They get took upshore, in the savannah, 'n put comf'ble, 'n when you go, they go!"

"So I have Big Mary to thank?"

"Nobody else. She d'plain boss!"

"Isn't the Superintendent going to have something to say?"

"He don't last. The Po-lice they all ma'd or they
198

wantin' get ma'd. They don't do what they own led-dyfolk tell 'em, what they' goin' 'eat? Where they sleep? What they do, the night's cold? They turn around, never hear nothin', take care thieves an' such, and mind the house, an' see d'chicks don' get squashed. What else they do? On'y what Big Mary tell 'em. *Nothin'!*"

We walked through a blue-painted side gate between rows of smiling women. Air was quiet, except for drumming behind us. I hadn't the faintest idea where we were. A well-cut lawn took the dust off my shoes. I was a little hot, and grateful for the cool shade of a grove of trees. We walked through for a few minutes, and although I wanted to ask questions, I didn't because the little woman seemed to be telling the beads. She wore dozens of necklaces, of teeth, dried berries, shells, and what looked like bottle-tops.

We turned a curve to the left, going toward left-and-right hand paths. In deep shadow, at the tip of the divide, a white shape knelt before the wine-red lamp of a shrine. The shape stood, almost impossibly tall, opened her arms, and looked up in a ray of sunlight.

She was still whispering when we stopped, but I didn't hear a word.

Big Mary looked down at me. She was half a head taller, dressed a little better than the others, in the same white cambric jacket edged with lace frothing at neck and cuffs and down the front, to the broad deep-green sash, skirt edged with lace to the ankles, green slippers, a mass of beads round her neck, head tied in a colored scarf. A Pucci. One of Consuelo's.

Barbarically beautiful, I thought, but it was no barbaric or common intelligence behind that smile.

"I been shakin' about these pas' few days!" she said softly, as if surprised. "I knew something was near. I couldn't see where, but when my broth' call' me 's morn', that's when I knew. I didn't tell the leddy Con'swell. She got a full 'nough head. She' be passin' this way, two minutes. This the bridal path. You go on, and she meet y' on a steps with Little Mary like she said!"

"This is little Mary?" I said, and held out my hand. "I owe her a great deal. Mary, I'd like to make you a pres—"

"Mary an't her name, any more'n mine!" Big Mary said, a little sharp. "I'm *Big* Mary, 'n 'at's *my* name. She's *Little* Mary, 'n 'at's *her* name. 'n *this* fam'luh, we don't have Mary. We *do* have *Big* Mary 'n *Little* Mary. 'n we' different, like streaky bacon 'n lean gammon, same fam'luh!"

"Who taste better?" Little Mary asked, in a giggle, down below.

"Somebod' get his teeth in, he fin' out!" Big Mary giggled, up there. "You say a present. Mist' Trothe? Tell you. The holy beads. Rosary, blessed by the Pope. That's all. Both of us. Nothin' else. Mine, longer. More to stretch. But *blessed*. By the Hol'ness. An' I want the gua'*ntee!*"

"You've got it, the moment I get back!"

She held up a long, thin fingered hand, pointed a thumb over her shoulder.

"She' down there now!" she whispered. "Hear the child'n just a minute. Hurry, you, Little Mary. Going to make him late 'n unlucky. Fine *ma*tron you are. Fly outa here!"

CHAPTER TWENTY-FIVE

Once out of the heat, and the cheering crowd of Consuelo's arrival, the service became one of those twenty-minute lacunae which seem to pass in a moment. A ransack of memory brought only phrases, tones of voice, the glory of massed white flowers in sunshine filtering colors through stained glass, a chant of women, a rumbling basso of men, the scent of a bouquet of lilies-of-the-valley, Consuelo leaning on my arm, the extraordinary liquid depth of her eyes looking at me when I put the ring on her finger which I suppose I'd known before, but hadn't realized with such a gentle sense of shock, and the childlike, dancing happiness of the crowd outside singing muted under the porch, and we went out in the sunshine.

That's about all I remembered, standing in the Mid-Room, holding a frosted glass, and yet I suppose I'd been wideawake. I confess my ears had been on yardarms for any sound of a police car or hint of further trouble, and it hadn't helped concentration on what went on.

Consuelo appeared, at any rate, to me, nothing less than flower-like.

"Flower-like" applied to a woman, we'd been told by Mr. Bissenley, our cricketing English master, those years before, was a thoroughly reprehensible misuse of the world's one, truly, commercial language. It had certainly been juggled by poets and poetasters, but its most noble usage was reserved for the sober realms of trade. An acquaintance with the best in literature was necessary, naturally, as evidence of schooling, and an apt line, or quotation, would always add grace to correspondence or conversation, and, pari passu, inform the recipient or auditor that he wasn't dealing with some jackanapes.

Despite Mr. Bissenley, I thought Consuelo flower-like, and again, I sent him and his teaching to the devil, wondering how many hours of enjoyment had been denied to me, and to all the others who'd come under that stultifying aegis. No wonder we regarded English, as a subject, from that time on, as nothing more than a necessary mark-getter in Business Correspondence. But then, dear Mr. Bissenley compounded a felony by teaching us how to take a book to pieces in terms of character, action, structure, and style. From that moment, I regarded any book as a laboratory specimen to dissect at leisure. As small boys, naturally, we delighted in taking things to pieces, and I wasn't aware of damage until my Mother gave me *Marius, the Epicurean* for my birthday, and to show her all I knew, I gave it the Bissenley treatment, much to her folded arms, distantly staring, almost wordless disgust.

"Edmund, you're a pagan *brute!*" she said. "Now go back and *read* it!"

I've had occasion to use that lesson in many other ways since, not least in dealing with people. They're rather more complicated than any book, and dissection can be fatal, especially in starting from a wrong premise.

It all went through my mind while Perkins poured me another glass of champagne, which I raised to Consuelo's in a ring of women on the other side of the room, and Superintendent Leverson came over, smiling as if nothing had happened.

"Sorry about this morning!" he breezed, putting a shine on it. "I knew there was something fishy but I had to make sure. Even the Justice got taken in, can you believe it? Somebody must know their way about, though. There was a message to Government House these three were arriving in a bomber, and asking for all facilities in arrest and deportment. Well, they were met, their papers were in order, or seemed like, and the Justice got in touch with the Minister. There's a lot of red tape this end, of course. But these three were barefaced. No other word for it. They showed the sergeant on duty downstairs this paper, and he only had to see the color and the print, and that was it. Big stuff. Besides, he knew I was here, and this is where they wanted to go. But what they didn't know was that he's Big Mary's brother. He got on to her, and she told him. So they all came over, and fell in behind you on the way. Then the girls set about them. Three of them were armed. As it is, they got back to the airport in the police car. And that's it!"

"Any idea where they went?"

"Well, they took off without orders from the control tower, and damn' nearly tangled with a Caribbean Airways jet coming in. Apparently they headed for Cuba. That's the last I got. What do you make of it?"

"I'm very worried about leaving my wife here!"

He laughed, looked into his drink, and round at the people.

"No need to be!" he said, easily. "You'll always have a safe spot here. The biddies are worse than the men. Take my word. I know what goes on, but I don't interfere. They could try to come here any way you like. Wouldn't get them anything except a rough knock. Those three this morning won't be much good for a time, I can tell you!"

"At night?"

"From this time out, they'll have to get in at the airport, first. That won't be so simple. Come in from the ocean? They can try. They'll never see the beach. These chaps may be village boys, fishermen, farmers, black as the ace. But you don't get a second bite. You see, I haven't got long to go, so I'm not much more than a figurehead. I deal with the office, mostly. Believe me, Mrs. Trothe's safe. The biddies'll watch it, for a start. Specially Big Mary. She's a bloody witch!"

"She's probably the reason I'm not en route to Cuba. What makes her a witch?"

I looked at that stare without the smile.

"No use trying to explain," he said, throwing it off. "It's a place set in its ways. They know things we don't. I leave them strictly alone. Big Mary's a very good woman, in fact. But keep on the right side of her!"

Consuelo came toward us, smiling here and there, stopping to talk for a moment, though I knew she was trying to reach me. I seemed to feel it coming out of her. Leverson nodded a smile, I gave my glass to Dilyard, and when I was a couple of yards away, she put out her hand. Her clutch surprised me.

"I've just heard about this trouble this morning!" she whispered. "What on earth was it?"

"Our friends having another go. They weren't among them, though. I'm sure of that. How does anyone know I'm here?"

"Newspapers. Radio. But how could they expect to run you out?"

"I don't think they'd have tried. They didn't get a chance at a clean shot. They'd have got away easily enough. As they did, in fact. Thing is, can they do it again? With you or me? I feel you'd be safer in New York!"

She shook her head. She still wore the little coronet and the lace and the heavy pearl satin dress threw a warmer shade over pale gold cheeks, lightened the blue of her eyes.

"No," she said, quietly sure. "I feel safer here than anywhere. I'm coming with you to Beyfoum, and straight back. I'm only worried about *you*. I think you ought to come here whenever you're able. It's only a few hours flight. Pretend we've gone back a century. It took your grandfather longer to get to Onslow Close from London, didn't it?"

"By coach, yes. What we want here for at least the forseeable future is a private army. I've got to have a radio net working—"

"All very simple!" she said, taking my hand. "Supposing we leave these delightful people for a few hours? I know a much more comfortable place to talk!"

"How d'you feel?"

She held my hand on the heartbeat under the lace fall.

"I don't know!" she whispered. "I'm in a dream. It's such a *free* feeling. Nothing's real. Everything's wonderful. Not in the least as I imagined. Darling, look!"

She was staring over my shoulder, and I turned.

An enormous cake went up in a Babylonian staircase of white icing to a confection of silver bells, flying doves, boots, horseshoes, anchors, and on the ends of flying ribbands, our names, all tied in a huge true-lovers' knot.

"I never saw anything so beautiful!" Consuelo crooned. "I could eat every single bit, to the last crumb of cardboard. It's all de*lic*ious protein, isn't it?"

Big Mary came from behind with Little Mary and a troop of people in the estate's dark blue and white livery. She held the cutlass taken from over the mantel in the dining room, and when the men put down the platform banked in white roses, she presented it, hilt first, across her left forearm to Consuelo.

"Cut deep, cut straight, cut well, 'n that first piece, cut with a heart full of love, it go in the silver box for the silver weddin'!" she said, with that extraordinary smile. "After twen'five years, don't matter nothin'!"

Waiters brought round the champagne, and in the cheering crush, Consuelo took the cutlass, and with a little help from me, drove the blade in, cut down, withdrew, pierced and cut again, bringing out a clean wedge. Little Mary took it on a slice, wrapped it in silver paper and a napkin, and put it in the square silver casket. The cooks, in laced whites, drew their knives, and began to cut for the plates held out all round us.

Consuelo led through a crush of people raising glasses, calling toasts, trying to stop us, but she went through like an ice-breaker, out to the vestibule, to the stair. We had to pick a way between people handing up plates of cake, reaching for filled glasses, passing down the empty, and Big Mary came behind with a tray, a bucket and bottle, and I heard what she said when people reached to take them. Obviously, she came from a seafaring family.

"Leddy Con-*swell*'!" she shrilled, at the stairway turn. "You got to fling the booky!"

Little Mary threw the bouquet of lilies-of-the-valley from down below, and I reached out to catch it.

"A l'l prayer, 'n throw!" Big Mary whispered. "Out go the ol' life, in come the new!"

Consuelo pushed her nose among white bells for a moment, looked at me, held it out for a sweet sniff, and threw it high. Dozens jumped, arms waved, and we turned to see Dilyard with a telegram.

"This's urgent, sir!" he said, looking appealingly at Consuelo. "Man brought it, he want the si'nature!"

I initialled, and Consuelo took the envelope, holding it by opposite corners, looking at me over the top.

"I ought to reach for this, but langorously, in about six or seven hours!" she said, pensively bovine. "Since it's urgent, I'll toss you for it. Heads you get it, tails me!"

"No coin!"

She took off her shoe.

"If it comes down lefthandside, you open it now," she said, taking the other off, and sinking to my shoulder. "If it's the righthand, you open it when I feel like joining the party, not before!"

She threw up the shoe, it circled, and fell in the copper bowl of the overhead lamp. Without waiting, she took off the other shoe and made a nice shot in the next.

"Best luck there is!" Big Mary said, behind us. "Lose one, that's what you done. Lose two, you'all new. Doing, thinking, all past. Sir, can I promise the children a party for Christmas?"

"Best they ever had," I said. "Now I'm going to open the bottle, and you can hop it!"

Consuelo gave me the yellow Western Union envelope.

"I have a feeling about this," she said. "There are hundreds downstairs. I told them we didn't want to know about any of them for the moment!"

Big Mary had barely closed the door, and she opened it again.

"Mis' Edmun', like it or not, you got another urgent!" she said, and held it out. "This one got the urgent red, looky here!"

Consuelo sighed, and seemed to float to me. She had no feet.

"Eeneemeenee," I said, between the two. "Which, first?"

She opened the one she held, and gave me the form.

TOILSHORE. LONDON.

FOR EDMUND TROTHE. BUT HOW CAN OUR LITTLE BROTHER MARRY WITHOUT US QUERY. AND WHAT SHALL WE DO WITH THE CHURCH AND ALL THE FONDNESS PREPARATIONS QUERY. OF COURSE WE FORGIVE IMPATIENCE BUT THE ROCKET IS SO BEAUTIFUL AND OUR FAMILY IS SO SAD. ANSWER TO YOUR SCANDALIZED AZIL.

"I'll patch this one, now," I said, and went over to the desk.

H.H. PRINCE AZIL. KHADAZ EL MERIF. OMAN.

THIS WAS THE CIVIC SERVICE WHICH AS YOU KNOW IS NECESSARY. THE CHURCH CEREMONEY WE SAVE UNTIL THE DATE SET. PLEASE TELL THE FAMILY TO BE PERFECTLY HAPPY FOR OUR SAKES. KINDLY UNSCANDALIZE YOURSELF. SHALL BE AT BEYFOUM ON SATURDAY. IMPATIENT TO SEE YOU. EDMUND.

"Let's see if the next wants an answer, and they can go off together," I said, and Consuelo ripped the other envelope. "You read it, and I'll think what to say!"

She looked at it, turned her head, and held out the form, print up.

PATTI AND BABY INJURED FLYING LONDON CLINIC PLEASE HELP ME EDMUND. OB.

Consuelo put an arm round my shoulder, held tightly, let go, and drew a deep breath.

"Big Mary, you go down and find Captain Bulkeley, and tell him to be ready as soon as possible for a London flight," she said. "I'm going to pack a bag. Come back and help me. Ask Groves to prepare a change for Mr. Edmund. We'll go out by the side door. Have the car there. Keep *that* bottle till we get back. I'm going to leave everything to you. Make sure Brother Teague has his meals regularly. And see that everything's put back in order. But *don't* let the party be spoiled. There's no need to tell anyone we've gone, d'you see?"

CHAPTER TWENTY-SIX

Life Guards trumpets were sounding, and Miss Purcell waited for me, nodding a smile when I reached the Blur's suite, and went in front to open the door.

The Blur seemed to have aged. The top of his cranium had always pushed a conical eggshape through the white bush above his ears. Now there was more egg, less bush, and the pouches under the washy grey eyes were bluish, heavier, and his mouth drooped, making the nose seem longer than usual. That air of Holier Than Thou, which I'd been told he'd adopted on the day he was accepted for the Athenaeum, and that in my experience had got holier with the years, appeared to have subsided into a sort of hedge-priest glower, coupled with a strange-ish laugh, not quite a whinny, perhaps, but a quavery nhu-huh-huh! strange to him, and I found, unsettling.

The Lane-Cawle, and other lesser enormities had taken serious toll.

"Ah, Trothe!" he greeted me, in that laugh, which had begun in the chair, standing, coming over with a hand out, wide, sweeping in to make a catch at mine. "What a *very* agreeable—ah—"

"I wish I had something agreeable to discuss," I said, and brought things down to cold water level. "My daughter and grandchild have been seriously injured in a grenade attack. I have good reason to believe that the Lane-Cawle pair were behind it. I've come to ask if anything's known of their whereabouts, or if you can give me any information about them. I've staged a fairly defensive operation until now, but it hasn't worked. I'd been hoping to drop them. That's what I'd like to do. But I'm afraid they're a little too sharp. And very well organized. Is there anything you can tell me?"

He nhu-huh'd, swinging here and there in the chair.

"I shall begin by telling you that your failure doesn't

surprise me," he said, almost patronizingly. "We've failed. I don't attempt to palliate. You're not facing a couple of common or garden criminals, Trothe. You're up against two of the best brains we ever employed in the Service, much to our—inexpressible—shame, and humiliation. They're masters, in any sense, in what's of use in matters of enquiry, or eliciting detail, or in the schematic destruction, shall we say, of an enemy. They were trained in our methods over the course of the years they served, as you know so well, and they were fully informed of all developments in every sphere. Up to the moment. They knew the moves. They worked during that time without any suspicion. It's no use asking how it was done. The simple answer is, we don't know. Until almost the hour we'd decided to arrest, there wasn't a hint of suspicion. Not a hint!"

I let him get as far as that.

"I sent you four reports, and I know others did, all of them detailed," I said. "You took not the smallest notice. You never sent me a word. Why?"

He shifted, smoothed both sides of his face, looking through the window.

"I think I told you before, Trothe," he began, in the tenor-y drawl I loathed, which he used when trying to play down a bad patch. "I had to find out, to my cost, what inroads had been made even in my own section, here. It was found later that many reports I should have seen were either truncated or destroyed. You may have noticed that my secretaries are new? Not new in the Service, but new here. That was one result. Again, I don't attempt to excuse. One has to trust somebody, though, really, it's rather difficult, what?"

"Is anything known of the pairs' whereabouts?"

"The last solid information we had, both were in the Soviet Union, at a resort on the Black Sea. We're just as anxious to obliterate them as anyone else!"

I felt I wasn't going to get very far.

"Do you know anything of their organization?"

"Only that it's as good as anything we ever had, plus,

we suspect, the enthusiastic help of the KGB, which isn't by any means to be belittled!"

"What evidence is there that they're working with or for the KGB? Why should it be the Russians? Why not someone else?"

"There isn't anyone!"

"China?"

He threw back his head, apparently in pain.

"Oh, Trothe!"

"Why? Is a third of the human race to be discounted?"

"I think so. And for some time to come. Let the Russians worry about them!"

I got up.

"For the last time, you have no information that might help me?" I said. "I show my cards. All that I have. I shall tell you that I've been trying to protect a business. So far as I was able. Now it affects my family, I'm forced to use other methods. You're not inclined to help me?"

He looked upwards and sideways at me. His eyes were tired, but wary. His attitude, I thought for that instant was that of a dog uncertain whether to fang, or sit. I could almost see what was passing in his mind. He, more than any, had been bitterly wounded by the pair. He'd personally had to explain their defection and give reasons for their impunity—for him possibly the most exquisite punishment which any fiend could have devised—to the Prime Minister, in abased and abashed excuse for the incompetence of the Service which he directed, and the remarkable stupidity—if that were all, and some of us didn't *quite* think so—which he'd displayed with such fruitcake aplomb, down the years of their rot.

"I'm very much inclined to help you, Trothe," he said, dry-lipped, so that I thought I heard the *pop!* "But I'm given cause to doubt, d'you see? The pair are known to be on the most intimate terms with your Arab friends. Many of them are your directors, or their close relatives. Why don't you ask *them?* They might be able to tell you far more!"

"I'm aware that there are links. But that's because of Soviet help to the Arab states. I understand the Arab attitude. It's natural. They make no secret of it. And that's where my bread and butter is, and I'm not for one moment quarrelling with it. That's beside the point at issue. Can you give me any help in the matter of the pair?"

"None whatever, I'm afraid!"

"You won't, or you don't know?"

"We don't know. We're getting a mass of conflicting reports. But we don't know which are planted, and which aren't. They have to be sifted. That's going on!"

"You knew that Dorothea Ferrers was working for them? Sending her reports through the diplomatic bag of a certain country here? To M.I.?"

"It didn't go unnoticed. Nothing very useful, I'm afraid. Rather too meagre!"

"Have the West Germans any hand anywhere?"

"If I knew, would you really expect an answer?"

"Why not? I believe the organization I've got—it's not in optimum condition for the moment—is fairly good. It's my intention it'll get better. You wouldn't consider an exchange of information?"

He got up in that nhu-huh! and stretched, but limply.

"But, Trothe!" he deprecated, pulling that sort of face—which covered another, I thought, of sudden fear—brought out for naughty children. "You know too well that's heresy. No. I believe we both have to plow a lonely furrow. I think it better—"

I was sick of it. I turned to get my hat and coat.

"There's a matter of a stolen rocket," I said. "I know very little about it. Do you?"

"Not much more!"

"Dorothea Ferrers?"

"Less!"

"Paul Chamby?"

"I believe your friend Von Staengl might be able to help!" he said, suddenly, in a different tone of voice.

"See what he has to say. Chamby got him out of a very awkward corner, didn't he? By the way, where *is* Chamby?"

"So far as I know, taking a cure," I said, unwilling to lie, since I knew that his links in Egypt were fairly sound. "Where's Alethea Cawle, these days?"

"Ale—ah—oh, yes," he tremoloed, and straightened the curtain. "Well, I suppose she's—ah—enjoying herself, somewhere, what? She's no longer with us, if that's what you mean? Rather a shame, really. Nice girl, I always thought. However. Circumstances, y'know. No. I don't know where she is!"

There was never a more hairless lie.

"I have reason to believe that you're monitoring my Company's radio traffic, in and out, telex, telephones, and doubtless correspondence," I said, putting on my coat without looking at him. "Tell your radio operators to be extremely careful, won't you?"

"They do very well without advice!" he said sharply. "I don't know what you're talking about!"

"You still have a warm nest here, obviously. I'd enquire about that diplomatic bag. Remember, from this time, I make no distinction!"

"Threats mean nothing to me!" he said, looking out of the window, waving a hand, a gesture, for him, more than strange. "Thank you for your visit!"

"I believe *some* good came of it," I said, opening the door. "I regret there was nothing more. Goodbye."

I smiled at flat-faced and rather pallid Miss Purcell on my way to the stair, and went down, convinced as never before that the Blur had indeed something to hide, and more, was deeply worried. He had every reason to be. With George Whitborough from the Far East going in as Chief, and Neil Collinson already there as Vice, he had a couple of Class One brains on the other side of his desk, and I'd that morning sent them a five-page report, which didn't name anyone, though the pointers were plain enough. If he had anything to hide, I didn't envy him one scrap.

I walked back to the office for exercise. It was one of

those stingingly cold mornings, grey, with a whistling flurry round any corner, women holding their hats on, skirts down, men gripping bowlers spreadfingered, sheets of newspaper twirling in tatterdemalion ringaroses, The Mall a polar stretch, and Pall Mall offering a little less bluster and a short cut. I hurried in front of a taxi turning into Cockspur Street and almost ran into Anthony Bretherton.

We gaped at each other. I hadn't seen him for years.

"Good God, Edmund!" he bellowed, always the hearty one. "I've been looking all over the bloody show for you!"

"Here I am. What is it?"

"Well, look here, I've got an appointment at the War Office in exactly eight minutes," he said, looking at his watch. "Where can I find you?"

I gave him a card.

He looked at it, and his face seemed to sag.

"Great God!" he whispered. "It can't be. What are you doing *there?*"

"I own it," I said.

He looked up at Nelson's Column.

"Well, I'm damned!" he murmured. "You *own* it? But that's where I've just come from. I was to meet a Mr. Alvin—"

"What were you hoping to talk about?"

"An order for bullion—"

"Pipe-dream. But I'd like to hear about it. By the way, Chapman Ryder does all my business!"

"But it wasn't for your Company. I understood it's for an Arabian syndicate—"

"Get your appointment over and come to the office. We've got plenty to discuss!"

Had Lane persuaded the Prince Abdullah to let him have a credit for purchase of gold? It would be simple enough. If I knew Mr. Lane, he'd play the gold market. In the present state of affairs, it was about the easiest way of making a lot of money in a short time. I went into the Carlton Club and called Sir Chapman, but he was out, and his deputy took my message. It was just on time to call the nursing home, and the operator put me through to Consuelo.

"Patti's much better, and the baby's *gurg*ling. The stitches come out tomorrow. Then they're going to do a plastic in a few weeks' time. Now, let's just think. Supposing I have a comfortable bed put in one of the jets, and fly the three of them, let's say, on Saturday, to Banbury Cross?"

"Marvelous idea!"

"I think I'd better go with them. I can always go on to Beyfoum, can't I?"

"Just take care of Patti and the baby. Plenty of time for Beyfoum. Did you find anything about Alethea so-and-so?"

"Yes! I was going to tell you. It's being said she's in a convent in France, nobody seems to know for certain. But my source said she can find out, and I told her to. What does Mr. Berry say?"

"Drew a blank everywhere. You didn't hear from Gillian?"

"Not yet. They may have moved elsewhere. Matron told me Ob missed a breakdown by nothing at all. He's having sleep therapy. Mild form. I'll fly and have lunch with you. Yezzz?"

Life went very well. Consuelo changed subtly from secretary to wife. She took care only of the matters between myself and the Princes, and Miss Burrows, Miss Toverell, and Miss Greig saw to the rest. The apartment over the office became a temporary home where she reigned supreme. I didn't interfere. Domestic matters weren't business. So far as I knew, it all ran like clockwork, and she'd already been to Onslow Close and put everything in order, and we'd promised ourselves a day there if we could fit it in.

I was a little worried about Ob. He'd been in a bad way on entering Sir Roland Ainsworth's nursing home. It was purely psychosomatic, Sir Roland had said. If Patti had died, there was every possibility he could have committed suicide. He'd arrived in London with her and the baby like a madman, and had I not ordered an ambulance to meet them at the airport, he might have done some damage, so the Matron told me. As it was, the night physician took care of him, and he'd been put to bed before Patti and the baby were operated on that night. The only time I saw him, a few minutes while he was fed, he simply held my hand, whispered thanks, and fell asleep. I hadn't a notion what was happening to his business, no messages came to the office for him, and I didn't get in touch with his London managers because Sir Roland thought he should have a few days of absolute rest.

"He's on the very narrow verge," he said. "Let him alone. Do him the world of good. He's been using his nerves. Let him put some weight on, wake up the giant he is. He *is* a big fellow isn't he!"

The office was quiet, there were no messages, field reports were in, but I thought I'd look through them after a nap. I called James Morris, and the secretary said he'd very much like to see me, but he had a luncheon appointment, and could we make it the Ritz bar in ten minutes?

It was only round the corner.

He must have gone in the Piccadilly entrance when I went in at Stratton Street, and we met on the stairs.

"I shan't take my coat off," he said, in the bar. "Save time. Look here, what do you know about this Barnbruche affair?"

"Supposed to have been flown out by a Company aircraft. I can prove it wasn't!"

"I *know* it wasn't. But I wish I knew who's got it. Absolutely, not a trace."

The bar was full, we spoke standing, heads together, he with his back to the wall, I at the end of the counter. I'd already had a look about, and I knew he had. I didn't know a soul.

"It's one of mine," he said, pretending to show me a paper. "It's a new type and brutally destructive. How the devil they were allowed to get away with it, God only knows. But it's the way things are run in these

216

days. Miles of paper to sign, every long-eared ass with a collection of rubber stamps, barbed wire, hush-hush, top secret, all the other idiocy. And one night, in the heart of this fortress, three chaps wheel out a handcart, take it across an enormous space under the guns of the sentinel towers, put what's on it in a car—it's supposed to be Christmas decorations for the hospitals, but nobody thought of looking—and off they go to the airfield, lift it on a waiting plane, and that's that!"

"Did they get a medal?"

"For waking us up?"

"Who's behind it?"

"No real idea. Just a guess. One of those essentially simple jobs that come off because of a touch of the mustard of audacity. Three odds'n sods, and a handcart. What could be more innocent? But what they took was a weapon that could wreck everything for half a mile round this hotel!"

"What's the meaning of 'warhead,' exactly?"

"An explosive head used on a projectile. I'm wondering what next they're going to get away with. We're corrupt in certain sectors, y'know, Edmund. Some of them would sell their own mother's bodies!"

"You think they were our people?"

"Behind it? Certainly. Who else knew what we had there?"

"But they were Germans who carted it off?"

"Naturally. Three ordinary chaps working there. Honesty carried the day. They believed what they were told. That's half the job. They were given an order, and they delivered a handcart full of Christmas decorations to a car outside the gate. The center piece was a large Santa Claus. It wouldn't go in the car, and everybody had great fun breaking the rear window and helping to push it through. That was the warhead. The rest was dressing. So simple!"

"Can't weigh very much?"

"Out of its casing, no. What's really important is the

detonator. The warhead's safe as houses without it. But the detonator's the jewel. They were both mine. What *is* the use of working in secrecy? Or taking an oath of fealty? It's blown to the winds!"

"What damage could it do?"

"Hard to confine it to general terms. It could flatten everything from here to Hyde Park Corner, down to Piccadilly Circus, to Marble Arch. Rubble. Nothing human would live. Nice thought, isn't it?"

"What could it do, let's say, dropped from an aircraft?"

He looked at me in narrow-eyed surprise.

"Aircraft?" he said, and lifted his drink, still looking at me. "Permit me to say this, Edmund. We know each other well enough, I think? If you have any ideas, can't you tell me?"

"Supposing it were used on a building project, my own, for example. We've almost finished a large complex in Arabia. It's an area perhaps four times larger than the one you've just mentioned—"

"Depending on the height of delivery, don't hope for a whole brick on top of another. It's one of the best weapons we had!"

"German brain behind the coup?"

"I believe it was one of us. Must have been. And he passed it on to a German confrère. Also at the top, obviously. Now, how do they set about getting just one of them out? Just one. That part of it, the simplicity, the audacity, was one of us. There's every sign of the old business of singeing the King of Spain's beard. They've got a perfect wriggle of vipers over there. And more than one serpent over here. I'm certain of it!"

He was half-smiling, but I saw his glass. That tremor was rage, from the gut.

"There's a lot of steel in the project I mentioned—"

"Make no difference. Depending, I should have said, on how much of its full potential is used. It has a five-part exploding pattern. Five charges in a pentagonal design. Use a fifth, and it does about a fifth of the total

218

damage. And so on. Look here, I shall be late. If I hear anything, I'll call you immediately at this number!"

"Please. D'you suppose the Lane-Cawle pair had anything to do with this?"

He laughed with the last sip.

"Who else *could* it be? They knew all about it, didn't they? We're looking forward to meeting your wife. Her brother was a great friend of mine. 'Bye, Edmund!"

I walked back with plenty to think about.

The idea I'd had about that warhead was taking solid shape.

Destroying Beyfoum would set us back at least a couple of years, re-ordering, re-building. And we were wide-open to air attack.

I didn't enjoy my lunch, and the nap slid out of reach.

CHAPTER TWENTY-SEVEN

Invox flashed yellows. There was a D.D.—Don't Disturb—sign downstairs, so that it had to be important.

"Mrs. Homer Tregwiss Preese, the second, Roman numeral two, of Rosscommon, New York State, to see you!" Miss Burrows said, in her warning voice. "An appointment, sir?"

"Immediately!" I said, and leapt shoeless for the door, went back for them, couldn't get a heel in, tried to squeeze, cursed, and yellows blinked.

I padded over, touched the button, and the door slid.

I had to stare.

I'd made a mistake. I'd thought the caller was Druxi, in one of her vast selection of what she called her Social Register monnikers.

This was a stout order in black, double breasted, with a silvery something running through the cloth, a lace fichu overlapped by jowls, dark trifocals, snub nose, a large black hat, sitting more to the front than rear, slanted, rather like a pendant nest, grey hair in two thick loops past the ears, a large bag in black leather with a silver buckle, and a stubby collapsible umbrella.

I hadn't an earthly notion what I'd let myself in for.

The whole thing stood there and studied me.

"Well, come on!" it almost snarled, and a touch would have done it. "In? Or out? Y'like me? Or y'don't? What d'ya have to do? Pick a daisy?"

"Who—um—" I began. "Have I the pleasure to mee—"

"Ah, come off it!" she said, in a large square-toed-black-patent-shoe-heels-apart waddle for the nearest armchair. "Je*sus!* Some' you guys. Make up your goddam minds!"

Miss Burrows looked at me, eyes wide, hands in appeal. I shook my head and shut the door.

Mrs.—whatever-her-name was—pivoted on her right foot, swung the left up in a high kick, heel above the shoulder fell back in the chair, dropping one knee over the arm, and haa-haa-haa'd.

Druxi.

"Worried about the get-up?" she said, picking at the dewlaps. "It's something new. It's all over me. Type of latex, I think. Hot as hell. Pinch me. I'm nowhere near!"

"What's the play?" I asked, airing my knowledge of American football. "You look frightful!"

"All in a day's tough luck," she said. "I got in here just ahead of a guy called Bretherton, and another Stather. They've both worked for the pair. Whether they know it or not. Any idea what they're here for?"

"A purchase of bullion. I can let you know the details, later. I saw Lane without being able to talk to him near Basra three days ago. Cawle, no report. I've been looking for his daughter!"

"Miss Alethea? I can only tell you what I'm told. She's teaching math in Switzerland. St. Ursula of the Snows. Convent for girls. Hardly be for boys, would it? The report tells she's probably going to become a nun. She's doing an Ophelia over her daddy. Moss, streamers, veils, 'n all. But the informations's third or fourth hand. I'm not sure of it—"

"Her mother?"

"Has a house there. Always had. Near Basel. Daughter can run home weekends in her Volks. One way of suffering!"

"Do I detect a note?"

The trifocals were down the nose, but the eyes pierced, pale-blue, smiling.

"You're teaching class all week, marking papers, driving that little Volks three hours to, three hours from Mummy's villa, and it's being given out you're all misericordia? Doesn't do, Edmund. I have a pretty smart little contact there. We're waiting for the wrong move!"

"Where do I enter?"

The eyes still smiled. The knee came off the arm. Feet were together.

"You know the Graf von Staengl, don't you?" she said, softly. "How does he strike you?"

I thought back for a moment

"The only time we met, he gave me the right word about Hauerfurth," I said. "He's a friend of Paul Chamby's. That's how I met him. Why?"

"Von Staengl gave you the word, did he? *My!* If you hadn't had something pretty smart for an out, where would you have been?"

I thought of The Blur.

"Why would Von Staengl have something to tell me?" I asked.

"He's just left the War Ministry. One of the few high-ups who didn't swallow poison or blow their brains out. At least, he hasn't yet!"

"Any danger?"

"Why not talk to him while you can? He's with the NATO team in Brussels. Lots of money and all the pretty girls in the world!"

"I've been told he's something of a hot pump, if that's the term?"

"Maybe. Way things are today. We used to know—or we thought we did—what went on. Men were just that, and wonderful. The other stuff kind of crept in. After my time, thank God!"

I looked at the ceiling.

"What do you suppose might be the outcome of a discussion with him?" I asked. "Are the pair involved?"

"They certainly are. So is he, so are you, so am I. I often curse I'm not a man. I hate using a gun. I wish I could just use my hands!"

"The Blur advised me to see Von Staengl not two hours ago!"

"What else? Lord Blercgrove's nobody's idiot. See Von Staengl, get the story, and take the heat off *him!*"

"Any idea what the story might be?"

222

Druxi got up, gathered her handbag, and generally pulled herself together.

"This is like wearing a suit of cold hot water bottles," she grumbled. "I don't even know when I'm sitting on my own ass!"

"Question of bones?"

"Bones, hell. I slip off where I think it's at. Let's get back to Von Staengl. He knows where the x's mark *all* the bodies. He's been everybody's secretary. In every Ministry, and some that aren't. He was in Washington at the time of the pair. A dozen of the people he worked with either committed suicide or disappeared. This doesn't count in others we don't know about. Weaponry's missing—"

"Warheads?"

"Oh, well. Lots of things. I keep having the feeling the world I knew's changed right around. French don't sound like French any more. Germans don't act like Germans. As for you British, I don't know *what* got into *you*. There isn't even room for a bad joke—"

"Your visit, I take it, isn't simply to needle me?"

"Oh, Edmund! I pay you the compliment of not considering who you are. I had a hurry call to attend a Labor Conference in one of those icy places up the coast. Know why? It's believed Mr. Joel Cawle in person's been talking in private session as a delegate of the Garment Workers Union. Name's Colman Marcus. Spoke about the decline of unionism. He'd gone before I caught up. Garment workers? Shades of Sam Gompers!"

I knew it would be a wrong move to ask her where she got the word.

"I'm trying to decide where the pair can be attacked," I said. "Seems to me the wife and daughter are vulnerable, in Cawle's case?"

"Daughter, perhaps. Doesn't give a damn for his wife. Has his own piece!"

"*That's* what I want to hear! Who?"

"We've been getting a whiff of Chinese cooking all along, perhaps you've noticed?"

"Indeed!"

"Well, the pork subgum-and-bamboozle platter's been going to Venice these past week ends. She stays at the Gritti Palace. She's a Miss Feng Tung Truc—here's the name—and she's supposedly attached to the Vietnam chop going on in Paris. She's at this address in the Avenue Kleber. We hope she's somebody called Lily Hong. Been with Cawle a couple of years. She gives the parties. Doesn't appear at the sessions. But she's a big lug, has bodyguards, won't date. It's been tried. How's your Mandarin?"

"Fair. I just got married, you may have heard?"

"And congratulations. You'll be getting the family gift in a day or so. Elevate your mind a moment. You can still remember a few words, can't you?"

"I can probably defeat anyone who wasn't born speaking it. I hold a Portuguese passport. I've lived in Macao, Goa and Angola for most of my life, so I'm a little rusty. If they then want to switch to Portugese, or French, or a few others, I can oblige. Why?"

"I'll be there the day after tomorrow as Madam Ming T'ang Wah. I own restaurants in Hawaii. World tour. If we meet, and you know me, we can ho-how-hang for a few minutes, lapse into something else, and who knows? I understand with her own people, she's sociable. My contact says she never sees anyone anymore except her own playmates. And Joel Cawle's been there twice. First as this American Labor speaker—the nerve!—then as a Deputy in the Italian Communist Party."

"Must admire his range!"

"Uh huh. You'll get there, what time?"

"The day after tomorrow. For luncheon?"

"Then I'll fly in from Milan that morning. Meet you where?"

"I never enjoy a cocktail so much as on the terrace of the Grand Hotel. That's next door. The Gritti used to be part of it. There may still be a way in. I'll have to find out!"

"Could be useful. I'd like you to meet somebody who wants to join you, by the way. Friend of Gillian's. She'd like a little experience in Arabia generally. I don't want her *too* far in the rough, if you know what I mean. You'll see for yourself. There was nothing, by the way, at that Grosvenor Street place. Clean move. They're far too good!"

"How does Georges look at this Chinese bit?"

"Has to be careful because of the Vietnam talks. She's virtually a guest of his Government. He's tied. But he doesn't mind a brawl in somebody else's backyard. What do you suppose we might get out of her? By *any* means!"

It was borne in that Druxi was out for Miss Hong's wherewithals. I was more than willing to go one better.

"The headquarters of the pair, what they're doing, who's behind them. Make a nice start, wouldn't it?"

Druxi put her gloves on.

"I never wanted so much to lay hands on anybody like those three!" she said, in effort of buttoning over swollen wrists. "I've begun calling it my swan song. If I could put the three of them away, and know their organization was dead, and most of them in it were watching that lovely green damp spread over the walls of comfortable stone cells, I'd retire happily!"

"You? Retire?"

The dowdy bundle shook, and seemed to wheeze itself back in its other skin.

"Okay, Miz' Tooth!" the voice grated, in hormonic alto. "Nice see'n ya! How's the argot hit you?"

"Tangentially. Any reason?"

"Two downstairs. Call you!"

I touched the button, and went to the door.

"Hey!" the voice bellowed. "Da shoes. Gal don't get to come in here, some punk off widda shoes?"

I got the shoes on, and opened the door while the yellows flashed. Miss Burrows stood there, mouth tight, mute.

"Well, s' long, sweerie!" Mrs. What's-her-name coughed. "See ya down the Garden. Slop up a bucket o' blood, huh? Hi, there, hon'. Come up for me? Boy, you sure got the juice working for y'!"

Miss Burrows stood aside for her to go in the lift.

"I keep you gentlemen waiting?" I heard her voice boom from below. "Real nice of you, sir. I appreciate it. And thank *you*, Mr. Sergeant. Don't tell me it's raining *again?* Ah, *brother!*"

There was a mumble in reply, and the lift came up with Anthony Bretherton, and a man I didn't know.

"Sorry to be late, Edmund," he said. "The old duck asked if she might go in first. I think I've seen her before, somewhere?"

"Probably saw her on TV. Collects funds—"

He turned to the other man.

"I took the liberty of bringing along Jeremy Stather. His business seems very much to do with you. He'll explain later. Edmund, I'm very worried. The more I think of it, the more I'm sure I have a case against this Company. On the strength of these letters, almost a contract in themselves—"

"Why don't you take them to the Fraud Squad? I've told you. They're forgeries, and four 'directors' aren't—"

"But I interviewed this man Alvin, here, in his office!"

"Have you made quite sure of the financial side of this business?"

"Everything's in order. One doesn't go into this sort of thing breakneck, y'know. I've been extremely careful. Step by step. Banks. Brokers. It's the biggest deal I've ever handled. I'm talking like this because I know *you*. I went into it because your name's on that letter heading!"

"That, and the Company's name and address, telephone and cable items are the only parts I acknowledge. There seems to me to be a criminal charge—"

"How can there be?" he almost howled. "The money's *there!*"

"How do you know?"

"Know? I've verified. I've seen the copies—!"

"How did you meet this man Alvin?"

"At the Bath Club. He was there with Ted Knollys. Flew over with him. Ted's going to be shocked!"

"Mr. Knollys should find out his friends' antecedents, surely?"

"Oh, I don't know," Bretherton said, and got up. "If the fellow's his wife's cousin, I don't see why there should be any fuss, do you?"

A large red light flashed and burned between my eyes. I'd known Edward Knollys and Mary, his wife, through Mel. I hadn't seen them for years. I'd never heard she had any American relations. Mel would have been the first to tell me.

"I see absolutely no reason why," I said, in a throwaway, and went for the drinks sideboard. "Look here, we can't talk without a quaff. I've got some sherry. I suggest a trial?"

"B'all means," Bretherton said, and Stather nodded. "I'm not a bit happy. I'd—uh—put everything in order, y'know? I mean, that sort of buy doesn't come every day. Makes me look, uh, I'm not sure. Look here, Edmund. I believe I *have* a case against your Company!"

"I warn you. You haven't!"

"Those three letters—"

"I've told you. And I haven't any directors at all. None. Who *is* this cousin of Knollys' wife?"

"Mary. Mary Phillipson before marriage. Some relation of Angela Masters. Isn't she working here?"

"Did she make the introduction?"

"I believe she spoke to her boss. Paul Chamby. Isn't he the Director-General?"

"Hasn't been, for a long time. I hope you didn't put any money of your own in this?"

Bretherton shook his head, looking from the glass to Stather.

"I'm sorry!" he said, up at me, "I've simply got to consult a solicitor. I'm in a nasty spot. I don't owe anything, thank God. But I've taken on certain commitments, you see?"

"Others have bought on assumption?"

He nodded, finished the drink with a head-back swig, and put the glass down, turning it, looking at Stather.

"You'd better look at that cheque," he said. "Mine was all right. Better see if this one is!"

"How long have you known Edward Knollys?" I asked.

"Oh. About five years, I suppose. My wife met Mary at the Henley Regatta. I used to do a bit of sculling. We've seen them off and on. Had a few deals. Fairly small. No trouble. Till this!"

Stather looked at his watch and got up. Palish gingery combed-back hair sparsed the top of his head, left the forehead a bony shine, and his eyes seemed round, bluish, spread nose, pouty mouth, the type I've met before, apparently shy, perhaps not too bright, though in reality, rather sharper than that.

"Cheque's been cashed," he said shortly. "Expect anything else? That type of con always forks up the clover to Santa-Claus things. Mr. Trothe, I didn't come here to discuss anything like that. I asked Mr. Bretherton to bring me here only for one reason. Mr. Seymour Logan I believe, is General Superintendent of this Company in the Middle East?"

"He is. Why?"

"He was a friend of my father's. I last saw him when I was at school. About ten days ago, a representative of his brought me a letter from him. He wanted to buy certain items which aren't easy to find, and they're costly. Anthony rang me today and said you'd told him the letter-heading's a forgery. That made me look at the letter I'd got. It's the same!"

He held out the letter. Logan's signature was a clumsy copy.

"It appears to me you're both unlucky," I said. "I'm perfectly sure Mr. Logan doesn't know anything about it. What sort of items were they?"

"I don't think I shall say anything more until I've heard direct from Mr. Logan. You'll notice he writes from this address?"

"Disregard it. I'll send a message to him, now. I ought to get an immediate reply. Would you care to write what you want to say?"

I passed him a blank, he took out a pen, and we listened to pen squeaks. I wondered when some device might also listen and present the words. I pressed the button, and Bretherton got up, watching the chute ingest. The sherry seemed to have tinted his worry.

"Look here, Edmund!" he burst out. "I've *got* to have this clear, d'you see? Apart from three letters from this Company, I've had five cables from El Bidh, a place in Southern Arabia. I know the cash is available. I've made quite certain it *is*. My clients wouldn't accept that sort of risk without strict enquiry. But you say the whole thing's a fraud. How *can* it be?"

The cables from El Bidh rocked me for a moment. I felt I'd been right about Bernard Lane. But how the devil could the ten million in bullion be switched from a rumor about my buying aircraft, to a hard deal in London for a purpose not yet known, by a director who didn't exist?

"Where's the bullion to be delivered?" I asked, filling glasses.

"We aren't as far as that yet. Look here, I've got to go, I'm sorry. May I come back a little later? I'll have more news, I hope."

"Do," I said, and gave Stather his glass. "Meantime, we'll wait for a reply from Mr. Logan!"

Miss Greig took him down, and Berry's men waited to tail him.

"Miserable business!" Stather said, looking at a screen of fusil oil on the side of his glass. "First real upset I've had. Thing is, there's a lot of money left over. If the fellow doesn't exist, what?"

"Give it to charity?"

"Explain how to my accountant so that he can explain it to the tax lads. I don't understand it. Why couldn't Mr. Logan get on to your own man here, Gouldsden?"

"If it *was* Logan. Did Gouldsen buy through you?"

229

"Quite a lot. I understand he's left?"

"He has, yes. Did he pay with this Company's cheques?"

"No. It was Intramed. S.A. On the National Provincial, down here. All good. Where is he? The stuff's waiting for him!"

"He was never employed by this Company——"

"I was in this office twice. Here!"

"I said, and please follow me closely, he was never part of this Company. Whatever he bought had nothing to do with this Company. And we don't bank with the National Provincial!"

He shook his head, putting the glass down, and got up. The green tweed tie was askew in the aircell shirt collar. The grey-black-brown tweed jacket hung out at the back of the neck.

"Two of them, both something to do with this Company," he said, as though listening to himself. "Plus the Bretherton nonsense. What's the answer?"

"You'll do well to get in touch with me if anything like this happens again. It looks as though no money were involved. Next time, there might be. Then where are you?"

Blues were flashing, and I reached for the receiver.

"Logan here, sir!"

"Trothe!"

"I'm a bit puzzled by this message"—I touched the button so that the voice came over the yawp—"I knew this boy's father, certainly, but it's years since I saw the boy himself. I've never done any business with him. How could I? I don't even know where he is!"

I motioned to Stather to stand near the mike.

"Here he is now. Talk to him!"

"Jeremy Stather, here, Mr. Logan——"

"Well, hullo, my boy! I'm sorry there's not more time for the courtesies. Now, what *is* all this? What am I supposed to have bought? That's the first thing!"

"Well, sir, as you may guess, I'm very sorry indeed to trouble you. Supposedly you ordered—and paid for—with a balance of about two hundred pounds—a

230

small generator, the sort that works on batteries. Then there was a light cell unit for a computer, the computer itself, a mini, and a special timer—"

"Just a moment now! This is all absolute tosh. I've ordered nothing. I've paid for nothing. Put me back to Mr. Trothe, will you?"

"I heard. All right, Logan. I'll straighten it this end. We'll speak tonight. Out?"

"Out!"

Hands in pockets, Stather was pacing slowly toward the door.

"I'm really most sorry to have wasted your time," he said, over his shoulder. "I don't know what to think!"

"Where's this stuff at the moment?"

"Olympic Airways freight for Athens!"

"Addressed to?"

"This Company's office. To J. S. Logan. What am I to do with the rest of the stuff? It's all paid for!"

"What's the name of Mr. Logan's alleged representative, and where's he staying?"

"The name's Redmond, and he's supposedly in Birmingham at the moment. Going on to Glasgow. Back here next week. He was at the Savoy. What's my best move?"

"Get in touch here, immediately. I have the means to deal with it!"

He nodded. He seemed too far gone to talk. I watched him as far as the top of the stair, and shut the door. Berry's men would attend to the rest.

I sent cables to El Bidh, to Logan, and to Argyopoulos in Athens. I got Miss Burrows on to Olympic Airways freight department.

Sir Chapman Ryder called while I was dictating.

"Bretherton's absolutely in the clear," he said. "The money's there. This appears to have nothing to do with your Company. It's being done through London and New York with a little help from Zurich. What it's designed to do—I mean, the buying of that amount, with further promise of a great deal more—or what it's to buy in turn, or if it's simply to stay in a vault, I don't

231

know. I do know it's sending up the price of gold. Now, is that the idea?"

"Putting up the price?"

"Can you imagine a gentler, or more formidable blackmail than the buying of gold, when it's known what it threatens to do to the franc, to the sterling and the dollar? To mention only three? Who's got the money to spend? Who doesn't care about loss? Who wants certain items which the sterling, franc and dollar Governments can't, or won't, supply? Who's able to shake their currencies? Until those Governments give them, or let them buy, what they want? Have I said enough?"

"Plenty. Oil does the talking!"

"I don't mind that. Most of the business goes across this desk!"

"Bretherton was at the War Office today. Same deal, perhaps?"

"Possibly. I shan't know until Thursday. Call me if you hear anything, won't you?"

Yellows flashed.

"Commodore Kopfers, sir!"

The Company's senior pilot was a veteran of KLM, late fifties, silver hair, red face, two of the bluest eyes I ever saw, a healthy laugh, and a magnificent Dutch don't-give-a-damn about everything. Except flying. He'd retired not long before, and I'd been lucky to get him. He'd already saved us a mint in maintenance and flight schedules. There's a trick to everything. He knew them all.

I showed him the blue flimsy, with the instructions for a paradrop.

"It's what I thought!" he almost bellowed, and put his fists on his knees. "I'm over Switzerland? I have to drop? No permission? But, you know, sir, the Swiss, they are very strict. They are *hard*. They don't permit. And where is this Kretzgros? I look on all the maps. Nothing. But I cannot break international flight regulations. I refuse to have the bale on my aircraft!"

"Good!"

"Then this administrator there, Holtby, he shows me on the map, under my flight line, a marked spot. I ask what is in the bale. He says it is mountaineering supplies for a team going up. It saves time, he says. The bale is the size of this desk. I find the place, it's grass, full moon, on a hillside, sheep, I think, some cattle, a farm, a river. But I fly on—"

"What happened to the bale?"

"I don't know, sir. I left instructions to other crews not to touch it!"

"It came from Germany?"

"I don't know, sir!"

"Show me where this place is. Then tell me about the 'administrator'—"

Miss Burrows managed to wave the pad in my eyeline.

"You have an appointment at the nursing home at four forty-five," she said, getting a word in edgeways. "With your son-in-law at five o'clock. Both appointments are for fifteen minutes only, sir. And Mr. Frederick Trothe is downstairs and would very much like to talk to you!"

"Thank you. Get on to Bell's Fosse. I want the flight office, and Customs!"

CHAPTER TWENTY-EIGHT

Frederick had changed amazingly, touchingly, since I'd last seen him. It was the subtle sort of change that happens in a boy sloughing infancy, and now, in youth, ridding the callow. He was much more a man in voice, a newer light in the eye, more decision in the set of the mouth. Mel had always said he favored me rather than her, but I failed to see it. Startlingly he reminded me of her in gestures, a laugh in the throat, so very much like Mel as I remembered her. He had a good voice. I listened without paying much attention.

I had a fair idea of the sort of time he must have had, serving his sentence—as he called it—at the Vicarage. But it was better than prison, and he'd not only thrown off the drug habit, but had no further desire, and proved it by going back to his old haunts for the past five days, finding old friends, refusing every kind of offer, and coming back with a sense of utter relief.

"I did it deliberately," he said. "I gave it long enough. I slept in the old dosshouse in Taverner Street. Same push. My God, what a frightening lot they've become. They don't *look* unhealthy, y'know? Well, not quite that. They look simply awful, in fact. But they can still trot about. That's what surprised me. They were taking terrific stuff. I don't want to name anyone. You'd be shocked. It's the girls I'm sorry for. How long is it? Ten months? Well, almost a year. Since I've been away, I mean. They look ten years older. They're on the streets, of course. To pay for it. I don't know what's going to happen to them. I feel like going back there and starting some sort of Drugs Anonymous biz. But it wouldn't work. Too far gone. That state, it's hopeless, Dad, how about a job?"

He tried to make it casual, but it came a little too fast. I put a hand on his shoulder.

"In what?"

"I'd like something rough," he said. "After these past few days, I feel, oh, not soft exactly—I've kept fairly up to scratch, football, boxing, that sort of thing, I mean, I'm not going to fall down—but these past few days, I've sort of become afraid of being *here*. As if I might be pulled back again. I don't think I could be. I gave it a good trial, I think. Any idea of going back, living that sort of miserable dry-out, Christ, I freeze. The old type of bohemians, you know, were champion choirboys by comparison. They live in stys. On the floor. Twenty, thirty, who comes? Lay your filth alongside. Sleep your dross. Bath? Soap? Water? What are they? Syphilis is dear companion. So's the smell. Lavatory? Wherever. Clothing? Buy new. No, Dad. It's probably the aesthete, rather than the athlete, talking. What I'd love at this moment is a job in the desert. A long way from anywhere. Fresh air. Heat enough to burn out the canker. I believe it'll save me. Finishing touch. I'll stay there, I'll bake, I'll burn, till I'm sure. Then if I'm good enough, you'll perhaps give me a better job!"

While I listened to him, wanting to bounce him on my knee as I had when he was a dumpling, I'd already seen him as assistant to Heumann on the northwest line from Beyfoum.

But the gem glittered between my eyes. I had *the* great idea of a lifetime. He was made for it.

"You've got a job," I said, "Start next month. What are you doing at the moment?"

"Nothing. I mean, nothing, except going absolutely spare. I'll go back to Onslow Close tonight. If you'll give me some cash. I'm broker than that. But it's simply marvelous to be there, Dad. If there were anything to do, I'd stay there for the rest of my life. But that's moonlight and mandragora. Perfume and lozenges. I know much too well what I need. Hard graft and no mercy. I've seen the other stuff!"

Time to air the idea. I wondered how much to say.

"You're going to get all you can handle," I said, carefully. "Before that, I'd like you to do a little job for me. Take a Company jet tomorrow. Fly to Tobruk.

235

See a friend of mine. He'll be your contact throughout. You'll simply be a hopster, hippop, whatever they call themselves. About a hundred or more of them have a camp not far from Derna. All nationalities. I want you to join them. You'll pretend to be far from bright. You know just enough to get there, and wear whiskers. I want you to keep your eyes open, ears needled, that's all. For me. Until I get there. We shan't know each other. Got it?"

"Got!"

"Take my car home. Bring it up tomorrow morning. What do you think of Ob?"

He hesitated, stood, straightened his tie.

"I hate the thought of it on one side. But I think he's the devil of a smart chap. I like him. Thing is, I can't see him in bed with Patti. I can't see *her* with *him*. How the hell did it happen?"

"Ask Patti. Probably she found a man for the first time?"

He turned one of those "looks," grey, piercing, his mother, that sent a knife through me, and the smile started all the way down.

"I suppose so," he said, nodding. "Probably right. The girls all tell me they're about three hundred per cent louder and far more workmanlike than the rest of us. Funny thing is, I know girls who've told me they're not all that good. We're only talking about a piece of muscle. No, Dad. I'm sorry. This color business hasn't settled in my mind yet. I used to think it was all right. After all, I've run around with most of them. Bedded them. Anything. Anywhere!"

He hesitated, turned away.

"Well?"

He pulled a deep breath.

"Well, the only one I got really tied up with came from Malaysia. She *wasn't* ordinary. I'm not sure what she was. I can't find her. The others didn't know where she went!"

There was a note in the quiet voice. I didn't like it. I heard myself. I know that state too well.

236

"That's why you went back?"

He nodded, looking down at joined thumbs.

"Supposing she'd been there?"

The thumbs opened.

"Not sure!"

"Right. Now tell me how you met her!"

"That chap Aunt Pam married. That swine!"

"But you quite liked him, didn't you?"

"I don't like thinking about it. We got sucked into it. He very nearly got Patti, too. He started giving those Sunday parties at their place in Barnet. All very showy, lights, big grill at the pool, remember? Well, you weren't there. All fun. That was *the* big word. Marijuana. Smokes. Lots of music. Then the needle. In fun, of course. Very clean and scientific. More and more fun. More needles. Sniffs. Everybody sloshed. Bucking in the bushes, and that sort of thing. We really did look forward to our weekends. Then he started coming round to my place with the girls. Two or three nights a week. More pot. More of the other stuff. Then LSD. That really got me. That's where she came in. I never imagined anyone like her. I seemed to go, well, quite mad, looking back. And I really *don't* want to!"

"Where did she live?"

"In Curzon street. She moved a long time ago. Couldn't find out what happened to her. I think she worked at a tourist agency. Nobody seemed to know. I believe only that fellow could have told me. He knew what he was doing. He gave the stuff to her, and she gave it to me. And I did the selling. That's what I can't understand about myself. Why did I do it? I didn't seem to be using my brain, at all. I was half drunk, months on end. If you looked at the work I was doing at that time, you'd see it. As I had to. Frightful!"

"You never met her outside your rooms, and the place in Barnet?"

"Twice, I think. Once at the Trocadero. I took her to dinner there. We went to a theatre club. Saw a Kafka play. I don't remember much about it. She took me back to Curzon Street, that night. That's how I knew. She must have been earning a lot. Beautiful place. The other was in the house where we got pinched. That was an accident. Diana Beales woke up in a panic. Didn't know where she was. That happens, of course. The rest of us were blupped. Poor kid. She managed to remember their phone number and called her father. Do you know Morton Beales? I was just getting into the shades when he got there. I've heard women screaming. I never heard a man *scream* before. Absolute madman. It could all have blown over, except for him. Wouldn't hear of it. He got the Police, had everybody arrested. Drug Squad down from Scotland Yard, every damn' thing in the book. I blacked while he was in the middle of his act. Looking back, I think he was absolutely right. It stopped a great deal more nonsense. Di-di and a couple of others were hoicked off to Switzerland. She wrote to me all the time I was at the Vicarage. Have to buy her something nice, one day. She had a hell of a time. It's worse for girls, y'know. She said the nuns were very kind, but she had the violet wobwabobs and black graggers. I know all about that. It's when you'd willingly die just for one shot. I had Doctor Norris. He was a real giant. She had a team of specialists from Geneva, or somewhere. And her father flew out a couple of times a month. She seems all right, now. She doesn't want to *hear* about it. Like me!"

"Is she still at this convent?"

"She'll be there for the next year or so. She'll take her degree there. I thought of, well, trying to fly en route. See her. Give her a kiss!"

"No reason why you shouldn't. Buy her something *really* nice. By the way. What was this other creature's name?"

He turned away, ran a fist up and down his chest.

"Lily!" he said, loudly as a shout. I went on writing. The cheque made him stare. He looked underbrow at me. He had a good direct eye, I was glad to see.

"Thanks, Dad. I can buy some kit, send some flowers to Patti, and the Vicarage. A lot of pretty jobs. What's this Tobruk thing?"

Again, I had to consider what to say. I took out my wallet and gave him a card.

"That's every useful number when you want to speak to me," I said, as it were, carelessly. "Now, Tobruk and Derna. A lot of youngsters have got together somewhere near there. Maurice, your contact, will get you there. You'll have to rough up. I have an idea there's somebody there working against me or the Company. I don't know who, or why. It's an idea formed on slight evidence, and that's all. I want you to lounge about and see who runs things, what they do. I'd like to know where the money comes from. Particularly keep your eyes open for any radio installation, never mind what kind. Think you can do that?"

"Certain!"

"The aircraft will be ready at Bell's Fosse tomorrow at whenever the Captain says. Telephone and find out. I'll ask him to fly to Tobruk via Basle or Geneva and give you a day or so there. Or more, if there's good reason!"

"When do you appear?"

"You won't know me, anyway. I'll be a plumpish item from the purlieus of Didonc-la-Bas, selling kitchenware from a van, in somewhat scattered French!"

"Odd!"

"Surprise you?"

"Not a bit. I'm rather glad. Mummy always said you were something of a chameleon!"

"Really?"

"Oh, yes. I'd rather like to be!"

I looked at him, he looked at me, eye to eye, and I found no swerve, no give.

"If you insist," I said tentatively, "I'll take you on as a helper, when you find me. But if there's anything there that gives me the slightest cause for worry, you'll be in the middle of an up-'n'a-downer!"

He rubbed his hands in small glee.

"Sounds more like it! Right. Shan't see you till then? Bye, Dad. Thanks for everything. That's a tremendous lot!"

I gave him a hug, he pecked my cheek, and I must say I saw him go with a great deal of pride. And elation.

The matron came to tell me that Ob still had a high fever, and took me up to Patti's room. The place was like a flower shop. The baby's cot was in the next room, where she could see it. Heavy bandages covered her face, head, and both arms. I couldn't kiss or touch her.

"A fine way to meet you!" she said. "But I'm not complaining for a moment. I really don't know why we're here!"

"Deliberate?"

"Oh, of course! We were coming from Marrakesh, and it's a wild road for a long way. Well, this car came up behind us, and braked as it passed, and somebody threw the grenade through the window. By the grace, I was holding Mel in my arms—we were both dozing—and it fell in the crib. It's a heavy withe and iron affair made by Ob's family, and covered with lace and a fly net. It held down most of the explosion, but we were cut about by bits of wood and things. Nothing serious, really, but so much blood, I was sure I hadn't a drop left. I didn't know one more thing till I woke up here. Ob's been absolutely wonderful. But it's done him a lot of damage. I'm rather glad you can't see him for a day or so. He's in a very ugly mood, indeed. I've never seen him angry before. He's quite frightening!"

"Not to you—I mean—"

"But he's *marvellous* to me! No, it's the people who did it. He thinks it's the party trying to get him out of everywhere. He doesn't tell me much. But he's awfully worried. Now he doesn't want me to go back to Morocco, and I love it!"

"Why not stay on Onslow Close? It's very different, you know? After all, you were born there!"

"Well, I'd love to. If Consuelo agrees?"

"Of course she will! You could take the garden suite. Frederick won't be there. Neither shall we. By the time you're fit to travel, everything'll be ready for you. And you'll have Constable Parnes to guard you!"

I intended a far stronger guard. I called Berry downstairs.

"My son leaves on White Horse One from Bell's Fosse tomorrow. He's going first to Switzerland for a couple of days. Then on to Tobruk, in North Africa. I want him under strict surveillance at all times. The tails should be fairly young. I'll see you when I reach London, anyway. Second. Would you please see there's a strong twenty-four hour guard on Onslow Close? You might get the radio patrol on net. Instant alarm. Have a look at the place and decide for yourself, will you?"

"That'll be done, sir. Question of Edward Knollys. Do you know him?"

"A nodding acquaintance, yes. Haven't seen him for ages!"

"Not surprising, sir. He's been dead a bit over three years. The Secretary of the Bath Club just told me. Nobody of that name's a member, now. They never heard of Alvin. I'm waiting for my men behind Bretherton and Stather to report. My colleague at Corledge Trans is still working on that Cawle business—"

"I'm told she's teaching mathematics at a Swiss convent!"

I could almost see Berry's expression.

"I take everything I hear these days with a drop of vinegar, sir!"

"Don't blame you in the slightest. How could a non-member of the Bath Club invite another non-member to have a drink or a meal? Did you discuss that with the Secretary?"

"He doesn't think it happened, sir!"

"Mr. Bretherton's suspect? Or did this Alvin tell a lie? He's the one I'd like to find!"

"I've got a couple of men going through the incoming shipping and airline registers, sir. He could have changed his name, of course, couldn't he?"

"With a couple of dozen passports, he wouldn't have to worry!"

"I'll report within the hour, sir!"

"I'm leaving the country tonight. I'll be back on Saturday. Good luck everywhere!"

Had I known Knollys was dead, I could have nailed Bretherton then and there. I called Sir Chapman Ryder.

"Do you know anything about Bretherton? Trustworthy, that sort of thing?"

"Absolutely, so far as any transaction here's concerned. I knew his father. Very fine man. He was on the Baltic Exchange. The son went into bullion. Doing very well, Anything wrong?"

"He met this so-called director of mine. The bullion cook-up. If you hear that name—Alvin—mentioned, and he pretends he's anything to do with me, would you please call the Police?"

"With great caution, yes. But if the money's there, and he's prepared to pay, then what?"

"He's using forged letterheads, and a directorate he isn't entitled to. That's quite enough, isn't it?"

"Quite. I'm waiting for the sale at any moment. I think it might be a very good idea if you were here!"

"I've done rather better. I've been in touch with Chief Superintendent Hockley at Scotland Yard. He's very interested indeed!"

I called Berry again.

"You'd better get a few enquiries going in the City. Among the bullion brokers. We're looking for John Alvin. Banks, everywhere. I'll give the man who finds him a thousand pounds!"

"You'll see the dust from where you are, sir!"

"Good. Watch Bretherton closely. No reports yet?"

"Nothing, sir. They must be having a proper chase!"

I signed everything put in front of me, and went upstairs to loll in a comfortable chair with nothing to do, for once, and have a cup of tea. I called the nursing home and found the patients comfortable, but the Matron said Ob was still asleep, and it might be wiser to leave it until tomorrow.

I asked to speak to my man on guard, and he told me that Mrs. Trothe had left in the Company car, there had been no suspicious moves or visitors, and the night reliefs were due in an hour.

Consuelo came in just afterwards, called to me from the lobby, asked the housekeeper for vases, gave

Groves an armful of flowers, and ran in to throw herself in my lap.

"Cuddle!" she whispered. "I'll be warm for the first time today. Darling, that place is like an icebox, didn't you think? I'm sorry we couldn't see Ob. They think he's got a touch of Honkonk nonsense. Baby's a darling. She won't be much darker than Patti. But *her* daughter might be black as Ob. Still, by that time it'll be quite fashionable, I suppose. Do we want to go to Onslow Close tonight?"

"Not in this weather. I've got to disappear for two days. Back on Saturday. We'll dine and see anything you want. If Berry calls me, or anything else that's urgent, get me on clix at twelve one and midnight one. And I've got a call now. Sit on my knee upstairs!"

She had both arms round my waist going up, and she stood over me while I netted. She wasn't wearing a bra. She didn't need to. Felt good. Eight stations sent NOR which meant they were busy on something to do with the pair but not ready with a report. The others didn't come on. The last, my prize on the Soviet-Turkish border, hit me in the ear with HII, meaning urgentest. I took the letters down, tapped CO3, for congratulations, and three dots meaning emphasis. I took the sheet to the desk, and deciphered.

"Cawle en route Iskanderum Soviet ship Blagarov. Flying Milan Paris by Air India or Air France. Name Franc Baszkas Czech passport profession agronomist specialist viniculture believed going Tunisia. KGB alert on all points great care."

I sent long cables to Kober in Istanbul, Argyopoulos in Athens, Genia Pearlman in Rome, Madame Berthe in Paris, and called Berry. He was out, but Miss Hammond put it on tape. Hockley's deputy took a complete note.

"Mr. Hockley's having a look round this bullion business, sir. Sounds as if this Alvin make a nice fit for a pair of cuffs!"

"That's how it sounds to some of *us!*"

243

While Consuelo watched, I took my lucky sovereign and steadied it on my thumbnail.

"The Blur, George Whitborough, and Neil Collinson should know about this," I said. "Heads, the Blur, tails George. One or t'other, then Neil. Right?"

"*Should* you tell them?"

"Public duty?"

She shrugged. She was wafting through her demure days, as she chose to call them, and vitality wasn't a feature.

"If you must know, I don't trust *any* of them!"

"Poor us!"

"It's been that for too long. Don't spin it. Tell the Blur. I'll bet you Mr. Franky Backswhacks gets away!"

I called Grass Tree 14, and a manservant went to find z'ludship.

I read him the message without saying a word about source.

"I believe we've got that, Trothe!" the voice crackled. "I think we may have the same contact. Any idea about intention?"

"None. Am I to leave it to you?"

"Absolutely. Once he's in Iskanderum, he won't move a foot without our people like gnats round him. I dearly look forward to that meeting!"

"No news about Lane?"

"Nothing. Trothe, this was most kind of you. Thank you so much!"

Consuelo opened those blue, blue eyes in a simply ravishing stare.

"Now we'll know more or less, shan't we?" she whispered. "Darling, what a *pity* we can't rumple a carpet or two!"

CHAPTER TWENTY-NINE

Mimi had done a splendid job on Liao Cha Pei.

I was the tall, slender type from Szechwan, citified in clothing and manners, goldish rather than yellow, irregular teeth with large canines, which made it easier to keep my mouth open to breathe, rather than through my broken nose. A special fit of contact lenses lifted my eyelids at the outer corners, and the eyebrows were plucked to coincide. Mimi really showed her genius in my wig. It was that black Chinese bristle which stands on end, resists comb or barber's scissors, and simply sprouts up from the head, not even decently *en brosse,* yet extraordinarily fine to the touch, and I worked on that mannerism, enough, at least, to convince anyone I wasn't wearing a wig. It was like all Mimi's wigs. Once it was on, it stayed on. I could bath and swim in it. I'd made that a *sine qua non* from the beginning. There's nothing more embarrassing than a wig that slips. It had happened only once, long before, and I still thought of it with shut eyes.

I remembered it on the terrace of the Gritti Palace, watching the gondolas prance in the wake of motor boats driven by a type of ruffian, so common these days, able to do as he pleases because of a little more money.

I was thinking that a flogging with a salt rub might cure a few of them, when the white-enamelled prow of a pinnace slid beneath the terrace rail, and along to the pontoon.

A seaman jumped with a rope, another came behind to offer a hand to a positively opulent Chinese woman, hair piled and pinned, showing a beautiful leg almost to the thigh in the divided skirt of a green and blue *cheong sam,* neck roped in pearls, diamonds in wicked glint at ears, wrists and fingers, little-fingernails curving a couple of inches in gold sheaths, holding a miniature griffon in the crook of her right arm.

I wondered if this were Miss Feng Tung Truc, or Lily Hong.

She really was beautiful, not heavily made-up, rather tall for a Vietnamese, and she carried herself magnificently, half smiling in the brilliant black eyes, knowing everybody alive was looking at her, oblivious, walking down to a table at this end, and by some small miracle of grace, sitting down without showing anything except an ankle and a jewelled black satin shoe. A young man, in clothing and bearing a footman of sorts, bowed, she nodded, and he spoke to the waiter. A young woman, possibly a secretary, sat with the young man at a nearby table. The pinnace turned out and went over to the Dogana.

I sat there, impassive, smoking a Turkish cigaret, drinking a modish Campari and lime, looking at a party of tourists going into the great door of Santa Maria della Salute as a shoal of fish into a leviathan's maw.

I went on looking at a large Thomas Cook & Son's tourist folder. I'd almost decided to go over to Burano, and a shadow fell across the page. I looked up. The young man had thoughtfully put himself between me and the sun. He bowed in the old manner, palms against the inside of the knees, feet together, and while I sorted my wits, I heard the kind of Mandarin I hadn't enjoyed since my time at the Oriental School. It's a difficult language to translate without floweriness, but the gravamen was that a daughter of heaven wondered if I were the son of the savant Shiao Cha Pei, and invited me to join her in a drink to the early disembarrassment of catsmeat in Pekin, and freedom from the blasphemies of anti-culture.

I put out my cigaret and stood, said—loudly—in Mandarin just as good as his, that I would enjoy even so much as the personal air of one thinking as I, and walked out of the window, and, in the bow-legged jolt, hands at sides, knuckles front, through the foyer to the terrace, bowing from the waist, palms inside knees, eyes lowered to about a foot from the shoe.

246

I took a hand, a slight squeeze, and at its gesture, sat. Druxi.

She was perfect. She looked, even in that strongish sunlight dappling off the canal, not more than thirty-five, though how she did it, I couldn't attempt to guess. Her face was healthily plump, a slight chin, skin satin-smooth, barely a wrinkle, the black eyes were contact lenses, and everything else was stuck on, but I'd defy anyone to tell me so.

She began by saying how much she'd enjoyed my father's lectures at Pekin University, though it seemed years ago, and yet it was only just before the little brutes hung their books on the Walls, and spat in the face of the Great Mother. Her family escaped to Formosa, and then to Hawaii.

"Though I find it pleasant to speak my language again, I prefer to use another until sanity comes," she said in the quiet voice, in French. "If you prefer another language, please, I have Spanish, or Portuguese?"

The waiter brought her drink, a gin tonic, and another for me. I saw her hand around the glass. It made the thumb-out-and-bent-down sign for Beware of Microphones. In reply, I smoothed the back of my right ear with a forefinger.

"I have met nobody from Macao since I left eleven years ago," I said in Portuguese. "I have lived in Goa, in Angola, and in Portugal. I am a salesman from the company of Noronha, da Silva and Cha Pei. We specialize in pulp and paper. I hope to receive an order from the respectable company of Thomas Cook, here, this afternoon!"

I did. It was all planned, set.

"I am a working widow taking my first vacation," she said, and her Portuguese was good as mine. "I married a chain of restaurants in the Hawaiian islands. I come to find new dishes, buy wines, make contracts, find cooks, waiters. It is difficult. If you are lunching here, could we not join? I have an appointment immediately after with the manager of Florian's Cafe. You know it? I think it so beautiful. I shall make one like it in Oahu. It will be a sensation!"

"Of course you speak English?" I said, in the clipped vowels I'd copied. "Hawaii, yes, nojelly?"

"Oh, natchally!" she said, in perfect Chinese American, which is more of the mouth than the tongue. "I lived there eight years. Come on, let's eat, talk same time, whaddya say?"

The young man and woman went somewhere, perhaps to the staff room for their meal, and we had a table at the window, with fresh sweet peas in the vase, a bottle of Soave in the bucket, and the best spaghetti I've had for years. We talked about everything, in six languages and twelve accents, each pulling the other's leg, and I was enjoying myself tremendously, always well within the bounds of Liao Cha Pei, salesman, once of Macao, Goa and Angola, and I saw the slightest occlusion in the light of Druxi's eyes.

A moment, not that, but warning enough.

I turned aside for the waiter, and caught the broad back of Georges Pontvianne going through the door of the smaller room, and in the mirror, a flash of the golden beauty I'd last seen on the musical stairs going up to his office.

"It will take fifteen minutes to walk to my appointment," I said, standing. "I must go upstairs for my case. I am sorry I cannot take coffee. You will please permit me to leave after such a pleasurable meeting?"

"I'm a businesswoman," she said, with all those splendid teeth. "I'm in twenty-nine. Drinks're just as good there as in the bar. Hope we meet later!"

I bowed, she lowered her head, and I left in that jog for the lifts, up to my room, and shuttered windows keeping out flies, a darkness where I fumbled for a moment, and stood still.

A tiny red glow on the dressing table sent a thin blue whiffle away in the draught.

I went closer. A joss stick burned in a glass finger. A long envelope leaned. I reached to switch on a light.

It was by hand, embossed print gave the Gritti

248

Palace, but the superscription was in the most beautiful calligraphy, a perfect rendition of my name, infinitely more graceful, than I'd ever been able to achieve however laboriously, in what, by comparison would be our monkish script, disciplined, taut, scholarly.

I opened it. Had I not been something of a student, I couldn't have read the ideograms on a page of rice paper ribbed and silky, rough-edged from the mill, brushed in black with red uncials—I suppose we'd call them—of honorable address, inviting me to a meeting—a free translation might be a click of tea cups, a Madame Hoc Dang Ky at six of the bell, to honor the memory of Shiao Cha Pei, a scholar, reverend senior, my father, to felicitate his son, placate the Shades, kiss the memory of a mother's small feet, quiet voice, gentle wisdom, now silent, though doubly beautiful in memory's flawed mirror.

I wondered.

I hadn't expected that "things" would happen quite so soon, or quite in this manner. I called the maid, and she came in, bobbed a knee, a big-boned striped-gray-and-white madonna with the fresh smell of clover and the cowbarn behind her. I asked when the envelope had been delivered. She said the page brought it up before she went to lunch at midday, or not more than ten minutes after I had arrived at the hotel.

I didn't like it.

Georges Pontvianne was downstairs, Druxi was somewhere, Madame Feng etcetera was next door, and I, unheralded, get an invitation in about the time it took to go from my room to the terrace? Who knew I'd be there? Who could know Liao Cha Pei, paper salesman?

I took out my cane of brushes and bottle of ink, and wrote an acceptance, sealed it, and gave it to the maid, cow-eyed, watching me as if magic were afoot.

I put in the silk thread traps across the bathroom door and the door of my room, hung out the PLEASE DO NOT DISTURB sign, took my case, and walked down the stairs, out, to the back alleyway, turning right at the end for St. Mark's Square. I climbed the slope of the small bridge by the Bauer-Gruenwald, rested the case on the balustrade to fasten the catch, and made sure nobody was following—most Venetians were enjoying a siesta—and turned left, before the Square's archway, to the office of Thomas Cook & Son.

The contract was ready, the manager was most affable, papers were signed, and I was back in the narrow street in ten minutes. Only the pigeons moved in the Square. Florian's tables were so many colored discs. I wanted to keep out of the hotel for at least an hour. If anyone had a notion to search my room, I made them a gift of ample time. I walked across to the gondola top by the Luna, woke a gondolier, and told him to go behind the Dogana, along the Canal to the turning of the Accademia. I enjoyed the plash of the sweep, the sunlight, the feeling in closed eyes of being someone from the Fifteenth Century going home. The gallery was quiet, two people were in front of me, a man and a woman, German from their speech, and we went through the same rooms at the same distance from each other, standing in front of pictures, looking. I came out without knowing exactly what I'd seen, though the faces, the colors, an aura of mastery and mystery brought me hard up against what was missing in my clerkish, selfish life.

I hadn't time to ponder about it. I took the steamer down to the point at Harry's Bar, and went in for a coffee and cognac. Nobody in the place. A barman came out of the kitchen, and started the vapor. I opened the caes and went through the papers as if they meant something. I dropped a few, so that he could pick them up. I intended him to remember me. I went to the telephone and dialled the Gritti Palace. Neither the Mesdames Hoc Dang Ky, nor Feng Tung Truc were registered at the hotel. I didn't insist. Wealthy clients are protected.

The sun was strong, heat made me sleepy, and the cognac had slightly blunted a feeling of unease. Something—it's no use going against instinct—was piling up somewhere, but I wasn't sure where, or what. Georges Pontvianne had as much right to be in Venice as anyone. He was at least himself. Druxi and I were somebody else. But why, at the same time as ourselves? The Vietnamese? I put it out of mind, jogged back to the hotel, thinking of bed, and at least an hour of superbly dark nothing. The traps, of superfine silk, had been broken. Somebody had been in there. I lay down, quite unworried.

Softly insistent taps on the door woke me, and I turned, looking at evening sun reddish through the shutters. I tied a gown and went over to fiddle with the key. The lock was one of those brutes that require this way and that, stick, push the door, turn, pull the door, stick, rattle, and it seems to open by itself. Bloody thing. That made me realize I'd forgotten who I was supposed to be.

The page went back a foot, wide-eyed, to see my face, but I smiled, which I suppose was worse. I took his package, tipped to bring a healthy grin, and shut the door, looking at Boldi, Florist, and a large red plastic bow. Nobody I knew would send me flowers. I hardly thought Druxi would.

More than anything I wanted a cold shower, and that's what I had. My blue shantung suit was pressed, and I put the links in a starched linen shirt that seemed still warm from the iron. The watch said 5:21. Plenty of time. I poured a drink, pulled the bow apart, took off the lid.

Under the tissue, a small bunch of white sweet peas crinkled delicate petals at me. Under another tissue, a second bunch.

White.

Two bunches of white sweet peas? Nothing accidental about it.

Two bunches of *white*?

In other days, two white anythings, flowers or balls of paper, had always been a signal to drop everything and clear out, get going, don't dally. Danger.

I didn't bother to argue with myself. I threw everything into the suitcase, called Reception for my account, and asked for a porter to take my bag across to the airport for the nine o'clock flight to Rome.

The lift took an age to come up, and seemed to be

deflating a stolid balloon on the way down. The vestibule was quiet. The porter scribbled pinkfaced under a green light at his desk. I went down to the Reception, paid, tipped the page, and asked him to call a gondola. The clock said 5:54.

I showed my envelope to the hall porter, and he reached below for the telephone as though he were putting a hand up my hostess's *cheong-sam*.

"Hall porter!" he said, at the ceiling. "Number thirty three!"

A voice replied, he nodded, and lifted a finger for a page.

"You will please wait, sir, and the secretary of the lady will descend!" he said, apparently well-rehearsed. "It will not be long!"

I lengthened my mouth, squeezed my eyes, jerked my neck, and followed the page up to the mezzanine, left, to a double door.

A drawing room, cool, no sign of use.

I sat down.

My watch said one minute past six.

I lit a cigaret, thought of my life in detail, that is, Liao Cha Pei's life, reeled off the names of our neighbors, my schools, teachers, local headmen opened a window an inch to look down at a side canal, heard the bell strike the quarter.

I strolled down the corridor, turned a corner, found a Service, and went in. An elderly waiter sat, chairlegs back, feet on the sink, smoking, reading a paper.

"Oh, so sorry!" I said, all smiles, note at the ready. "I forgot, please. Which way Madame Hoc Dang Ky, you please? I lost, yes, up, down, no good!"

"They don't know what they're doing downstairs, that's why!" the waiter said, happily taking the note, and thumbnailing the end of the cigaret to drop it in the space between his heel and the shoe. I hadn't seen that done before, but it's intelligent, since it saves a smoke, and prevents a smell in clothing, though I turn from any thought of taking a draw at the fagend. "This way, if you please!"

We went down the way I'd come, up the main staircase, to the left, to the right, to a white door, and he
tapped.

We stood there.

"Always keep everybody waiting, sir!" he whispered.
"I've stood here fifteen minutes at a time, dinner getting
cold, while they're dreaming. Not me. I like my food
hot!"

He tapped again.

We stood there. The corridor held the alien feeling
of a museum after the closing bell.

The waiter tck-tcked.

"Just a moment, sir!" he said. "I'll see if I can get the
other key and go round the side door. Sometimes
they're on the balcony. They can't hear. Keep ringing,
will you, sir?"

He flat-footed away and turned the corner.

I rang twice. Twice again. Silence seemed to buzz.

I tried the handle. It didn't turn.

Suddenly a key cracked, the handle swung down, the
door opened and the waiter ran, shouldering me away
in a violent heave, hobbling, sobbing in a curious lung-
choking squeak to the corner, pushing himself off the
wall and away.

I went in to a dark room, with a window showing
pale evening, a star, a shadowy vase of grey blossom.

I walked between heavy gold and plush furniture, to
a smaller, perhaps a dining room, and on, into the
bedroom. Clothing littered the floor, sheets hung from
the double bed, a broken bottle pointed jagged glints in
the carpet.

Light glossed a naked body. From the shape, a
woman.

I went closer.

I was back in James's office looking at the hologram.

The face was a black mask, beaten flat to the skull.
For a moment I thought of Druxi, but I picked up a
cool hand and made sure it was not. The girl might
have been dead two or three hours, no more.

There was nothing in any drawer, or in the handbags

253

or suitcases, no letters or books. I had no time for a careful search. I didn't want to be caught here.

A light was on in the small kitchenet. The door was still open. I went down the back stair, passed the laundry room, out of the service entrance. The watchman called as I shadowed the window, but a note made him put his bit of Tuscania back, and puff, and I went through the arch, out to the canal, turning right. Two alleys along, I went to the left, counting the doorways. I made sure of the number, rang, and the door swung.

My friend Rinaldo met me at the top of the stair, and pointed to the bathroom.

It took fifteen minutes by my watch to clean my face of stain, take off the wig, remove contacts and teeth, and turn my clothes, including shirt, tie, hat, shoes and raincoat, making me into somebody else called Eric Howard Smeath, with a passport in that name in my pocket. Rinaldo gave me a professional inspection, found I'd forgotten to turn my socks, had me hopping one foot to the other, and finally saw me downstairs and out, with a whispered "Good luck!" as he'd done so many times in other years.

I walked down to the Gritti Palace, filled a pipe going in, went through to the terrace, just in time to hear a police launch scream down, swirl about, and join two more.

"Scotch, and a baby polly!" I told the waiter, looking up weak-eyed in halfmoon specs, between puffs of latakia. "Bring the bottle, will you? I want to see the label!"

" 'sort o'scotch'd you like, sir?" he asked, in copybook Cockney. "We got the lot, here. Black Label do y', sir? Bottled it meself, this morning. Straight out' the canal!"

CHAPTER THIRTY

I watched the come and go of Police, the arrival of gentry whose importance could be gauged by the bows and nods between porters and the manager from landing stage to doorway, listened to the constant ringing of a variety of telephones, the chatter of a gathering crowd in every sort of small boat, and the toll of Santa Maria della Salute's great bell.

I asked no questions. I read the day's Continental editions in English, smoked the pipe till my tongue felt boiled in its own juice, tried again to find Druxi in the name of Ming T'ang Wah, but she wasn't known, took a quiet walk up to 29, as she'd told me, found an empty suite, tried to call Georges, but he wasn't registered at either hotel, and down I went to the bar for another scotch.

I felt a let-down. I'd gone to Venice expecting to find the pairs' oriental hangtail and my son's light o' love, and I was keyed to deal rather sharply. As it was, I didn't want to think about that girl's body. She'd been European, well-cared for, from the perfect finger and toenails, and the short hair, even in that light had been fair.

What really puzzled me was that invitation. Beyond the manager of Thomas Cook's, and perhaps a secretary, nobody except Druxi knew I was going to Venice. I'd had no reservation at the hotel. Had it been full, I'd have gone over to the Lido. Yet, in about fifteen minutes of arrival, I'd had a letter. But the number of the room I'd been taken to wasn't the number Madame Hoc Dang Ky had given. Apart from that, if the girl had been murdered between three and four o'clock, there'd been plenty of time to cancel the visit. I wondered if Druxi had been invited. I was fairly sure that any Chinese visitor would come under suspicion if only because of nationality. Were the women Druxi was after, Feng Tung Truc, and my would-be hostess, Hoc Dang Ky, any relation? What was the murdered girl to either of them?

But the question that burned a hole at the back of my mind, which I wasn't free to examine, and for the moment didn't choose, was wholly concerned with the murderer's identity. Bernard Lane? Joel Cawle? Was one or other in Venice? I didn't want to examine the possibility, but it stuck, worrying as grit on the eyeball.

Quite suddenly, in a stinging sense of error, I knew I'd put myself out of the game. Unintentionally, of course. I was now Mr. Howard Nonsense Smeath, or whatever. But had I not gone there as Liao Cha Pei, would I have got that invitation? Had it been sent purposely to lead me to that room, to link me to the murder? If I hadn't gone there, hadn't hung about, hadn't met the waiter, the body might still be lying there. Meantime, what would have happened to Liao Cha Pei, sitting in the waiting room? Supposing the body had been found without my help, and the Police had come in to question me. Could I have protected my identity? How could I explain a disguise? What might be said in my defence?

I was wide open to the nastiest clout of my career. I saw it coming.

As I sat there, dear Mr. Smeath, tourist, of Durwood, Kent, puffing latakia, bibbling scotch, shoes outwardly rawhide, no heels, inside black horsehide, stylishly Singapore, with heels and rubber tips, what—if I were searched—could I say? How many pairs of socks were blue inside, beige out? How many suits were made to be worn blue one side, beige the other? Raincoat, tweed lining, yes, but a felt hat, brown one side, blue in, with a headband that snapped out to fold in the underbrim, would, I thought, take some explaining. Passport, yes. Fairly safe. That is, until H.M. Consul-General was called in to verify detail, and the Passport Office sent him a reply.

Then?

Debâcle.

There was no defence.

In sudden access of light, it appeared to me that I'd been playing the pairs' game. All they need do was point a finger. They didn't have to appear. Enquiries would do the rest. In my position as Director-General of Overland Holdings and allied companies, what reason could I give for disguise?

That warning light began to glow red. I'd been played as a fat salmon. The pair knew me rather too well. I was wrong man, time, place. But if I sat there, I was finished. I couldn't sustain interrogation. I'd waltzed into it. I heard the foxes yap.

A turn of the head brought the waiter over, and I put down a note.

"They won't let you leave, sir!" he said. "Nobody allowed out. Everybody, one by one. Questions!"

"What's this for?"

"Been a couple of murders, seems like. Can't get the tale right, yet. See they don't let nobody in the place, don't you? Gen'lly, we're skatin' about, this time. Look at us. Ain't even breathin'!"

"Listen to me. We speak the same language. I want nothing to do with this sort of nonsense. I have an appointment in St. Mark's Square in ten minutes. Don't want that mucked up. Let them play their own funny games. How would you like to earn fifty of the best? In fivers?"

He flipped the napkin under his arm, looking across the canal. Water slapped white tatters up the Salute steps, tore them back.

"I'll see the color of 'em, first, sir, you don't mind?" he said, down at me without moving his eyes. "No hard feelings? Know how it works, sir, don't you?"

I fumbled with the wallet under the table, pulled out a wad, bent it, counted, palmed them, put the wallet back, and showed the fanned corners.

He flicked an eye—there's no mistaking five-pound notes—and nodded, still looking through the window.

"At the back of you, sir, turn left, you got the restaurant. Go through that passage, find me waiting. One minute from now!"

A young man and woman in beach clothes sat at a

corner table. I could hear others talking. The barman read a pink paper. I watched the second-hand mark off a minute, put the pipe in my pocket, and walked out, carrying hat and umbrella. The hallporter stood at the doorway, back to me, talking to a group of Carabinieri. I made no sound in the carpet, along the wide corridor. At the end, a door swung. The bar waiter held a long blue overall coat.

"Slip this on, sir!" he whispered, and pointed to a lidded box. "Carry that out and put it alongside the others. Bar's rubbish, that is. Take the coat off, chuck it anywhere. Don't take no notice of nobody. Thank y', sir!"

I crushed the rolled hat in my trouser pocket, gave him the overcoat and umbrella, lifted the box on my shoulder, and walked through the door he held open, passing the white lights of the watchman's box, out, to the darkness of the canalside quay, put the box down with the others, slipped off the coat and hung it over the rail, and walked along to the main way, left, to the station, right to St Mark's.

I went into the bar on the corner for a coffee I thought I deserved.

I tried—I'd have given anything—to walk out backwards. The dorsal width in front of me could belong to none else. Georges Pontvianne stood at the bar talking to a uniformed officer of Carabinieri and two plainclothesmen.

"Coffee, and a Strega, please!" I said, in my Smeath voice, an adenoidal croak-cum-scrape which I was rather proud of. "In a large cup!"

I'd forgotten I'd left the pipe in my overcoat pocket. I went over to the tobacco stand for cigarets, which put me, as I turned away, almost eye-to-eye with Georges. He didn't look at me. He seemed shaking with anger, whispering to the three, all head-down, listening. Whatever he was saying drew short nods, as if they were acknowledging orders.

As I struck a wax match, he stood straight and raised his head. I was appalled at his eyes. He appeared to have been weeping. They were red, murderous. But of all men, Georges was a gentle soul, I'd have said, one of the world's kindliest. It seems ridiculous, but I felt I simply couldn't pass by as I'd intended. I wanted to put an arm round those shoulders, try to cheer him up.

The officer saluted and turned to go out. The policemen followed. Other people in the bar looked across, and away. The barmens' frowns had warned them, though in any case, the Venetian man-in-the-street is curious to a point, and then, in an ancient Roman sense, courteous. He keeps his nose to himself.

But I—I suppose with *my* ancient Roman sense —had to show respect for friendship. Left fist clenched, I patted thumb and index with a flat right hand three times, an unobstrusive, natural gesture not to be remarked except by the knowing eye. Cup off the saucer, about to drink, he paused, put the cup down, took out the handkerchief, blew his nose twice, tucked it back, twice, two deep pushes, pulled down the jacket, tweaked the lapels, picked up the cup, drank.

I tasted the Strega sweetening and cleansing my palate, and walked out, right, toward St. Mark's.

It was a time of Venetian evening I love. A mauve glow burns flagstones and church fronts, lights canal water in deep green, red, and gold, whitens the faces of passersby in the comi-tragic mask of Policinello, dresses them all in those rags and colors, and the Doge reigns again.

Georges caught up with me by the newspaper kiosk outside the Post Office. Thumbs sagging jacket pockets, I gave him my number, bought a couple of papers, he bought Punch, and we turned together, strolled down to the further arch, under the arcade, to the cafe, and took a table not quite in the open, fairly dark, and close enough to the band to drown talk.

"I haven't time to discuss anything properly," he said. "I've lost an agent. A wonderful girl. I don't think you met her. She'd been working outside. That's why we were caught at disadvantage. I didn't get her report until last night. That she was here, that is. I came in this morning. Any idea where Druxi is?"

"She was here at lunchtime—"

"I've been trying to find her. I don't know what to say to the girl's parents. 'Your daughter has been murdered. We shall pay a sum in compensation?' Mh? Is that it? And the murderer?"

He lifted those huge shoulders, let them slump. I knew the reason for red eyes.

"You have nothing to tell me?" he said, more statement than question. "Can you believe there have been a dozen Asiatics of one type or another on this little mudbank for the past two days, and they can't find *one* of them? Eight servants between them, passports checked, hotels paid for, and they vanish?"

"By sea?"

He raised an eyebrow. It was almost a shrug.

"What do I care? They've gone. My girl was killed in the most brutal manner. I assure you, if I rest my fingers on the one guilty, I will not permit one bone to stay in place! I pray to know what to say to her father!"

While I watched the strollers under the arcade, my mind had been reaching.

"This girl hadn't been working in Switzerland, had she?" I asked. "No link to the pair, for example?"

Elbows on the arms of the chair, he cradled his fingers and looked at me, nodding.

"So you are out of the business, mh?" he said, waiting for the sodawater to pour and lifting a thumb for enough. "I shall tell you. She *had* been working in Switzerland, and there was also a link to the pair. Someone we would like to harvest, ah, with such hospitality!"

"An assistant mathematics tutor to the daughters of wealthy families?"

"I know it. But the people my little girl was determined to take, where are they? It is extremely difficult for them to appear as any of us. They may pretend themselves Mongol. But not Caucasian. It is one advantage we enjoy. What, then are we to surmise? I shall

260

not waste time with catalog. Can we ignore the fact that more than a dozen people of another part of the world, instantly recognizable, turn into air?"

"They could have gone by ship?"

"The Italian Navy and Air Force is as good as any other. There was at most three hours for them all to leave. Apparently they took nothing with them. It's all in their rooms. Nothing very much. Nothing of use to us. Only two ships left in the past four hours. Both were searched. Nothing. No other thing floating escaped. Roads, cars, trains, planes, nothing. What is the inescapable conclusion?"

I pretended to be daft.

"They might have gone underground here?"

"Over a dozen of them?"

"What's the inescapable et cetera?"

"They established their own theatre!"

"Eh?"

His stare was a wide-eyed blank.

"No more Chinese or Vietnamese or Annamese than we are!" he said. "Any of them. They washed paint off, stuffed wigs in the toilet, and walked out. By this time, they are on their way all over Europe. Who should we look for?"

I raised my glass.

"Perhaps that's what the girl had found out," I said. "Didn't have time to pass it on?"

"She got through late last night to say where she believed she was going. That's why I am here. Of course, we can't act as if we ruled creation. I had to wait. An empty barrel on the beach. And what? Disaster!"

"Any idea who the murderer might have been?"

"None. But, Edmund, what horror has escaped from hell, these days? What has our life become, I ask? Crimes of passion, drunken crimes, crimes of robbery, very well. But this deliberate extirpation of the human being in such a way, this premeditation, this cold destruction of beauty? I forget how to speak. What shall I tell her father? Her mother. How are they to attend the funeral? How shall they be shown the body? *There is no face!"*

Through a vision of the mask in the hologram, and the other that evening, with memory of the weight of a curled, cool hand, I heard the Campanile's bell strike the hour. Georges lifted his drink to go.

"No news of Lane?"

"Nothing!"

"Any detail on Alethea Cawle?"

"No more than you know. The young woman's had training. She's done well. She's clever, apparently. Druxi put me on to it. That's why my girl was there. A little over a month. But there's no proof that this tutor was in fact Alethea Cawle. None. She's supposed to drive to her mother's house outside Basle. Does she? No. She takes the train to Geneva. Last night, she came here. But where *is* she? With the Chinese?"

"I wish I could see a pattern anywhere. Where is this place?"

"The convent? Terrible hole. In the mountains. Cold as hell. Nearest habitation is a farm that supplies them with dairy produce. The bus stops just below the village. Kretzwoche. You walk the rest. The convent's strictly *clausura*. They don't permit visitors. There's an auberge in the village. But it wouldn't be found in Michelin-"

"Kretzwoche? Near Basle?"

"Well, reasonably. The road's a horror. You go via Grossenbalde, turn at the bridge, up the mountain. Why? Thinking of a visit?"

I nodded to the waiter.

"Just time for the other half. I'm leaving immediately. I suppose you've checked the area? Maps? Ever hear of a place called Kretzgros?"

"Of course. That's the name of the farm, there. How do you know?"

"Finish this, and walk to the boatpoint, there. Let me regale you!"

CHAPTER THIRTY-ONE

I hadn't a notion what position Tengler held—I couldn't see him in a dark morning—and I didn't bother to ask. He simply told Mohr he was ready, and to lead on, and when we reached the convent of St. Ursula of the Snows, he presented a letter which opened the gates and put us in the waiting room. That, for those who know what *clausura* means, is a little piece of magic.

The convent must have been an old castle. We couldn't see much when we got there because of the mist, but inside, with a fire in the chimney a dozen of us could have stood in, tapestries on the walls, high-backed leather chairs, slate-flagged floor, a long table with a wooden dish piled with clove-stuck oranges—I hadn't seen pomanders since my grandmother died—it was bleakishly comfortable, though the atmosphere "seemed" against us, as if resenting our sex.

"Extraordinary, if you consider all this was built by a religion of the soul!" Tengler said suddenly, in excellent English, and surprised me. "No other civilization except ours takes care of something without proof in so many different ways. Nobody else cares about the soul. We're beginning not to. I ask myself why? I don't know. Just grown out of it? Let everybody do as they wish. Seems to be the modern way? And in ten years, what is 'modern?'"

"They certainly have a feeling for protection," Mohr said. "Children especially. I don't know how many girls they've got it here. All ages. All done something. Put away. And the nuns, they've left it all outside. Even when they're dying, they won't let a doctor look at them, I mean, properly. All he comes up here for is sign the death certificate. He was telling me. Nobody's ever been known to leave those gates, once they're in. We're an exception!"

"Obedience!" Tengler said. "Matter of fact, it's the same with the Russians or the beehive. The top says what it's to be. Do as you're told or suffer. Minute you let things go, finish!"

"Where d'you draw the line?" I asked. "Here, it's all lines. In my business, there are certainly lines. Drunkenness, late on the job, absence, so many things aren't allowed. Or a business can't survive. Looked at from that point of view, it's also, in a way, protection of a kind of soul, don't you think?"

"Depends on what a soul is," Tengler said, and sat nearer the tremendous blaze of logs. "I suppose I could smoke? Blow it up the chimney, won't hurt, will it?"

"Join you," Mohr said, and stood under the cowl. "Did you ever see such a road, coming up here? I didn't know there was anything like it in the country!"

"Part of the scene," Tengler said, and lit from a twig. "Imagine this, even a few years ago. You'd come up by coach. Take you three days from Kretzwoche. Now try to escape!"

"Hard life," Mohr said. "They're very hard on themselves, I think. They've got the idea pleasure's a sin. Is it?"

"It's like the word soul," Tengler said. "You've got to specify your terms. Then you're among the philosophers. And *they* don't seem to know what they're talking about, either!"

"More you look at it, the more of a mess it starts being," Mohr said. "I made up my mind, I'm going to do what I've got to, and potter along in my own way till I drop out. I think that's the only way. Rest of it's a waste of energy, if you want my opinion!"

"No after life?" I said. "These people here, and more outside, all wasting energy?"

Tengler had to bend to look at me, one side of his face gold in flamelight with a touch on the bald spot, a gilded gash in a line under the eye socket to the jaw. Small grey eyes glinted laughter, with a touch of malice.

"I've never seen any sense discussing it!" he said. "Hindus talk about reincarnation. Buddhists, trans-

264

migration. When I was a youngster, I read them all. And what? We talk of the life to come, hell, and all the rest of it. All right. So far's I'm concerned, we'll know when we get there. That'll be the right time to do something about it. Or it'll be a bad job. This moment, there isn't enough proof about anything to convince a ten-year-old. As they are today, anyway. Take them to church, let them decide later. That's what we do!"

"All right," Mohr said. "Why take them to church, then?"

"I think it makes them cleaner people, more character, stronger later on," Tengler said. "More discipline, even that much, gives them a better chance, anyway. Does them no harm. It—"

The door opened wide, silently.

A veiled nun in black, a ghost in that shadow, raised the flat of a hand to Tengler, and turned for the door.

"Does that mean all of us?" he asked.

Again she raised her hand—under the veil—to him, and turned to walk out.

"You ought to come too!" he said, to me. "It's your business!"

The nun raised that hand.

Tengler shook his head, and followed her, and another shadow reached in to shut the door.

"Give you the creeps!" Mohr said, and pulled the chair nearer the fire. "This helps, though. I think we've had a useful morning, sir? If he's not long, it won't be late when we get back. Do it in three hours. That was a good dinner she gave us down there. Haven't had a piece of boiled ham like that for years. How do you see this thing being used, sir? I mean, the innards. You think Tengler's right, saying it's a 200-pound bomb?"

He looked at me sideways, hands over his mary, feet out, comfortable. He was one of those men who look fat and aren't. He was solid muscle. I'd seen him use it that morning, to the eternal surprise of Kretzmolle's owner, Roltvich, and three of his men, in lifting a metal cradle they'd found, and forcing it open, something they hadn't been able to do, and they said they'd tried.

The cradle had nothing in it. They'd seen it at the pond's edge when the cattle went down to pasture.

I was deeply shocked. I hadn't expected to find anything. The flimsy in the file which Prince Abdullah had given me was genuine. We knew that a bale *had* been flown from Ehrplatz to Bell's Fosse. The cradle we'd found, painted olive green with a red band, was proof that a drop *had* been made, at the time, date and place. What was I to say in rebuttal? The bale had "disappeared" on the night Commodore Kopfers had issued an order not to accept a paradrop instruction. At a new field, where people hadn't been working long enough to know each other's names, a Holtby, odd instructions, and defiance of Customs were possible, though not any longer. It was no solace to me.

"Why didn't you report this at the time?" Mohr asked Roltvich, worn, shrivelled, in patched leather jacket and trousers, an almost mauve face, rheumy grey eyes, shifty between the three of us as the swifts under the eaves outside. "Couldn't you see this was military property?"

"What's it doing up here, then?" Roltvich yelped, in ageing falsetto. "If they want to leave things about, does that mean I got to lose a day's work, telling them something they know?"

"What time did you hear the plane?" Tengler asked, in sabre-cut German, that took the grins off their faces. "Make up your minds!"

That was when the women joined in. Their voices were shriller than the men's, but not one of them seemed to have got it right. Two in the morning, till past six, all shouting at once, all in fine kitchen argument.

I looked on, wondering where it could lead

Farming people know the time without looking at a clock. Kopfers had told me it was bright moonlight, and flight time over the drop would have been 4:38.

Until then, Tengler and I had only shaken hands, and his car had followed ours. I'd wanted to go to the convent to find out about Miss Alethea Cawle and Kretzgros, generally, and Mohr had said that an official would come with us because the place was on the border, touchy, out of common bounds.

In that bucolic wrangle—I was reminded of a Breughel interior—Tengler looked at me and gathered what I was thinking. Till then, I hadn't said a word except in English, and Mohr translated. Nobody knew I spoke German.

"You have perhaps something to say, sir?" he said, and his frown stopped Mohr's translation. "You find the soup a little uncooked, perhaps?"

"They're lying," I said. "Find out who brought it here, and how much they paid!"

Nobody, so far, had mentioned any payment.

Even Tengler was surprised, and frowning, he turned away from me, and threw the question over their heads. Eyes went one to another. Roltvich began in gulps of self-righteous nonsense, and a few joined in. They'd obviously rehearsed the story, but not the denial. Tengler leaned on the umbrella—I noticed it was in perfect furl—looking up at the hams and sausage hanging from the beams. He, Mohr and myself, in felts, overcoats and carrying umbrellas, were ridiculously out of place. Part of the malaise of our time.

One by one they stopped talking, eyes down, fidgety.

"Well, then!" Tengler said, dryly bright. "Perhaps you'd rather talk to the Police? You'll all go together, of course. Who's going to look after this place while you're away?"

"Wait, sir, please!" Mrs. Roltvich said, both forefingers erect, a sensible woman. "We don't want any trouble. No need for it. I heard the thing come over this way"—she pointed to a spot about 40 degrees off our flight plan, I was reassured to see—"and I called down. I was just getting up. It was almost half-five. The woman slept in that chair. The men were in the barn. Three of them. She ran out before I got down here. There was plenty of light. They had the truck down there at the gate. That thing you found, that was in it when they came. I went down to get the eggs while they had supper, and I saw it. So did he—!"

Roltvich lifted stubby hands, turning away.

"All right!" he said, wearily. "All I wanted to do was make some *sbrinz,* no? A few more cattle—"

"Name of the woman?" Tengler said, head on one side.

"Down there at the convent. Name's Tauperman. Came in here, couple-three weeks ago, said friends of hers were climbing the mountain, so they wanted to drop the tents and heavy stuff because here's the flattest place. Just in case of damage, hitting an animal or something, she'd pay five thousand francs. We wouldn't have to do anything. Only keep the mouth shut. I said yes!"

"Number of the truck?"

"Didn't see it!"

"Get yourself ready to welcome the Police!" Mohr said. "I advise you to milk your memories, friends. Save blood!"

I'd been trying to decide, ever since, if a drop was made by another aircraft—I felt I had to believe Mrs. Roltvich—and the cradle left there to incriminate the Company. If copies of our flight documents were in possession of the Swiss authorities, then, had Kopfers not asserted his command, there might have been gravest difficulty in making a case for defence.

But where had the "bale" gone which had disappeared from Bell's Fosse with somebody called Holtby? If it *had* contained the Barnbruche warhead, what had since happened to it? Had the aircraft Mrs. Roltvich heard dropped it, and the cradle we'd found put in its place?

I didn't know how to answer Mohr.

James Morris had told me that the detonator and warhead together weighed about thirty pounds, which didn't sound much of a size. But if, as I'd imagined, it might conceivably be used to destroy Beyfoum, why bring it to Switzerland?

"I'm not sure what to say," I said. "What could they do with it, here?"

"Always a big market for something new, sir," Mohr said. "Take that sort of thing to pieces. Photograph it all. Give a team of men and women a little piece each. Send them to places outside the country. Gather them all in one place at odd times. That's how it's done. If it's right, you don't have to look for a buyer!"

"There's *still* somebody in the head office, sir!" I heard Berry saying, angrily, tiredly, again. "The Holtbys last just long enough to do the damage. Whoever it is, they're making mugs of us!"

The wide door swung in without a sound.

The nun held out a hand—under the veil—to me. Tengler stood behind, in the darkness.

I went out, the nun shut the door, and we followed her to a dark staircase, up three flights, to a long corridor, turned left, to one longer, and went almost to the end, and a door.

A breath of incense and candlewax teased.

The nun lifted the right hand, pointing to a slip in a polished brass holder, in Gothic capitals M. R. TAUPERMAN and put a key in the lock, opened the door to a small white room, a narrow bed with a rolled mattress, a prie-dieu with a crucifix, a small table with a washbowl and ewer, a larger table with a chair, and on the slats of the bed, a knotted bundle.

"Open that," Tengler said. "Examine the contents!"

I unknotted, threw back the ties, and found a rag-tag of soap ends, dusters, an almost bald nailbrush, a towel without label, laddered stockings, a cotton reel, a used tube of toothpaste, an empty jar of face cream, a down-at-the-heel pair of sandals, cotton cleaning gloves, a chewed pencil, a ball point refill, a little pile of torn up paper—which Tengler took over to the table and tried to put together—and the most interesting exhibit of the lot, so far as I was concerned, a small piece of blotter, glazed on one side, with the advertisement of my bank in Zurich, asking clients to save and offering 4 percent per annum.

The dress had torn away from the zipper. It seemed fairly new. A perfume came from it, a little too tenuous to be caught whole, but different from the soap ends. Perfume? In that type—or any type—of convent? It seemed curious. The sandals were handmade, well used, and I found the faint inked maker's number on the inside of the arch.

"Letter from London, West two," Tengler said, and pointed toward an envelope almost entire. "The woman's careless!"

It was an ordinary envelope, by air, regular postage, addressed to Miss M. R. Tauperman.

I was startled by the handwriting, large, clear, I suppose what we'd call Germanic. I thought I knew it. I couldn't place it.

"Not much to go on," I said, playing down.

"I've seen a lot less than this come up for twenty years hard labor!" Tengler said, with every satisfaction. "Whoever this is, take it from me, she's new. We take the lot?"

"Of course," I said, and folded everything, knotted corners. "How do people like this get a job here? Doesn't anyone make enquiries?"

"I saw the paper downstairs. Seamans' Mission, Hamburg. She'd been employed there, wanted a month's retreat. The Bishops there and here did the rest. Innocently, of course. They have great difficulty in getting suitable staff. And she was very able. Well-bred, devoted to work, popular with her pupils, nearsighted, short, strong personality, wart on the right side of the nose, large teeth, sense of humor, but restrained. And deeply religious. As you see from the dress and stockings, quite tall, slim. Very careless!"

"How did you get the details?"

"We've already been in touch with Hamburg. Miss Tauperman was in the fifties, short, 48-52, and went to Africa some months ago. They think, Lambrene. We're enquiring. Obviously, this job was planned carefully for a long time. It fits. But the detail is careless. There should be no cloth, no knots, no pieces of soap!"

"Could I telephone London from here?"

"Of course. This is a mountain emergency call station. We're up on the northern border, you know. Come with me!"

This time, the nun came behind us. We went down the stair, to a long room, brightly lit. Three operators in grey veils sat at the switchboards. A fourth, at a desk, took my calls to Consuelo, Berry and Argyopoulos, and I offered Tengler a cigaret. Before I could take the match from him, my call to Berry came in at box two.

I took the sandals out of the bundle, read off the number, described the leather and style, and told him to find out which shoemaker used that serial.

Argyopoulos came in as if he were down in the village.

"Sir, I am desperately sorry!" he said. "The two cases addressed to Mr. Logan, we re-routed to Geneva. They should be there now. I can't get through for the moment."

"Airline?"

"Olympic, sir. In the name of Miss Toverell, as you said in your telegram!"

"Was the telegram in Company code?"

"Yes, sir!"

"Sent from London?"

"Yes, sir. Signed Eoptic. Correct, sir?"

"Correct. I'll get back to you!"

Somebody had made a grievous error.

Eoptic, cablese of my initials, was known only to my personal office staff, Consuelo, Miss Burrows, Miss Greig, Miss Toverell, Robarts, in the Legal Department, Berry, and the six European office managers. Its use meant that I was making a direct request apart from Company business. The message was invariably in code, not the Company's, and each office had a book in the safe. The cable could only have been written by someone with access. Moreover, my operators in London would not accept any message without authorization, and that could come only from my office.

I got back to Berry, and explained in detail.

"Pulls the strings very tight, that does!" he said. "All

right, sir. The shoes. I picked it up first one out of the box. Lobb St. James's Street. They got it right away. Sandals were made four years ago. Name's Angela Masters, address—"

"Angela *what?*"

"Angela Masters, sir. Heronbury Grange, Leicester. Right, sir? Anything wrong?"

CHAPTER THIRTY-TWO

The Kretzmolle casing, as I'd thought, wasn't part of the warhead stolen from Barnbruche.

The telegram, relayed by Army Signals, lay on the table.

Dr. Buders, my attorney in Europe, Dr. Dessier, the bank director, Inspector Mohr, General Tengler—of the Intelligence Branch, we'd found, of the Federal Army—and Luis Monners, a counsellor at the Foreign Ministry, sat in conference on the top floor of our office building in Geneva, waiting, while I spoke to Consuelo from the glass annexe.

She'd tried to be diplomatic, but I caught the note in her voice and asked questions. Ob refused to go to Banbury Cross. He'd let Patti go until she and the baby were fit to join him in Lagos. His excuse had been pressure of business. But in fact, and Consuelo had forced it out of him, he didn't like the idea of going to Jamaica and "pretending to live a white man's life."

Consuelo caught his tone exactly.

"Another form of 'racism' or a quirk of his own?"

"Patti told me he'll have nothing to do with Negroes in the Commonwealth or the United States. He says dealing with them complicates life. She wouldn't say any more. She knows a lot more than she tells. I don't mind that. I'm thinking of flying them off tomorrow afternoon. Am I still having dinner with you?"

"I'm flying in half an hour. Did you get tickets for something?"

"Of course. The newest. Message in from Superintendent Berry. There's no record here of any radio message sent to the Athens office on that day or time, or with your signature. Nothing else that mentions Olympic Airways or the Athens office. His enquiry is proceeding. Second. He's been in touch with Angela Masters' mother. Angela's in Sicily, staying with an aunt. She left Gillian and Errol in Barcelona about a week ago. They were going to Madrid. She doesn't remember whether she gave the sandals away. Three. Sir Chapman Ryder of the Canal Banking Syndicate called to say that the purchase—doesn't say what of—is final, and the consignment is being flown to Zurich, but he's not sure when. The amount, he says, is authorized by the Prince Abdullah and others, and that a future purchase is expected and being prepared for. He emphasized that neither your name nor the Company's is mentioned in connection. Four. Mr. Denis Lincoln says the London office will be quite ready for work on Monday next, and the model of the Beyfoum township is ready, and so is he and the construction company. Five. Just in. Message from the Constantinople office. Blagarov called Iskanderum. No passengers aboard. No Bakasz among the crew. Airline offices blank. It's signed Kober. That's all!"

"Well done!"

"Would this mean the Blur got to work?"

"You pays your penny. That's all. Tell Berry I'm anxious about that Athens telegram. It's a key!"

I went back to the table.

"Sorry for the interruption," I said. "The shoes didn't belong to the Tauperman woman. Where she got them from, we'll have to find out. It's easy to 'plant.' Question is why? I hope to get a full report by tomorrow anyway. That should be the end of it!"

"It might even be the beginning!" Tengler said, quietly. "I have already given the opinion that this girl, whoever she is, is not trained. Nothing here is professional. Small things. Small? She is twenty or thirty years younger. This piece of blotting paper, here. It has two kinds of ink. Two colors. She uses a fountain pen, thick nib, one, and another, perhaps an ordinary pen. At the school, possibly? It is being studied. We have specimens of her writing in the pupil's notebooks, and her reports. There are also a few distinguishable letters on the blotter, and some figures. We are looking into it. The comb gave us enough samples to decide the color of the natural hair, and the dye. The towel was used for cosmetics. We know which. The dress has been dry-cleaned many times. The marks are there. We shall find the companies. The sandals give an impress of the foot, or feet. I shall demonstrate the plaster casts. The Bishop in the Grossenbalde diocese, naturally, is outraged. I don't know about his Hamburg colleague. He says that the matter was conducted by correspondence, the woman presented herself and she was accepted. Her forms gave her age as thirty-two, schools, University, home address. The *real* Miriam Amelie Tauperman was Alsatian. She spoke French and German with that accent. The other didn't. The Mother Superior had no fault to find with her. She said, with great feeling, that she was an excellent teacher, and they would miss her. Unfortunately, we find no record of this woman entering the country. She visited a supposed sister in Geneva each week. We cannot trace the address. Of course, a convent lives in terms of generations. Everyday matters are only spaces between one Mass and the next!"

"Who is this woman, Tauperman?" Mohr asked. "That's the basis of the matter. Who's behind her?"

So far, I hadn't mentioned the pair. My Xth sense was at work. Other people didn't think as I did, and moreover, didn't have any problems. I trusted Tengler, but mention of Lane or Cawle could put the Company under surveillance. I had to be careful, above everything, not to jeopardize our interest, and more importantly, my usefulness.

It was the moment to open the despatch case, and give Tengler the El Bidh file, a slim steel job with a special key. I saw his surprise.

"It begins here," I said, showing the blue flimsy. "That paradrop instruction was made entirely without authority. Luckily, we have an ex-KLM commodore. He refused the order, and as you see here, he put it off the aircraft and issued this order to our pilots. No paradrops anywhere in Europe. This is the storeman's note that the bale was taken off the Company register, and trucked out that morning, to Kings Cross. It's a rail terminal. This certifies that no bale was received there, and this is a declaration by H.M. Customs that no bale of this description appears on the Company's books. We don't deny that a bale *was* flown from Ehrplatz to Bell's Fosse. That's a subject of enquiry by the German police. We deny categorically that the casing picked up here was flown by a Company aircraft!"

"Let us for a moment accept all this," Tengler said, holding up the file. "Why is your Company used? Why not another?"

"Because, I suppose, we were flying a consignment of tubing over a period of weeks from Ehrplatz, near Neussen, in West Germany to Genoa for shipment to Lebanon. The flight line we're allowed passes over the Kretzmolle farm and almost over the convent. If we accept the blame, is there any need to look further for a culprit?"

"Do you suspect anyone in your Company?"

"The intelligence section is in charge of Chief Superintendent Berry, late of Scotland Yard. There are suspects. But we have to be excessively careful. We're looking for bigger fish!"

Tengler's small grey eyes were acutely bright, quite without humor.

"The original warhead is what I'm most interested in!" he said, quietly. "Is that what was taken to Kings Cross and didn't get there? What happened to it?"

"Why not get in touch with Scotland Yard? They're handling the matter. They've known from the moment I did. And they're not less interested. They think it may have been flown in a light aircraft to Northern Ireland. West Coast. It's quieter. Transferred to a larger plane and flown where? That's the line they're working on. Mrs. Roltvich said that a plane *did* come in at just before six that morning—you'll remember she pointed to an area well away from our flight plan—and *did* drop something which the men took away in the truck. Are we stretching anything if we surmise that was it?"

Tengler nodded, tapping the file on his knee, looking out at the lake, greygold in raincloud.

"A woman, three men, and a truck," he said. "What would they do with a projectile? I need hardly tell you there's strictest vigilence at all points of departure. This isn't an easy country to get anything in. It's *very* difficult to get anything out!"

Nobody moved. Monners seemed asleep.

"The Mother Superior told me a couple of interesting things," he said, reaching for his overcoat. "She didn't agree that this woman should leave the convent during what was supposed to be a retreat. But she said she was having medical treatment, and she sometimes left in midweek. This was perhaps to keep in contact outside? She always came back at night. That's a very bad road for anybody to drive up. Points to courage, at any rate. The other thing is, she got on everybody's nerves playing on a dummy keyboard, but she wouldn't play for the Services. So there was a little feeling about *that*. Well, now. If Inspector Mohr's coming with me, I'll give him a receipt for this file. It will have to be seen by others in my department, of course. No objection?"

"None!"

I saw them out to the lift and went back to find Breguet serving coffee. Dr. Buders stood at the window, talking to Dessier. Monners hadn't moved.

"Tengler'll have a copy of this when he gets back," he said, lifting an envelope. "I didn't want to say anything while he was here. We prefer to keep things in airtight compartments, if you understand me?"

"Perfectly. I had a few years of official life!"

"It's a report from our investigators at Basle. About the Cawle estate. It's taken them some time. The place hasn't been lived in for the past year or more. The family hasn't been seen. Wages for the caretaker and gardener are paid through a lawyer, here. He gets a yearly cheque. The last, last month, from Paris. That account belongs to a legal firm. They got it from Tunis, paid against Intramed S.A. Enquiries are going on. In your report, you say that this Tauperman woman went every week-end to this house. That information must be wrong, surely?"

"Wouldn't surprise me!"

The dark eyes watched me without expression.

"Do I infer that you feel there's a link between this Tauperman woman and the Cawle family? We know, of course, who *he* is!"

"I should have thought of the theft, and the circumstances. I must say I'm profoundly disappointed. I'd thought we had a strong lead. But if she didn't go there—and she *must* have been followed, or there couldn't have been a report—then where *did* she go? Is there another Cawle property in Basle? In another name?"

"It's all being thoroughly looked into. In this other matter, of the consignment of gold. I understand five companies bought. What is your query, there?"

"I only want to know about the number of boxes going to our bank. I don't want them mixed with the Company's property. They might well be, because the Prince Abdullah and his associates are my Company's principal shareholders. You saw in my report that canard about our buying gold to pay for Israeli aircraft? I want to know the number of boxes, officially, by Customs entry, and I want them identified, and set completely-apart. They have nothing to do with me!"

"Should be simple enough!" he said, and got up. "I'll call later?"

"I think you have a point about the boxes in the vault," Dr. Buders said. "Things can get badly mixed up. In book entries alone. I've known it!"

"Ah, to the devil!" Dessier said, normally a staid member, never much to say, as if he'd retired to permanent isolation behind a long grey beard. "Everybody talks inessentials. I'm very worried about this Barbruche thing, whatever it is. I didn't like Tengler's attitude, I know him far too well!"

"He seemed to accept what I said?"

"You don't know Tengler!"

"Are you thinking of leaving the country?" Buders asked, suddenly. "It might be difficult!"

"I intend to leave in ten minutes!"

"I wouldn't waste any time if I were you!" Buders said. "And don't attempt to use the Company plane, will you? I fear it won't be available. There's been a violation of air space, to begin with."

"Not by this Company!"

"Proof?"

I looked at two men of entirely different personality, though curiously, both pairs of eyes held the same light.

"You can't think I had anything to do with this affair, surely?"

"Remains to be seen!" Buders said, with restraint. "But we, your colleagues, are placed in a most uncomfortable position. If you are arrested, it will be on a Federal warrant. There, I am helpless. I can only plead Law. The rest must wait, pending the formulation of a charge. I advise you to leave while you are able!"

"I'm damned!" I said. "Never thought it possible!"

"You don't know what other information Tengler may have!" Dessier said. "I told you. I know him. He'd arrest all of us. Only on suspicion. It's enough!"

"That's my worry!" Buders said, nodding. "How do we defend ourselves?"

Breguet paused in the doorway.

"Sir," he said. "An urgent call from London in your office. The caller doesn't want to be switched through here. Mr. Berry, sir!"

"Pardon!" I said, and hurried, shut the door, switched on the scrambler.

"Yes, Berry?"

"I'm afraid this is a bit of bad, sir. That message, signed Eoptic? I just talked to Clissold, the chief operator. He'd been taking his two days off. He says he sent that message. It was brought up by Hanley. The office runabout? Yes, well, I got hold of him. That message was given him by Miss Burrows, and I've—"

"Miss Burrows?"

"I knew you'd be upset, sir. She hasn't been in the past three days. Sent in a medical certificate. I just sent a man to see the doctor. He can't be found. Nobody at that address. And she's left the place she was staying at. No trace. Nothing there. But that envelope you sent by wire photo, sir—"

"Yes?"

"Same handwriting, looks like. I've sent it to Tilley, the expert. I believe she knew I was near putting her to rights. She knew I got some details from the school she said she went to. Mrs. Trothe's here, sir. Like a word—"

"Thank you, Berry!"

"Edmund? I'm absolutely spun-dry!"

"I can well imagine it—"

"But listen. I'm *the* most. When I was putting that El Bidh file together—"

"Yes?"

"Well, I hadn't really been in the office for ages, just in and out, now and again. I went in the girl's room—very few of us use it—and found her doing something extraordinary to her face. I thought she was taking her teeth out, or something, but I simply wasn't using the turnip. I thought of it after Mr. Berry told me. I got Mummy to send up my school album. There's one of me with the junior girls. There's no doubt whatever. You can't do much about a profile. She always wore wigs. Well, who doesn't? But if you really *look* at her, and then *think*—because I always felt I'd met her before, though she told me she came from Rhodesia, and went to school in Dehra Dun—well, there can't be a doubt about it. This photograph's enough—"

"What are you talking about?"

"The highly efficient and most charming Miss Deirdre Martine Burrows, late, I regret to say, of this office, and of my own school, and all sorts of other giddy heights, including Washington—"

"Just a moment—!"

"That's right. We've been paying Alethea Cawle!"

CHAPTER THIRTY-THREE

The Brecht play first-night seemed to have brought everything out of the tank, including, I suppose, us. I never saw so many odd get-ups, from turtle neck jerseys worn with dinner jackets to embroidered mechanic's overalls, quite a number of young women in dresses of filmy stuff which showed their breasts, and one, in a lengthy mink coat, with nothing underneath. She'd thrown the collar back from her shoulders, and put a hand under, I suppose to assure herself that things were still, as it were, *en place*. The delectable sequin-spangled thrix I saw could hardly have been anything else. Her partner, in a mauve velvet nehru, trousered in jute, seemed to notice little except *his* spangled mop in the mirror.

Consuelo looked at me, widest, bluest, blankest.

"I feel dreadfully old, wizened, and completely *not!*" she whispered. "I'm ancient *stuff*. Next time, I'll appear in a mini-apron. Or a mini-bib might do it. But darling, tell me. When the goods are so much exposed to the weather *and* to the naked eye, is there still a spell?"

"There certainly is. Here, anyway!"

"I'm disappointed. I'd thought yours a far nobler nature?"

"It's embarrassingly noble, at times. In fact, positively Morte d'Arthur. Except when it's shoved in my face. Then, I confess, I revert. After all, these are the basics. As you see for yourself, agog's the word!"

"Then I may go home?"

"No, my darling. If you took *your* clothes off, they wouldn't be standing about like this. Turn round, now. Slowly. Look at the tall, fair man, over there, left hand side of the doors. Tall girl in black with him. That's the Graf Von Staengl. I'll stay here. Go over and give that attendant a note. Find out where he's sitting. I have a feeling I know that girl. Have a close look at her!"

Von Staengl's long waves in a fair head glowed in the lights. He wore evening dress and an order flashed under his collar. The girl with him seemed to me someone I'd met, but she was oddly flittery. I couldn't think of a name. She wore a black stole which at that distance seemed part of her smooth head. The long black dress fell in a line which spoke of Yves St. Laurent. Consuelo had almost the same thing in pale amethyst. Together, standing for a photograph, they made a couple from another world, not old-fashioned, but rather a new or newer fashion, absolutely distinct from the paintfaces, odd skelets, and rag bags round about.

I stood in shadow, under the portieres, and took three good double heads with the telelens in the Minox. Consuelo came back, followed by the stares of the more discerning. She was worth a stare. Her great advantage, at distance—and it didn't by any means become a disadvantage nearer to—was a height of leg from heel to thigh rather longer than from thigh to shoulder. It made her seem taller, slimmer. The waist, on better days, I could almost span, a toucher, no more, and the rest was flat where it ought to be, round where it should, and my idea of all perfection.

"You're looking at me in *that* way," she said, eyebrows up, eyes down, everything over on one side, pulling her gloves, redbrick virgin, one lid stuck. "Can't you think of *any*thing else?"

"I'm thinking of about a little over an hour ago, *a deux*. Perfectly willing to go home. Better play there, I'll bet you!"

"I want to see the first act of this. They're supposed to be naked. I've never seen more than two naked people at a time. One of them was me, in the glass. When d'you suppose they'll share an apple in public?"

"Give it time. They'll need at least four casts for a week's work, I should think. Where's Von Staengl?"

"In a box. He won't be able to see us. I don't know the girl. Curious looking creature, close to. A little scraddly-raddly, I thought. But quite smart. Shall we?"

We got to our box just before the lights went down.

282

Von Staengl was far right from us, unseen. The stage was below us, and when the curtain went up, we weren't far above the actors' heads. I prefer a stall about halfway up the aisle, where I can't see the grease-paint.

I couldn't get "in" to the action. Whether the translation didn't quite fit the German or not, I don't know. It seemed arid. The actors didn't look comfortable. Apart from that, I was too engrossed in my own business to pick up the theme, or in any way empathize with what went on. It's not quite the way to go to the theatre.

That's not altogether why I'd gone there. Consuelo didn't know, but Berry had reported Von Staengl was in London to present an award for a Brecht play and would like to talk to me. I didn't want to see him in public, still less invite him to the office or the flat. I'd asked Consuelo to change the musical tickets for the Brecht with a promise I'd take her next time, and there we were.

I leaned back, listening to the voices, trying to follow. I believe that all problems have a solution, given brain and patience, and often, patience is the more important. But I had a feeling that time was against me. The Burrows-Cawle business had been a really painful crack. There was little that had gone into my office or Consuelo's that she hadn't seen. Her being there explained so many "mysteries" and the pair's constant one move ahead. They might just as well have been using my desk.

Yet, her going destroyed any notion that Alethea Cawle had been at St. Ursula of the Snows. We'd gone all through that with the calendar. She'd been in the office without an absence for months, and for a couple of hours on the two Sundays prior to her leaving. Berry couldn't find any trace of where she'd gone, which surprised nobody.

But who was Miss Tauperman of St. Ursula's? How could she have got a pair of Angela Master's throwaway sandals?

The crates sent to the Athens office for Logan, and redirected to Geneva, had been collected by somebody

283

with a duplicate of Athens transfer. Our Geneva office knew nothing of it. Argyopoulos still had his copy on file. There shouldn't have been others. But the Olympic Airways waybill seemed genuine, and on that, the two crates had been released. The Customs declaration and payment for odd items was in order. The description of the various units matched those on Stather's invoice. Berry hadn't been able to find him, either. His secretary had said he might have gone abroad. He often did. Bretherton had taken his wife and children to New York.

My real worry was the Branbruche business. The West German Military Court had yet to publish the result of its enquiry. Whether the blotch of suicides in various West German departments were caused by it, nobody knew. There were guesses. I wondered if Von Staengl knew that a Company plane was suspected of flying it out. I could very soon put him right, there, and so could transport control at Ehrplatz. We had a clean sheet. All our flights had been correctly loaded with tubing. There had never been a cubic foot to spare. We couldn't prove the projectile hadn't been flown in. We *could* prove that it hadn't been flown out, that is, if it had been in the bale which Commodore Kopfers had refused to accept. Dealing with any matter the pair had a hand in was like trying to pick up mercury with a toothpick.

The curtain came down in a scatter of handclaps, lights went up, and Consuelo turned to me.

"You saw a great deal of that, didn't you?" she said. "A real Brechtian fan. But I'm terribly disappointed. There isn't anyone who isn't absolutely *sweat*ing in broadcloth. If there'd *been* a nude, I suppose you'd have been drooling over the ledge? Now tell me what it was about?"

"You tell me. While we have a drink. They serve in the boxes, don't they?"

"If they don't, usually, they will tonight. I'll go. The girls' isn't far. You're luckier. It's almost opposite!"

I closed the door and sat down again.

The root of my worry was how that warhead was to

be used. When I reached the office, I'd called James Morris from a gloaming walk in his garden, and told him what had been happening.

"We've been studying it from another point of view," he said. "It had obviously been planned with meticulous care. There's no evidence that it *was* the warhead they put in the Volks. That may have been a little byplay while the real job was being done elsewhere. It has yet to come out in testimony. There's no real proof it went to Ehrplatz. Something *did* go there, but it was too small to be the projectile. We know how long it would take a team of technicians to dismantle it, and there wasn't time between the theft, and its appearance at the airfield. It's the length of the thing that's the trouble, and then the fins. It's all special tooling, so it couldn't be a garage job. I'd say it'd have to go inside something about six foot by two foot, or so. That is, once they had the fins off. It's the devil of a job!"

"Do you think it was flown to East Germany or some other satellite?"

"We've got the border watch logs. No flight of that sort could have happened without being known, whether it was chased or not. We don't think it was flown out on that side. Far too risky. The theory most favored is that it went in hiding somewhere while the fins were taken off, and possibly the casing. The explosive's in a five-part container, with the detonator separate. Both'd fit into a medium sized suitcase. But they wouldn't be the ideal companions. A signal in the right sequence of a variety of wavelengths, and up she goes!"

"It's not a contact weapon?"

"If you mean by that, the things of the dear old days that went off when they hit something, no, Edmund. We've developed—if that isn't a rude word—radio control of flight, direction and moment of explosion. Simple as that. I need hardly tell you we've been putting out that signal ever since!"

"Why hasn't it blown?"

"Well, either the detonator's been detached—it helps

285

our theory that the thing's been piecemealed—or else someone knew enough to disarm. But the moment both come together, and armed, up she goes!"

"I'm thinking of the Beyfoum complex. The warhead wouldn't have to go by air. Simply deliver it there, and send a signal. Enough?"

"If the signal were known, yes. Took us a little time to work out. Take them rather longer, I imagine!"

"Time's on our side?"

"I don't find that at all comforting, unfortunately!"

Neither did I.

It seemed to me, then, that the pairs' idea might be to wait until Beyfoum was in working order, and then destroy it. I could imagine that blast going through the pipelines. The lives lost. The horror.

A tap at the door brought me up, but while I reached, it opened.

A large shadow blocked light from the corridor shining whitely smooth across gold waves.

"Mr. Trothe?" Von Staengl murmured, heels together. "Permit me, please?"

I felt I'd been outgeneralled. He was lucky. My first solid thought was to ask him to leave. But I imagined I saw his reason for what was nothing less than a discourtesy. A small box, without light except from the theatre, a closed door, gave privacy complete. He didn't want to be seen with me, that was obvious.

"Come in," I said, in no welcoming tone. "I was expecting a drink!"

"I could certainly do with one," he said easily. "Mr. Trothe, I put aside formality and all diplomatic fanfarol. We have no time. I draw to your attention Mr. Bernard Lane. I believe he will end my career!"

"I suggest that will depend on you," I said, in no great hurry. "You're not expecting physical violence?"

"No," he said, almost amused. "If that were all, I could support it. No. A few more years, I could possibly be at the top. I don't think it's going to be allowed!"

I stared at him. He seemed absolutely serious.

"By your own people?"

He nodded. There were taps on the door. I reached to open it. A waitress brought in a tray with, I saw thankfully, a bottle of scotch, glasses and a siphon.

"Thank you," I said. "Would you please come back later?"

She was the pleasant sort of woman London's theatres seem to find, and she nodded, half-curtsied, and went out.

"It is his influence among certain of my own people," he said, while the door closed. "We have not much time, and I am flying to Bonn after this performance. What I have to say cannot be repeated. Many of my friends—colleagues of years—have committed suicide. Or it has been made to appear so. Because of a variety of scandals. I cannot go into it. The last, Barbruche, concerns your Company, and so I come to you. You are implicated because, apparently, your aircraft flew out the rocket. It did not. It was flown on a plane of a fleet serving Western Germany and the Low Countries, Spain, and the North African litoral, from Morocco to Egypt. The company's called Intramed Air—"

"I've heard of it—"

"You'll find many interesting people on the board of directors, notably Lane and Cawle, if not in the printed list, then financially. You will be the first to know what influence they might have had, whether in establishing the airline or asking favors. If you think of the years they worked in closest cooperation with the European intelligence services alone, you have some conception of the way the airline was founded, and what it's done since. Any complaint now, and you can imagine the sort of scandal they'd cause by passing certain stories to the press. The people involved couldn't deny anything. It's all fact!"

"Are you caught up in this?"

He laughed, looked out in the theatre, moved out of the light.

"But that's why I'm here, partially!" he said. "If I

287

must topple, I'd like to know that someone like yourself holds an ace or two which might be played in my behalf!"

"I'd be more than willing!"

"Then let us consider the company behind the airline. It is strong financially. We happen to know this. That wealth goes into politics in most of the countries in Europe, and to the satellites more and more. It isn't for Communist cells or propaganda as we first thought. It's for small movements of students and workers outside the unions and syndicates. Outside, I mean, not copying the usual communist or socialist attitude. The word anarchy begins to appear more and more. More and more of the student body everywhere, and the younger workmen are being filled with ideas which take them away from the traditional labor or socialist movement. This is of course a serious matter for all of us. I cannot tell you where it's coming from, or where it leads to, exactly. The overthrow of present governments, obviously. But how? When? Whose is the mind behind it all?"

"You've formed no opinion?"

"Nothing tangible. It leads hazily to Lane and perhaps Cawle, I can tell you that. I've never found anyone able to separate the two. The over-all plan seems simple enough. Disturbances begin in Universities and factories. Certain conditions are asked to be met. They are reasonable on the surface. The parrot-cry is modernize. Change with the times. Very well. As in most places, my country, yours, France, Italy, many of those conditions *were* met. But giving that inch has meant arguing about miles. Sessions, convocations, meetings, fares, hotels. People forget it all costs money. Where does it come from? I can tell you that Intramed and allied companies have a great deal to do with it!"

"Where am I of use, here?"

"First, Intramed is a carrier for smuggling. Every description, chiefly gold and narcotics, diamonds and precious stones generally, the proceeds of the more important thefts, people unable to present themselves to

288

passport and police officers, criminals of one kind and another, together with legitimate commerce, which is their excuse for existence. What is not intended for passage over frontiers, or for Customs inspection, is dropped by parachute in chosen places. That is how the Barnbruche projectile was disposed of!"

"In Switzerland?"

He appeared surprised.

"You know that?" he said. "The Grossenbalde drop?"

"Why not tell me what it's going to be used for?"

He shook his head.

"We don't know. We have no firm thought about this. Three theories were advanced. First, it would go to Russia. Why? They have as good. Second, it would go to Israel to be copied by their engineers. Third, it would be used in five different places. You probably know the explosive is in five parts. One detonator. But the Swiss have the finest micro-technicians. They could copy the detonator in a very short time. As a result, five weapons, each of brutal force. Very well, let us then suppose that there *is* a cupola Conference in Europe this year. The participants? The President of the United States, of Russia and all the others. The weapon can be carried unobtrusively. It is exploded by radio signal. Let us suppose the session is under way. Nobody would survive. If, choosing time and opportunity, four other weapons were exploded, in the House of Commons here, in the French Assembly, in the Bundestag, and in the Senate in Rome, the entire political machine of Europe is almost destroyed, and that of the United States paralyzed to a point where public opinion in both continents and Russia might be moulded to another form of thought. Panic is poor bedfellow for reason, and the general level of political thinking anywhere is low. And what could be the result? A form of anarchy, military dictatorship, perhaps, economic disaster on a scale not even thought of, and an eruption at the level of students and young workmen? Is it impossible? Absurd? Is it? What happened in Russia those years ago?

Or in China at this moment? If he went back now, with a government for every state, and a central government ready to work, would Chiang Kai-shek find it an easy matter to rule? Peoples' minds have changed, Mr. Trothe. They are no longer amenable to old ideas. There are two new generations, plus the one now coming of age, plus the one in formation, plus the one behind. Generations now aren't counted by the age of breeding. It's not a thirty year gap any longer. It's ideas, not breeding, now. But they are permitted to do as they please. Which, of course is why an army takes command as a last resort. It restores at least a semblance of discipline. As in China!"

"This is all very interesting, but where does it concern me? What's the reason for this meeting?"

He put the drink down untouched.

"I have reason to believe that your Company and others of comparable size will be subjected to increasing attack in all sectors," he said, almost in a whisper. "Even armed. Land, sea and air. That is my information. As I have said, I have been moved to another sphere of action, and so I shall not be in a position to amplify—"

"Is this present move part of the process working against you?"

"It can only be that. I should have been much more the politician, more the servant of creditmongers. That way is lined with prizes. Property owning, bank accounts, ministries. My way? Via crucis!"

"I see. Is that all you came to tell me?"

He looked at me from about two yards away in deep shadow. Even so, I felt his eyes, saw the strange shine. The theatre had filled, voices became a breathy drone, a woman laughed oh-hah-hah!, glasses clinked in the corridor, and the warning bell rippled tinnily. I was wondering where Consuelo could have gone. Von Staengl moved, settled the decoration under the tie, pulled the ends, and picked up the glass.

"This is perhaps the last time we shall toast, Mr. Trothe!" he said, half bowing, heels together. "I came to say this. The other was preamble. The present disturbances among students and young workers will become much more serious. The attack on your Company and others are part of an overall plan. Lane and Cawle are two of the planners where it concerns Europe, the Middle East, and those countries in Africa that were once part of the British Empire. In this, your son-in-law is closely involved. He is a commercial and banking power in many countries in Africa. You were in North Africa recently. You escaped by favor of Mr. Paul Chamby. He gave false information. How do I know? But then, how do I also know that Lane at this moment is in El Bidh? How do I know that the former General Klaus Reis has been in Ben Ua to assure its defence? How do I know about Dorothea Maxwell Ferrers and Renée Saddler, and John Alvin and Bertram Gouldsden, and the rest? It was my business to know. Georges Pontvianne was in Venice recently, to his sorrow. I hope you will have no sorrow in Banbury Cross!"

"There may be an attempt there?"

"Where you can be destroyed, there will be attempts. They have all the resources they require. Everywhere!"

The bell rang again.

"Now tell me why you risked coming here!"

Von Staengl finished the drink, put the glass down, looking up at me.

"I can only hope that some of what I've said's penetrated!" he whispered, almost in a cat snarl. "I pay you the compliment of considering you an honest man, a European, whether you like it or not. I know that you work to eradicate the Lane-Cawle partnership. Very well. In the next weeks, a meeting is to be held of all the principals of these nuclei. I don't know where. The tickets are being bought and distributed, I know that. Those tickets will take them so far. Others will meet them with other tickets to take them on, small expenses. It follows the same pattern as other meetings in Europe. What is such a meeting for? To formulate and synchronize strategy for the next year, two, three years.

All under the direction of the Lanes and Cawles. Ask which power has the necessary funds to employ the Lanes and Cawles? Or what makes the Lanes and Cawles work so willingly? Devotedly? At great risk? Why?"

"What am I supposed to do? What *is* there to be done?"

He went to the door, and half opened it. I saw people passing outside.

"To be done?" he said, in a cracked laugh. "By me? Nothing. Nothing at all. By you? But you must choose. Time is a luxury. Good night, Mr. Trothe!"

The door closed in a *snap!* behind him, leaving me in further shadow as the house lights went down. I was finishing my drink, when it opened quietly and Consuelo slipped—I've never seen the word more gracefully illustrated—in.

"Where the *hell* have you been?" I said, toning it with an arm about her waist. "I was getting worried!"

"That's how it looks!" she said, leaning to put the top on the bottle. "I saw that man come in, and I stayed away till he left. His companion's a very odd piece. I was next to it for a few minutes. Darling, that's no girl!"

"Dear me," I said. "A *'poufiasse'*?"

"Says it *exactly!*" Consuelo whispered, in the silence before the curtain went up. "Isn't it a little horrifying? Even in these rather bottom-y days? How can he? An occasion like this?"

"Isn't he presenting an award, or something?"

"D' you think they'll ever take the place of girls?"

"I doubt it!"

"Why?"

"A sphincter's not much competition!"

"Darling, the theatre's *ringing* with your voice!" she whispered. "What on earth's that?"

There seemed to be a lot of running in the corridor, heavy feet, doors slamming, a sshhhhh! in the theatre, and someone fell against our door, sounded though he slid off, and more feet ran the other way.

"I don't like this a bit!" Consuelo said, and sat nearer. "Unusual isn't it?"

I'd straightened to look over the ledge at the stage, and the unmistakable flat *smap!* of a .38 muted nearby, shouts, a long high shriek, and most women in the theatre seemed to scream together, except Consuelo.

"Don't go near that door!" I said, and led her into the corner against the wall.

I stood to the side, turned the handle and looked through an inch of lit space. The noise seemed to be to my right, near the stairhead. Our pleasant waitress, looking rather pinched about the gills, came in view, bending forward to see round the curve of the wall. She had a small bald patch in the middle of her scalp.

"Listen!" I whispered. "Come over here!"

"Oh, my God, sir!" she quavered, fingers to lips, staring. "I don't know what's happened. They reckon a poor man's been killed down there. Run after whoever it was. Went in a dead faint up there, the lady did, with him!"

I got her in the box, and shut the door.

"Look, this pays for the bottle and the rest's yours. Now, how about showing me the way across the stage so that we can slip through the back?"

There were more shouts and screams from nearby, the theatre's lights went up, and a glance showed the audience filling the aisles and the actors standing, uncertain.

"We want nothing to do with *that!*" I said nodding at the noise. "Never mind the coats. Just take us to the door. I'll look after the rest!"

She picked up the tray, bottle in hand, and led down to the left. Two doors were open. In the large box nearest the stage, chairs tipped against each other and one had fallen. A long black glove lay a curlicue on red carpet inside the door. I reached in to pick it up while the waitress shouldered the iron door open.

Bowler-hatted shadows moved in front of us with the opening weight.

"All right, sir!" Berry said. "Been waiting for this.

I've got two men down the other end. Any idea what happened, sir?"

"None!"

"I just spoke to the manager. He doesn't think they'll ever get the audience settled down. You want to leave, sir, the car's outside!"

"What was that shot?"

Berry looked at me over his glasses.

"Wouldn't I like to know?" he said. "I've got Miss Hammond and a man after that woman with him, and I'm waiting here till they report!"

"Where's the Graf von Staengl?"

"He left your box, sir, he done no more, he went out. His cape's still in the cloakroom!"

I looked at Consuelo. Those eyes were telling me what I was thinking.

"Do I understand that the woman with him left by herself?"

"They had three people with them in their box. Two of them were Germans. The other one was something to do with the play. The two Germans went out with her. One of them went left out of the theatre, and the other went right, and she got in a car down here, on the corner. I've got them all taped, sir. I'm just waiting for the calls!"

"Well done. Any idea who the woman is?"

Berry flicked a glance at Consuelo. She pretended an innocence which I thought quite devastating.

"Can't talk in front of Mrs. Trothe, sir!" he said, into his chin, while we made way through people talking to the actors. "Fact of the matter is, she covered the ground a sight faster than my two after her. I'm not sure if they didn't lose her!"

"How about Von Staengl?"

"He left your box, sir, and he went through the door we just come out of. I'm hoping my man down here picked him up. I don't see him here!"

A fireman, with a splendidly crisp black bow tied in his cap, touched Berry's arm and whispered, and Berry turned to me.

294

"Don't go for a moment, sir!" he said. "Got a call, here!"

He went in the glass-panelled doorkeeper's cubby, and took the receiver off the table.

"That Von Staengl man's really very attractive, isn't he?" Consuelo said. "But the woman—is that it?—with him, didn't leave their box after she went back. I had the whole curve in sight. Did he have anything interesting to say?"

"Tell you later. Make a nice nightcap. What's wrong with Berry?"

He was looking wide-eyed at me through the glass. I put my head round the door.

"That woman, sir!" he said, covering the mouthpiece. "I've got Taylor on the line. He followed her to Curzon Street. It's the beauty place, you know, used to be owned by that Renée Saddler. She's gone in the side door to the flat upstairs. She had the key!"

"Report it!"

"All right, Taylor," he said in the mouthpiece. "You hang on till Beasley gets there. Keep an eye on who goes in and out!"

"I understood the place had been shut up," he said, ringing off.

"It *is* a little surprising!"

We were in the street, and the car backed out, holding up two cars turning in. The chauffeur went forward to let them pass, and somebody in the leading car waved.

"That's Inspector Bateson, sir!" Berry said, "Murder detail, C.I.D. What're they here for? Let me find out!"

Consuelo got in the car. Berry hurried down to the stage door. The plainclothesman saluted and stood aside, but he stopped two others from going in. I was thinking of the *smap!* of that .38 and linking it with the Murder detail, and Berry came down the steps two at a time, and about half a dozen followed, but running for the two police cars.

"Von Staengl's been found shot up there, sir!" he coughed. "I told Bateson about the woman. We're off round there. Like to come, sir?"

"Follow you!"

Consuelo sat away in the corner.

"Darling!" she whispered. "I don't want to spoil anything, but I'd much rather go home, please? Any thought of it, and I'm sick. Why *can't* people stop murdering each other!"

"All right, my sweet, home you go. You won't mind if I leave you for a little while?"

"Make it that, please? You know I can't sleep when you're not there!"

Only one answer to that, and I had the enormous pleasure of watching night time London pass by with all the beauty in the world in my arms. Surprisingly, we didn't hit a red, and Pall Mall was a long width of satin. Kerrigan came down the steps and Bledsloe waited in the doorway.

"Take care of Mrs. Trothe till I get back. Is Groves upstairs?"

"Yes, sir. Anstey's up there with him. Ferriss is on the second, Mills on the third, and there's three of us here. Ought to be all right, sir!"

"Don't care if they've got a regiment up there!" Consuelo said, over her shoulder. "I only feel safe with you, that's all!"

"Not more than an hour!" I pleaded. "Play patience, knit, listen to the Footles, anything. Shan't be long!"

I watched the door close and the two guards fall in behind her to the lift.

The car moved, and I sat back, trying to find a reason for Von Staengl's surprising remark about Paul. What "false" information could he have given anyone? Had he ever worked for the pair, knowingly, or had he ever been in any sense a traitor? I refused to believe it. Illness, drug addiction, whatever it was, might have induced him to think and act in strange ways, but I was certain his basic character was solid. Yet he'd told Kheif a miserably untrue story which might have put at least four of us in prison without hope of a hearing for many a month. There was certainly that.

For the rest of it, what, exactly, had Von Staengl been trying to tell me? Why did he begin to say it and then meander off into detail which I found sobering enough, but hardly germane, considering that most could have been put in a letter, or told over a meal. Could he have suspected me—or others—of planting a microphone? Did he fear that it might appear as evidence in some future trial? He'd seen it happen, and so had I. Had—my turn to wonder!—that box been wired or miked? I hadn't thought of it.

"Hutchins, go back to the theatre with Beasley after we reach Curzon Street," I said, down the speaking tube. "Ask him to look at this box—take these stubs—for anything that might look like a mike. Then have a look at the royal box further up, same side. The C.I.D.'s there. He won't have any trouble. Report back to me at Curzon Street!"

"Sir!"

I'd gathered he had enough evidence that the pair were working for Maoist China, and he was warning me that the campaign would move gradually from public relations through the various media, to armed attack on the larger companies, first, and then to political machinery. Since economics are the basis of stable government, I thought that sound reasoning. But I found most interesting the meeting of students and workmen, somewhere, at some time. I had to get Druxi and Georges into it to find out where and when. It seemed to me that one or other of the pair might be there, and I certainly had all intention of joining them.

Police cars, and a small crowd shadowed near the garden at the end of Curzon Street. I found Beasley and sent him off, and went through the crowd to the doorway. Berry and two other men were talking to a uniformed Inspector.

"Second murder here, sir!" Berry said, leading upstairs. "The other was a nice, clean job compared to this one. We got round here too quick. The murderer just had time to half-do the job. Got away over the roof at the back. Must have took the weapon with him. Nothing here, except a lot of clothes and stuff. Inspector Bateson, Mr. Edmund Trothe!"

Dark hair greying, a cool bluish eye, thin face,

freshly shaven, tallish, jacket off, sleeves rolled, he looked as if he were enjoying himself.

"The Superintendent told me you had reasons for wanting this woman followed," he said, in a soft Yorks accent. "The matron in there's just told me she's—or he's—not a woman!"

Ah, Consuelo!

"I have a curious idea we'd met, somewhere," I said. "An idea, that's all!"

"If you had a look at the body, d'you think you might remember?" Berry asked. "Do no harm, once the make-up's off?"

"They're taking his nails off, at the moment!" Bateson said. "It's getting more and more like the Bible says, sir. Sodom and Gomorrah, I mean, it's all round us. A broth of abominable things, eh? Here we are, sir!"

The body lay under a sheet. Blood had soaked through at the head. A hand protruded. A policeman tweezered a plastic nail off the thumb. The other fingernails were uncovered, looked unwashed, and bitten down to the quick. But closer, they weren't bitten, but squared as if deliberately. And I'd seen that opal ring before.

Bateson threw back the bloodstained sheet.

Beyond the horribly battered face, bones glistening white in a torchbeam, there could be no doubt.

I took the Minox from my waistcoat pocket and gave it to Bateson.

"With an enlargement of any one of the three negatives in this, you'll be able to reconstruct and identify," I said. "The fingernails are additional proof. This is the body of a concert pianist of the modern order. The name's Joh Pensen. May I use the telephone?"

CHAPTER THIRTY-FOUR

I don't think I've ever been so angry, pained, disappointed—whatever the word is and I don't think there *is* one to describe what I felt—as when I went into the Sloane Square make-up room and found Mimi absent, five empty bottles of scotch in the sink, two port bottles in the sauna, beer bottles here and there, a broken sherry bottle on the wig rack, and that stench everywhere.

I'd just seen the girls and the baby off to Jamaica on White Horse Two, with five extra men for safety, and I still held sharp memory of the grip of Consuelo's arms, heard her whisper, a scream of jets, an aircraft climbing in flashing lights, the pale blue dreary ride back in London's dawn.

My Bézé clothing was on its hanger, but there were no shoes, no linen. I couldn't find the wig, the other pieces, or the personal items for the pockets. I was dished.

I hadn't time to put him together.

I gave the clothing a pat, told M. Bézé he could be of use later, and sat down in the outer room to think. The place was in a frowse. Mrs. Lindhurst hadn't been able to get in, evidently. Dust matted everywhere so that Mimi, poor soul, must have been carousing for at least a week. She drank until she couldn't climb the stairs, and then she disappeared, and Mrs. Lindhurst, deaf and dumb, without a key, couldn't get in.

"I don't make a ni*sance!*" Mimi told me once, hand upraised. "I go. I finish. Enough!"

It was, indeed.

I had to go to Ulla Brandt Ben Ua's house to make sure that all damage had been repaired, and to Hamoun to find out from Maurice what had happened, but far more importantly I had to get into the hiphops' camp to find out what, if anything, was going on there, and then visit the house near Derna where I'd last seen Joh Pensen and that German girl. I wanted very much to find her.

Druxi, Georges and I, over a three-way line had decided a course, but it depended rather too much on perhaps, and if, or but. They were going to find out where Von Staengl had gone after he'd left the theatre. The man found shot hadn't been identified, except that he appeared to be a German, but without papers or any identifying mark. It wasn't even known where he was staying.

But all that didn't get me very far, and I had a flight to Algiers at ten o'clock as Evariste Fromentin Bézé and a passport in that name.

I had to cancel, and use another idea. I picked up the telephone, and began dialing.

The line was dead. It shouldn't have been.

The clock said 5:12.

Quietly, I went in the next room to a telephone with a direct line to the office. It was dead.

Thoroughly warned, I felt for my little friend in the shoulder holster. I used the backstair down to my suite, opened a door which only I knew, and went to the telephone on my desk. Almost as I was about to press the button to call our switchboard, I pulled back. The set didn't "sit" square in its shallow, polished steel trough. I used the beam on my keychain to examine it. Two wisps of copper wire led down, behind the desk, along the wall to the bookcase. I took out about eight volumes of the Cambridge History from the bottom shelf.

At the back, a neat aluminum block with a small copper excrescence made a dullish shine. A closer look showed an intricate clockwork job, a small battery, and a radio set made on the pattern of my clix. I opened my rummage cupboard, chose a small plier, and gently undid everything undoable, and took to the table what I was quite sure could only be one fifth of the Barnbruche warhead. There was no doubt about it. The markings were stamped.

It took a few minutes to find the cuts in the telephone cables outside in the box, less time to join up. I called Scotland Yard, got Hockley's night deputy, gave a description of Mimi, and then got James Morris out of bed.

"I'll be there in about thirty minutes," he said, through early morning gravel. "Don't let anyone mess about with it. The warmth of the hand here and there can set it off!"

"Really? I'm nursing it!"

"Oh, for G—!"

I was talking to Robarts, the Company's legal advisor, when I heard the first Police car arrive.

"Tell Simmons to present any figures they need. And remember, I want this woman protected in every way possible. I repeat, all articles of clothing and theatrical stuff came up from Onslow Close while it was being altered, and she looked after it while she ran her own business from this address. Is that clear?"

"But the Police aren't coming there for that, are they?"

"For an entirely different reason. But they may want to know all about who works here. And she's been taken seriously drunk?"

I went down to open the door, and three uniformed men of the Night Patrol came in, but before I could close it, two cars from Scotland Yard stopped, and Superintendent Maybell and three plainclothesmen came down the ramp. Maybell looked a little tired, but his bulk moved easily enough, and the hornrims and toothy smile made him appear far less awesome than the bane he was known to be. We'd met years before, and while my mind was able to store what he was saying, and reply, the greater part was with Mimi Prôche, and wondering how on earth anyone could have got in to my suite without the keys. It had taken that length of time to sink in, a sort of retroactive knockout.

I knew Sloane Square was denied to me from the moment.

"Mr. Hockley's been telling me about all this

Barnbruche business," Maybell said, when we went in the big room. "He's very worried about it. Well, now, this woman Prôche. You say she's been living here?"

"In the terrace flat in the adjoining building."

"Better have a look round up there, hadn't we? Just to make sure. Boulters, take a detail, make sure of the state of things. This Mrs. Lindhurst, the cleaner, she's deaf and dumb, sir? No key?"

"Mrs. Prôche always let her in. She ought to be here at any moment."

"Kyles, send a car back and get the D'n D man here, case we have to do some talking, sharp!"

He put on another pair of spectacles to have a good look at the pack, but without attempting to touch it.

"Cold blooded lot, eh?" he said, in a smile. "No danger, as it is?"

"None. I'm a little worried about how they got in!"

"How many people come in here?"

"Mrs. Prôche, Mrs. Lindhurst. Absolutely not a soul, with the exception of those two and myself!"

"They're here every day? How often do you come here?"

"Perhaps once every ten days. Often, longer."

"She could drink all this by herself?"

"Never had the slightest trouble!"

"You never made any enquiries about her?"

"Yes. Twelve years ago. When she first came to work for me. M.I. cleared her!"

The moment I'd said it, of course, I realized what an utter dolt I'd been. In the positions they then held, the pair must have known about her, and since the trace had been made, an agent would now and again make a routine check to keep items up to date. In all that time it had never occurred to me. At night, any catman could enter and roam where he pleased, except here. To get in the steel outer and inner doors he'd need the barrel keys Mimi wore around her neck.

But then she'd have to tell him the serial numbers to turn the dial that unlocked the door.

Nobody else knew them, except myself.

The full meaning began to percolate in what I felt as freezing drops.

Without a word I went to have a look at the outer door. The lock showed no sign of a scratch. The inner door showed none.

Maybell watched me try the key, dial the numbers and open.

"Oh, I see!" he said, half-frowning. "If she didn't open that door, whoever did'd have to know the serial, eh?"

"There's no other way, and from my knowledge of her, unless she suddenly went mad, it would have to be done by force!"

Those steps coming off the runner and on to the parquet brought back that sense of a failing heart.

The sergeant halted in the doorway, saluted, held up his keys.

"Had to get in with these, sir," he said quietly. "The woman's up there. Been dead about three days. Job like the one round Curzon Street. Only this one got done *right!*"

"Very well, sergeant, call the detail!" Maybell said, almost tiredly, down at the floor, and looked up at me. "You'd be about the only one to identify her, wouldn't you, sir? Care to come with me?"

The sergeant had gone down the stairs to get up to the other house, but he'd come back along the top corridor that went directly to the terrace, and left the doors open.

All the way along that shining parquet with the blue canvas runner, I had the strangest feeling that a complete part of my life was being stripped away. I could never again use Sloane Square except as a workshop, perhaps, but even then, so long as the pair were loose, there was risk to the men working there. I suspected I'd come through scatheless, so far, because the pair could never depend on when I'd arrive. That particular handset had been wired because they'd known that only I could use it. We'd had that special type of telephone in the Service.

The blue and white terrace tiles shone in light rain and the awning dripped. Violets budded in pots along the window sill. A plainclothesman opened the door. Maybell went in first, and I stood in that horrid smell beside him. The room was tidy except that the table was on its side, a vase had smashed, and the flowers were crushed brown.

Maybell stood aside.

A policeman turned back the sheet.

The white mop was bloodied black. The face was a black mask. The earrings were Mimi's. The hand I saw with the diamond and pearl ring on the little finger was Mimi's. The dearness in them, the craft, the most womanly mind behind them, the kindliness and humor, everything I'd known and depended on as Mimi had been battered deliberately, with progression of time and choice of movement into dead horror.

"That is Mimi Prôche," I said, listening to my voice coming off the wall. "For reasons which I shall give later, I believe she was held here or elsewhere in the building, for some time before she was killed. We shall know from Mrs. Lindhurst how many days it's been since she cleaned my place down there. Notice these flowers. I shall also hope you've noticed there isn't a glass or bottle or trace of alcohol in this room!"

"Been took note of, sir," Maybell said. "Didn't know of any friends of hers, I suppose?"

"You'd have to look among theatrical people for that. So far as I knew, she had none. It was a lonely life. You know, I never gave it a thought. Never. We're a heartless *bloody* lot!"

"See a few like this, y'get to know it, sir. I don't know what some of them deserve. Right, Boulters, nobody else in here. Wait for the detail. You off anywhere, sir?"

"I'm flying to Madrid at ten something. I should be back on Saturday. Why?"

I looked at a clear hazel stare.

"I advise you to wait till Mr. Hockley gets here, sir."

You're the only one knows anything about this. Serious charges here. See that, don't you?"

My turn to stare.

"You don't suspect me?"

"Never use the word, sir, you don't mind? A talk with Mr. Hockley'll do it. You go down to your place with the constable, and I'll wait for the detail back here. Won't be long, sir!"

I felt like kneeling beside that bier.

But in presence of witnesses, the thought stuck, robbed any movement.

Instead, I followed the rainspun, scintillant shoulders of the policeman, past the violets she'd planted, across the tiles that so often sung for her.

I knew in all certainty how it felt to be a traitor.

CHAPTER THIRTY-FIVE

"We can't make a plan, and setting traps is talking non-sense," Superintendent Hockley said, pouring more coffee. "They've got the advantage of being able to go anywhere they like. We don't even know what to look for. This series of killings—I can't call them murders—appear to be the job of one man. I've got files from everywhere. The details check with what we've got here. Whether that man is Lane or Cawle, I don't know. Might be somebody else. I thought the Curzon Street case'd give us some pointers. But he's too careful. I've had reports they've been seen here, in Paris, in Geneva, Rome and Athens. You say Lane was in El Bidh. Means nothing to me. I've either got to get them here, or ask for extradition where I can. Did this woman Prôche have anything to do with the pair at some time? Or with M.I.? Sounds like it, to me. You never heard she was employed by M.I.?"

"No. It was I who gave her name for the trace!"

"He did a good job of going over her stuff," Maybell said. "Took everything in the way of paper. Postman says she always had a fair foreign mail. No sign of it. Why?"

"Might have been a postbox, and a very useful information point for them," Hockley said, putting the cigaret out. "All she had to do was pick up a phone!"

"I can't believe that!"

Hockley turned down his mouth.

"Doesn't matter much what *we* believe, does it? There's a reason behind everything. Even a dirty killing like this. Whoever he is, he doesn't all of a sudden take it into his head. He likes to go about it a step at a time. Must take him at least a couple of hours, the surgeon said. But it's always people who could tell a tale. They know enough to give him away. Looking at things as they are, I think this idea of yours about this place in

North Africa, there might be a lot in it. I know about it. There's a couple more here and there round the Mediterranean. A lot of our bad'uns get down there. Wouldn't surprise me if you didn't turn something up!"

"And if he does, what?" Maybell said, running three fingers up the lines of his forehead. "An extradition order'd be a bit late!"

"I don't doubt Lord Blercgrove'd take good care of it!" Hockley said, and he wasn't joking. "I saw him yesterday. Very nasty temper about everything. Got a map there. Everywhere the pairs' reported seen, there's a flag. Red for Lane, yellow for Cawle. Looks like an orange carpet. That's only the past month. They've used every airline in the business. Must have dozens of passports. For what good they are, these days!"

"Did Lord Blercgrove tell you who sent in the reports?" I asked.

"His own people, I suppose?"

"He's been in the tease business too long. He's started pulling you in. I'll give you a hundred to one, again, he asked you to leave everything to him!"

Hockley looked mild surprise, half smiled.

"You'd win," he said, quietly, almost with satisfaction. "Not very good friends, are you?"

"At root, it's cold enmity. We don't mix. I wouldn't trust him as far as I could shift New Scotland Yard!"

"Interests me," Hockley said, resting chin on clasped hands. "Why?"

"Reports my friends and I sent in over a number of years, all ignored. Then, for no reason, the pair got away. Mark you, in Washington, with everybody after them. Who gave the word?"

Hockley stood, and Maybell pushed from the table in a shriek of chair legs.

"Outside my area, that is!" Hockley said, in a different, sharper, tone of voice. "My job's to find a couple of traitors and one murderer. You knew Mrs. Meryl Armitage at Plummy's Club, didn't you?"

"For many years. Why?"

"She didn't go in on Monday. Hasn't been seen since.

Can't find her. Nothing wrong with the books. Thought I'd mention it!"

"Not another victim?"

"Well, look at it. She was there for years. Those two were founder members, with you, and the Lord Blercgrove, among others, weren't they? Another information drop?"

I suddenly saw Meryl in her red velvet dress—she was never in anything else—a la Empire, the string of pearls we added to each year, hair—black at first, whiter with the years—piled and wound about by a plait, pinned with a diamond comb, her smile, her invariable greeting—"*Hul*lo, Chuckles!"—standing on the counter on big nights, singing "My ol' man's a fireman in a big gorblimey 'at!"—not so innocently, magnificently, and all of us cheering the place down. Why? She was simply a woman who loved living, and we knew it, knew that she lived only for the Club. I sicked any thought she might have been bought by the pair.

"Impossible!"

"First time I've heard you raise your voice, sir!" Hockley said. "I'll let you know if you're right or wrong when we find her. She's a priority at the moment. Hope you're taking good care of yourself?"

I thought about it on the way to Alec Roivers' place. I took some trouble to see I wasn't followed.

CHAPTER THIRTY-SIX

The wardrobe at Sloane Square was out of reach. I could go anywhere in the world as myself, and in my own aircraft. Simple enough. But I couldn't go to North Africa and expect to stroll in. I had to use cover.

While I'd been talking to Hockley I'd got the idea.

Frederick was already there, I hoped, by this time. He'd be waiting for a French salesman of kitchenware. That was out. Instead, I'd thought of Harry Kells, wood carver and general roustabout, whose appearance didn't require stain or wig.

Alec Roivers had often worked with me. He owned a chain of small hotels in the Paddington area which were rarely empty day or night, and took rather more than a paternal interest—when they went to Court, he paid—in the women who brought their custom there. He was an ex-paratrooper, with excellent gifts in both hands, not above using his feet, and if his head was never his strong point, he was still an excellent companion in a rough-house.

I walked in by the back way of the Diss Hotel, and went up to his office on the first floor. He was still in bed. The room, the smell, I ignored. I've never known anyone sleep in so many tatters and find a way out.

"Up, Alec!" I said, rapping my umbrella on the door. "I want a couple of old khaki shirts, socks, jacket, corduroys, shoes, raincoat, anything in the way of a bag, a clean room and a pot of tea. I don't want to be here more than thirty minutes. Shift!"

Alec wasn't the talkative sort. He was about my size, which simplified things, and he knew from old that everything I was then wearing was his. He barefooted along worn linoleum, opened a door, and stood aside.

"Back in ten minutes!" he said. "Tea up in three!"

The room was clean, threadbare, quiet. I undressed to singlet and trousers and lay on the bed to consider

309

things. I didn't get very far. A *crack!* on the door brought in a large woman—no word from me—with a tray of tea, buttered toast, and strawberry jam with whole fruit in it, something I hadn't seen for too long. Before I could say anything she shoed the door open, caught it, went out and slammed it. I suspected he got the butter and jam from West Country people coming up through Paddington Station, just down the road. The tea was equally good, in a mug that felt an inch thick. I was enjoying myself when Alec came in with a brown paper parcel.

"Tell me what y'don't like in this, I change it!" he said, ripped the paper in a grab, and spilled everything on the bed. "Cost y'couple o'bars. All right?"

Even I couldn't have done better. It was all secondhand, but washed. The khaki shirts were cottony with wear, the corduroys were almost bald at knees and seat, and the shoes turned up at the toes, clumped thick in the sole, nailed, fitting where they touched. But the socks were new—Alec was sensible—grey, Military surplus, and so was the webbing pack. While he went down to get a couple of blankets and a strap, I got out of Edmund Onslow Perceval Trothe and into Harry Kells, washed my head under the tap, towelled it into a mop, put in a pair of blue contact lenses, added a clip to each side of my upper back teeth, chewed some toast, drank tea, and went over to the long looking glass on the inside of the wardrobe door.

I even surprised myself.

Clothes makyth the man.

Alec opened the door, and stood there, looked about, stared back.

"Well, Christ, you are, you're a bloody swipe!" he said, and cackled. "Often thought about you, sir. Wished I could get in, have a basin. Old times. Bit of a barney, like?"

"Want to come with me?"

He held out his foot.

"Try this one. Made of rubber!"

310

"I'll give you ten minutes to decide. Fifty a week, all expenses. Perhaps a *real* barney. On?"

He walked out, and I heard him feather the stairs. He could put his toes on the edge of a top stair and slide down as if on a chute. I've practised, to my cost.

I'd just packed everything in the webbing rucksack, and he came up the stairs two at a time. I couldn't have designed anything better.

He wore a beret, an old military overcoat, patched flannels in tints of oilstain, a holed claret-colored pullover, a tweed jacket, and a red and black tartan satchel bulged overarm, with a walking stick, carved in a bulldog's head and bright eyes of ballbearings, sticking out of the right fist.

"Best I could dig out, sir!" he said, almost pathetically.

"You'll do!"

He feathered ahead of me, and I tried, and might have broken my neck. We got out in the street, and I led to the Tube.

"Who's going to look after things for you?" I asked.

"Chunner. Her what give you the tea. Been with me years. All I got to say is 'Take the clutch, back Sunday!' I say Sunday, she won't wait up!"

"Clutch, I take it, is money?"

"Course. Nobody can't clutch more'n she can. See her the first time, she was sat on the stairs, there. I says, what you want? She says, got a job? I says, yes, I says, clean up down here. This is two o'clock in the morning? She got in, there, hot water, soda, the lot. You see it now? Shoulda see it then. So I says, here's the key of 16. It's your'n. Best job I ever done. Never heard her say two words. Get on like 'house afire!"

We must have made a curious duo, walking into the London Air Terminal, but nobody took the slightest notice, possibly because oddities are the norm in these days, and I was at the ticket counter before I thought of asking Alec if he had a passport. He had. I was surprised to see quite a number of pages stamped.

311

"My business, I got to go there, ain't I?" he said, bashful Billy himself. "Want girls? Got to get 'em. Lads like a bit of foreign, see?"

"I should have thought they got enough of their own?"

"Bit of foreign does it. Y'own's the same old thing, ain't it?"

I didn't pursue it. I chose an Air France flight to Tunis, and read and slept. He lay back and slept. We ate a very good lunch over the Mediterranean, and I was still asleep when we landed. What amazed me was his command of French. He had one word in three, but perfectly understandable, and I let him take charge. We got the next flight for Sfax, via Sousse, didn't have time to go into the city, and had another excellent meal on board. We reached Sfax in the afternoon but, again, unfortunately we couldn't move out of the airport because the Derna flight was a couple of minutes later, a better plane, a delicious kous-kous, and excellent claret. I opened one eye a couple of times when we landed, slept again, and woke up at Derna.

What really *did* knock the breath out of me was to see Maurice, in a white shirt, outside the airport with his jeep.

As one, when I sat on the step, so did Alec.

"Eyes down!" I warned.

Maurice waited, one hand on the windscreen, smoking a Gauloise from the extreme left hand side of his mouth, bending his head to miss smoke. People with us came out, went off in cars, the air crew left in a limousine, a few came out to get in a smart bus.

Maurice stood there.

The only cab driver came over to look at us. We took no notice, he put his hands behind to kick sand back to darkness. The bus lit us in turning, the cab lit us, the beams went away coloring green and red till the sound had gone. Insects churred. Mosquitoes micro-whined.

I saw the white shirt coming toward us, heard the thump-dot in the sand.

I thought I'd try the outfit, and kept quiet.

"Pardon," he said, with uncommon diffidence, I thought. "I was asked to meet a couple of passengers on this flight. Didn't want to go to Tobruk, did you?"

"We wanted to get to a beach a little east," I said, in Russian-accented French. "This flight ended here. We were waiting for the next!"

"You've got all night to wait, didn't they tell you?"

"Suggestions?"

"Stay here at the hotel, and get a taxi in the morning. He won't get all the way to the beach. You'll have about an hour's walk, that's all!"

"How about by sea?"

He nodded.

"Best. I can get you a motorboat. Friend of mine. I'll leave the jeep, come back with him. I've been there a couple of times. Lot of lunatics living there, nude, that it?"

"Could be!"

The tooth which Alec drained sounded like the tip of Etna's crater. But it made a break.

"Out of the frying pan, eh, Alec?" I said, trying the accent on him. "Might be some new business?"

"Right pro's don't give it away!" he said. "Not even a look!"

"I'm in accord!" Maurice said, and spat. "They're going to be expelled at any moment. The fishermen don't come back to their wives, the gardeners down there don't, so there's a howl from the women. Wouldn't surprise me if the Army moved them this week. Most of them come in by fishing boat. No passports. Look, get in, we'll go down to the harbor. Not far. But who sent that message?"

"Nobody we know," I said. "Did a Mr. Frederick Trothe call you, by any chance?"

Maurice took his good foot out of the jeep and turned to me, folding his arms.

"Aha!" he said, under his breath. "Now we are a little nearer, perhaps? He *did* call, and I took him down there. How do you know him?"

"His father's a friend of mine!"

313

He wagged two fingers.

"What's the connection?" he asked the darkness. "My wife took this call this afternoon. Wait. I'll ask the Police board to enquire where the call was made. Easier. I'll also warn my friend to prepare the boat. About ten minutes!"

They were some of the sickest minutes I ever lived through.

If Haza took the call that afternoon, then somebody must have known I'd flown from London to Paris, bought on' to Marseilles, to Tunis, via Sousse to Sfax and Derna. How could anyone decide where I was going to be at this time of night?

I went back to follow the moves. I'd left the Sloane Square house in a police car with Chief Superintendent Hockley. He'd dropped me at the office. There, I'd made a routine sweep of clix without result. I'd taken a Company car to Hyde Park Corner, changed to a taxi for Piccadilly Circus, watched closely at the newspaper stand, made sure I wasn't followed, and went down to the Tube, doubled about on one line and the other, and got out at Paddington.

I'd taken normal precautions.

But up against the sort of agents the pair were using, the most abnorm would have been wiser. In that agent's shoes, I'd have had no difficulty at all. To underline, Alec must have been seen going out to one of the slop-shops along the street, and coming out with a parcel.

A small bribe, the right questions, and the agent would merely have to wait till someone in corduroys and that jacket, with a webbing bag, came out, follow to London Air Terminal, verify the flight, call his off-number in Paris, and he'd pick me up, and call on. So easy.

"What did you say to the man you bought this stuff from, this morning?" I asked Alec. "Tell him they were for a friend of yours?"

"I wanted everything clean. That's what I said. I says you was proper particular. I says, any complaints, I come back here, I do the pair of you!"

314

That settled it.

The telephone call to Haza meant that the pair had their fingers rather nearer me than I'd imagined. Was Maurice suspect? I couldn't believe so. He wasn't the dissimulating kind. He was like Alec.

That made me ask myself. What was I? I hadn't an answer.

The white shirt came thump-dot, clanked into the jeep, lit a cigaret off a sog, flicked it off in a sparky comet.

"The call came from Tobruk!" he said, switching on the headlights, nodding, holding out a hand as if balancing. "So why don't *they* meet you? I didn't want to come here. But I don't like to bite my nails, eh?"

"Could Tobruk localize the call?"

"I'll find out tomorrow, don't worry!" he said, wheeling for the road. "The boat will cost money. He likes to be paid first!"

I got into my inner shirt, took out the smaller wad.

"How much?"

"Show him the money, I'll make the price. He's a bandit!"

Lights spread an arc just below, and we passed along the back way, honking through crowds in the noisy soukhs, oil lights flaring among electrics smells of meaty stews, coffee, dried fish, and clattered over the quay.

We were in the boat and moving out over still water almost as we stopped. Maurice spoke to the pilot behind. Alec moved nearer me.

"D'you know this bloke, sir?" he asked quietly.

"Very well. For years. Why?"

"He's looking at you proper chance-y!"

"He's no fool. There's something about the cut of my jib. You go up in the prow. I'll talk to him!"

He moved off, and Maurice stepped over a coil of rope, dropped on the canvas beside me.

"Maurice," I said. "How's the house?"

"Foh-ho!" he exploded, slapped his hands, looking up, feeling for cigarets. "My friend, I was dragged be-

315

tween two camels. But you are very good. I have two cables for you at Hamoun. I'll bring them tomorrow—"

"Stay away, and let Arefa bring them. Tell him to look for the one with the red handkerchief tied round his head, and the other, wearing a white sweatband. He will not come direct. He will not come on the beach. He could be recognized. He's known by some of those people. He must hide. You understand?"

"Perfectly. Very well. I make a report. The helicopter put down two people that day at the airstrip. Both boarded the plane and flew north. The helicopter went to the west. It hasn't come back. Two planes of the same company have been in, one the day before yesterday—"

"Intramed Air?"

"Exactly. They brought in stuff for merchants here, nothing important, wines, clothing, shoes, and they took out goat pelts, carpets for Paris. I have the address. In the house here, three arrivals. Two men. One woman. They left the following morning before I could get there. They made a great scene about the radio material we took. I believe they came to get it. They had to use an interpreter. A woman!"

"French?"

Maurice looked at me one-eyed, smoke scrawling grey, shaking his head.

"Chinese!"

That was a stopper.

"You verified?"

"Of course. They had curious passports. Their papers were in eight languages, and the last visa was Dutch. They were going to Paris. My friend's head of passports. He took the details. Get you their names if you want?"

"Get them. And you come for me tomorrow night. Where you put us ashore, here, seven o'clock? I'll send answers to the cables by Arefa."

"You have a fair account. Repairs, complete, and the people of 'moun al Amoun!"

"One cheque!"

The pilot shut off the motor, and we slid up the beach. Only then, I saw the pale arc of sand on both sides of us. In the breath of surf, there were drums, down on the left, lights, and Maurice pointed.

"Sand all the way, about three hundred metres. They have a camp among the pomegranates. Careful near to. It's all vegetable plots above the tideline. Don't walk across. You won't see the gardeners. You'll feel the knife!"

We shook hands, and dropped over the ankle in froth. While we put our shoes on, I heard voices in gusts, guitars, drums, a trumpet, an *ah-hah!* of laughter, and a few screeches. We had to walk almost there, until I saw the place was screened by vines, behind the long furrows of vegetables. Oil wisps burned in about a dozen rush-roofed huts among the trees. In front, a space was trampled flat. A group sang in chorus, lying about a fire in a ring of stones, from the silhouettes and the light on those further away, about a hundred or more. Behind me, some distance off, another fire glowed under trees, and sparks showered up in yells, and dwarf laughter.

I waited till the singing stopped, and went forward.

"Evening!" I called loudly, in fair to middling Cockney. "Any chance for a couple of bright 'uns? Heard you was all here, come down to see you. 'jections? Matelots, all we are!"

A man I hadn't seen—I couldn't see any of those I'd met—stringy, bearded, with a rush apron just covering the jolly, stood up almost beside me.

"Y'can have what's here," he said, in a Lancashire accent. "We've nowt of our own. What are you? I mean, just plain blokes are y'? Sailors?"

" 'at's all, mate!" I said. "Dead plain. Deck hands. Why?"

"Well, you might help us rope up a raft we've been trying to put together. Float down t'coast a bit. We're getting slung out 'next few days. Can't leave us well enough alone nowhere!"

He spoke as if half asleep, little enough life in the voice, not much in the scrag of arms and shoulders.

"Expect we might give y'hand, me and my mate," I said. "Any grub?"

"Hut four, down there," he pointed over his shoulder. "Y'll find cheese hanging up. Bread i't netting. Wine i't barrel. What there is. Don't leave crumbs. Ants!"

The group seemed to ignore us, and started another chant. The man turned away, climbed over the figures nearer, and wandered across the fire stones.

"Dead funny do, eh?" Alec said, following me to hut four. "What, barmy, is he?"

"Drug of some sort, possibly. Grow what they want, here!"

I counted down to hut four, and went in. The small wick floated in a cigaret tin. Two couples slept on straw mattresses. Two others in a bunk tier, and a naked girl sprawled on a mat. Milk dripped in a hanging bag, and I took down the sack of bread, chose a couple of crusts of Arab unyeasted bake, spread them with soft cheese, and Alec tipped the barrel for two clay mugs of bitterish green wine. I took some black olives from a bowl, a red pepper, and a lettuce, and we went out to a smooth mound about fifty yards from the songsters.

"Did you see all those bunches of dried leaves hanging up near the sack?" I asked, munching. "Reason that fellow's half-out. And the others in there weren't asleep. That was hashish. Ever try it?"

"Never see no sense in it. Paying game till they get on to you. Do five inside? I give it up. Who d'you reckon these people are? Kid, asleep there, not a rag?"

"Haven't made up my mind. They seem to have a system. Unemployables? That girl was drugged. But safe enough, apparently. Quite a lot of Arabs among them. White skins don't tan beyond a certain tint. Take your shirt off for more than ten minutes tomorrow, you'll get a burn you'll never forget!"

"I ain't taking nothing off. Not that I'm no lady. I just don't hold with it. That's business, that is!"

A goat cheese sandwich with that doughy bake of grains, fresh lettuce, strips of pepper rind, a black olive now and again, and a mouthful of thin claret, night air, the breath of the sea, and a chorus of voices can make an uncommonly satisfying meal. I looked about for sleeping space, and Alec waved a warning match, held out the pack of Woodbines—I hadn't seen them for years—and over the light I saw two men coming away from the fire.

"Just come in?" one of them called. "Didn't see any troops up there, did you?"

"Come off a boat." Alec said. "Why? What's on?"

"Getting a bit worried, that's all," the younger man said, and squatted. "Them lads, you know, they don't try too hard, come to handling the birds. Make 'em lay eggs!"

"Couple there, I see, asking for it!" Alec said, ill-temperedly. "Laying about here, bollock naked? I mean, take y' chances, don't you?"

"That's their business!" the first man, older, bearded, sounding possibly Wessex, said, peremptorily. "Everybody's their own self, here. Pick your own, make your own, if that's what you want. But nobody can't tell you. Don't want it? Don't have it!"

"Can we help?" I asked.

"Comes to a scrap, you can," the younger said. "Won't do much good, though. We sent a message to the Consuls. Don't know if they got there. We couldn't find the German and Belgian, and then there's some Swedes, and a couple of Russians, I think they are. If we could just get a lift down the coast a bit. Start up there!"

"Start up what?" Alec said, in a cone of smoke.

"Another commune," he said, with simple candor. "We like the way we live. That's why we're here, if they'd just bloody-well leave us alone!"

"What, don't you do no work?" Alec said, grieved.

"I was your age, I had to keep a family. My Dad died. Did your'n?"

"*We* died!" the older man said, looking back toward the fire. "We let go of families. We're here to *be*. No. All we want's a fair go, and leave us alone. We're doing no harm. Taking what's handy, being our own selves, growing what we want, fishing, all that. Listen, if you're here to preach the other stuff, you can sling it. We're not standing for it!"

"Keep it *lento!*" the youth said, looking up. "Don't go round with the tape. Fact is, we don't care *who* comes here. You got to find your own way, that's all. Listen, down the beach a bit, there's a lot more. Lot from all the universities. Y'know? And ours. Same lot. You just find out where y'arse sets best. Where you can talk to people, see? Some birds I can talk to, see? Down there, I can't. Same shape, same everything. Can't talk to 'm? I come here. Blokes the same. Talk to some, fine. Others? It's orbit, no suit. Here, I'm right."

"What d'y'mean, orbit, no suit?" Alec said irritably, in night air. "I mean, let's hear what you're talking!"

The youth looked at him sideways, and away.

"Try going round the moon, cock-raw!" he said, tiredly. "What I say, some people you can talk to. Others, Christ!"

"Come on," the man said, walking away. "Night watch, up!"

"What's that for?" I asked, and stood, with the youth. "Worried about something?"

"They can come in any time. Birds in roost can't do much, can they? The other lot up there come down here and try. Arabs try. Don't get too far. 'less we had too much pot. So we keep off it one night, do a trick, and the others take it the next. We give 'em a do of oil balls. Burn 'em. They don't like it. Had no trouble, the past week. Get hit with one of them, take a foot of skin off!"

"Listen!" the man shouted, almost at the fire. "Don't move about too much. Be unlucky!"

The youth raised a hand, let it flop, walked off. Alec looked at me.

"What d'*you* make of it?" he said worriedly. "All sound barmy to me!"

"How do we sound to them? Better look for a place to sleep. Out of the way. Tomorrow, we can help them with the raft, pay for supper. I want to look at the 'foreign' lot up there!"

CHAPTER THIRTY-SEVEN

I woke in pink dawn. Running feet pounded under my pillow. I lay in a hollow of sand, with the branches we'd torn from olive trees under. A sharp scent of woodsmoke carried aromas of baking grains and coffee.

The beach went pale to green water. Dozens of long-haired girls, and men, were running down to leap, knees high, and dive in the small waves. Breeze took sound away, but voices lazed in the hiatus, a wheeling of gulls, children's laughter, strange notes of pathos, innocence.

Alec had gone. I sat up, and saw him at the sea's edge, trousers rolled to the knee, shirt off, sluicing head and shoulders, using sand for soap, taking no notice of the really lovely nudes in front and on both sides of him.

I went down in briefs, plunged, swam out to the high breakers, turned and came in on a crest. Alec dried his head in a shirt, looked up bloat-eyed, saw me and paused.

"Well, what'd'you make out of *this?*" he called, nodding at the dozens on the beach. "I never see nothing like it. Not even in 'em films. Worried about nothing. I mean, they ain't even got their hand on it!"

"Why should they? They're used to each other. Perfectly natural!"

He looked at me in baffled amazement.

"Can't make you out!" he said, and half-heartedly wiped his neck. "Here, I thought you' be the first to be proper disgusted, and you go and say *that!*"

"Looks healthy enough. The girls're all beautiful. Except that I find a naked man with a beard slightly ridiculous. Let's get up the beach and see if we can get something to eat!"

I folded the red hankerchief in a pirate's cap, and Alec tied the sweatband. His trousers were rolled to the knee, shirt outside, and I wore blue shorts, with a looped shirt around the shoulders. We made a pack of clothing between the satchel and the rucksack, hung them in a vine, and started up the beach, to the east.

"All aboard for Margate!" Alec said. "I could go a nice cup of Chunner's best, and a couple of slices of toast, eggs and bacon, and the *Mirror*. Can't believe I was in the Smoke yesterday, and this, today. I mean, *look* at 'em!"

I was looking. There must have been at least a couple of hundred girls up and down the beach without a stitch between them. Men generally wore the leather thong or nothing. They were all a magnificent sun color. Most of them threw a rush-ball in circles of twenty or so, or fours played netball, and others lay in the sand, eyes closed in the rising sun, or covered themselves with mud down at the water's edge.

I've never seen anything more idyllic.

But I felt disastrously out of place. Out of time, out of context. Simply not in the game. I didn't belong. I tried to analyze, and found it beyond me, except that I managed to unearth a part of myself unwilling, I wasn't sure why, or unable, or fearful of entering the mental climate. Then I had to laugh outright at myself. It was, of course, nothing but a residue of impacted Puritanism clogging the filter.

Alec stared. I wondered how to explain.

"I feel I'm in another world," I said. "Dreaming. But it's a good dream!"

"Gets tastier b'the minute!" Alec said, smacking his lips. "Y' know, guv'nor, I never see nothing open, I mean, like this. Dead funny do. They don't even care if you *look* at 'em, do they? My old lady ever see this, she drop dead. She would? But I do, I like it!"

"I'm glad!"

"So'm I, guv'. Glad I come here. And thank *you*. You done me a favor, did you know? I was getting sort of down, like. I been abroad. Had me good times. Seen it all, like. Nothing much, come to look at it.

323

This is something else, this is. Dead new. Nobody looks at nobody, and every one of 'em looks right. I think that's what it is. They look *right!*"

I agreed, privately.

"Could I ask you question?"

"Of course!"

"Why did you ask me to come here?"

"As a bodyguard. But you knew that!"

"Ah. Won't need much of one here, will you? I seen nothing I couldn't chew in handfuls."

All this, at about six o'clock—my watch was in the rucksack—nothing looks sillier than a wristwatch on a beach—or worn with evening dress, which is funnier—I don't know why—and as yet, I hadn't seen anyone I recognized. But the little boy standing one-legged just behind the beanrows seemed to be looking at me and away, at me, and away. I touched the red hankerchief, and turned off, up the narrow path between beetroots and tomatoes, and he went through the vines. I followed, went on, through the pomegranates to the olives. I heard the familiar jingle, and in green gloom of foliage, Arefa stood in front, though I hadn't noticed a move. He touched heart, mouth and head, and gave me a plastic package.

There were three cables, not two.

PLEASE PRESENT OFFSHORECO VAULT KEYS GENEVA URGENTEST DOES NOT ADMIT DELAY

MOHR

Those keys were in a slit in my right shoe. One had been Paul's, and I'd taken it from him on the night he'd entered the clinic. The second was mine, given to me when I'd become his vice, and the third was in keeping of the Director General of the bank. All three keys had to be used to get into the Company vault. I had a curious rumble in the Pit. Premonition, it seemed, was valid.

DARLING MINE, ALL WELL WONDERFUL EX-
CEPT YOUR BEAUTIFULLY LAUNDERED AND
IRONED AND BEFLOWERED PILLOW. BIG
MARY SAYS PLEASE RIDE ANY WHITE HORSE
TO BANBURY CROSS AND ME. KETTLE BOILS.
PATTI MEL SEND KISSES TO DADDY AND
GRANDADDY. I SHOULD SHAY SHO.

CONSUELO

In that red flush, which turned the forest to a scarlet
shimmer, and brought a blast of heat thudding in
temples and groin, I could have thrown everything to
hell and walked, singing, to the airport.

I hesitated over the third.

BETROTHED LONDON
REPORTS SAY EL BIDH IN DANGER ATTACK.
CANNOT FIND FACTS. SENDING THIS DES-
PERATE HOPE YOU CAN DO SOMETHING LOVE

ULLA

That was enough.

"Arefa, you tell your father to bring the truck here,
with horses," I said. "I want to ride from here to the
road, and I want him to tell M. Maurice to get me a
flight immediately to Cairo. Take these messages. Ask
M. Maurice to send them priority. Try to be back here
by ten o'clock. Yes?"

He nodded.

"Go with God!"

I went back to find Alec sitting in a path between
onions and lettuce, arms about his knees, smoking. The
sun was high, the beach shone white, all the scores
walking, lying, running, were the same deep gold tint.
Human beauty hymned, a green sea flowed, voices
chorused, and a red and yellow fishing boat raced for
the beach, dropping brown half-moon sails, and girls
ran with baskets to take the catch.

Alec looked at me over his shoulder.

"Never see *no*thing like this!" he said. "Look, down there, they got coffee. All right?"

It was then, in a cloud of worry, barely seeing anything, that I caught Frederick, lankily arms about two girls, as I'd have expected, walking up the beach toward the long, laughing, line. That's, I suppose, what really got me. Everybody seemed to be laughing.

He saw me as we got closer, flicked a look at Alec, said something, and turned back. I walked toward him, the girls went on, wet hair stuck to their shoulders, clean, of the air, quite lovely, and only Alec's sandstuck feet seemed gross.

Frederick watched the pomegranates until I was a couple of yards away, and I looked sideways at Alec.

"How about getting in the queue!" I said. "For three!"

Frederick turned toward the surf.

"You don't look too excitingly French!" he said.

"Wasn't on. Find anything?"

"I've had a fairly comprehensive chase round. There's no radio here larger than the miniatures some of them carry. They can't get batteries, so there aren't many. I've been all the way up in the olives at the back there. There's nothing up to the road. Fair distance. I haven't heard anything really political. lot of opinions, of course. There're quite a number of Sorbonne people here. Nanterre. Madrid. Barcelona. Other places. Americans, too. Men and women. It's a mix. Wouldn't have missed it!"

"Nothing pro-Soviet?"

"I've heard a lot worse at home. No. They just seem to come here, and get together, and like it. Dad, I want to ask an enormous favor!"

"All right?"

"I'd rather like to stay here for a little time. I've found a sort of basis. I'm sorry for them in a way. I don't quite know how to tell you. I'd like to borrow some money, if you agree, on what Mummy left me. I

326

don't want much. I'd like to build a decent shelter, here, where the girls, at least, can have a hot bath now and again, get their nails done, that sort of thing. Where we can sit down to a meal, kitchen, tables, chairs. Place for talks, plays. Debates. Electric light. Iceboxes to keep stuff in. A place off, for lathes and whatnot. Where the lads can make what's wanted. Power for looms. A lot of the girls are really good, linens, carpets, all that. Would you consider it?"

I was deeply, tragically, even stupidly touched. He looked so much like his mother. Sentimental humbug? But it exists.

I realized I was of an old, old generation.

This was the new.

Alec came down, balancing two mugs, one atop t'other, three grainbakes piled in the steam, and carrying another with a lid of smaller biscuits.

In that time, thankfully, my throat hardened.

"Of course," I said, out to sea. "How much d'you want?"

"Well, I've been into it with a chap from Rome, and a few others, they're students of architecture. Plenty of them here. I thought about a thousand pounds, to kick off. Too much?"

"Here y'are, me lucky lads!" Alec bawled. "Grab it while it's hot. This your boy, guv'? Thought so. Here, one for you. Your young ladies said they'll be waiting round there, at the herb garden!"

"We planted a little parsley and mint," Frederick said, in the air. "How do we manage this?"

"Maurice will come to see you. But if the authorities here won't let you stay?"

"I think if we built something, sort of hotel fashion, where people could sleep decently, live a, well, a more civilized sort of life, lavatories, baths, that very usual nonsense, they'd perhaps be inclined to a rather more reasonable line. If they want tourism, we can bring in most of Europe. Nudism's tourism!"

"Lot in that," Alec said, and gave me the other mug

and bake. "Guv', I made up me mind. You're going off today? You don't mind, I'll hang on. Shove a tent up, time being, what more d'you want?"

"I have only one small doubt," I said. "Supposing they won't let you?"

"Never heard of nobody turning money away. I can show 'em mine. I suppose you can? Like he says, reasonable. What are we, insulting somebody?"

"Talk to Maurice. He's a builder, and he's shrewd. How do you see the capital paying dividends?"

"What's made, and the little we'll charge for services," Frederick said. "We can sell the cloth and carpets. Other things. It's all here. All it needs is money!"

"You've got it. If Alec stays on, I'll feel more confident. What're you going to do, first?"

"Build a fairly strong one-storey affair. Then bath houses. Then see what we want. I'll take care of buildings and the books."

"Ever rain here?"

"For a couple of months in the year. That's when we move to dry quarters. We could also use one of your radios!"

"Send it this afternoon. I'll call you from time to time. You haven't asked about Patti!"

"I telephoned before I came here. She sounded wonderful. I'm very grateful for all this——"

"Nothing of the sort. Question of drugs. I saw it drying up there. That's not the main attraction, is it?"

He looked out at the sea, down at the mug.

"No!"

"But it's used?"

"Some of them, yes!" he said unwillingly.

"You don't? I'd like to be sure about it!"

He shook his head.

"There's plenty of stuff here," he said quietly. "Anything you want, at any time. I don't know where it comes from. I think, from down the beach. Some of them are in a quite hopeless condition. They're few. But they could grow. Another reason I want to stay here. I feel I could prevent it. Or some of it!"

"You're thinking of staying here? A career?"

I was joking, but he reddened.

"No!" he said, in a dander. "I told you. I'm *sorry* for them. Really sorry. And I'd like to do something!"

"Good. Your friends are becoming impatient. Back to the herb garden. I'll probably be here again in a few days. Take good care!"

He nodded, half-smiled, shook hands, and went in through the vines, a fine, healthy-looking chap, I thought, heavy shoulders, good calves, and from the greetings in the line still going up for coffee, not a bit unsightly to the girls.

"I find any drug lark going on, I tell you what I do!" Alec said. "I bet that's the cause of the chuck-out. I don't blame 'em. But what's the *idea* of drugs? I never see nothing in 'em!"

"What's the idea of booze? What you *could* do is find out, quietly, who's got the stock. If these boys and girls haven't any money, how are they getting it? Why? Who's behind it?"

"I see what you mean. Why's he giving away cash, that it?"

"If a lot of them *are* students, they've got to get back fairly soon. Universities are opening. If some of them go back addicted, they'll create a demand. They'll be followed by others, human nature being what it is. A circle forms, gets larger. Good for the peddlars. Rotten for society. What you could do's stroll about, sleep here and there, get to know people, and nail him, or them!"

Alec raised a finger, smiled almost dreamily.

"Now y'talking, guv'. But supposing they come in with the troops, what then?"

"Get back to Derna. Come again another day. Be careful. They're the old-fashioned type of Arab. The best. They don't stand any nonsense!"

We'd walked a fair way. The beach curved inland, in a bay perhaps five miles along to a headland, the same vegetable plots, pomegranates, vines, olives, not a tiled roof that I could see, though I knew that nearer the trunk road there were the considerable properties of

329

landowners, mostly Italian, French, and Arab. I wished I'd brought a map to see how far we were from the house where I'd last seen Joh Pensen and that girl. I wondered again about her. She wasn't the type able to hide for very long, and too many people were after her.

I didn't want to think about El Bidh or Banbury Cross, still less about Geneva, but I had to. I'd already decided to go first to El Bidh. That was absolutely a keypoint. I had to talk to Ob to find out what he'd done about arms, ammunition and mercenary troops. I had the aircraft to fly them in, and I knew where to charter helicopters. I only hoped the Princes were safe.

That nagged.

The Geneva business puzzled me. My two keys, and the Director General's would open our vault. But for what reason? We had nothing to put in or take out. It was I who normally gave that instruction. What was "urgentest" that permitted no delay?

I became aware that the sun was a blazer, and my shoulders were cooking even under the shirt.

"Better double that cover," I told Alec, and showed him how. "A few minutes of this, you'll be a steak!"

"How is it they ain't?" he asked, nodding at the girls. But then his eyes seemed to change color, and he looked at me. "Hi! I didn't see that, would you believe it?"

All of them wore a collar of leaves. I don't think I ever saw anything prettier than those girls, all in a woven short cape of pomegranate leaves, with little conical caps of grape. The men wore much the same, and some, burnt as Arabs, nothing, though most of them stayed in the shade.

We were about halfway along the bay. I'd already been surprised by a change in the type of girl. The young men seemed cleaner cut—soap and water cleaner?—better formed?—a more classic shape?—I'm not certain. The girls "seemed" more feminine. They moved with more grace. I wasn't at all sure about it. But I seemed to hark again to the theory that schooling counts. It was here, plain, for that matter, nude.

"Hold tight!" Alec said. "I see a pub over there? Don't tell me there's something cold?"

A drink was what I wanted. We walked across sand a little too hot for my feet, behind the plots and the vines of green grapes, and sure enough, there were plank tables on trestles, stools of sawn trunks, and men serving behind a counter of two doors laid across a couple of small boats.

"Not too promising!" Alec said. "No barrels? I can see a lot of room for 'provement', here!"

But they kept the bottles in pits dug to the water plane, and a boy down there threw them up into expert hands that flipped them, acrobat style, to the barman. It was the weak beer of the coast, but cold, and good, and with a *kifé*, a flat of pastry with mince meat, we sat down in vineshade, and let things take their most pleasant course. The girls and their partners went by on both sides of the table—I tried not to hear what they were saying, but I heard French, English, Spanish, and Italian, and a Roumanian girl sang something that brought an unbearable memory of Mimi Prôche—and Alec chewed *kifé* and drank his beer, and looked across at me.

"Know what?" he said, just over the noise. "I never had nothing like this when I was their age. I reckon I'm worse off!"

"Cheer up. At least, you're in time to share it!"

"I wish I was *in* it. I ain't even got the guts to take me trousers off!"

"Close your eyes and drop them!"

"What, an' show me truss?"

"They won't mind!"

"I notice you don't!"

"Very odd place to get burned!"

He held out the Woodbines, I lit a match.

"You reckon it's all going to be like this everywhere?" he asked, over the flames. "I mean, youngsters, like this lot? What's going to happen? Who's going to do any work?"

"It'll get done one way or another. Examinations

have to be passed. People have to learn a trade. Iron laws. Some of them say they've finished with the whole thing. They'll ram their heads against the realities. Hunger. And age. The dream-killers!"

"Pity, though. I *like* this!"

Alec, I was beginning to find, had to be led carefully by the hand. He was willing victim to sudden enthusiasms. I knew that Frederick was far more inclined to pour cold water, a further "accident" of schooling. I wondered if Alec would accept a pointblank order from a boy almost half his age. I hoped he would. The knowledge inherent in the order, the look, the tone, the accent, might do it, I thought.

I had a hand over my eyes to shield from sunrays dazzling through breaks in leafage, and I looked over the tall tomato plants of fat green fruits turning pink, suddenly warned by the appearance of a number of men I hadn't noticed before, all in the buff, most bellied, in towels or shorts, a few behind fully dressed, all my age, older, some perhaps a few years younger, but certainly not students, and from their faces, not professors of anything except licence.

Instantly I was reminded of Cosa Nostra. No mistaking the type. I'd had a few brushes with them at other times. Their base was just a few hours off, across the Mediterranean. Many of the "students" came in on fishing boats. No passport?

It fitted.

They went along the back of the vines. I sniffed cigar smoke.

I hadn't time to do anything about it. We'd walked about four miles. It would take at least an hour to get back, and I had to fly soonest.

I stood, and gave the boy some money. He was digging for change, and I sat down again.

The golden marvel I'd last seen swaying a song on the creaky stairs of Georges Pontvianne's office had just come in, with two other girls, and a couple of extremely well-developed young men, shorter hair than most, shaven, in blue briefs. The glory wore a yellow

332

flowered bikini and top, but it didn't do anything except emphasize everything, and it was all extremely emphatic, some of the nicest emphasis I've ever seen. She was about a match for Consuelo, though, out of loyalty, perhaps not quite. I couldn't see her face, and the two lads sat one across, one beside her. Three other young men, all footballers, came behind me and sat at another table. I'd have made a large bet they were of the same party, and had Georges come in, I wouldn't have been surprised. But the very fact that she was here gave me a most pleasant lift of spirit. If she were anything like her mother, I pitied the Cosa Nostra team—if that's what they were—their fat, their cigars. Obviously, there had to be a large catch, either in view or being played for.

I got up, very well content, and set a fair pace.

"What, you off to a fire, guv'?" Alec said. "Proper tearing it up, here, ain't you?"

"I'm catching a bus. Did you see that girl?"

"Did I what? 's what I'm staying here for!"

"Right. Now, listen. Make a point of hanging about. I know her family. Spot her, and just dawdle about in reasonable distance. There could be some trouble. Then again, not. If there were, I'd like to know you were there with those lads round her, putting in a few!"

Alec closed those fists, and looked up at the blue, almost in armor, lance at ready.

"Guv', I get the chance!" he whispered. "I just get the bloody chance, that's all. By Krice!"

CHAPTER THIRTY-EIGHT

I had the luck at Derna to catch a private flight of tourists going to Athens, by jet, and Maurice sent on a cable asking Argyopoulis to hold White Horse Three Romeward. All I did, there, was cross the tarmac, shake hands with Captain Lester, and walk upstairs, to a hot shower, a good meal, and a first-class radio operator.

Logan was in the desert, and I asked his office to make an appointment for next day at Basra, with a team of our best explosives men. I got on the scrambler to Berry, told him to find Ob, and ask him to call me in Rome within the next couple of hours.

"Nothing much new, sir," Berry said, a little wearily. "I believe Mr. Hockley's office's got a couple of lines. But they don't say too much, as you know. Ah, yes. The glove you picked up in the box, sir? Pair of the one Pensen had with him. Blood on it, and on the dress, same group as the dead man. So Pensen must have been there when the shot was fired. It was something like a .38 bullet, strange to us. Not lead. Don't know what it is, yet. Don't know the type of weapon, either. The bullet spreads. No sign of the man Von Staengl. The West German people just closed up. Nothing on the Prôche case. One more item, sir. Mr. James Morris sent in to say he'd like you to call him!"

I got on to Mohr and heard that "aaahhr!" of sheer relief.

"But what's it all about?"

"Sir, I cannot say anything, you understand. But please be here no later than three o'clock this afternoon!"

"I'm sorry, I'm flying on to Basra tonight!"

"I must impress you, sir, please, to speak to the Director of the Bank, Dr. Brille, but immediately. There is no recourse. No option!"

For many reasons, principally because of the diplomatic files held there, I didn't want that vault examined by anyone. But something was very seriously wrong if, as I gathered, somebody—and it could only be done by Federal order—intended to go in without my permission. I saw that El Bidh had to wait.

I sent forward to Captain Lester, and asked him to change course for Geneva. Within moments I felt the seat tipping gently right, watched the horizon disappear on my side. The London operator asked if I'd take an urgent call to Rome, and Miss Pearlman came on, bright as a trivet, read through a summary of engineers and stores in transit, auditor's certificate, and a favorable report by Miss Toverell on the personal files of the staff.

I checked surprise, played a small card.

"Has she finished there?"

"Almost, sir, I believe tomorrow morning she goes to Athens. She has to verify with London this afternoon—"

"Are you sending the dossiers by courier?"

"One's just gone. We shall have clearance on them this evening—"

"Is Miss Toverell with you now?"

"Downstairs in her old office, sir—"

"You work well with her?"

"Excellently, sir. I always did. When I met her in London two years ago, I thought her so much older. But she is so talented. For a young woman, such a brain, so *English*. I should learn again English as Miss Toverell speaks. It is so *Ox*ford!"

But then, Miss Pearlman, as a student of English, would never confuse an Oxonian with the Doric Miss Toverell, especially having met her. I was being given a smart, most diplomatic tip.

"Is anybody with you?"

"No sir!"

"Pay the strictest attention to what I have to say. I do *not* want Miss Toverell to have any idea that I am, as it were, supervising her work, do you understand?"

"Perfectly, sir!"

"You will therefore not say that we have spoken. I don't wish to find it mentioned in her report. Is that clear?"

"It is perfectly clear, sir!"

"Very well. Call London immediately. Ask for a Company aircraft to take Miss Toverell to Athens tomorrow at eleven o'clock. She may wish to fly elsewhere. You will instruct the pilot to obey my order. If there's any misunderstanding about this, ask Commodore Kopfers to talk to me in Geneva at six o'clock this evening. Is that understood?"

"It is understood, sir!"

"And my name, or any breath of this conversation will not be mentioned. Are you using your brain?"

"I am using it very much, sir!"

"Very well. Miss Pearlman, I rely upon you!"

Evidently, I'd picked the right girl in Miss Pearlman. She'd put two and two together, played along, and, with any luck, we had a fat bird in the trap.

Miss Toverell was by no means "young," God love her. She was fifty-sevenish, tall, thin, a Highland Scotswoman, of the bluest and best, and she spoke the Doric, which has little to do with Anglo-Saxon English, though to listen to, it's possibly the most enchanting English of them all. I also knew—because I'd seen the accountant's report—that she was in the middle of month's rest at her home in Argyllshire.

I called Teddy Taphamides' office in Athens, and got on to that quite lovely quasi-English voice again, and she put me through. I knew some day I'd *have* to go the Athens just to look at her.

"Edmund! I have been calling your office—"

"I'm in mid-flight between here and Geneva. Tomorrow, at some time, a Miss Emma Toverell—T-o-v-e-r-e-l-l—of this Company is flying to Athens—"

"Got it? Yes?"

"She's an imposter. She's travelling on a false passport. She should be kept in close custody. It's possible she has links with the pair—"

336

"Ah, Edmund, what a nice fish!"

"Get her tanked!"

"She is *truite bleue,* believe me. Now. New for you. We had a ship at the Piraeus, Blagarov, from Tiflis and Dolmecde—it's in Turkey—two passengers, one, British, Reeves, had some trouble. He gave the name of your Company, and stated they were both employees, engineers on leave. The other is South African. Neither had a passport, and the Captain declined to help. He sailed without them. They now wish to get to Malta!"

"I'll pay all expenses to have them flown there, but under escort. You will please get in touch with the authorities there, and have them both shown into a comfortable cell. If it's the Reeves I know, he can cool his heels till I get there!"

"They go tonight. When shall we have the pleasure of lunch?"

"Lunch? I'm thinking of a bacchanalian dinner!"

"I shall wait. So impatiently!"

Reeves, an oilman of wide experience, had been bought by a "competitor" and had left the Company without notice, together with dribs and drabs of others, until, not long before we'd been in serious lack of supervisory staff. I'd never found out who was behind the buy, or where the men had gone. Now, it seemed, there was some chance of an answer. But how did he manage a passage on a Soviet ship? He'd need a passport. But his passport, as with everybody's, had been held by the Company until he had to travel, and we still had it. Was it Reeves? How did he get into the Soviet Union? How, without papers, had he left, and what was he doing in Piraeus? How did he, or they, expect to hoodwink the British Counsul? It was a nice series of questions, and if I knew the Maltese, there'd have to be solid answers.

I had a feeling I was closing in.

We were touching down while I was in the middle of the day's diary entry. Mohr waited with Dr. Buders, in heavy rain, under an enormous red umbrella, and we got in a small runaround with a flat canvas top that douched water when we turned, and did nothing to keep the raingusts out of our faces and laps. I've often wondered why people go to the trouble of making something perfectly good that doesn't altogether fit the told me about the consignment from Rome and the job.

"We are in a very serious situation, Mr. Trothe!" Dr. Buders said, loudly, over the squalls. "I wish you had other, from London. It was embarrassing to admit I knew nothing!"

I sat back. Hard rain became encouragement of sorts.

"Dr. Buders," I began carefully, and paused. "Nothing of any kind has been sent to the Bank. Nobody has authority to use the vault. What, exactly, is the complaint?"

His eyes, wide, sideways, crimped in gusts, glared disbelief.

"I have your telegram announcing the arrival of the Rome consignment!" he shouted, sounding like a child. "The other, from England, went to the Director, and he telephoned to me. General Tengler, of course, was immediately informed. He acted as you might expect!"

I wondered how long it would take me to speak German as perfectly as he spoke English. There was a stilt, but no real accent.

"I sent no telegrams to anyone!" I shouted.

He shielded his face from a stinging spat.

"I don't understand!" he said, and got well down in his coat collar.

"The other came in the day before yesterday," Mohr said, from behind. "They are both in the Bank's vault. Your London office did not acknowledge the Bank's messages. Two days we have been trying. But then General Tengler enters the matter, and so we have nothing to do!"

I had a distinct feeling.

I was very glad I'd decided not to go to El Bidh.

Beneath all, a memory of Consuelo hurt, burned. It's

not too much to say. I could feel the warmth of her pelt under my hands, hear her whispers, sniff the scent of breasts, feel that first, thick thrust, and the cling, all her neck between jaw and ear, taste the sweet of her shredding in dream after dream, while I talked and listened, and others thought I was myself.

Guards let us into the side tunnel to the Bank, Mohr showed a pass which took us into the carlift, and down we went, I don't know how far, to the vault doors, the grilles, the striplight lanes, that enormous arched pale-blue space, that led to another, and another, all piled with crates under huge Capital letters, and the guide turned in under O.

OFFSHORE OIL was stenciled on one of the crates.

That was a mistake.

"This is the consignment from Rome, billed from Athens and London," Mohr said, hooking a finger at an overalled guard. "Dr. Brille will be down in one moment!"

"Offshore Oil is a subsidiary, a book term, convenient for accountants," I said. "It has nothing to order, and doesn't. This is not my property!"

Mohr stared.

"The invoices are from your London and Paris offices, via Athens and Rome!" he said. "It's gold!"

"That makes it all so much plainer. It's not mine!"

The nearer liftdoors opened, and a group came out.

"Dr. Brille!" Mohr said, almost as a prayer.

I wasted no time on introduction.

"I want these boxes opened immediately!" I said. "I want the contents verified, and I want the Police here. These are addressed to a subsidiary of my Company which exists only for the purpose of buying a variety of tubing. I am absolutely in control. Nothing moves anywhere unless I say so. I have not recently bought any gold. Nothing has been sent to this Bank. Open them!"

"I should first like to read to you the relevant paragraph in Swiss Law, *verbis*"—Dr. Brille—whom I'd never met—started saying. "We are in a curious situat—"

"Open those boxes and let's find out how curious!" I

insisted. "Was any representative of my Company here to sign them in?"

"No, sir!" Dr. Buders said, cold, distant. "It is why I asked them to be put here, in the Bank's reception vault, instead of in the Company's own. I was given no notice until they were here!"

Dr. Brille's sign to a supervisor brought a couple of guards trotting over, one with a toolkit, and the other pushing an automatic scale.

"We have already noted a discrepancy in the weights of the several boxes," he said, copying Dr. Buder's tone and manner. He was the thin-upstairs-potting-out-about-the-belt type, quite bald, gold rimmed half-moons, washy blue eyes that could be focussed, as now in points, and a surprisingly full bottom lip which shone spittle. "All boxes of bullion should contain the same weight. If there is a lesser weight over, it is marked in the delivery copy, and also on the box. We have nothing in paper, or on the box!"

"Good!" I said, watching the men put a box on the scale, check the weight, and compare it with the invoice. "I'm here to see that the name of my Company is protected, and I'm very grateful to Dr. Buders and Inspector Mohr for insisting that I come here!"

That "tight" feeling in the air seemed to loosen. I saw by their faces that I'd said the right thing. I believe they thought I'd been playing a game. I was certainly wondering what the devil the game *was*. I'd no doubt the pair were involved, but I couldn't see how, in a pile of boxes.

The last came off the scale, and the guard brought Dr. Brille a paper with a neat list of weights, box by box. He looked at it, and gave it to me.

Only six of the weights tallied.

"You see reason for our doubt?" he said smilingly. "Each box, I repeat, should be the same weight. I should say, *of* the same weight!"

"Sir, permit me to felicitate you upon a command of English. Kindly have those boxes opened. I have the

340

right to request it. Or, if you prefer, let us wait for the Police!"

"I am the director here," he said quietly, with a smile, and turned to the men. "Empty those boxes!"

"If they'd gone into the Company vault in the usual way, I suppose they wouldn't have been weighed?" I asked, looking at a row of gold ingots flush with the top of the first box. "I feel someone gambled on it!"

"A client's property is sacrosanct when it comes in correctly designated for that vault. Then we expect the Company representatives to be present, each with a key, and I, or whoever is on duty, present the Bank's, the vault is unlocked, the property is deposited, the doors and grilles are locked once more, and generally, we adjourn for a glass of sherry, or a whiskey!"

"They probably supposed it would go in the strong room upstairs. Might anyone have made enquiries about it to find out?"

"Unless they were substantial clients, wanting to hire a private vault, no enquiry would be met. Anything in the strong room upstairs comes down here. We do not draw plans, or invite disaster!"

"But it begins to appear!" Dr. Buders said, behind me. "What is *that!*"

Under the first two of a top row of ingots, black enamel reflected the gold. The guard tipped the box slowly on to a canvas sheet. I knew what it was.

"That's a generator which can be switched on and off by radio!" I said, and knelt to turn all dials to normal. I wasn't surprised to see that "normal" was its setting, and couldn't be altered.

"Is there a jeweller's nearby?" I asked. "I wonder if I could borrow a set of watchmaker's tools?"

"Inspector Mohr!" Dr. Brille said, almost as a command.

Mohr went at a trot to the lift.

"What would that be used for?" Dr. Brille asked, looking at it sideways. "Is it dangerous?"

"Not now. I'm going to dismantle this part, here, and put the whole thing out of action!"

341

Other boxes were opened, ingots piled, and then, under the top row of a heavyweight box, they tipped out an oddly shaped scarlet affair, with a small keyboard, rather like a cashier's adding machine.

"A little beauty" Dr. Brille said. "We have many of its grandparents upstairs. But I've never seen a computer so *small!* What next, now?"

I had a curious feeling about what we were going to come across. Here, obviously, were the stores which Stather had ordered—as he thought—for Logan.

"These things are expensive," Dr. Buders began, a little doubtfully. "But why are they sent to this Bank?"

"We'll probably come across a fairly good reason," I said. "I wish Mohr would hurry himself. Didn't you say there was another consignment?"

"Next bay," Dr. Brille nodded. "A large affair, and a small crate."

"Wouldn't it be as well if somebody started taking the lids off? Save time?"

Dr. Brille spoke to a supervisor, and our men emptied a sixth box filled with gold, adding to the long dully-shining stack in ringing *dings!*

"But is somebody ready to lose all this?" Dr. Buders said, in amazement. "After all it's a considerable sum of money!"

"I shall claim it!" I said, while the guards were taking a second row of ingots' out of another box. "For their purpose, presumably, it was going to be worth it!"

"Past tense?"

"Hopefully so!"

The guard slowly lifted out a weighty box, about a foot long, and four inches by three, satin-finished, at a glance, a radio, not European or American, and possibly not Japanese. There was no way of telling how it was set, and rather than dial-fiddle, I used the vade mecum on my key chain to take off the back. I cut all the wires I could find, took out the capsule battery, and had a good look. Wrightson, my chief radio technician would have called it a ruddy marvel. It had rocket engineering written all over it.

I began putting things together. We had a generator, a computer and a radio set. Both generator and computer were fitted with small radios. I had no way of finding out if all three were set to the same frequency, but if they were, then what? Would a radio signal, passed through this ultra-powerful set operate the other two? For what reason?

Mohr came in breathless with a leather fold.

"Sorry I was so long!" he said. "Had to go to the head office. Is this what you want?"

It was, exactly, and I put all three radio receivers out of business, and then found that the large radio was also a transmitter. That set me back. There was no morse key, and I couldn't find ducts for microphone or headset. It was a doughty job, of extraordinary range, which received and transmitted but what for?

Dr. Brille stood with Mohr watching the last two boxes being opened. Dr. Buders, sitting on the stack of gold, caught my glance, and grinned, eyebrows up, opening his hands.

"I support myself on more wealth than I shall ever see!" he said. "If I have piles from sitting here, they will be gold-plated. *Such* a pleasure!"

"Something here!" Mohr called.

The guards were lifting out ingots packed about an amorphous shape in a nylon wrap. Mohr used his penknife to cut the tape binding, and it took the three of them to unroll some yards of stuff finer than silk.

But it was the wired bronze and platinum artistry inside that I reached for, and recognized instantly as James Morris's pet, the detonator.

"Don't take the wrap off!" I said, and made a cushion of the nylon, and put it down, slipping off my jacket, going to work with a loup and screwdriver to dismantle the leads into the main chamber. At the top, under a flat hood, a radio set about the size of half a box of paper matches was more than strong enough to relay a signal.

"I understand nothing of these things, Mr. Trothe!" Dr. Buders said, looking over his glasses in open admiration. "Are you able to say what this could be for?"

"I can only guess. Nothing in the other boxes?"

"A little more money, that's all!" Dr. Brille said, pulling his waistcoat over the hump. "We now go in the other vault, if you please!"

Mohr strapped the fold, I got into my jacket, and we set off, a procession of guards, two supervisors, our party, and when we passed through to the larger vault next door, General Tengler and three other men waited beside the desk.

Under T were two cases addressed to *TRU-CIALGAS*, and that, too, was a mistake. It was a cable cipher used only for a message to me, in person, aboard an aircraft east of Cairo.

Three sad mistakes, one after another, but the first and worst lay in not making sure of me. At that moment, I wondered if the El Bidh cable from Ulla might have been a fake.

"Well, Mr. Trothe, you are ready?" General Tengler said, in a breezily military manner. "I shall require a complete report about this matter, and I must warn you I place an embargo on everything addressed to you here!"

"Perfectly all right," I said, watching the large case without the lid, carried on to trestles. "None of it's mine. But I shall claim the gold, of course!"

Eight men had all they could do to lift, and lay it flat. A supervisor reached over to pull off a green baize felt-lined cover, and an expanse of walnut gilstened.

"A piano!" General Tengler said.

The case's hinged sides let down. The keyboard was padded in a rubber cushion. I lifted it for long enough to see *BECHSTEIN* in gold letters. In the curve of the piano, the guards took out two metal files of music, a metronome, a case of piano tuner's tools, and three more heavy packages. Two guards had to call a third to lift the largest.

"Be careful how you handle that!" I warned. "Put it on the floor *very* gently!"

With Mohr's help I lifted the piano's lid. Enough wiring stretched to fool perhaps a cursory inspection. But a closer look showed most hammers and the longer strings missing. In the space, steel shapes were well-packed in sacking. They had the twist of propellors, smooth to the touch. The larger package, set down on the floor, had been stripped of canvas, and an inner wrap of new chamois leather.

No mistaking that dull shine, or the little copper excrescence on top.

The entire business became very clear indeed. A series of correct signals, fed to the computer, and the entire Bank would have gone up, with every piece of paper. The Company would have lost all documentary reason for existence.

"Inspector Mohr, you will please call Chief Superintendent Hockley at New Scotland Yard," I said, and stood, to put on my jacket. "Inform him that the piano belonging to the murder victim, Pensen, has been found, together with the second part of the Barnbruche warhead, and the original detonator. Dr. Brille, if you'll kindly provide a secretary, I'm ready to dictate a report. General Tengler, would you care to witness?"

CHAPTER THIRTY-NINE

Below me, the Hellespont's lights stretched a jewelled mouth in a half-grin, and I wondered what might have excited the Emperor Alexander's mind when he first saw it, and if he'd been half as worried about his army as I was for the 103 mercenaries in two jets behind me, and the outcome of the drop we'd planned for the morning.

Commodore Kopfers had given a before-sunrise time for arrival at the Company's airstrip south of Basra. Major—'One Eye'—Plenn, late of the Congolese Liberators, commanding the troop, and Captain Racoude, ex-Foreign Legion, were in the aft compartment office, adding the details. I had the Company's D.C.-4's waiting to fly the men in, and a couple of helicopters, one for the medical team and one for me, afterwards to take out the Princes.

They were my main concern. El Bidh radio was off the air, and from Logan's message of half an hour ago, there was no movement in or out, and locals seemed to have been told to keep away. Two forces, number unknown, of Prince Abdullah's family, were at two points about thirty miles apart, coming down from the mountains.

With El Bidh in mind's eye, thinking of a few marksmen behind automatic rifles, I didn't give horsemen much of a chance. My paratroopers had far better. Their weaponry was in advance of any I'd ever seen, the men were veterans, and none of them, apparently, had any fear of being killed. I could accept that in war a man could take his chances for the sake of his Country. But here, they were simply being paid to kill, or be killed. I'd looked at them fairly closely while they answered their names to go aboard. They all looked quite ordinary. I saw nothing that would mark a killer.

The youngest was twenty-three, the eldest forty-eight, most were French, Belgian and German, some British I couldn't identify by appearance, Swedes, Finns and Russians. But they all had not less than five year's fighting experience, others far more, and Major Plenn told me he'd never done anything else since graduating at Louvain. He seemed a perfectly normal type of the officer class, used a monocle—which gave him his nickname—and the men obeyed his orders in the manner of well-trained troops.

I'd told him I was curious to know why they'd adopt such a risky profession, and he'd taken out his monocle to blink.

"Actuarialy, no more risk than crossing a street in any big city!" he said, smiling, slightly supercilious. "And where else could they earn as much? When they finish this, they can go off and buy a business somewhere. Or stay on, earn more. At least, while they live, they live well. How many can say as much?"

No conscience, there, and so far as I was concerned, no profit in further talk. But was I so different? I didn't have time to go into it.

Ilse Pedersen brought in the dinner tray and a fan of messages, one, blue, from Kopfers, and the others from the radio cabin.

SIR, WE HAVE A SMALL TAIL WIND WHICH WILL INCREASE AND SO WE SHALL ARRIVE ABOUT ONE HOUR FIVE MINUTES EARLIER. WE ARE AT 31000 FEET AND RISING TO 36000 TO ESCAPE ALL TURBULENCE. PLEASE EXPECT A FEW LITTLE BUMPS IN THE NEXT FEW MINUTES. BOTH AIRCRAFT BEHIND IN GOOD ORDER. WE ARE FOLLOWED BY THREE TURKISH FIGHTERS. WE HAVE NECESSARY CLEARANCE AND SO DO NOT BE ALARMED IF YOU SEE THEIR JETS ON YOUR SIDE. THEY ARE TURNING AWAY.

KOP.

I opened the first message, in Company cipher, decoded in the radio cabin.

BETROTHED LONDON RELAYED XX2D IIJ.
FOR TROTHE, NEED TWENTY THOUSAND STERLING BAIL CAWLE AND TOP MAN/DEROVSKOY. WILL CHARTER PLANE FLIGHT LONDON MAKE ARREST. WAITING.

GILLIAN. HOTEL BEL AMI.
VALETTA. MALTA.

A large rat nittered from the page. Gillian would sign her code name, first, and second, all the money in creation wouldn't buy anyone out of Malta. Somebody was being clumsy. Relying on known links? I'd never heard of Derovskoy.

I wondered about Gillian and Yorick. I hadn't heard a word from them. Who'd know their names in Valetta? How could it be known that I'd promised to fund her, and why, as daughter of one of the world's wealthiest bankers? And why hadn't Yorick signed the cable? That was a worrier.

I wrote:

ROULEBROS LONDON
ANY IDEA WHERE GILLIAN IS QUERY WISH CABLE IMMEDIATELY REGARDS

EDMUND TRUCIALIST BASRA

and:

LADY IMBRITT MELLONHAMP SUSSEX ENGLAND
NO NEWS YORGILL. WISH TO CABLE NOW. REGARDS

EDMUND TRUCIALIST BASRA

My desk began to quiver, which my seat translated in a long slide, a thump, bump, more slide, and I held the tray, watching the wine slip up the glass, steady, slip the

other side, bump, thump, slide, and then we were clear.
The same type of motion in a car on a bad road would
pass as nothing, but in the air, for some reason, I always feel we're about to founder, plunge, explode, and
curse though I may, I've never been able to cure some
idiot part of myself of that ridiculous fear.

OFFSHORECO XX2D IIJ.
BIG MARY PROMISES TO TIE YOU IN A
ROQUEFORT BLUE BLOW IF YOU'RE NOT
HERE FOR PATTI'S BIRTHDAY NEXT SATUR-
DAY. LITTLE MARY SAYS BLESS D'BOSS,
CAUSE HE COUNT. I AGREE. MY DARLING.
WORLD OF LOVE
CONSWELL

Again that tide struck, that almost uncontrollable
desire to throw it all up and go to her. She, in pro-
foundest fact, was all I wanted in the world. We had
more than enough to live excellently well as long as we
might. That was her wish. Secretly, it was mine. But
there was that sense of responsibility to the Princes, of
loyalty, of gratitude, and an unutterably final sense of
some day having to look myself in the eye. I had to
shoulder the consequence of all I'd so willingly accepted. Apart from that, I was forced to admit that I
liked what I was doing, had no real wish to do anything
else, and Consuelo was crown, orb and sceptre of my
empire. I felt more than a little pride in her, and it, and
that was all.

Smug, perhaps, but then facts are facts, and I lived
with facts and made decisions on them.

But in those moments I wished that with a clear conscience I could have ordered a turn around, a course set
for Jamaica, no further nonsense with paratroopers and
the drop, no thought for my friends, and to hell with El
Bidh.

As well ask the Commodore to fly headlong into the
ground. I've often wondered what loyalty is, or where a
sense of responsibility comes from. I had no notion

what impelled me to put aside all I wished to do—I had no real idea what a wish *was*—to go and help my friends.

I felt I had to, that's all. I suppose any ass in the street waving a placard, pro or anti, had as much, or as little reason. It didn't matter. Certain things had to be done because I found them proper, using a sense of honor, reason and knowledge. That I couldn't explain any of them satisfactorily, even to myself, was beside the point. They had to be put to use to achieve certain ends which I thought correct, and that I hoped would save my friends, and in part, my Company and its future.

Recrudescence of god-ism? I wasn't sure, and for the moment didn't care. But I knew in my heart that I could never go back to being second man, anywhere.

Ilse's tap brought in Major Plenn in khaki shirtsleeves, belted leaf-camouflage trousers, paraboots.

"Here is the scheme, sir, and I shall be glad to change anything you don't like," he said, and put a map of El Bidh on the desk. "We shall drop at roughly six hundred feet. Prevailing wind we hope will help us. The two D.C.'s will have time to drop a stick each of ten. But the area isn't large enough. We shall have to see when we get there how many times we must come in. I shall drop with the first stick to command the attack. Racoude will remain in the air to direct the flights. Could you tell me something of the nature of the ground?"

"Go for this area, here. It's all lawn and flower beds, plenty of cover from the palace, and a covered approach to the car lifts in this wall. There must be a stairway, there, somewhere, but I never saw it. If the lifts are out of action, that rock wall has plenty of hold for a climb. It's about forty feet. I'm going to drop with the first stick, as well. Detail the rest of them to follow me, and you stay behind to bring up the main body. Surrounding the place'll do no good. It's too big. We want plenty of grenades!"

He nodded, saluted, picked up the map and left. He

had all the cool approach of the professional soldier, and he smelled of carbolic soap. I decided that I'd do well to offer him the Chief of Police job at Beyfoum. He was exactly the man.

I opened the other message, decoded.

FOR TROTHE RELAYED BERRY. HOCKLEY WARNS THAT CAWLE WISHES SURRENDER ANY EUROPEAN CITY EXCEPT LONDON MAKE TERMS FOR RELEASE OF DAUGHTER ALETHEA HELD ATHENS BUT G R E E K AUTHORITIES DENY ALL KNOWLEDGE. CAN YOU INFORM NEWSCOTCID? BREAK. TWO. MRS MERYL ARMITAGE, MANAGERESS PLUMMY'S CLUB FOUND DEAD IN BEACH HOUSE NEAR RUSTINGTON. INQUEST PROCEEDS. BREAK. THREE. SEARCH GOES ON FOR VON STAENGL UNSEEN SINCE LONDON DISAPPEARANCE. MAN KILLED THEATRE IDENTIFIED AS WILHELM KULMACHER, W. GERMAN CULTURAL ATTACHE AT THE HAGUE, HOLLAND. BOTH NOW BELIEVED PART OF COUNTERINT KGB ALSO PENSON POSSIBLY ARMITAGE, IN LINE MANY RECENT DEATHS OR SUICIDES HIGH LEVEL W. GERMAN AND OTHER EUROPEAN OFFICIALS. BREAK. FOUR. TAUPERMAN, TEACHER AT ST URSULA'S NOW IDENTIFIED FROM FINGERPRINTS BY SWISS POLICE AS ENTERPOL DOSSIER NO: 87753/55/GT. AO NAME NOT TRANSMITTED BELIEVED NOW ALGERIA. BREAK. FIVE. ALL POINTS WARNED MISSING PARTS BARNBRUCHE WARHEAD COULD BE USED SEPARATELY. NO INFORMATION WHEREABOUTS. CENTRAL BANK VAULTS CLEARED INCLUDING COMPANY'S AS TEMPORARY MEASURE BY ORDER GENERAL TENGLER. ALL CONTENTS NOW IN UNKNOWN PLACE. NO FURTHER INTAKE WITHOUT DETAILED SEARCH. HAVE ORDERED ALL COMPANY AIRLIFTS SHIPPING RAIL ROAD DETAILED

SEARCH WITHOUT EXCEPTION. SUGGEST ADOPTION SAME PRECAUTION PUBLIC OR PRIVATE DELIVERY. BREAK. SIX. URGENT JUST IN. BLERCGROVE GRASSTREE 14 WARNS VENEZUELAN GUERILLA TRAINING CAMP UNDER CUBAN COMMAND SUSPECTED ROUGH COUNTRY FAR SOUTH BANBURY CROSS ESTATE. JAMAICAN AUTHORITIES INVESTIGATING BUT ALL SAFEGUARDS SHOULD BE MAINTAINED. BREAK. SEVEN FINAL. ALL WELL LONDON.

BERRYCID.

I rang for Ilse, and wrote a series.

TROTHE. BANBURY CROSS. JAMAICA.
PLEASE ASK EVERYONE TO BE UNREMITTINGLY CAREFUL IN ACCEPTING ANY CRATE, PACKAGE, PARCEL, COURIER POUCH INCOMING FROM ISLAND OR BEYOND. ALL MUST BE OPENED AND THOROUGHLY EXAMINED. BE PARTICULARLY CAREFUL ANYTHING OSTENSIBLY SENT BY COMPANY OR ME. I SHALL SEND NOTHING AT ALL UNDER ANY CIRCUMSTANCES EXCEPT MY LOVE AND I SHALL BE THERE FOR PATTI'S BIRTHDAY. PLEASE TELL BIG AND LITTLE MARYS I HAVE THEIR ROSARIES GUARANTEED.

and:

LEVERSON POLICE HEADQUARTERS JAMAICA.
PLEASE WARN CUSTOMS AND ALL SERVICES EXAMINE CLOSELY ANY CONSIGNMENT FOR BANBURY CROSS. IN PARTICULAR ANY RADIO OR OTHER MECHANICAL APPARATUS SHOULD BE LEFT TO BOMBSQUAD SERVICE ENGINEERS. REGARDS.

TROTHE.

and:

BLERCGROVE IGLOO LONDON.
IN VIEW YOUR WARNING VENEZUELAN
TRAINING CAMP JAMAICA SUGGEST RIGID
CUSTOMS PRECAUTION AND BOMBSQUAD
STANDBY IN EVENT PART BNBRCHE FLOWN
THERE. REGARDS.

TROTHE.

I had a feeling I was teaching grannie to suck eggs,
but I didn't see what else I could do in way of warning,
and though I wasn't at all sure that the camp existed, I
was aware that the southern tip of the island was only
an hour or so's run from the Venezuelan coast, and
amateur fishermen and skindivers make the most
healthily innocent cover for guerilla training.

The last I sent to a friend of mine.

MANFREDO GERRONI. JUSTICIA. MALTA.
LORD IMBRITT AND GILLIAN ROULE FRIENDS
OF MINE REPORTED HOTEL BELAMI VALET-
TA WOULD APPRECIATE ENQUIRY TO ASCER-
TAIN. CORDIAL REGARDS.

EDMUND
TROTHE TRUCIALGAS BASRA

I sat back, looking at the roof, ceiling, whatever they
call the top of an aircraft, and started to sort things out.

I wondered what Cawle might have up his sleeve in
offering to surrender himself on terms. He'd know
rather better than most that there wouldn't be any. If
the supposed Emma Toverell had been identified as
Alethea Cawle, then I saw no hope of release. Intelligence services throughout Europe had suffered by
the pair's defection, though none more than the Greek.
I could well imagine why the Government of Colonels
would deny any knowledge of her arrest. They wanted

to hang somebody. I had one small qualm of sympathy for Cawle's desire to free his daughter. In her place I thought of Patti, and wondered what I'd do in his. Surrendering himself, presumably, meant a confession, perhaps to recant, possibly to render Bernard Lane. It might work. But I gave Cawle not many hours to live thereafter. I'd formed a fair opinion of the organization behind the pair. I was certain they were not the masters, but only leaders, here and there. They'd made errors. But neither of them were prone to error, had never been. On the contrary, both were known to be cold, skilful, exact. Financial power was certainly behind them, perhaps forcing the pace, either ordering them or by other means impelling them to action which neither, left to themselves, would have taken. I had no doubt that the attempt at the Bank must have succeeded with a little more care. The gold had been bought openly in the Princes' name, and sent openly to their—the company's—bank in the names of registered subsidiaries. If somebody had taken the trouble to equalize the weights and fill out the manifests correctly, the consignment must have been admitted without question, and I'd have known too late to do anything. The correct signal, sent to that radio, would switch it on to relay and amplify a signal to the generator, which would put the computer to work. The various signals sent by other transmitters would have been accepted, the correct code sequence chosen, and on a time signal—wherever the detonator and warhead happened to be—up they'd have gone.

Allowing that clever Alethea Cawle—Miss Burrows of charming memory—to leave the London office, and go to Rome to receive the gold and send it on was nothing less than a catastrophic lapse. It couldn't have been known that on her only visit to London, at the time she was put on contract, Genia Pearlman had met Miss Toverell and made friends with her. An innocent question would have uncovered it.

It was the sort of botch that the pair in their heyday could never have committed, and it was on that sort of carelessness—where success just managed to slip through their fingers—that I based my theory. They were not their own planners, or masters, and in sum, not themselves.

In itself, that was a lift of sorts.

For a moment I thought of poor Meryl Armitage, of all the pleasant years I'd enjoyed with so many friends at Plummy's under her most womanly care, permitted myself a traitorous thought that possibly she might have been suborned, dismissed it, remembered her in plum velvet, piled white hair—"*Hullo,* Chuckles!"— and rang for a scotch and soda to drink to her memory.

Good friends are few.

I didn't understand the Von Staengl business. His position was near enough to the top to know pretty well all that went on, whether in Europe or elsewhere. The Blur, in a sense, had gone well out of his way to mention him, which was most unusual, and so had Druxi, and neither played the cards far from their shirtfronts.

Recalling what Von Staengl had said, I had the strongest impression he'd been trying to tell me something, but without the courage to say it outright, and from what he'd said, I hadn't quite—and still couldn't—gauge all he'd intended to say. He'd made one statement, which I'd accepted with gravest reservation, about economic attack. I didn't see how, but then, I hadn't his knowledge.

Again, if Kulmacher, the man killed at the theatre, officially or not one of the many West German cultural attaches at The Hague, *had* been employed by the Soviet counterintelligence KGB, it was no surprise, since his use mightn't have been confined to Europe or the United States. Holland had one of the largest Chinese colonies in the world, and the Peoples' Republic was strongly represented. The essential weakness of their agents lay in their appearance—instantly identifiable and impossible to disguise—and hopelessly worse, their deficiency in languages and translation.

I'd since booted myself for not pressing Von Staengl, but then, I might have shut him up altogether. It hadn't been the place to press.

I allowed myself a couple of moment's luxury, wondering who Interpol dossier No. 87753/53/GT. AO could be, and what she was doing in Algeria, and Ilse came in with the tray.

"It's not so long, sir, now!" she said, pouring the soda. "The desert, when it's moon, it's beautiful, don't you think? I dream down there many times!"

"When you want to work down there, let me know!"

Her very pale blue eyes smiled, and she inclined her head.

"I let you know now, sir. I want the job!"

"You don't know what it is!"

She laughed glistening white teeth.

"I know you, sir. I like the job, please!"

"You'll be taking care of a lot of children. I'll talk to you at Basra!"

I drank the health of three girls at Banbury Cross, and one ex-Plummy's, in a cold and very good scotch and soda, and put my head back, always a silly thing to do, since I sleep as a baby at any time, anywhere.

CHAPTER FORTY

I awoke when Ilse brought in the coffee as if there'd never been a pause. Light was mauvish.

"Sixteen minutes we land, sir!" she murmured, a little swollen in the lids, washed clean of make-up, fresh linen. "Com'dore Kopfers presents his compliments, the morning's ideal, and should he turn over El Bidh?"

"Absolutely not!" I said, waking up. "I don't want them given any warning. Run!"

She ran, and I poured excellent coffee, went in the shower, got into the jumpsuit, strapped weapons, and buckled myself into the chair by the time the wheels bounced on our well-laid tarmac strip.

Logan waited for me, and we walked across to the storesheds where the men were breakfasting. Over orange juice, steak, eggs and toast, he told me what had been happening before he got there, the state of the pipeline, the rapid progress at Beyfoum, and the general well-being in all sectors, except schools and medicine.

"That's well in hand. What about El Bidh?"

"Confused's about the best description, sir. Shammad flew a scout over the southern tip last evening. He said he didn't see a move round the palace, but there were hundreds of horsemen coming down through the hills, there, on the northwest, but they wouldn't get there till later today. The posts on top of the ravine all seem to have upwards of twenty men each. That's unusual. Nothing's gone in from the town since the day before yesterday. Everybody's been told to keep out. I couldn't find out where the word came from, but last news is from a boy who got out over that rocky stretch east of the palace. He said the servants were getting killed off, and the rest'd locked themselves in the women's wing, upstairs!"

"Any idea who the attackers are?"

"I was coming to that. The sheikh, here, got it from his brother who runs a busline up the coast. He thinks a lot of Baluchis and Afghanis were recruited somewhere, and flown down to Faid, and then embussed for Tharaz, down here. Give them a day to regroup, that's three days in all, and they probably attacked across the top of the ravine last night. They don't fight by day. That way, they'd have the palace asleep. Rest's a matter of conjecture. Knowing *them*, I'd say you won't find much!"

The eggs had lost taste. I nibbled a crust, drank coffee. My watch said 0541 when Major Plenn stood on a table to give final orders to the troop.

"Any word about who's behind it?"

"General rumor, sir. Been going about a long time, now. Out-of-luck lads in the ruling families—the ones that get the bones without the meat—the younger officers, and the students, of course. But they're not showing themselves for the moment. Things might go wrong. But if they're successful here, and I'm still talking rumor, they'll go on. I've been a bit worried about Beyfoum, and one thing and another. We've nothing to stave off an attack like that, y'know, sir!"

"There're quite respectable forces of men to be recruited here, at Beyfoum—"

"Not if this place goes, sir!"

Logan's square red face, grey hair matted from a bucket wash, half-smiling grey eyes, sweat glinting in cheekcracks, red lobes, all, for some reason, turned into a question mark.

He was right.

I hadn't thought of it.

If the palace of El Bidh could be taken, then perhaps Ben Ua might be next, Oman, Kuwait, all the rest would follow, one after another, or all at the same time, with help of every nomad, every born pillager, murderer, now lying low, waiting, and at first whisper of success, coming out of their holes by the thousand.

It would take a sizable force, and a long time, to put them down, though if they had enough munitions and the right leadership, a terrorist campaign to follow might be difficult to break.

"Any hint where the arms are coming from?"

Logan almost showed his teeth.

"I gave a case of scotch for a couple of automatic rifles the day before yesterday, sir!" he said, pilling bread. "I believe we'd be wise to offer a few more cases. Let's say, ten dozen. With a couple of thousand rounds each. I'd feel a lot safer, I'll tell you!"

"Are they any good?"

"Best I ever handled, sir. They're Chinese!"

Major Plenn whistled, the troop turned out, I got up, and Logan helped me on with the parapack.

"Sorry I'm not coming with you, sir!" he said, and looked it. "I've the convoy of trucks and the lads ready the moment I get your signal the ravine's clear. Very finest of good luck, and put that in y'r pocket, and think of me with any dram!"

He gave me a silver flask with about a pint of scotch which I hadn't thought of bringing—that nicely balanced a weight of grenades in the blouse—and I trotted over to Major Plenn at the foot of the ladder.

"Drop next to last, sir!" he said, saluting. "We have twelve minutes in the air. On the ground, you will not move until I give the word. You will then be guide. *Bonne chance!*"

He went up in front, my hook was fastened to the bar by the sergeant, the door slid shut, and I sat on the floor slats with thirty or forty others. I couldn't see a face. Only two windows showed light. It was like being inside a hollow, ribby fish. The aircraft bumped lightly, swung to take off, the motors' thunder stung the bones of my backside, and we were rising.

I looked at my watch, remembering the ground below, trying to guess when we'd be turning right, seaward, and almost on the dot, we tipped, and I imagined I saw the little port, a surf line white in reddish sand, frills of waves outside, and we tipped again, plunging down.

The red light blazed.

Everyone pushed off the floor to stand. Major Plenn walked down on the right, talking here and there, monocle flashing, and clicked his own hook on the bar. The first stick formed, turning toward the door. Major Plenn pointed to me, and to a tall man I hadn't noticed.

"Follow him!" he shouted. "There's one behind you!"

The green light shone, silhouetting heads, the door rolled, and almost before it was fully open, the aircraft tipped left.

Plenn stuck a foot out of the open door and dived head down, followed by a second, third and the rest, and the sergeant took me by the arm.

Almost while the notion flashed, I was out, in the air, falling, a nightmarish feeling that yet was not. I saw the red terrain coming toward me as if I were passing through a wide-coned funnel. Breeze pushed at my eyelids. I seemed suspended in utter silence. But then the harness tightened, suddenly, dragged upwards, and as if the hand of God had grabbed me, the main parachute opened, and I was in a grip where cords were taut, whining in the wind, and I could have sung for sheer joy.

But when I looked down, the flower beds—I thought they were red lilies—were coming up at a frightening blush, and I had time to swing on the cords and kick out, to land feet down and roll headover. Most of the breath was knocked out of me.

I lay there for moments, savoring the luxury of flat, still earth, the smell of grass, and something like honeysuckle, somewhere, which reminded me of the side lane at Onslow Close.

Hands grabbed, and I found the sergeant manhandling me upright, unbuckling, pulling in the parachute cords, throwing them in a pile on the silk, shouting to others behind.

A rose arbor stretched left and right. I couldn't see palace. We went up a bank, and through the rose About three hundred yards off, I saw the gold onion tops, the white crenellated roof, two or three heads up there, but no move in front. I doubled across beds of carnations, a rosewalk, and the yellowy-red mass of wallflowers in the grey stone wall was in front. Both double-doors were open.

I signed to the sergeant to keep down, and ran for the nearer door. I made the most of cover, saw nobody on the way across, got under the lee of the wall, and stood, back to it, sniffing a delicacy of wallflowers, sweating, listening.

The two aircraft came in almost overhead, engines cut, and men fell like scattered rags.

I went in, to warm smells of oil and petrol in the garage. Long lines of cars gleamed in lanes. The lifts were waiting. I pressed the gate switch. It worked. I ran out and signalled the sergeant. He came on, autogun at the ready, watching the wall above, waving on the others. About twenty of us filled the lift, and I pressed the switch, starting a jangle that put my teeth on edge, but at least we went up, stopped, and the reverse gate slid open. We stood in silence.

I nodded to the sergeant, and led a single file along the corridor I knew so well, to the waiting room, and an unpleasant surprise of three bodies of palace servants hanging head down in the fountain. Their throats were cut. The water ran clear. I judged they'd been dead perhaps four or five hours.

I led on, into the rotunda, chose the same passage leading to the big room, halted while the sergeant detailed three men to guide the others, two to go back to the lift deck.

The sergeant followed me, trying doors on both sides, but they were locked. The men strung out behind us at about ten yard intervals, so that if a door opened, they'd have a chance of covering those in front.

I reached the heavy double grille. The gold bell was gone. I put my hand inside, felt the latch, raised it, and the outer grille swung out. The sergeant caught it, and let it rest against the wall. So far, in rubber soles, there had been little sound. The entire palace was quiet as a church.

I put my hand in to the latch of the other grille, and it slid up. I pushed it open without a whisper, so far, about a foot, and then had to push. Blood was black across the floor, bodies heaped, from the wounds, gunshot, and steel scraped on the tiles, scimitars dragging in dead fists, and more bodies piled further on. Despite air conditioning, a gross stench of dead meat hung. I went on, beside the long table, over fallen chairs, stepping across bodies of servitors in livery and others in odd brown uniforms, down to the far door, and when we pulled it open, the first faint sound, of shouting, somewhere beyond.

"Better wait for the others!" I told the sergeant, and he nodded, took out a cigaret, lit a match on his thumbnail—which I'd never been able to do—and sat one cheek on the table, at ease.

I heard the grenade bounce on the marble flooring as I saw the thrower—a whiskered bundle in the same odd brownish uniform—fall back in a spurt of blood from a burst behind me. We fell flat, the blue flash *cracked!* but most damage was among the bodies, and the rest in the length of the table.

The sergeant ran through the door with a dozen men, along the corridor to the other grille, and again the gold bell had gone, and once more I put my hand in to release the catch, swing the outer grille, feel for the inner, but it took three of us to shove it open because of the bodies on the other side.

"Sheer savagery!" Plenn said, looking about. "We know what to expect. No prisoners, sergeant!"

The sergeant saluted and passed the order.

The long room, possibly a refectory, from the crockery shards everywhere, heaped in bodies of servitors, most killed by grenade.

"They herded them in corners, and threw from the end there," Plenn said. "Shot the rest. How many floors are there?"

"Don't know. I've never been over the building. I

can't even guess where the women's wing is. But it's bound to be well protected. Why are we waiting?"

"Till my rearguard's in place, and the reserves of ammunition are up here. I consider it time to send a signal to your people to clear those outposts along the top of the ravine. I looked at them on the way in from the cockpit. Didn't seem much life. They might be sleeping, or they joined in the sack, here. Possibly?"

I switched on the little dreadnought in my pocket. The blue bezel glowed, and Logan's orange light shone.

"Hear me?"

"Perfectly, sir!"

"Send the column over the top. Tell them to take any prisoners they can for questioning. Shoot the rest. Understood?"

"Right, sir, I just gave the start signal!"

Plenn nodded, and we stepped over bodies to the further door. Most were henna-whiskered, of the household since birth, best of their kind. I could imagine what the Princes must feel at their death, and in such a manner.

The trooper at the window wagged a hand. Talk and movement stopped. In the silence a *cr-ack-ack-ack!* of automatic fire came faintly over the air-conditioner's hum.

"That's my men on the roof," Plenn said. "I told them to clear it, and work down. Come!"

We went at a fair pace through a series of small rooms, shadowed in the still-shut night lattices, some with bodies, all with fallen furniture, smashed vases, until the men in front came to another, larger bronze grille, and looked round for me. I reached in to slip the latch, stood aside for the weight to swing out, slipped the inner grille, and pushed it open.

The curious sound was a mass snore.

Bodies sprawled everywhere, inert.

We were at the end of the Palace, a long white-walled verandah on the shade side, with a rail overlooking the garden.

Empty bottles, most with the necks smashed, explained a great deal. But the true Arab doesn't touch alcohol, and that needed some explanation. The wine store must have been broken open. I didn't hear an order, but the troopers were taking cut lengths of steel wire out of their blouses, piling one body on top of another, and tying a right ankle to the other's left, a right hand to right, and since that wire's the very devil to bite through, I was inclined to feel sorry for the poor devils. While the binding went on, I followed Plenn into—as I'd thought—general food and drink store, butler's area, and the enormous kitchen beyond, with piles of bloodied bodies in whites, blood drying on the tiles, meats and vegetables in preparation, cindered in pots on the stoves and in the ovens, gas tanks empty, water still running in the sinks.

"I'd say the attack was last night, about eleven o'clock," Plenn said, bending to touch the back of his hand to the forehead of a cook. "These bodies aren't yet really cold. But what a lot of hyenas, eh? They didn't spare one!"

"Not the sort. They're hillmen. Recruited for the purpose. And somebody knew what he was doing. I'm extremely worried about the Princes. Let's get on!"

"As soon as these animals are *hors de combat*. My men are specialists. One thing but thoroughly, and correctly. You don't agree with my timing, sir?"

"No. I think the attack came, as you see, when they were beginning to cook for the higher echelon of palace servants. That would be after service had finished for the Princes. Two, three in the morning. Time isn't important here. If you've noticed, there isn't a clock in the place!"

Some of the sleepers had awakened, a few tried to fight but the troopers had only two answers. A rifle butt, or a bullet.

All the bodies were heaped down the middle of the room, and the sergeant walked along, counting.

"More than two to one, and many more on the roof!" he said, at attention. "Ready, sir!"

Plenn nodded, and the troop moved through the further door, to a circular stairway. I was surprised that so many men could move so quietly. But it was a little depressing to think that in piping times of peace, they'd learned their business in odd corners where nobody, except those who paid them, gave much of a damn who lived or died, so long as the day went well.

The moment I put my head over the top balustrade, I knew we were on the floor where the Princes lived. Corridors stretched left, right, and ahead, carpeted, lit in Venetian crystal, panelled in the tiles of ages past. Bodies sprawled in the length of each, more to the right, heaped against the end.

Leading troopers pulled them away, and Plenn pointed to the grenade-scarred bronze door.

"Have to use explosive to go through that!" he said, "No way of getting it open?"

"That's a highly old-fashioned job. There's a wheel that pushes a heavy bar across. You'll have to destroy it!"

Plenn gave an order, two troopers ran with a strapped bag, another wiped the wall beside the jamb.

"We don't go through metal," Plenn said, waving everyone out. "A hole in the wall will do!"

We turned the corner, and walked up the mid-corridor. The sergeant came out of the far door.

"All bedrooms up here, sir!" he called. "Not slept in. No bodies!"

Looking at a mind's eye plan, I thought we should be at the western end of the palace on the sheltered side from the sun, and obviously where the women's quarters might be. So far I hadn't seen the body of a woman. If the ruffians had managed to get in somewhere between one and two in the morning, most of the day servitors would be asleep, and the night staff would be on the upper floors, either serving the Princes and their numerous families, or waiting to eat their own meal then being cooked.

The pile of those brownish uniforms below the stairs

was proof of shotgun prowess but the weight was too much, and the space too cramped, and they'd all got back behind the bronze door.

The three-man team ran in to squat, and one jerked the tripwire. Not much more than a *fnn-nf!* brought dust in a gold puff, and a thick cloud.

We ran through, trod on bodies, got out in the free air of a room stretching the length of that side of the palace, carpeted walls, parquet floor, chandeliers. At the end, on top of a barricade of heavy furniture, an old man, a priest, long white beard henna-tipped, wearing the green turban, held out his hands.

"In the name of God!" he bagan, but I gave him no time.

"I make obeisance in that Name!" I shouted, and walked toward him. "We are friends. You are safe—"

A yell, a cheer, an extraordinary noise started behind there, and the furniture was being pulled away, men were climbing over, and Niz'r was among the first to jump off a pile of armchairs and grab me. I was right. He wore a bandolier of shot.

"Ah, Edmund, again!" he shouted, almost in a dance. "We are all here, all safe. By a miracle. We were going to let the Hakim talk to them and offer them riches to put down their arms and talk to us. We want so much to know who is behind. *Who.* That is all!"

Azil, red-eyed like the rest, pale, hardlined, came in a white burnous, arms out to wrap me, resting a moment.

"Edmund, we were thinking so much of you!" he whispered. "We wished you were with us, you know. Near us. We don't *know* what happened here. It was so quick, quick, *quick!*"

"You've got Ulla Brandt Ben Ua to thank. These are her men!"

Niz'r closed his ears to the hubbub, and Azil turned tiredly for the stair. We'd been trying to talk in a bedlam, a constant running of palace servitors, a crowd pulling down the furniture and carrying pieces away, teams settling carpets, a line trotting under yoke bouncing buckets of water, and processions of others carrying corpses, bringing louder screaming from women nearby, the nerve-lacerating back-of-the-throat sustained lament for the dead. Passing the open doors, I saw the women kneeling beside the bodies, trying to straighten limbs, and others carrying sewn shapes to the lift going down to the garden of the mosque.

Azil held out the palms of his hands, flat, and turned his head away, closing his eyes.

"We know shame!" he said. "We couldn't protect them!"

For the first time since we'd met, he seemed more Arabian then European, much thinner, and bowed. Perhaps it was the strict barbering of the beard and mustache, the white burnous and red sandals, instead of the cleanshaven, starched linen, tailored resplendency I'd always known, and I thought few would recognize H.H. the Prince Azil, of Park Lane and the Avenue Montaigne.

"I can see nothing to blame yourself for," I said. "How could you prevent it?"

In the small foyer of the stair going up, he turned to me.

"We are much to blame!" he said, direct. "We knew about it. We were warned. What did we do? Nothing!"

Those passing on the stairway flattened against the wall, touching heart, mouth, forehead, but he made no sign. We came out in glorious sunlight, on the expanse of the roof, with only the water tanks going up, a solid block, another fifty feet, and underneath, on the two sides I could see, a perfect reproduction of a Parisian cafe on one, and a barber's shop, with four men, feet astride, arms folded, waiting beside their chairs on the other.

"I'm so worried, Edmund!" Azil said, a few paces in front, speaking over his shoulder, with high morning breeze almost whistling his voice away. "We know we are under threat. Look what has happened. We had nothing here except the blades of our men and a

367

few sporting guns. This is not the first time we shall be attacked. We must put ourselves in order. If we are taken, everything is lost!"

"I'm waiting patiently to hear what Lane had to say. If anything?"

"He wants to buy the Company!"

CHAPTER FORTY-ONE

We were looking across miles of green garden, and further on, bare yellow desert going up black cracks to mountains, three ranges, the last, bluish in mist, all in red peaks where the heat shimmered. To my right, down a gorge perhaps five miles away, horsemen were riding hard in a cloud of almost pure white dust. Steel glittered. Far to the left, another cloud came on.

"Men of our name," Azil whizpered. "Many of their fathers, brothers, and sons are dead. They will require payment. Not in money. I fear there is nothing to be done. You see what they do?"

I leaned over to look down, about a hundred and forty or fifty feet, to the stone surround on the ground floor. Washing hung in loops dried less by the sun than heat rising from the stones.

Long lines of men wired together lay in pairs, and more were being dragged out and flung in place. I couldn't hear, but many were open-mouthed as if shouting, with the free hand trying to ease a new wire twisted round their foreheads. But those who managed to ease the wire were kicked back, and the wire appeared to get an extra twist.

"Azil, you've got to stop that!" I said.

He pointed to himself, in a faintest brows-up smile.

"I?" he said. "If I gave an order to stop, the women would take me in their arms. They have lost their men, Edmund. Those stones become hot in the sun. They will light fires to make them hotter. Those dogs will stay with their pretty ornaments of wire. In the day, they cook. At night, they freeze. It is very cold. In two or three days, they will be bones. If they arrive to their own women, they will be minus the ability to please. We shall care for them with great tenderness. Others will hear of it. They will not want to come here. That is the idea, you see? If you take advantage, prepare to suffer. You agree?"

"Something in it!" I said, watching lengths of timber being lit in lines at the edge of the stones, imagining the heat down there, the bite of wire, watching the couples fighting each other with the free hand and foot—I couldn't see why—until I saw one roll on the other, and lie there, off the heat.

"Voila!" Azil said tranquilly. "They have no honor. No desire to share suffering. They take all advantage. Later, the men on top will bite the other's throat and take the blood. Tonight, in the cold, he will roll over and use him as a blanket. Dog eat dog, you see? And you ask me to intervene? But my friend and little brother, Edmund, to whom we all owe so much, do you go to the director of the zoo, and ask him to open the cages? Remember, they would have done the same to us. And we remember our women. My mother is here. So old makes no difference. I think of her. This? It's nothing!"

Thin screams came up in gusts.

"That barber's shop," I said. "Am I allowed a chair? I'd like to hear more about this offer!"

"Of course, please," Azil said, and led the way. "Abdullah is at the mosque. Habbib is in Ryad. Now, this offer. He will give what we have paid, plus twenty-five per cent cash, in gold, at any bank of our choice, on any day, at any time we name. Fair?"

"Very fair, indeed. But for what reason?"

"On the day you left, he was offering us fighter aircraft better than those—at least, he said so—we could get from the Russians, better than the *Mirage,* better than the Americans. Well. This after all, is very interesting for us. We required proof. It is why I could not allow you to interview him that day. We told him he could have the order, secure, if we could see one fighter, and take the opinion of our own airmen. We called our pilots. They arrived here on Tuesday. That afternoon, the fighter came over. Ah, Edmund!"

We were in a better barber's shop than I've ever been

n. They must have collected shave lotions, soaps, colognes and assorted goodies from everywhere, including the squat majesty of a dozen or so bottles of everything from Trumper's in London, which almost made me homesick.

I took off harness and blouse, and sat back. The barber opened a large porcelain tub of shaving soap—the sort my father and grandfather had used—and began to lather, a thick munificence with a smell of the blossoming lilacs at Onslow Close.

"Lane was in charge of the affair?" I said, through foam

"But completely, and it was a marvelous machine!" Azil said, lying back where I couldn't see him. "It did everything. The four chief pilots were taken up. They said there was nothing like it in the air. They know. But, Edmund. It was not French, or Russian, or American. Nothing fashionable. It was Chinese!"

"You bought them?"

"Of course. We instantly made an arrangement for a transfer of gold. It was not even half so much money as a French or Russian or any other. We were so happy. We had a nice banquet, that night. Everybody. And everybody was in the radio room, sending messages. Very exciting. Well, you know, I have been in the habit of having a little drink with myself before I go to bed. I also listen to the radio. I like to hear what everybody is doing at two, three o'clock in the morning, what is the news, what interests the humble man in the street, everywhere. I have heard many strange things!"

The barber began to shave me with a razor I couldn't feel. I could still hear the screams from down there, tiny, horrifying. I could almost feel the scorch of stones, the binding wire, the misery.

"I think it was Hilversum," Azil went on, in that distant way of his. "I heard that the Red Chinese Chargé d'Affaires had first gone to the Dutch for asylum, and then to the United States. If you told me that the Prince Abdullah—I do him an absurd injustice!—had asked to become an Israeli, I could not be so flat. It was not five

371

minutes later that a majordomo looking after this Lan
came to say that he must speak to me with great urgen
cy. And so, I said, yes, of course, and he came up. *Sti*
with the buttonhole!"

I could see it, and him.

"He said he must leave immediately, no delay, light
on the roof, here, please, a helicopter is coming fo
himself and the Chinese pilots, they must go, so sorry.
said, it is something to do with The Hague? He said ye
I must be there to prevent any word of this transactio
coming out for the moment. I must make sure what'
happening. Very well, I said, you may go. Well, not a
hour later, my man woke me and said the radio roor
was burning and there was no telephone to the outside
I went up. It was all smoke. Since then, only this, of th
past hours. If I think of it, I cannot put myself togethe
I have to pacify my own people. I know them. The
wish revenge. How?"

Again I thought of those poor devils rolling on th
stones, or lying on top of the near-dead, wirebound, i
torment.

I pointed, and the barber handed me my blouse. I go
Logan making a call to El Humir, sent him a five
second harmonic to interrupt, and heard him cut.

"A successful job here," I said. "Things are bein
cleared up. How's your party?"

"The people going over the top ought to be at th
palace this afternoon. It's a rough climb. They've take
eight prisoners, killed the rest. Had to. No casualtie
our side. I'm sending the convoy in whenever I get
clear from that last outpost. Ryad's been calling, but a
mospherics are bad. I'll put him on the amplifier her
and see if I can't get rid of a bit. Stand by, sir, please!"

The barber finished the shave, I shampoo'd, towelle
slapped on some of Trumper's best, and felt brand-ne
again. But the screams, that new, horrid sound, we
incessant. I shut the door, and turned up the drea
nought. I could hear Ryad faintly through heavy a
mospherics, common in the desert for the time of th
year. I couldn't get a clear word.

Major Plenn came in, unbelted, took off his blouse, and sat down.

"Satisfactory, so far, sir!" he said. "We were a little unfortunate up here. Not us. I mean *them*. We disarmed them, and the palace people threw them all off the roof!"

"If they'd known what was going to happen to the rest, they'd probably have thanked you!"

"I expect so. How long do you wish us to stay?"

"I want you to leave, now, for Ben Ua. You'll report to Mrs. Ulla Brandt Ben Ua's representative there, and you'll also find two Generals, one American, one German, in advisory capacity. Liaise with them, do the best you can with the men you've got for the moment. You'll have another two hundred or so coming in before the end of the week. Put the palace in all-round defence. Second, the town. It's not big—it's a crack in the coastline—and most of the local men are loyal. Talk to the Sheikh there, and get his advice. If you have the slightest difficulty, call me. Did the prisoners tell you anything?"

He lay back for the lather.

"I asked no questions," he said, quietly. "Some interrogation was going on, though. Fingers were being cut off. Eyes taken out. Some were losing teeth. With a hammer and chisel. Tongues sliced. Ears. Noses. Other parts, of course. I should think they'll get some very interesting information!"

The barber's back was in my way.

"Were the Princes there?"

"No, sir. I didn't see them. It was only the women. Believe me, they are most capable. And especially attentive in what they do. The older women teach the little girls, and then the little girls try. Most interesting!"

"Any reason why it couldn't be stopped?"

The barber moved, the monocle flashed, and Plenn's left eye was grey, steady.

"If you will look from the parapet, sir, you will see, at an estimate, perhaps two thousand horsemen, and a little to your left, I think more," he said, under the razor's urge. "I ask you to consider, what is our condition when they arrive? I am responsible only for the conduct of my troop. So far, exemplary. The people here have their business. We have ours. For what reason should I put my nose into the affairs of women? And bring into question the lives of my men?"

"I know all that. But this *can* be stopped. There's no need for it!"

"But, sir, I am entirely in agreement. Except, of course, that we shall soon be at a disadvantage of at least fifty to one. If we manage to survive, how shall we reach the airport? And finally, sir, if you had not ordered this assault, what would have happened to the women, here? The old, the young, the little girls?"

"You consider they're getting what they deserve?"

He shifted his head to the other side, the barber wiped the blade, stropped, and lifted a jowl.

"I believe that to waste sympathy on such *merde* is an offence worse than theirs'. We condone. We should entirely destroy. I have seen too many of them. I regard my work as a cleansing process. The civilization which my father and his ancestors helped to create is being destroyed by these animals. Everywhere. I must practice my English, but I have so little opportunity!"

"You do very well. If I were to offer you the post of Police Commandant in command of perhaps five hundred men, possibly more, would you consider it?"

"I regret, sir. I must return to my wife within two months. We are near Tetuan, and the time is not good. The same type of animal will spoil everything there. If I find I can protect, very well. If not, I must leave. If I do, then I shall come to your office. You will not mind that I take six of the arms from those we took from the prisoners? They are the best I have seen!"

"By all means. I want the rest. What are they American?"

"No, sir, Chinese. The Viets are using them, also some of the Africans. Where the Chinese have influence. It is in many places!"

"Are you acquainted with many? I mean, personally?"

"With only two Chinese. With some dozens of their agents, yes. It is fascinating to see the plan begins to develop!"

"Plan? Did you say plan?"

The barber put a hot towel over a shining face, and opened a steamy geyser somewhere about the mouth.

"It is the Chinese plan, sir, for domination. Economically, to control through investment. If money will buy, it is not wise to fight. They copy the American system, but with different reason. The Americans invest and sometimes they control. The Chinese own completely. Through their agents. Bankers or businessmen. Then they begin to control politically, through the politicians. They are also bought. They don't always know it. In time, one learns, no? In our business, we have come to call it a Chinese affair, or a local. If it is a local, like this, I can immediately recruit better men. If it's Chinese, they know there is much to do, and little money!"

"Much to do, how?"

Plenn sat up, took the towel, and dried his face.

"It is generally an attack to erase a rival political party, or throw some fellow out of power, or destroy an industry employing many men," he said, as if it were all a matter of nothing much, which rather irritated me. "One is then expected to kill and destroy by fire or plastics, and they pay on the bodies, and the area consumed. It takes time, and we cannot always prove the numbers or the size. For this reason, many of the men refuse to work Chinese. Another reason is the difficulty of money. My men like to be paid in gold, or in hard currency at one bank. Chinese pay generally in the currency of the Country. It is often impossible to exchange. It is why Mr. Obijway is trusted. The men have worked for him before. He pays in any currency they wish, the insurance, the disability, the surgical operations, the sickness, and of course, the burial. He is a very good man. If he is in trouble anywhere, he can command an exceptional army. For this, I may say, he is respected!"

"Glad to hear it. There's one question I wish to ask?"

The monocle startled in a turning flash.

"But, sir, of course?"

"When were you first aware that Chinese were involved?"

He stood, stamped into his boots, put his hands into his pockets to pull down his shirt, and turned to the mirror to knot his tie.

"It was in the Belgian Congo, sir. A beautiful country. Wonderful to live. We had to go. We went to the French Congo. Another marvelous country. We killed, we destroyed, and we had to go. I have been here, and there. Always the same. I began to evolve an idea. At some time, somewhere, I must find a place where civilization is helped by my intervention. It is my hope and my wish. I am convinced that we must fight for our civilization. The rest is pretension. Here, I believe, I have done something useful. I hope to do something more useful at Ben Ua. But, sir, you know, here, in Arabia, we break ribbons, no more!"

"I asked you about the Chinese!"

The barber was helping him on with his blouse. I saw him take out the monocle.

"You know, sir," he said, polishing on the shirt cuff. "Everybody seems to forget the Long March of Mao Tse-tung, and that ragtail army. Without help. With nothing. Very well. Transfer the distance, and the effort, in a line directly pointed to Europe. With his present army, and the optimum conditions of the moment, how long would it take him to reach Paris? In the interim, in which place will you fight him? You confront five percent of his people. Let us say, thirty-five to forty million men. Is there a forty-million man army, anywhere, to stop them?"

"You think it's going to happen?"

"If you consider what has happened here, and what has been happening elsewhere, you might conclude that everything for the forward supply of that army, or those armies, has been well prepared. These things are not done in long term without a plan. Logically, what must we assume?"

"Arabia's a target?"

"A base en route. Supply point for petrol. Mid-march staging area. It is reason for Russia's preoccupation with the western border, the invasion of Czechoslovakia. They want that western frontier strong. Then they may turn full attention to the danger in the South and East. They are outnumbered more than three to one, ten to one, how many? They have a hard decision. Fight, or be surrounded, made slaves, exterminated. They have no choice, you see?"

Both helicopters swung over, hovered and set down. Captain Racoude got out of the second, and strolled over, smiling. I signalled the pilots to wait below.

"The top's clear!" he called. "We can use the trucks in the garage, if that's all right?"

"Your men deserve a bonus," I said, and shook hands with them. "You'll be in Ben Ua by what time?"

"An hour's flight?" Plenn said, looking at his watch. "Let us say, two o'clock, latest. I enjoyed this, sir. We shall hope to see you there!"

Any "enjoyment" I might have felt was soured by the shapes being carried over in slow file toward the mosque garden. I went down the stair to the long room. Sun lattices were up, fans hummed, furniture was in place, parquet gleamed between rugs, and there wasn't a soul, except, down at the end, masons were chopping at the gap beside the door.

They held back when I went through, down the stair to the throne room, quiet again, in order, except for damage to the table the carpenters worked on, and tilers were plastering the walls. Nobody seemed to notice me. From their faces, nothing might have happened. All was back to normal, every man at his own job.

I walked down the corridor of offices. Some of the doors were open, and as I'd thought, clerks were at work. Through a glass screen I had the luck to see Hassan Farad. He sat cross-legged, hands clasped, staring at a wide ledger. I went into an air-conditioned office. Somebody nearby wept long breaths.

"I'm leaving," I said. "I'll have the radio men here

today, and I'll call tonight. If the Princes are at the Mosque, don't disturb them. Kindly say I hope to meet them soon, and that I sympathize profoundly. If I'm needed, you may cable me at this address in Jamaica!"

He touched heart, mouth and forehead. He didn't speak. His hands trembled. The weeper let out his breath in a long ho-ooohh!

I didn't feel sorry so much as wretched. I had the most extraordinary feeling of inadequacy. My senses didn't seem to function, weren't sharp. I was glad to go, glad to get out of the shadow into white sun, glad to sniff the sweet sanity of wall-flowers, to see the door of the leading helicopter swing open.

"Oven in here, sir!" the pilot said. "Airstrip direct?"

"Don't go over the palace," I said, belting. "Just go!"

CHAPTER FORTY-TWO

Logan came with me to Damascus. Political trouble was going on, as usual, which didn't affect the Company, but he wanted to see that all went well at our base about fifty miles to the southeast, and to plan the precautions necessary if there were another general strike or a state of emergency. He took a dozen of the weapons and a box of ammunition. They were indeed good. We'd each tried a burst at the airstrip. There wasn't much noise, and they were deadly accurate at 100 yards, fast loading, simple, and we couldn't make them jam.

"Good job that El Bidh lot weren't properly trained in these, sir!" Logan said, in a serious grin. "Y'd never have stood a chance!"

I thought again of Plenn, and wondered which army would stand against Chinese soldiers trained with this weapon, and others perhaps more powerful, in the same class. I thought I saw why the Russians so urgently wanted all armies of the Warsaw Pact under one command, one system of weapons and training. It might hold a hope of stopping Mao's 40,000,000, or more.

I had to think about the offer to buy the Company.

It seemed stupid to build up an international complex and then in—however many—years lose it without recompense. Not that I accepted the idea of a Chinese breakthrough, walk-in, or any real attempt. But I did accept, and seriously, the idea of a nuisance campaign. It had worked well in far too many places to ignore, not least in parts of Arabia. Snipers, grenade-throwers, time-bomb experts, could make any community's life a hell, and Beyfoum was isolated, spread over a wide area, open.

The more I thought about it, the less I liked it, the more I wanted peace in our time, and the quiet years with Consuelo. I heard those screams again. I couldn't shut my mind to the thought of those womens' blades, or the little girls being trained in their use. I had to think about Beyfoum, and the people I was responsible for. In other years, the Royal Navy, H.M. Regular Army, and the Royal Air Force had taken good care of things. Now they weren't there, and nothing took their place. We were entirely dependent on local good will.

I'd seen what that was worth.

If El Bidh could be attacked, then so could we, with far less trouble, and perhaps by a better trained force. We'd need at least twice, perhaps three times, the number I'd thought necessary, which represented an outlay I didn't want to consider, thinking of barracks, supplies, and all the other costly details. My dream of schools, and a hospital, and similar flummery was only that.

It was then I realized what Azil's evasively sorrowful expression had meant. Without a word, he'd told me that the handwriting was on the wall, and they all knew it. That was why I'd been allowed to go off without a word from any of them. They didn't want to be asked. They didn't want to answer. They realized it would be a slow bleed, and nothing at the end. But they'd given their word to me, and they left it to me to make a decision.

I loosened my collar, toed off the boots, and lay down.

I decided against selling, and to hell with everybody. If we only went for three years, we could still make a better deal.

Meantime, I might possibly get a chance at one or both of the pair.

I couldn't pray for it. I couldn't light a candle. But I could wish, with the sort of feeling that seems to take meat away from the bones, scalp away from skull.

I think I know what a wish is. But not in words.

Ilse tapped, opened the door an inch, saw I was awake, and came in.

"Priority relayed from White Horse Five, sir. Mr. Kober has sent an urgent message from Istanbul. He couldn't reach you anywhere. He must talk to you. We shall be over in less than twenty minutes——"

"Let him know I'll be there, and tell Captain Tyne, please. Got some coffee ready?"

I had to shave, change collar, tie, the fashion plate, because even at that hour I knew Kober would be correctly dressed.

He was, and waiting at the foot of the stair when I went down.

"I have been trying to reach you since last night, sir!" he began, almost breathless. "We couldn't hear Ryad, and the other bases were impossible. Lord Imbritt is at the office, sir. It is most urgent, and Mr. Berry called everywhere, and all aircraft, to find you. I am so happy I succeeded!"

"So am I. Any idea what it's about?"

"He was in Rome, sir, and Miss Pearlman called first Athens and then me, and I managed to find El Humir, and they said you were in Basra. And so we went on, all day. Lord Imbritt is very impatient, sir!"

"But what about?"

"I don't know, sir, but it is Company business, most certainly. Lord Imbritt, sir, is very nervous!"

That didn't sound like Yorick.

"How, nervous?"

"He walks about, sir. He smokes. He drinks a bottle of brandy. And so *much* coffee!"

"Is there a lady with him?"

"She left this morning, sir. Not English——her tenses were incorrect!"

"Observant!"

Kober's eyes reminded of smooth grey pebbles. Lightless.

"I don't like people to come to my office, sir, and pretend to be your friends if they are not. Lord Imbritt speaks good German, sir?"

"Very good!"

"And the woman with him, a British passport, good German?"

"I don't know who she might be——"

'Why should they speak German when I am not there?"

"You've got a recorder in your office?"

"Not a word can be spoken anywhere which I cannot hear. If I am in charge, I am in charge!"

"Well done. What did they talk about?"

"I have not been able to take the second reel, sir. The first has little, only about Malta, and something in Rome, in Athens. It may be clear to you, sir. To me, it is confusing. I do not know what matters are being discussed. I got on to Mr. Berry, and he told me to put him on to the lord. But he said he would not speak to secretaries or people in a low position. The woman has gone to Cairo—"

"Did you find out where?"

"Inspector Achmed did, sir. He has the address!"

"I shall go to the accounts office and make some calls. Don't tell him I've arrived!"

We had a new building in the dock area, a fair-sized warehouse with offices over the top, plenty of space, useful, quiet at night. We reached the office by the back hoist, passing a couple of teams packing tube ex-ship to the airport, and I put in a call to Berry, poor man. He couldn't have been getting much sleep.

Hines, our London operator, answered, but Mr. Berry wasn't in, and neither was Miss Hamilton, his secretary. He'd try them at home, but I said no. There were two cables for me, not long in.

"We didn't know where you were, so we couldn't send them on—"

"Read them, please!"

"Coming up, sir. First one's Trucialgas Basra Message. Yorgill now Miami Fontainebleau Hotel and Palm Beach Wednesday guests General Pusey, and Saturday Plaza New York stop. Am joining them stop delighted see you all love stop text ends signature Miriam Imbritt. Right, sir?"

"Next, please!"

"Trucialgas Basra, sir. Message. Lord Imbritt not a Belami not in Valetta not in Malta stop. Shall entertain

im on arrival rest assured but would be overjoyed to
see you stop Embrace from Didi and self stop Text
ends signature Manfredo. Another one in, sir—"

"Yes?"

"Addressed Eoptic London. Origin's Paris, 1919 this
afternoon relayed a couple or more places, in code,
sir!"

I held up the receiver.

"Mr. Kober will take it. Thank you, Hines!"

Kober sat in my place, pointed through the heavy
plateglass door along the corridor, to the steel safety
slide opening into the main offices, and my own suite. I
passed the little kitchen sparkling in glass and polished
metal, waving at the huge white bulk of Angelo, the
chef, getting a flourish of his knife in return, and the
wonderful fresh sting of chopped celery over perhaps a
beef stew in red wine—from the bottles outside—and
the rich aroma of a damson tart—stones and peels were
in the refuse can—on the menu for the night meal of
the working shift.

"Smells good, Angelo!" I called. "When it's ready, I
want some!"

"If the patron can't get first plate, who can?" he
bellowed. "Serve it myself. A retsina, chianti, or the
local?"

"Wine and women of the country!" I said. "What's
wrong with the local?"

"Eheu, Muhamed!" he yelled, reverberating through
the building. "That's why *I'm* here!"

My master key opened the roller, it slid, and I left it
open, walking between glass walls to my office. The
clerical staff had gone. Flowers smiled on desks here
and there, and faint clatter from the loading bays
sprinkled the silence.

I opened my office door wide, and walked in.

I heard a throat cleared in the corner behind me.

Only one throat cleared like that.

Almost a trademark.

Bernard Lane's.

CHAPTER FORTY-THREE

"My *dear* Edmund!" he said, in that affected way o
his. "*Don't* be your usual impulsive self, *will* you? I
too, have a joytoy. At this range, even *I* could hardl
miss, what?"

I hung up hat and coat as if I hadn't heard, and sat i
the high-backed swivel chair, looking at the ceiling.
felt like something in a cap at a wake.

"*Heav*ens!"—same tone, in wonder—"It's *sulk*ing
*Real*ly!"

"Save time. What do you want?"

"Time, I agree, is short. Or *you* may find it so. Abou
an hour ago Joel landed at Havana. With som
presents. Your Patti's having a birthday? *His* daugh
ter's been rather badly tangled. She's by way c
being somewhat anile—in broad tradition of the famli
ly, apparently—and didn't verify her passport on
recent trip. Simply took what was given her. Whic
happened to belong to a Miss Emma Toverell. Joe
promptly lost one of his heads, and started cabling al
over the place. Even offered to submit himself to arres
if she were released. Fortunately, I managed to in
tercept, and did things rather differently. I—in you
name, of course—no apology—sent dear Emma a cabl
asking her in pathetic terms to fly via London to pick uj
the correct passport—which, as you know, was in you
office safe in conformance with Company orders—an
to fly on with all haste to release her junior colleague
poor Miss Whasname, from the official grip. Well, sh
presented the missing passport, and got back her own
and the wrong 'un went to right Miss Whasname, th
true owner. Meantime—in your name again!—I'
cabled Teddy Taphamides explaining the tangle, an
both girls went off perfectly happy. Miss Whasname ha
her various letters of authority to your offices here an
there, which helped, of course, and Miss Toverell wa

simply delighted to be back in her second home with so many of her old colleagues. At your expense, obviously, and on your cabled instruction, she's finishing her holiday there, as a reward. Hope you don't mind?"

I focussed on a light down the street.

That "joytoy" was twin of the one I carried in the shoulder holster. Any noise it made would be covered by the clatter in the warehouse. All he'd have to do was go down the stair, open the front door, and walk out. If he really meant to kill me, I stood little chance. A wrong move would be the last. He knew all the tricks.

I was inclined to laugh.

I'd walked into it. I'd expected Cawle. I could have dealt with him.

Lane was another type.

His face was remarkable in that it held at least a dozen others, each to be assumed at will. A series of small plastic operations had altered the line of the mouth, one nostril was slightly more flared than t'other without changing the profile, the outer corner of one eye—I believe it was the right—had been stretched, and the inner end of the left eyebrow was pulled up. All he had to do was half-frown, or raise an eyebrow, slightly lengthen the mouth, or distend the nostrils, or a little of each, and he was another man. He was equally adept with his voice, though sometimes he could thoughtlessly give himself away.

"Ive been at El Bidh, off and on, as you know," he droned, swinging keys a little above the blotter—an old dodge, intended to draw the unwilling eye, attract attention, hypnotise on occasion—but I looked at that light, thinking suddenly of Mimi Prôche, and the fingers-back handclap, the *yee!* of delight, and violets blooming on a windowsill. "I'm in the armament business, they may have told you? I sold them a number of aircraft. You've seen the state of the gold market? Extremely touchy. Well, chopping a verbal maze to manageable outlet, I offered to sell the aircraft, trainers and spares, and provide instruction for an agreed time, in return for the Company. Of course, plus a number of other benefits to be settled in principal, I suggest, here and now. Then our legal staffs can frivol with the details. The Princes agreed to sell, but they had to have your approval, d'you see? You *do* agree, don't you?"

"No."

"But Edmund, how *very* annoying of you!"

The keys hadn't stopped swinging. I knew he was smiling.

"Very well, then!" he said, in a brisker tone. "Let's talk of Joel, shall we? As I've already said, time's short. It's years since I heard 'Ride a Cock Horse to Banbury Cross,' but I must say I felt like warbling it when I got Joel's cable. Would you care to read it?"

"No."

"Then you'll permit me? Quote. Flight starts 0300 hours Havana time. Over target level seaward roughly 0325. Shall then follow your advice. Regards. Unquote!"

Even at that distance, I heard Angelo singing *Funiculee—Funiculaaaah!*

"I think I should impress upon you that he's not taking that flight for anything except the crudest sort of reason," Lane said, leaning back, smoothing an eyebrow between thumb and finger. "We want the Company, d'you see? All you have to say is yes. Because Joel's carrying a piece of James Morris's busiest, and, as *we* know *so* well, the old Banger's about the best there ever was. You can't be *so* indifferent, surely?"

"Do I understand you intend to destroy Banbury Cross?"

"But Edmund, *really*! Aren't you *the* most extraordinarily abrupt sort of chap? Of *course* not. You've decided to sell the Company, haven't you? Then Joel simply went for an airy stroll, shall we say? What?"

I suppose I should have felt something more than a thin sort of annoyance that I didn't feel angry. Murdering, killing were in my mind, of course. I was used to solving problems in that way. But the twin of my firearm lay under the hand swinging the keys. Any move, and I knew he'd shoot me, in this chair, and walk downstairs, out. It would mean the cheapest sort of

386

victory for the pair. The Company was theirs without a fight. With me out of the way, the Princes would make a deal for the aircraft, and feel themselves forever blessed.

I had to stop it.

There wasn't a hope.

There was only one way out, and two ways of going about it, though either way, the pair got the Company. The first was to agree—nothing else to do—to the sale, and thereby remove immediate danger to Consuelo, Patti and the baby, and let it go, thankfully, at that. I knew the pair far beyond any hope they might be bluffing. In the second, I could make a lot more trouble by holding the Princes to their agreement that half of everything, including the unissued stock and a share of the profits over ten years, together with unearned salary and all benefits over that period were mine, and I'd insist on payment in cash at Credit Swiss. That would mean the Company's coming to a halt for lack of working funds, and loud complaints from our American banking friends. They, too, would have to be paid. It wouldn't be easy to find that sum of money, wealthy as the Princes all were. The paper work, the movement of funds to cover gold or however it was managed, could take weeks. In that time, I might perhaps find a way of dealing with them, either singly or—as I'd so often dreamed—as a pair.

"The minutes are going, Edmund!" Lane warned, looking at his watch. "Joel's waiting, y'know!"

"But supposing I hadn't come here—?"

"I sent him the 'off' when Kober got your message. Do let's be clear about this. His jet does more than eight hundred and fifty an hour. He's got less than two hundred miles to go. Here's your original clix. Remember it?"

I recognized the Patek-Phillipe. I almost felt my heart sag with my knees.

There was no hope. Nothing I could do.

"I may send the signal, Edmund? Remembering that your family is intact, and all that sort of thing? I accept your word, you know? Would you please look at me?

You'll be able to tell which signal I'm sending. Let's have this straight. Do you agree to sell the Company of which you're now Director General? I'm speaking of Beyfoum, the several pipelines, ports, landing stages and airstrips, transport fleet, ships and aircraft, offices and real estate, together with the staff as at present constituted. You agree to sell, yes, or no?"

He was looking at the watch.

I caught a fractional glimpse of Consuelo in that bikini, with a garland of white flowers in a crown, and the ends caught and plaited with lustrous hair, another distracted thought of the baby, that was all, and it was enough.

"Yes!" I said.

"*Ex*cellent! Look here, will you?"

I saw the movement of his fingers tapping out the T—I—G—H—dot dot dot—That's It Go Home, three dots, emphasis, hurry or well done, the signal we'd all so often used once on a time.

"A most satisfactory night's work, indeed!" he said. "You're perfectly free to go when you please. There are one or two things. Please be good enough to send the people you wish to represent you immediately—I'd suggest tomorrow or the day after—to Nairobi. Here's the address. Our people are already there. Just send a cable to Corybant, Nairobi, and they'll arrange the flight, times, hotels, that sort of thing. Next, I'd be extremely glad if you'd stay on in your capacity as Director General. No need to put yourself out, of course. Just for appearances' sake, we'd prefer that you did, d'you know? The other thing is, you won't be in contact with the Princes other than to acquaint them of this decision. They, of course, couldn't care less. They get their aircraft. What heroes they'll be!"

I thought that my opportunity, and got up to reach for hat and coat.

"But what heroes *you* two'll be!" I said getting into the vicuña. "To whom?"

"I don't think you're going to be in the least surprised," he said, quietly. "Even if I thought you were interested?"

"But I am!"

He sat on the edge of the desk, and that face, which could change to a dozen others or more, in a moment, had become—I think "lit" is the only word—from the inside, perhaps some extraordinary livening of the senses which might project light, and I'm not normally takin by fantasy of that sort.

"We don't live long, Edmund," he said, head on one side, as though looking at something far away. "I've lived as much as most. Everywhere, everything. I saw a few of the 'great' days. My father saw them all, that is, of his time. He never tired of telling me what a third-class lot we'd become. It was only later that I agreed. When I saw the way he was treated. After a lifetime of devoted service. He was a man of ideas. Never accepted, of course. He knew India, he knew Africa, I mean, he *knew* them, but he knew Arabia better than any other Englishman of his time. He fought in all three, served in all three, and left the best of himself in each of the three. In legislation, roads, bridges, hospitals and that sort of thing. All for nothing. Everything he'd worked to construct or preserve, everything his father had done, and everything we as a people had done with a couple of thousand years of history and those sacrificial years of colonization, of law imposed, the trade which developed, the growth of cities, schools, Universities, civic bodies, local administration, all for nothing. In a few minutes, one dreadful afternoon, he saw a gang of our wretched politicians give it all away!"

I heard the plaint of his kind, robbed of their birthright for no more than Esau's mess.

"Gandhikaji?" I helped.

He got off the desk, opened his hands.

"India—imagine it!—no more than a buffer between two states of a nebulous-bloody-nowhere called Pakistan?" he went on, eyebrows raised, almost in laughter. "And—Christ!—this multi-atrocity was called *states*manship!"

Deliberately, I said not a word.

I didn't want to take his mind away from what was so clearly a fixed idea. I guessed perhaps accurately, at

389

the cause. I wanted to know the effect, that is, apart from what I could see and hear.

"Of course, I could go on," he said, sadly, ironically, contemptuously, or something between, which could only be savage. "Well, I got out. I began doing what I had to do for another idea. I think a better one. Clean. Prophylactic. Sweeps away social orders, classes, influence, money power, everything that detracts from the proper use of talent and appetite, wherever, or whomever. I thought at first that the Russians had it. I was wrong!"

"When did you find out?"

His mouth widened but there was no smile.

"When the Americans had to supply them with wheat!" he said, nodding in agreement with something he perhaps saw on the other side of the room. "That was the finishing touch. We went to the wellspring!—"

"We?"

"Joel and myself, and a few others. Fairly strong team. We've done pretty well. We'll do better now that you're with us!"

I don't think I gaped.

I simply stood there, overcoat on, hat halfway up, both hands paralyzed.

"Now that I'm—?" I asked, but gently, because the joytoy's satin-finish gleamed, pointing at me, muzzle down, as it were, by accident. "Now that I've *what?*"

I knew him too well.

"Don't humbug!" he said, almost amused. "Are you really going to tell people you signed your Company away, and you didn't know the buyer? Made no enquiries? Not interested? But will everyone be so—is irresponsible too harsh a term, d'you suppose?—when we all know you were virtually *given* the entire shoot? You don't know who *paid* you? *Can't* be right!"

"Then tell me!"

He put the gun in a pocket cut diagonally on the right hand side of the trouser, in front, just below the fob pocket, a better idea than the hip or shoulder holster.

"Poisoned with your own dead dog!" he said, almost

jovially. "Once you've taken our money, you're going to do as you're told, Edmund. Quibbling, or other forms of procrastination, will be met summarily. We have the means, of course. Presently, you'll be given a territory. You'll find it most diverting to see who's with us. Who's been with us for years. As I began by saying, we don't live for very long, do we? Might just as well play for the lot, don't you agree?"

"What 'lot' are you talking about?"

He stuck his hands in his pockets, head down, right foot making little circles in the carpet. We might have been sixteen again, talking in Main Hall at school.

"Ask yourself," he said quietly. "Without this oil business, what *could* have been your future? Leave the Service, pension, and what? Old age? None of the atmosphere of the corps d'elite. Courts, chancellaries, where? Like my father. Stymied. Governorships? Thing of the past. Commissioner somewhere? No. Blank. And no longer an Empire. Commonwealth? Sound of what, signifying owt, nowt. Zero. But, Edmund, we were born to rule, weren't we? Schooled, trained. But if there's nothing left, what, then? The moors and mists? Pheasant, anybody? Not my view of life!"

He lounged to the door, leaned there for a moment, looking down the sidestair. He seemed defenceless, vulnerable. I could almost have pitied him.

I realized, then, that I'd been wrong.

Pitiably, disgracefully wrong.

Patti, Frederick, and all their friends, whether at Derna or elsewhere, weren't of the "lost" generation at all.

But this brute, and myself, most certainly were.

No other generation would ever be so "lost" as ours. We had nothing to do and nowhere to go. No other generation had ever "lost" so much. Over our heads, all we'd inherited, that our fathers had built, was yielded, forsaken. Everything was stripped from us. We had nobody, and nothing, either to govern, or advise, maintain or direct. We couldn't follow our fathers. We had no road, or any land. It had all been flung away.

"What's your view? Let's hear it!"

"We'll talk when this agreement's signed," he said, and the curious schoolboy break in his voice became magnified in the stairwell's echo. "I think you're in rather a dangerous mood. I don't want to annoy you. Or lose you. And Joel, you must know, won't leave Havana till the papers are signed!"

"I shall want complete restitution in liquid cash before I sign anything!"

He didn't even turn.

"The Princes and their friends have already deposited enough for what they want," he called up. "The extra won't take long. Have no doubt about it, Edmund. You're one of us. I welcome you, and I warn you. Good night!"

The heavy door down there closed quietly. I went over to the window, but he must have gone along the wall beneath. A car started, turned, went away.

I saw my reflection in the glass, but very darkly indeed.

A rather more than wealthy Nobody, or exactly what I'd thought of being not long before, and for various reasons had shunned.

I felt sickish, impoverished.

The corridor was quiet, and the steel slide, I was surprised to see, was locked. I hadn't heard it shut. My key was still in the lock when it rolled, and through a foot of space, I saw Angelo's white mound lying in the corridor, ankles and arms wrapped in steel packing tape. I couldn't do anything for him, and ran on to the office. Kober bled from a small headwound, slumped in the chair, arms and legs taped. I went down the stairs to find a clipper. The place was quiet. All doors were shut. The men had gone. I found pliers, and went back, snipped the bindings, lay Kober flat, undid his collar, rested his head on a chair cushion, and went out for Angelo. He made me puff, pulling him along the corridor by his collar. I cut him free, made him comfortable, and picked up Kober's telephone list. I called Police, gave the operator the address, and asked for an ambulance. I didn't want to be there when they arrived, and waste time explaining.

I opened the back door with my masterkey, wondering where the packers had gone, and why a brutal attack on a couple of ordinary men should be necessary. But then, if he'd imagined he might have some trouble with me, he'd have to make sure of the opposition.

The car I'd come in wasn't in the garage. Most of the trucks were out. Even if I'd had the keys, I didn't feel like driving one out to the airport. I went along the street to the first lights and turned left, toward the nightglow of the city. My few words of Turkish came in useful at a bar, and after I'd spent some baffling moments trying to decide what could be put in coffee to produce that degree of mud, a rattletrap stopped, barely gave me time to get in, and we bounced till we met the asphalt, clattered on to the highway, and the driver held the wheel, palms under, fingers apart and extended, almost as if he were caressing the noise. We had to go over to the other side of the airport, and while my papers were verified, I sent the cab away, and went by carryall out to the jet.

I was rather glad to see it.

Maintenance spotlights were on, making the pale blue fuselage glow under a dark night, and a green reflection shone a round eye in our white horse galloping toward the nose.

But I felt divested, shorn.

There was a big difference between owning, and *being* Number One, and idling there on sufferance *as* a number one.

Curious "flat" taste about it.

CHAPTER FORTY-FOUR

There were two packages on the desk in my office, one corded in gold paper with our Jamaica tag, and the other in red, smaller, from Air France. I undid the wrapping on the larger and found a bottle of Krug, with a little blue bow—I could guess where it came from—holding a note.

Darling mine, I'm dusty and cobwebby and unbathed after a wonderful day in the attics. There's a treasury of beautiful forgotten things. We haven't been able to find you for a couple of days and London is rather worried about you. What do you do? I try not to think but sleeping becomes a trial. We all send our love, Patti and the baby, both are wonderfully well, and I send mine in multiples of plusultra kisses. I don't care what time it is, I want to meet you and put my arms tightly round you, so please send me a priority and I'll be there hours before.
Everything and the world

Consuelo
Do hurry. The roses are almost all out, but I refuse to see them with anyone except you.

While I read, almost holding her, feeling the lissome sweet of her waist, with a memory of her perfume tantalizing just beyond the edge of a deep breath, sensing the spiritual, mental, physical wholesomeness of a lovely woman rising from the page, I suddenly had an idea, a really fair idea, indeed, one that settled amost as a weight.

It wasn't that I reviled myself so much for giving up the Company, or that I didn't feel inclined to face an accusation of shameful conduct in having submitted to the pairs' will. I'd been forced under pressure of threat which I knew to be real and near, and I'd chosen, and with whatever bad grace, I'd accepted. But with all intention of making the best of a bad bargain.

True, I'd had other "ideas" which I'd thought good enough, but none of them worked. They'd all failed, at outset, and I quite saw why—at least now, at this moment, it was clear—simply because I'd constantly underrated the pairs' organization. They were considerably more powerful than I'd imagined—I was beginning to see good reason for the Blur's and Hockley's worry—and if, at times, a little haphazard, the machine they controlled or were part of was far better practiced than mine, a match, perhaps, for all the European Intelligence services combined, throwing in the CIA and the rest, KGB included.

But this new idea of mine was quite different. It was so new, so simple, I didn't want to approach it for the moment. I wanted to take it aside, quietly, and examine it. I knew I'd need James Morris's help and the hologram process, but that was as far as I went.

White Horse Two's windows were dark, the spotlights had gone, and the jets sang, shaking the bottle.

I wrote a message and rang for Ilse.

"Ask Blandford to send that priority for Mrs. Trothe," I said. "Put that bottle in the cooler, and about an hour out of Kingston, bring it in, and we'll all have a glass!"

She barely shook her head. I could almost see her Zuider Zee ancestors take stern control. A darkening of the eyes, a line of mouth.

"I'm sorry, sir, but Commodore Kopfers wouldn't allow!" she said, almost in preen of regret. "He is tee-tee, and the co-pilot, Mr. Dering is tee-tee, and so is Mr. Hawtrey, the navigator, and Mr. Gammans, and Mr. Blandford, and Mr. Henning, and Mr. Rush, and me. You forgive, sir, please?"

I thought of a team of tee-tees—minus one!—jetting West in vapor trails, and a stretch of stones at El Bidh cooling to below-zero in nightlong thrash of drums and tambourines, and the play of little girls' knives and the bite of wire. I heard Azil's grief, and the throat-rending lament of womens' voices in requiem for lost love, and horror of the lonely years, threading, merging with the engine's music, and for no reason, Consuelo wiggled white hips out of a bikini beyond the shower's opaque glass.

"A goblet in early morning can often liven things up," I said, turning on clix. "Help to soak a little of the evil out of the day before. I'm going to work for an hour or so. What I'd *most* enjoy at this moment is bacon and eggs, and a pot of good, *strong* coffee—"

She gestured regret with hands that seemed to speak.

"I'm very, very sorry, sir!" she said, and looked it. "This aircraft's been between Rome and Basra for the past month, and we haven't any more coffee. But we have excellent Oolong, or Soochow? The doctor says China tea's better for you!"

Her eyes were perfectly, liquescently innocent, I was glad to see.

"Very well, Ilse. You're absolved. In future, you will please carry a supply of coffee only for me. Meantime, a bottle of beer with the bacon and eggs. I'll have a classic English breakfast, and damn the doctors!"

She closed the door with more than usual care, and I undid the red package, took out a flat, square box, sealed with a thick plastic band. The vacuum envelope inside puffed air, and a small recording reel slid out. There was no label, no mark, and the tape was unlike any I'd seen, very narrow, dark blue.

I put it on my machine, switched on, and listened to a few bars of what sounded like an orchestra tuning without trying, and a sharp repetition of dots.

"This message is scrambled and will not last more than ten minutes now that the reel has been taken out of its container. Please switch off and put in the scrambler unit 11A22A. If it is not available, put the reel back in its container and place in an icebox. If, then, the message is faint, use an amplifying unit. Do not try to re-record. The tape is self-destroying. From the last sentence of the message proper, the sound will fade. Are you ready?"

I took the scrambler unit from the drawer, plugged in, and switched on. I had a notion I'd recognized the voice of someone I knew. I couldn't place it.

For the first few moments I thought it wasn't working.

An odd sound, a squeak wheedling into a groan, slowly began to resolve a rhythmic pattern, a slow pulse, and suddenly I could have laughed.

It was the plaint of the stairway leading up to Georges Pontvianne's office.

"You may soon learn that the Company you control has passed to others you may now know," Georges said, not very clearly. "The Princes, I am informed, have agreed to exchange their shares for an important purchase of armaments, I believe aircraft, with the help of other Arab states. The route of supply is via Kabul. Your landing strip at Basra will make a convenient base. You will recall our talk about the hundred-flower-petal tea? Very well. When those aircraft are delivered to their bases, ostensibly to aid the Arab cause, and training crews are established in their barracks, it will be found that the first requisite for the plan to subjugate Arabia has been accomplished without suspicion anywhere. The enemy is in the heart, and with adequate striking power. It must be remembered that he is no stranger to the nuclear tactical arm. But when the tea is being served on the shores of the Mediterranean, and Arabia and Israel are memories, what then? There are many matters we might discuss with a view to an over-all plan. In the period you have left as Director General, perhaps you feel it worthwhile to make this effort. It is my profound hope that we meet. I send the most cordial and fraternal regards, and a prayer that we succeed—"

The voice became a whisper, and the stairtread louder for three or four seconds, until I almost felt them underfoot.

But the sound was fading, in moments, nothing. I switched off, turned the reel over, but while I held it, the tape was shriveling, making a small crisp sound, flaking, scattering, and when I brushed the ash off my trouser, there was no mark.

The reel was bare.

I had to sit back to think. What link had Georges to the Princes? Azil had lived between Paris and London for a lifetime. His younger brothers were there for months during the season. Prince Abdullah had a house outside Paris, and another near Nice. Did Georges have a contact in any or all of their retinues? How could he learn something which I'd not even suspected? The princely family had every right to use their money as they wished. But they hadn't the right to sell any shares in the Company which I controlled, and more, those shares had no market price. Their value depended entirely upon my judgment, and any sale could only be made at my will, by my decision.

It took a little time for the idea's stain to blacken.

Yorick had told me he'd got his Ugo Primondi papers from Georges. Had the West German police been informed, they'd have picked him up immediately. But it was the *East* Germans who'd found him and taken him across the border to Hauerfurth.

Had Georges been the informer?

Worse, was he working with the pair? Was this message an attempt to trap? He must have known that I'd be in immediate touch with the Princes to find out whether they'd dealt behind my back. Or had Georges been told what Lane intended?

It seemed to me that he'd rather generously overplayed his hand, in keeping, I realized then, with other "mistakes" the pair had made.

Intercom flashed three red short, one long. Urgentest.

I pressed the button.

"Kopfers, sir. There is a message. I may bring it?"

"Do please!"

Some note in his voice, an nth of nervousness, warned me, brought on that curious moil in the stomach, that seems to respond with a prescience even superior to the brain's, and instantly thought roamed, a tumult which stopped with the tap on the door.

Curfew never cleared streets quicker than that little sound clarified the scurry in my head.

Commodore Kopfers stood in the doorway in dress uniform and cap—strange in mid-flight—but he looked at the foot of the desk. The peak hid his eyes, and that was ominous.

I answered that stiff-armed Dutch salute with a barest nod.

"A message I don't like to read, if you permit, and Mr. Blandford doesn't like to bring it, you will excuse?" he said, in that small voice, as though he spoke from the top of held lungs, and still not looking at me. "The message was received one minute ago. It is from Kingston. We are refused permission to land until tomorrow, ten o'clock—"

He pulled in the breath I needed.

I seemed to know what he was going to say. I wanted to stop him.

"Sir, the Banbury Cross estate is destroyed. The area is devastate'. No survivors. Only servants in Kingston for shopping. No names. Few victims identified. One, by a diamond—"

I saw the shadow look at a blue rag.

"It is all, sir, I turn for Shannon? London?"

I nodded.

"Sir, I must say we all are without words"—I heard the whisper from far away, so far, from the small, sere world all my own—"I am the Captain. I must say for everybody. We have a sympathy. So much feeling. So beautiful. The heart. We also, please. We loved her. I have leave to go, sir?"

I nodded.

The door *clicked!* A final mute, stone on rock. Sealed tomb.

Jets sang.

Love's fist paled in greyish blots. Her joyous name has no beginning, or shape, or end. In what whisperous ghost, her perfume shrouds. Calvary's plea retches over Golgotha, nails, thorns pierce, scourging bleeds warm salt, aloes clog, myrrh blinds.

As I had done unto others.

399

My turn. For so, so long, and all the gentle time I'd been with her, I'd known in my heart this moment must come.

Confessions had never absolved me. Prayers, candles, a laying-on of hands, for nothing.

Retribution's bourne.

Four yellow pills and a glass of her wine, and I could join her. Eyes shut in a deathly moment, an upturned chin, shaken head *No!*

Her voice *NO!* absolute.

My love lies a-dreaming.

Fear the wish, crave the touch, the finger-tips, and lips. And no. That meaning must be garnered. In a cowslip's bell. Void the sweet wonder.

Consuelo. Leddy Con-*swell*. Love's own diamond marks her beauty. My only wish grows in that glitter, whispering of her. In that tiny brilliance I hear my prayer. May I not repay?

They shall have mercy wherever they go.

Till these hands, wise of her beauty, touch them.

There's no candle I may burn, except for her.

I'll light them. Lovely white lady on a white horse, galloping off from Banbury Cross, light there shall be wherever she goes.

Sleep, my darling, my only heart. Sleep now, joy and sweet of my worthless life, sleep, sleep softly.

The night will grow its hours and age into days, and I must be myself, and rise.

I shall find them. If the most high God hears me, or not. Who is He to me? Who am I that He should be careful of me? There's a treasury of beautiful forgotten things.

Darling, sweetheart, princess mine.

The night is a child.